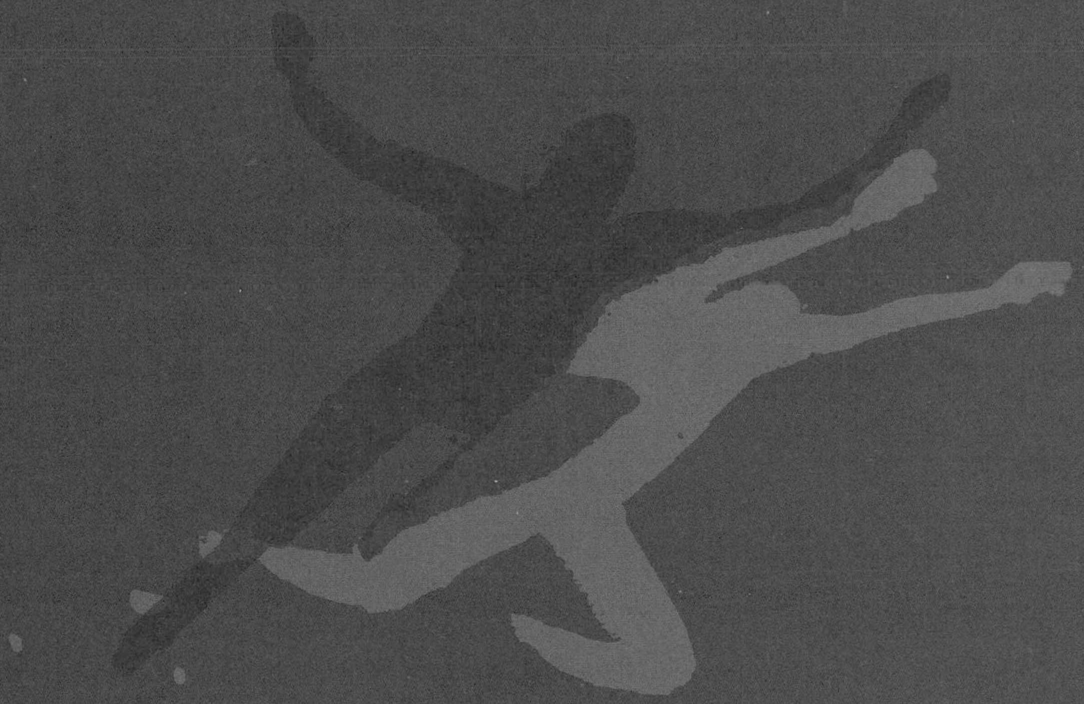

THE CLOVEN
BOOK ONE
WRITTEN BY
GARTH STEIN
DRAWN BY
MATTHEW SOUTHWORTH

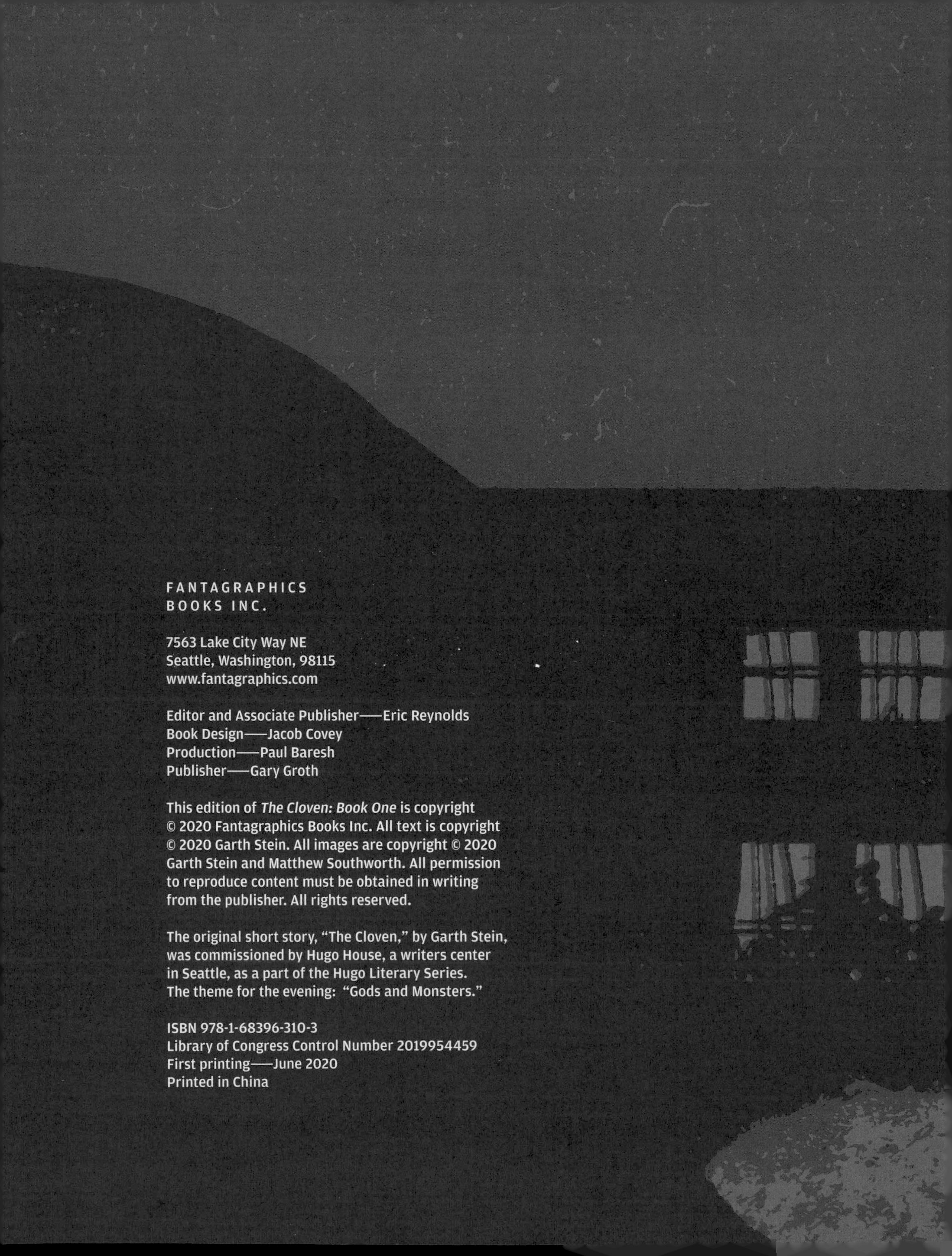

FANTAGRAPHICS
BOOKS INC.

7563 Lake City Way NE
Seattle, Washington, 98115
www.fantagraphics.com

Editor and Associate Publisher——Eric Reynolds
Book Design——Jacob Covey
Production——Paul Baresh
Publisher——Gary Groth

The original short story, "The Cloven," by Garth Stein, was commissioned by Hugo House, a writers center in Seattle, as a part of the Hugo Literary Series. The theme for the evening: "Gods and Monsters."

ISBN 978-1-68396-310-3
Library of Congress Control Number 2019954459
First printing——June 2020
Printed in China

THE CLOVEN

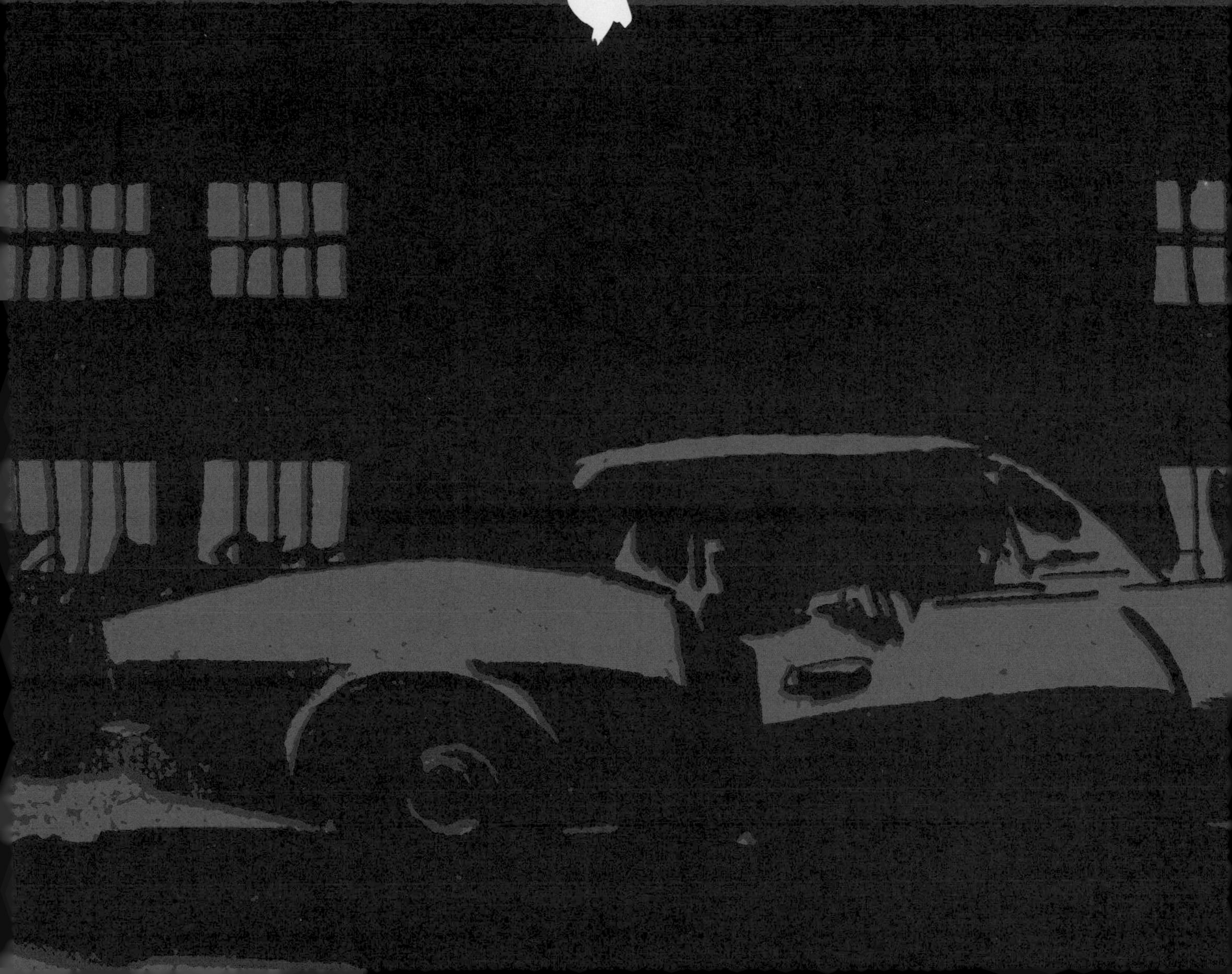

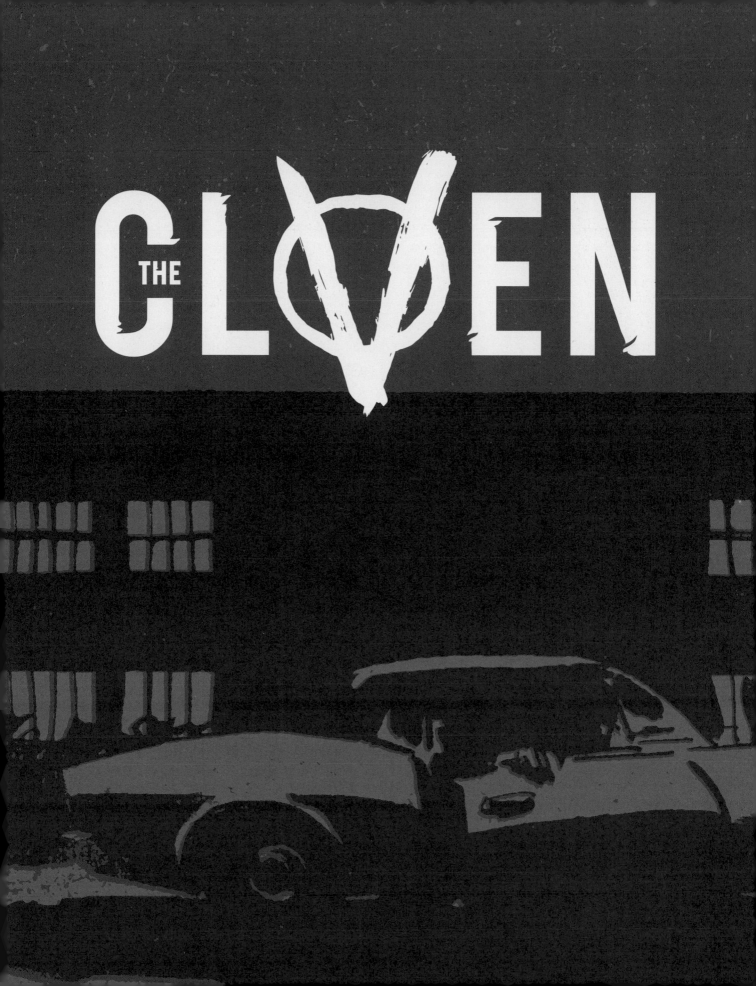

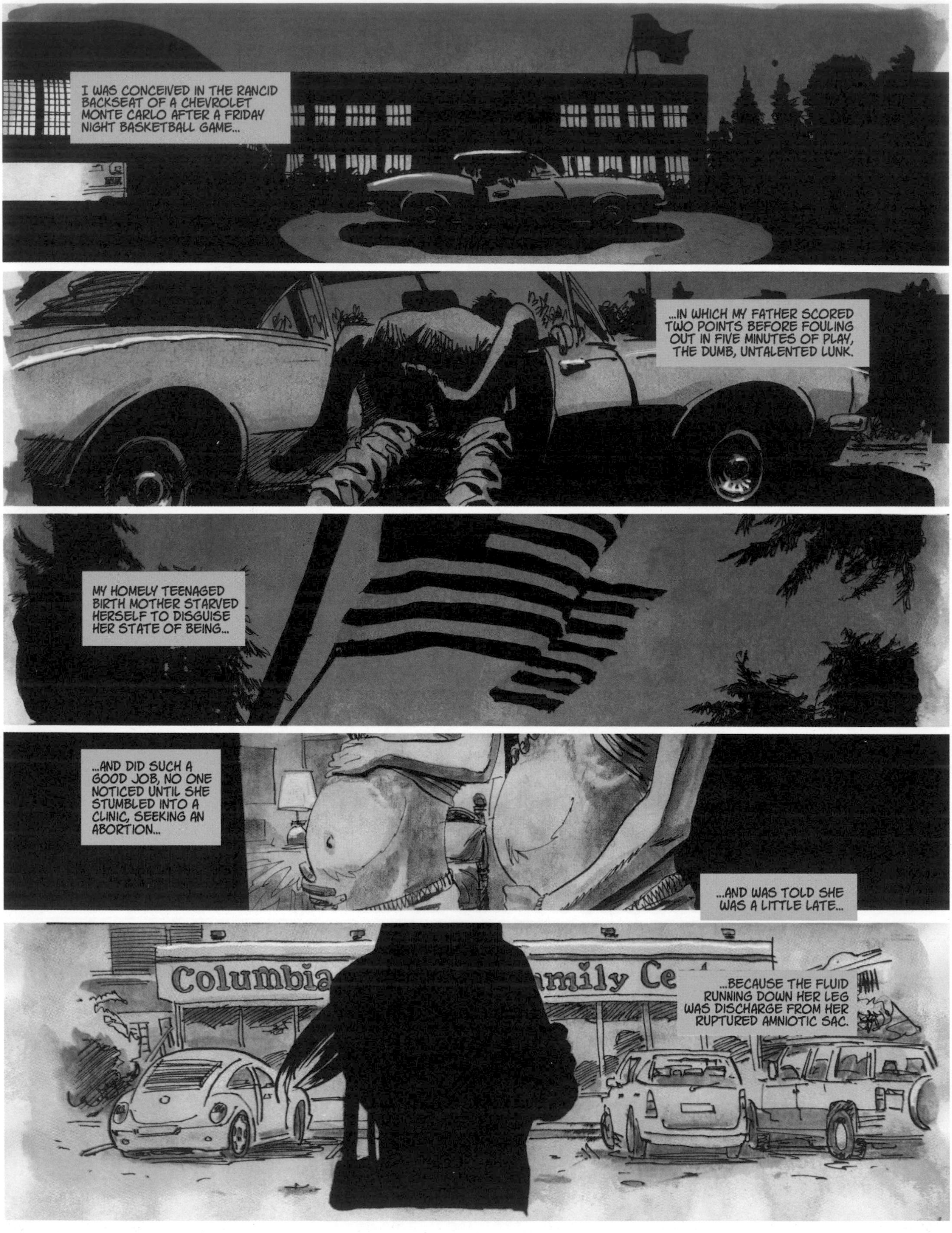
I WAS CONCEIVED IN THE RANCID BACKSEAT OF A CHEVROLET MONTE CARLO AFTER A FRIDAY NIGHT BASKETBALL GAME...
...IN WHICH MY FATHER SCORED TWO POINTS BEFORE FOULING OUT IN FIVE MINUTES OF PLAY, THE DUMB, UNTALENTED LUNK.
MY HOMELY TEENAGED BIRTH MOTHER STARVED HERSELF TO DISGUISE HER STATE OF BEING...
...AND DID SUCH A GOOD JOB, NO ONE NOTICED UNTIL SHE STUMBLED INTO A CLINIC, SEEKING AN ABORTION...
...AND WAS TOLD SHE WAS A LITTLE LATE...
Columbia
amily Ce
...BECAUSE THE FLUID RUNNING DOWN HER LEG WAS DISCHARGE FROM HER RUPTURED AMNIOTIC SAC.

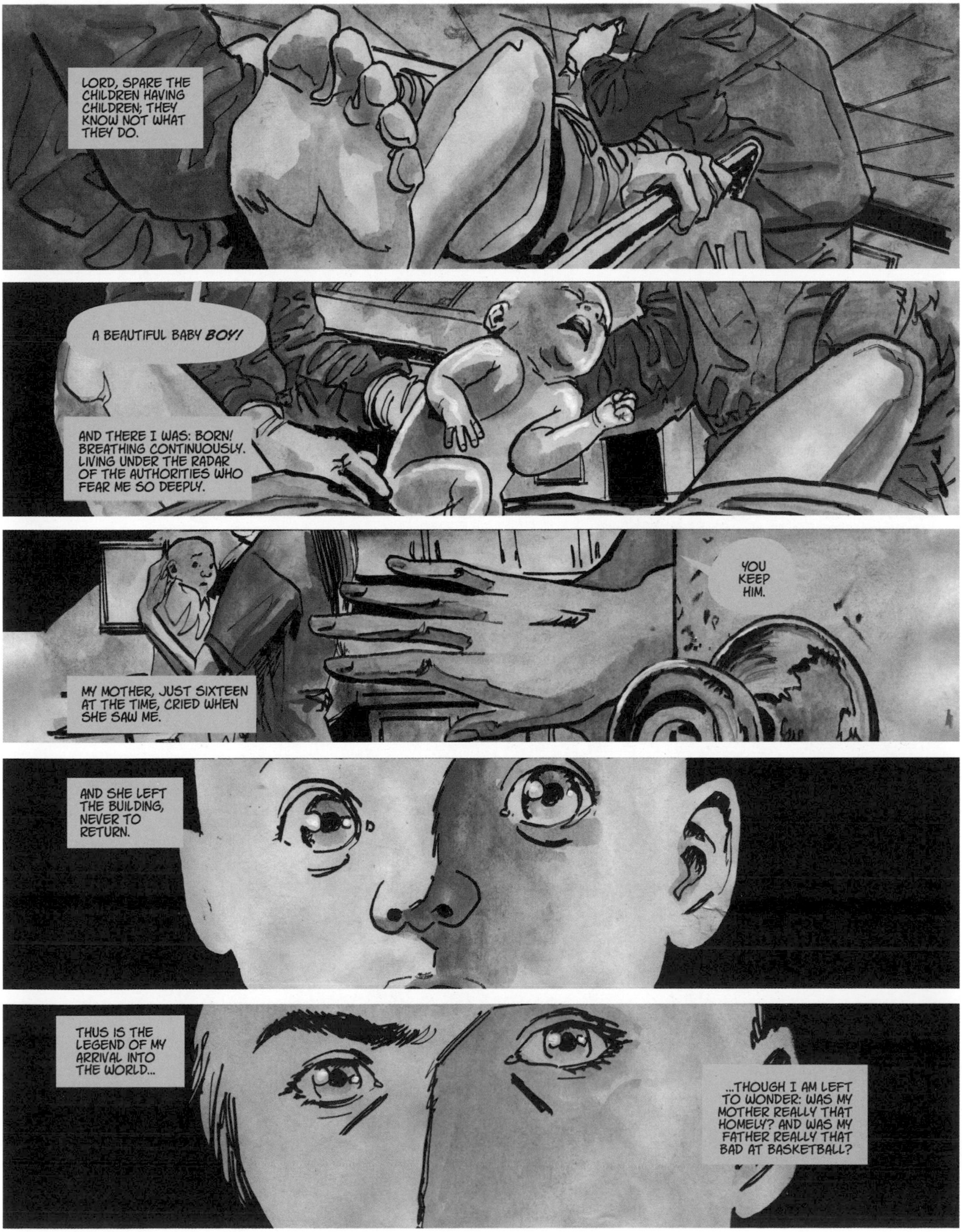
LORD, SPARE THE CHILDREN HAVING CHILDREN; THEY KNOW NOT WHAT THEY DO.
A BEAUTIFUL BABY *BOY!*
AND THERE I WAS: BORN! BREATHING CONTINUOUSLY. LIVING UNDER THE RADAR OF THE AUTHORITIES WHO FEAR ME SO DEEPLY.
YOU KEEP HIM.
MY MOTHER, JUST SIXTEEN AT THE TIME, CRIED WHEN SHE SAW ME.
AND SHE LEFT THE BUILDING, NEVER TO RETURN.
THUS IS THE LEGEND OF MY ARRIVAL INTO THE WORLD...
...THOUGH I AM LEFT TO WONDER: WAS MY MOTHER REALLY THAT HOMELY? AND WAS MY FATHER REALLY THAT BAD AT BASKETBALL?

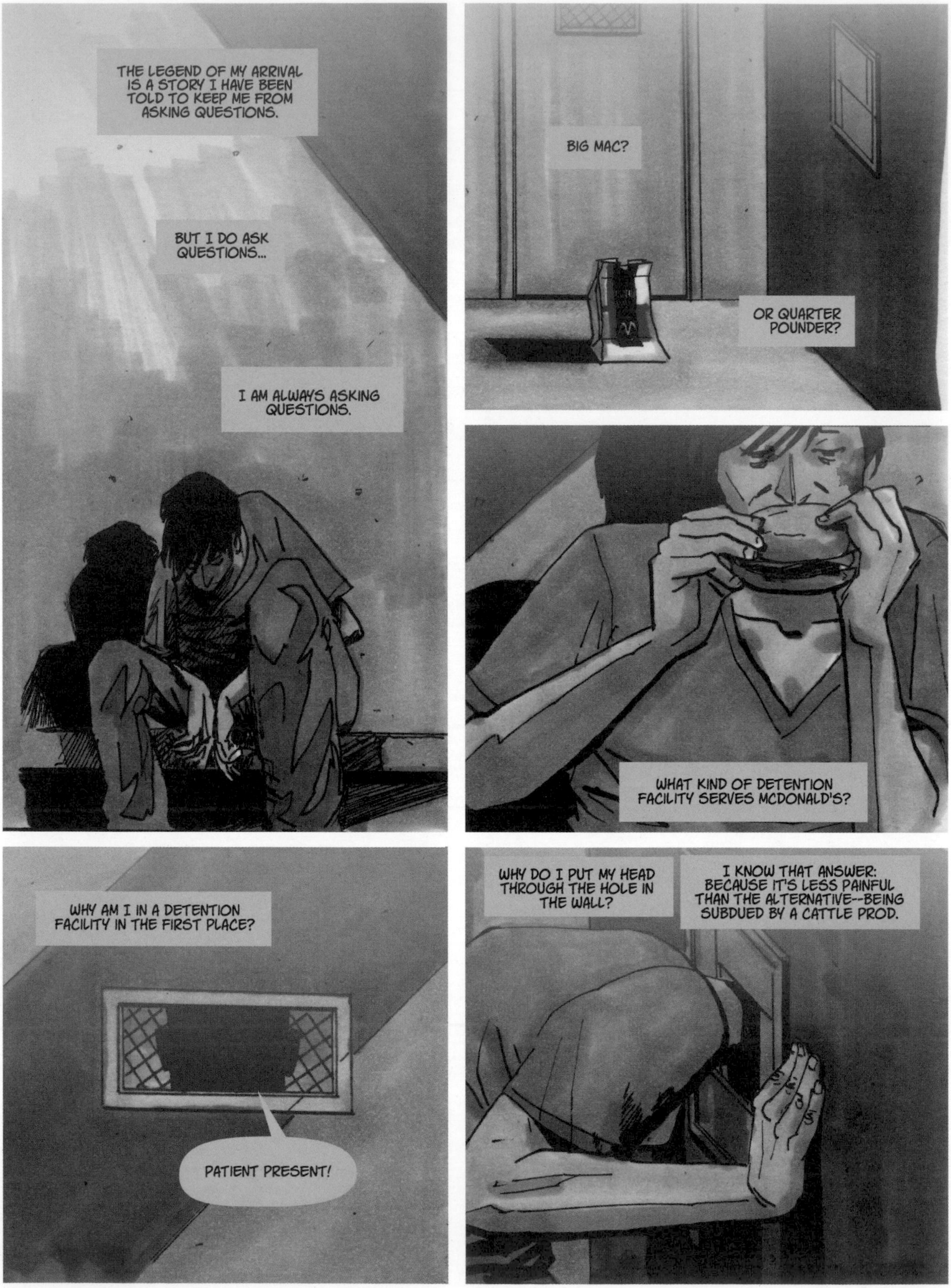
THE LEGEND OF MY ARRIVAL IS A STORY I HAVE BEEN TOLD TO KEEP ME FROM ASKING QUESTIONS.
BUT I DO ASK QUESTIONS...
I AM ALWAYS ASKING QUESTIONS.
BIG MAC?
OR QUARTER POUNDER?
WHAT KIND OF DETENTION FACILITY SERVES MCDONALD'S?
WHY AM I IN A DETENTION FACILITY IN THE FIRST PLACE?
PATIENT PRESENT!
WHY DO I PUT MY HEAD THROUGH THE HOLE IN THE WALL?
I KNOW THAT ANSWER: BECAUSE IT'S LESS PAINFUL THAN THE ALTERNATIVE--BEING SUBDUED BY A CATTLE PROD.

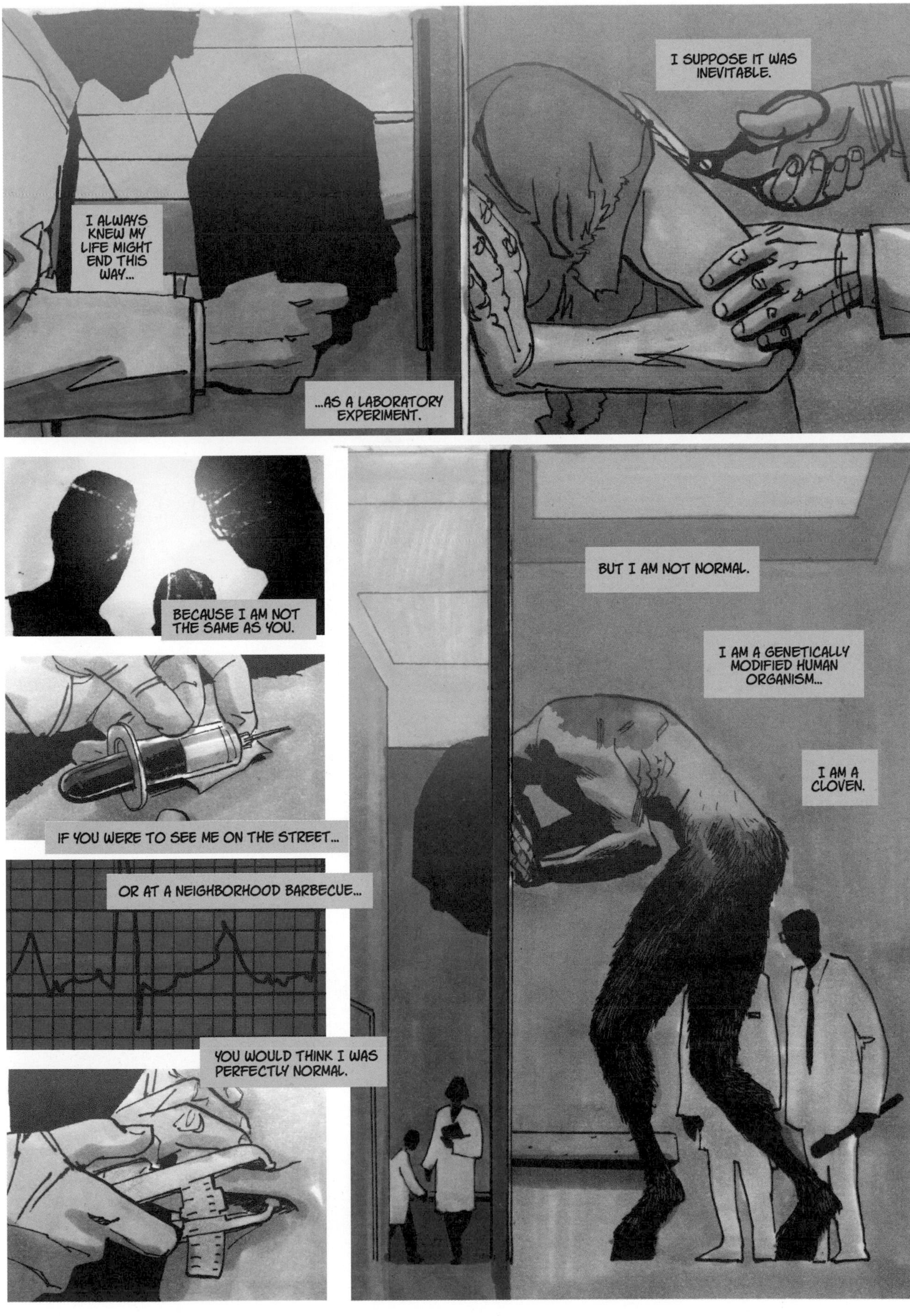
I ALWAYS KNEW MY LIFE MIGHT END THIS WAY...
...AS A LABORATORY EXPERIMENT.
I SUPPOSE IT WAS INEVITABLE.
BECAUSE I AM NOT THE SAME AS YOU.
IF YOU WERE TO SEE ME ON THE STREET...
OR AT A NEIGHBORHOOD BARBECUE...
YOU WOULD THINK I WAS PERFECTLY NORMAL.
BUT I AM NOT NORMAL.
I AM A GENETICALLY MODIFIED HUMAN ORGANISM...
I AM A CLOVEN.

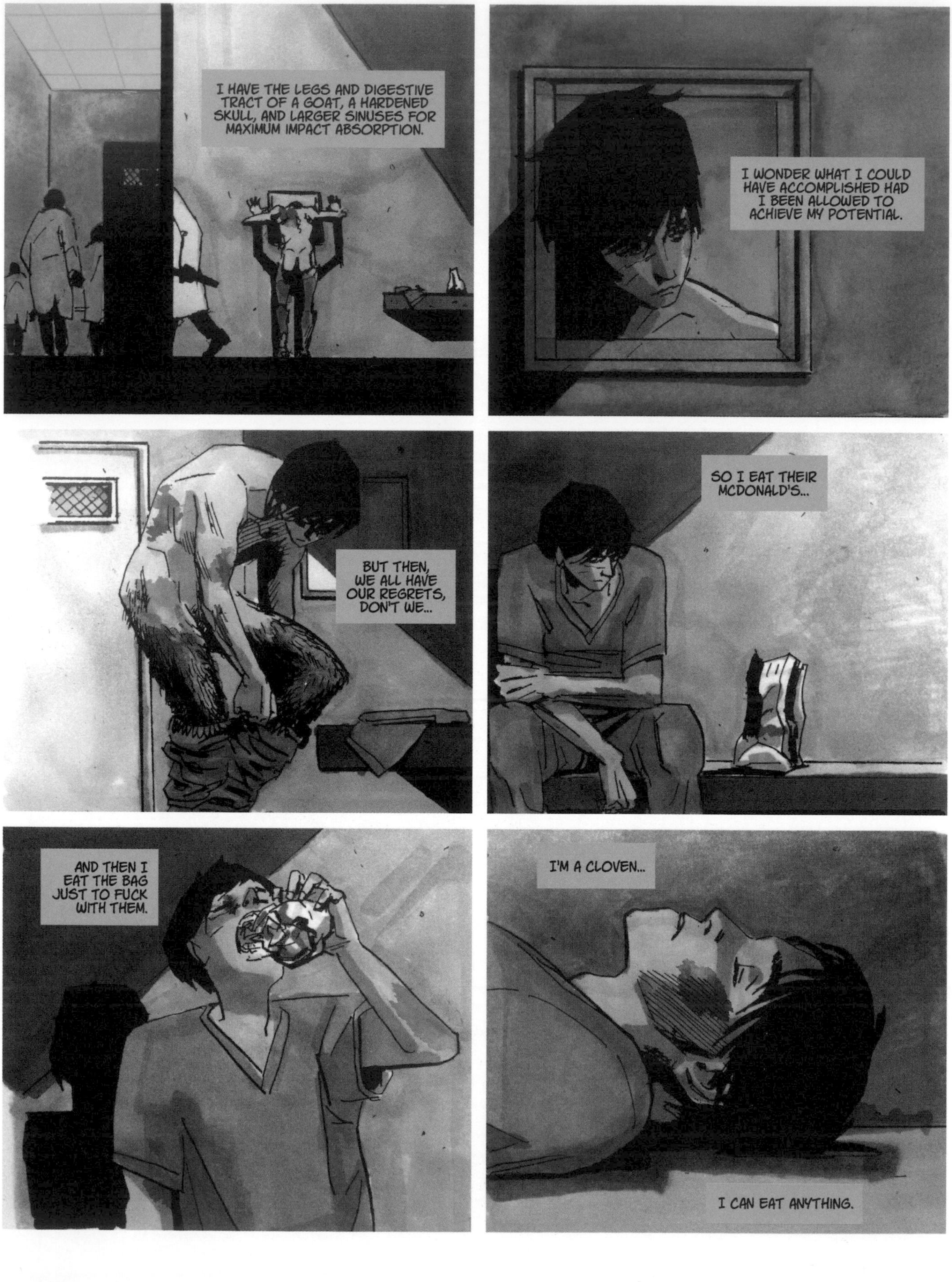
I HAVE THE LEGS AND DIGESTIVE TRACT OF A GOAT, A HARDENED SKULL, AND LARGER SINUSES FOR MAXIMUM IMPACT ABSORPTION.
I WONDER WHAT I COULD HAVE ACCOMPLISHED HAD I BEEN ALLOWED TO ACHIEVE MY POTENTIAL.
BUT THEN, WE ALL HAVE OUR REGRETS, DON'T WE...
SO I EAT THEIR MCDONALD'S...
AND THEN I EAT THE BAG JUST TO FUCK WITH THEM.
I'M A CLOVEN...
I CAN EAT ANYTHING.

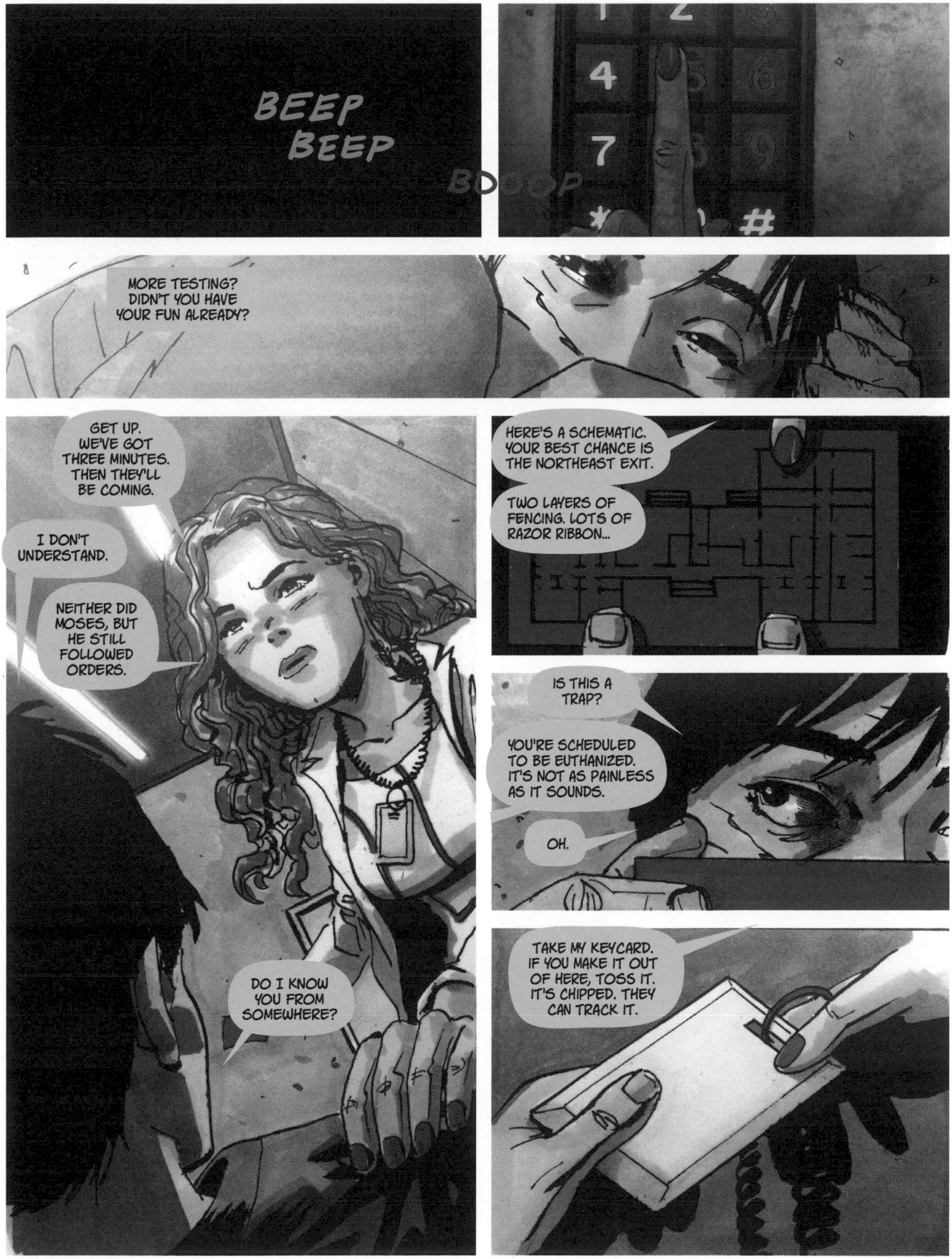
BEEP
BEEP
BOOOP
MORE TESTING? DIDN'T YOU HAVE YOUR FUN ALREADY?
GET UP. WE'VE GOT THREE MINUTES. THEN THEY'LL BE COMING.
I DON'T UNDERSTAND.
NEITHER DID MOSES, BUT HE STILL FOLLOWED ORDERS.
DO I KNOW YOU FROM SOMEWHERE?
HERE'S A SCHEMATIC. YOUR BEST CHANCE IS THE NORTHEAST EXIT.
TWO LAYERS OF FENCING. LOTS OF RAZOR RIBBON...
IS THIS A TRAP?
YOU'RE SCHEDULED TO BE EUTHANIZED. IT'S NOT AS PAINLESS AS IT SOUNDS.
OH.
TAKE MY KEYCARD. IF YOU MAKE IT OUT OF HERE, TOSS IT. IT'S CHIPPED. THEY CAN TRACK IT.

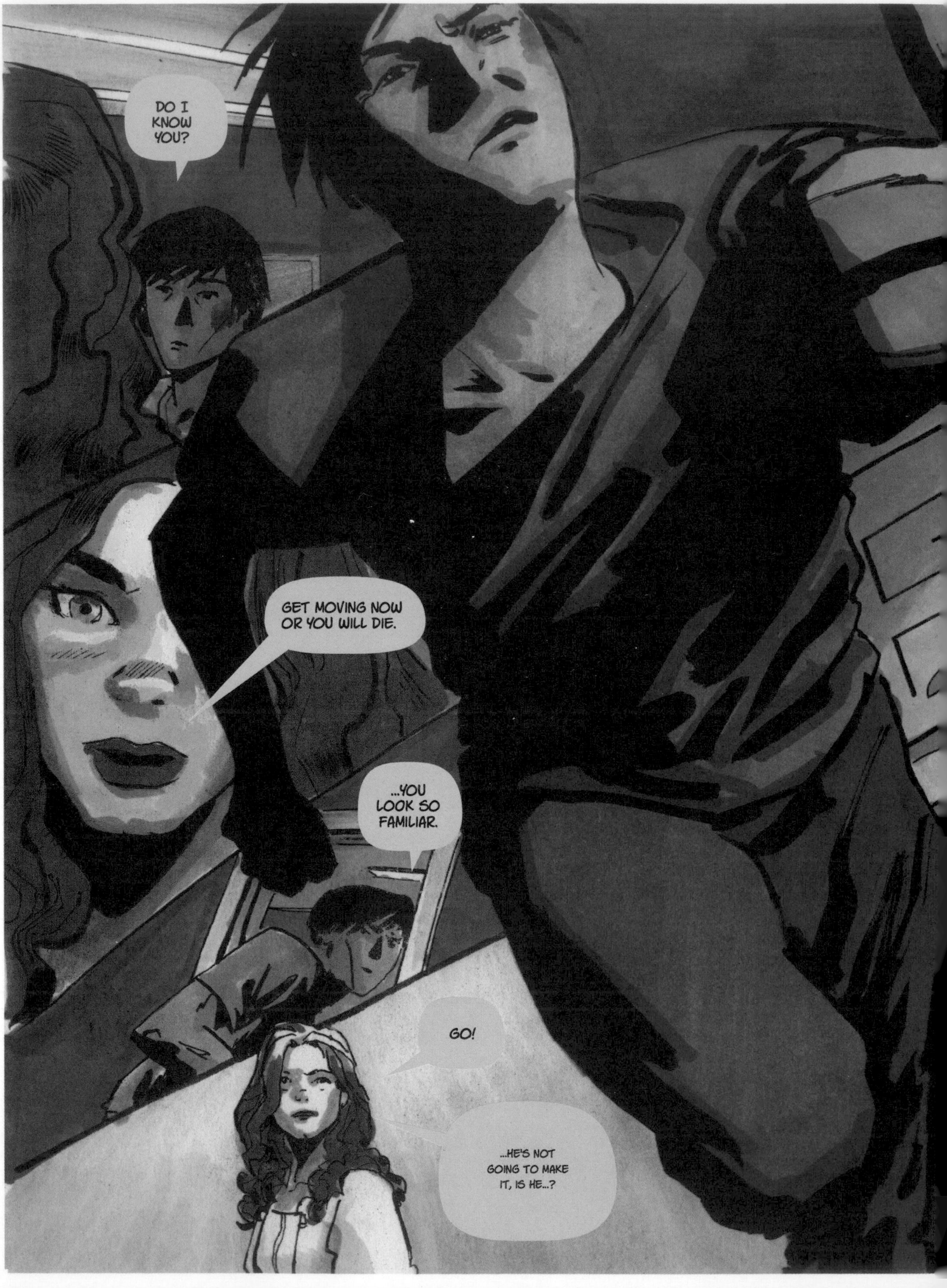
DO I KNOW YOU?
GET MOVING NOW OR YOU WILL DIE.
...YOU LOOK SO FAMILIAR.
GO!
...HE'S NOT GOING TO MAKE IT, IS HE...?

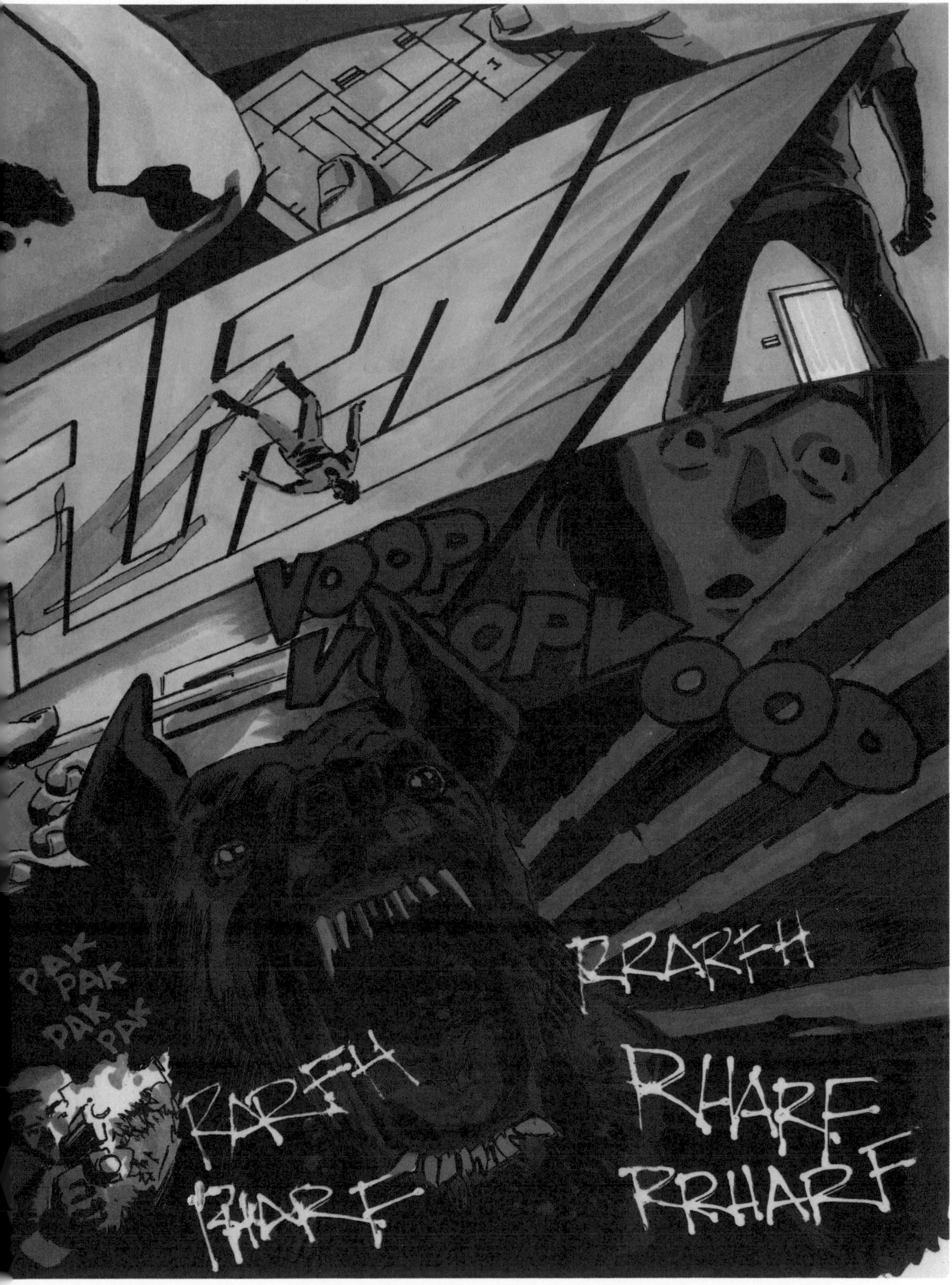
VOOP
VOOP VOOOP
PAK PAK PAK PAK
RRARFH
RARFH
RHARF
RHARF
RRHARF

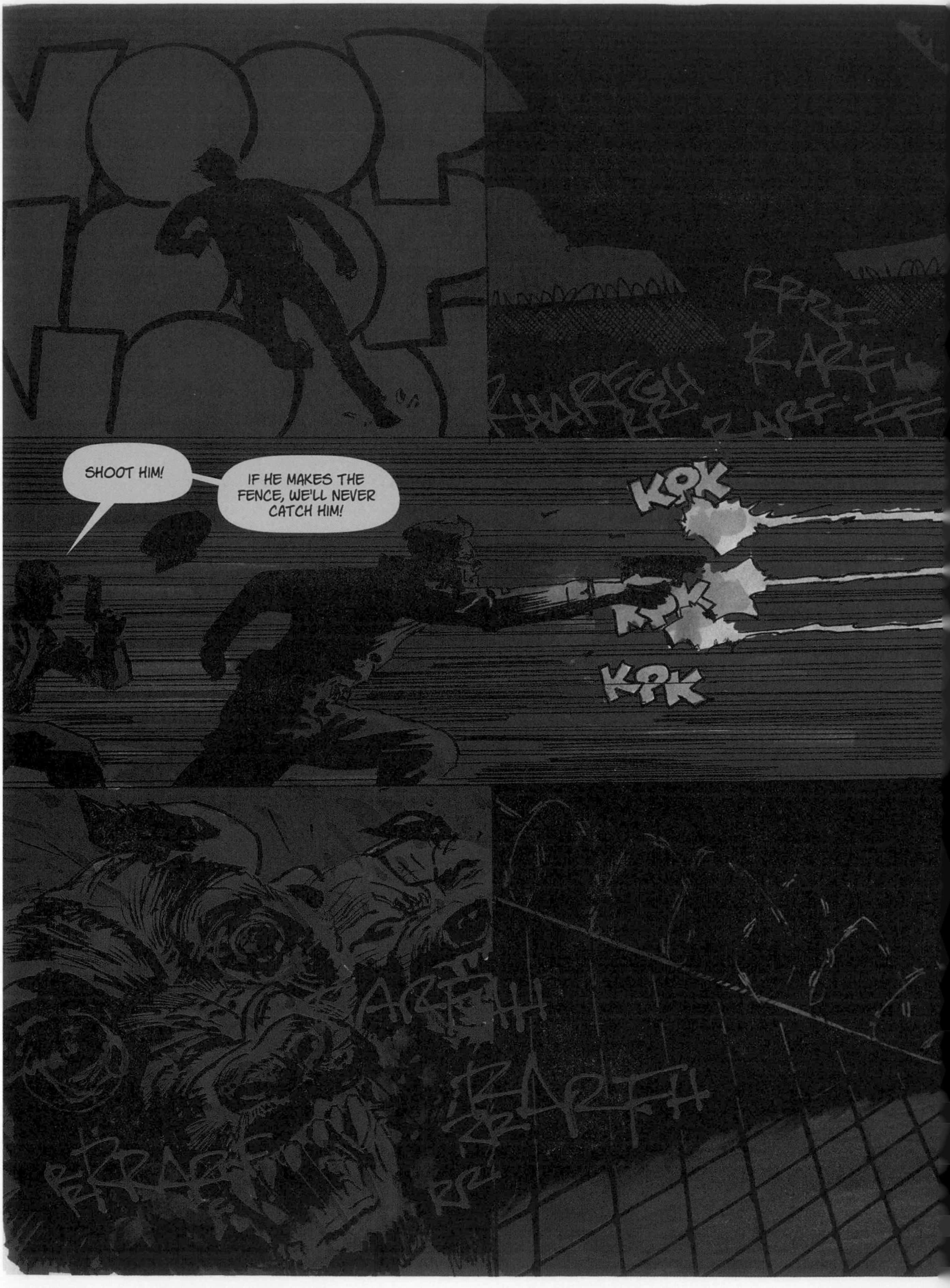
SHOOT HIM!
IF HE MAKES THE FENCE, WE'LL NEVER CATCH HIM!
KOK
KPK

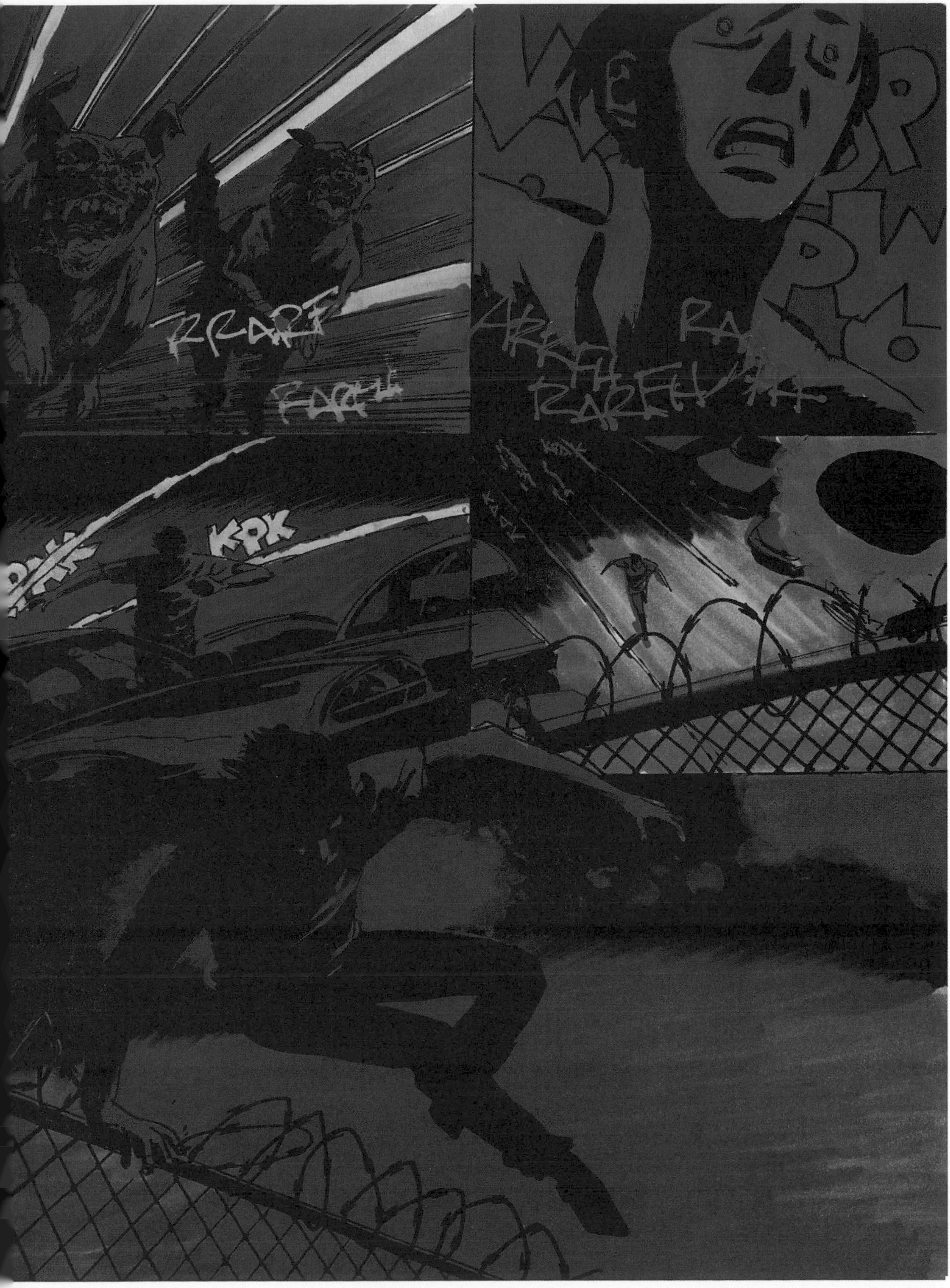
RRARF
KPK

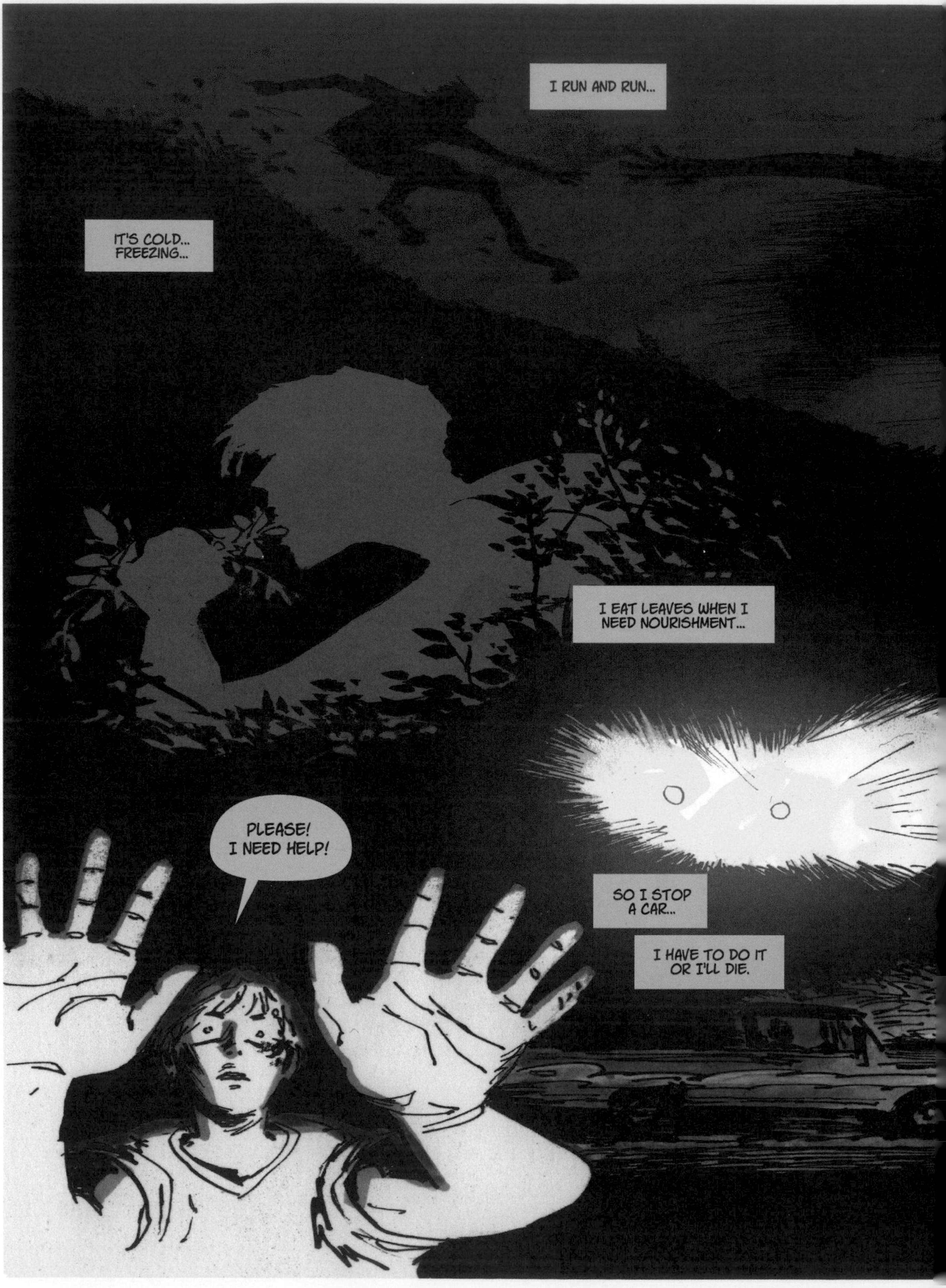
I RUN AND RUN...
IT'S COLD... FREEZING...
I EAT LEAVES WHEN I NEED NOURISHMENT...
PLEASE! I NEED HELP!
SO I STOP A CAR...
I HAVE TO DO IT OR I'LL DIE.

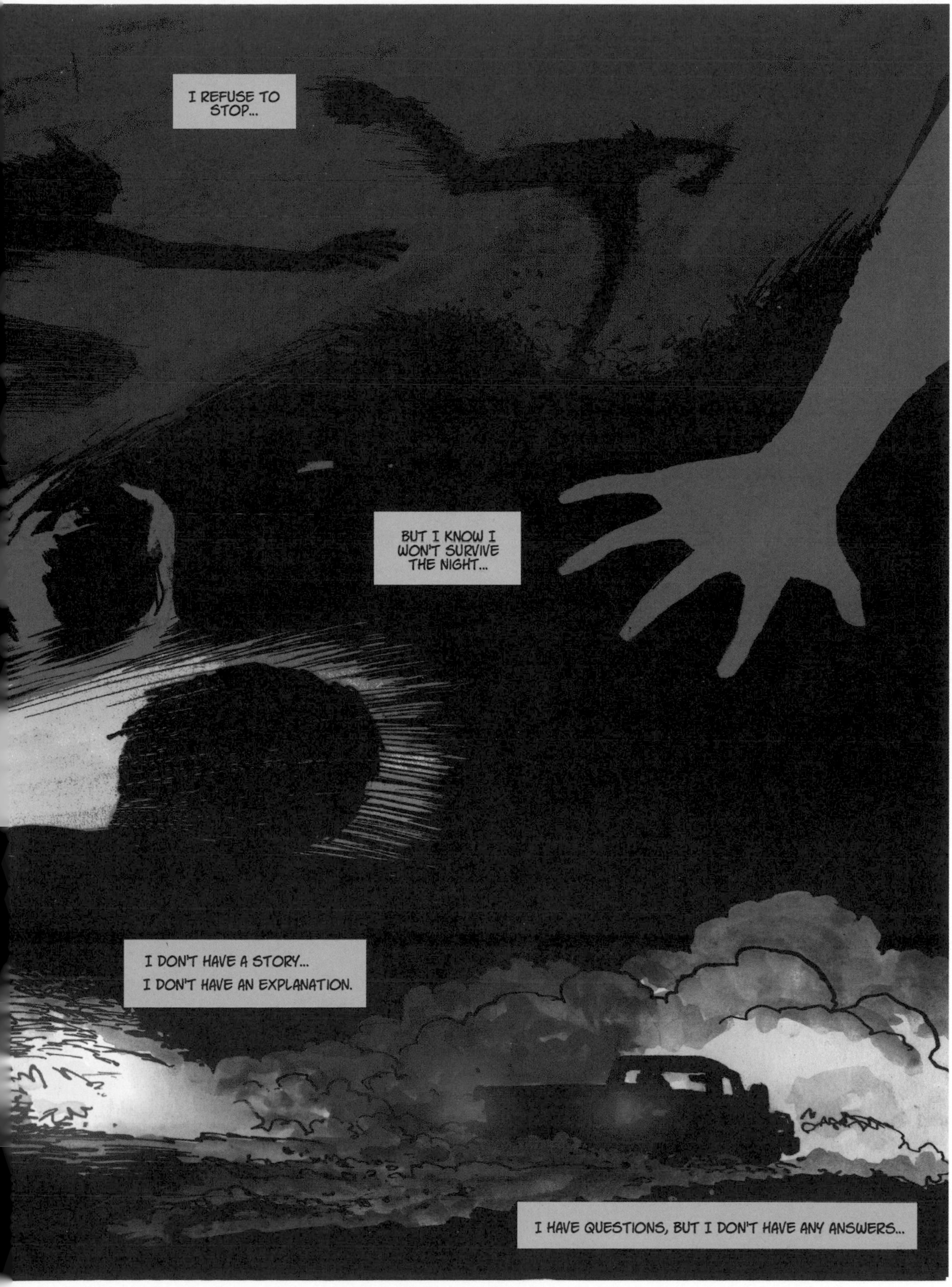
I REFUSE TO STOP...
BUT I KNOW I WON'T SURVIVE THE NIGHT...
I DON'T HAVE A STORY...
I DON'T HAVE AN EXPLANATION.
I HAVE QUESTIONS, BUT I DON'T HAVE ANY ANSWERS...

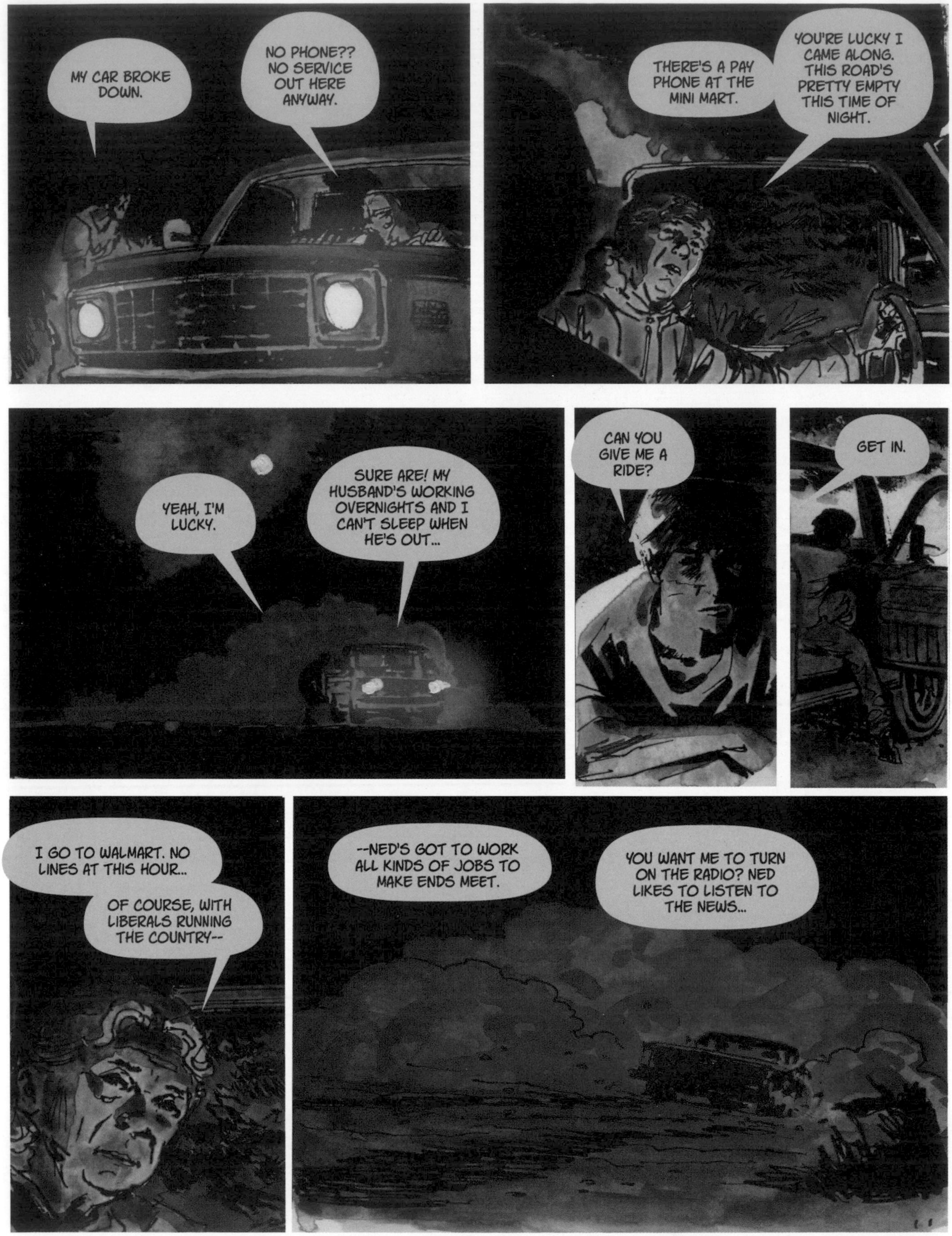
MY CAR BROKE DOWN.
NO PHONE?? NO SERVICE OUT HERE ANYWAY.
THERE'S A PAY PHONE AT THE MINI MART.
YOU'RE LUCKY I CAME ALONG. THIS ROAD'S PRETTY EMPTY THIS TIME OF NIGHT.
YEAH, I'M LUCKY.
SURE ARE! MY HUSBAND'S WORKING OVERNIGHTS AND I CAN'T SLEEP WHEN HE'S OUT...
CAN YOU GIVE ME A RIDE?
GET IN.
I GO TO WALMART. NO LINES AT THIS HOUR...
OF COURSE, WITH LIBERALS RUNNING THE COUNTRY--
--NED'S GOT TO WORK ALL KINDS OF JOBS TO MAKE ENDS MEET.
YOU WANT ME TO TURN ON THE RADIO? NED LIKES TO LISTEN TO THE NEWS...

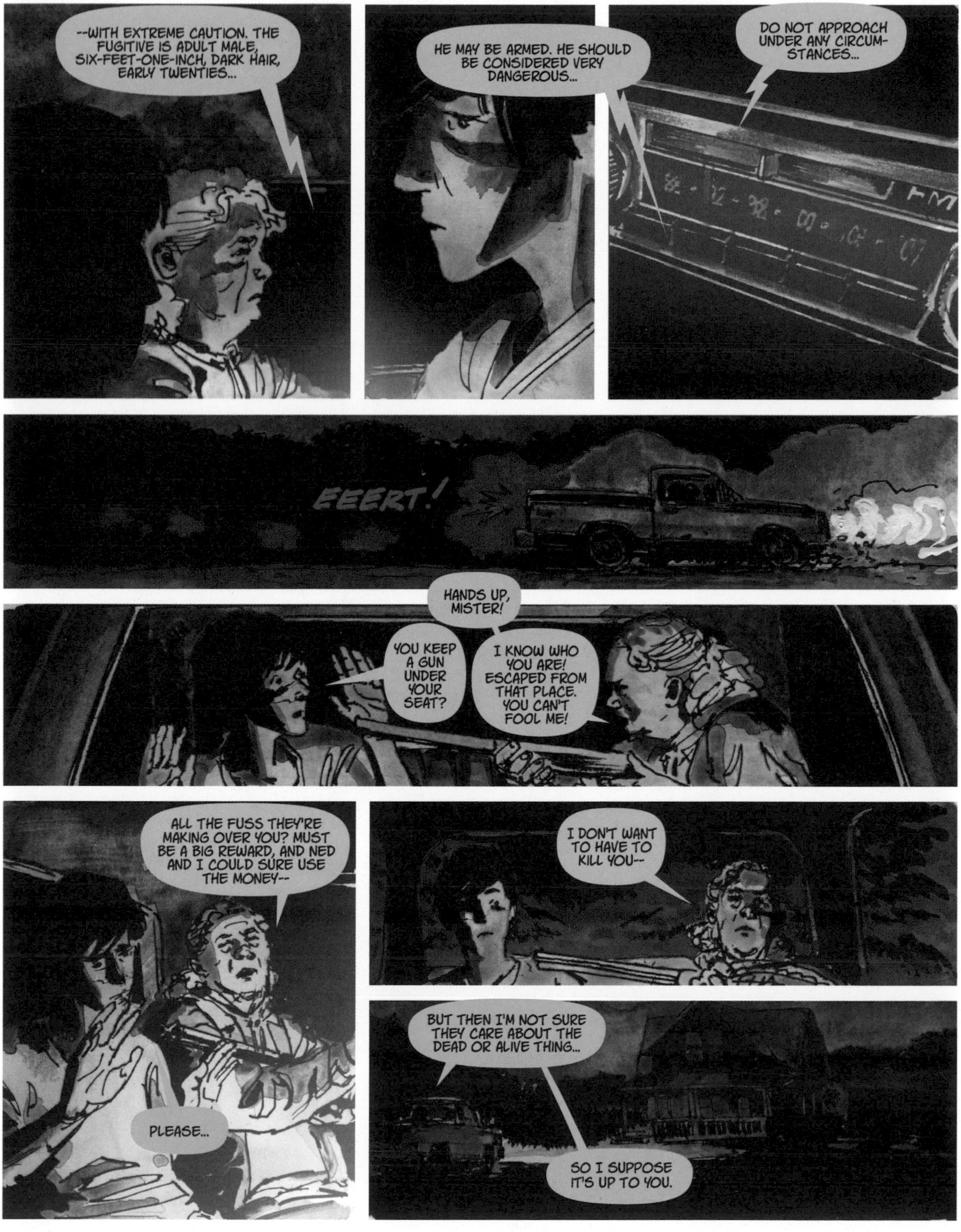
--WITH EXTREME CAUTION. THE FUGITIVE IS ADULT MALE, SIX-FEET-ONE-INCH, DARK HAIR, EARLY TWENTIES...
HE MAY BE ARMED. HE SHOULD BE CONSIDERED VERY DANGEROUS...
DO NOT APPROACH UNDER ANY CIRCUM-STANCES...
FM
EEERT!
HANDS UP, MISTER!
YOU KEEP A GUN UNDER YOUR SEAT?
I KNOW WHO YOU ARE! ESCAPED FROM THAT PLACE. YOU CAN'T FOOL ME!
ALL THE FUSS THEY'RE MAKING OVER YOU? MUST BE A BIG REWARD, AND NED AND I COULD SURE USE THE MONEY--
PLEASE...
I DON'T WANT TO HAVE TO KILL YOU--
BUT THEN I'M NOT SURE THEY CARE ABOUT THE DEAD OR ALIVE THING...
SO I SUPPOSE IT'S UP TO YOU.

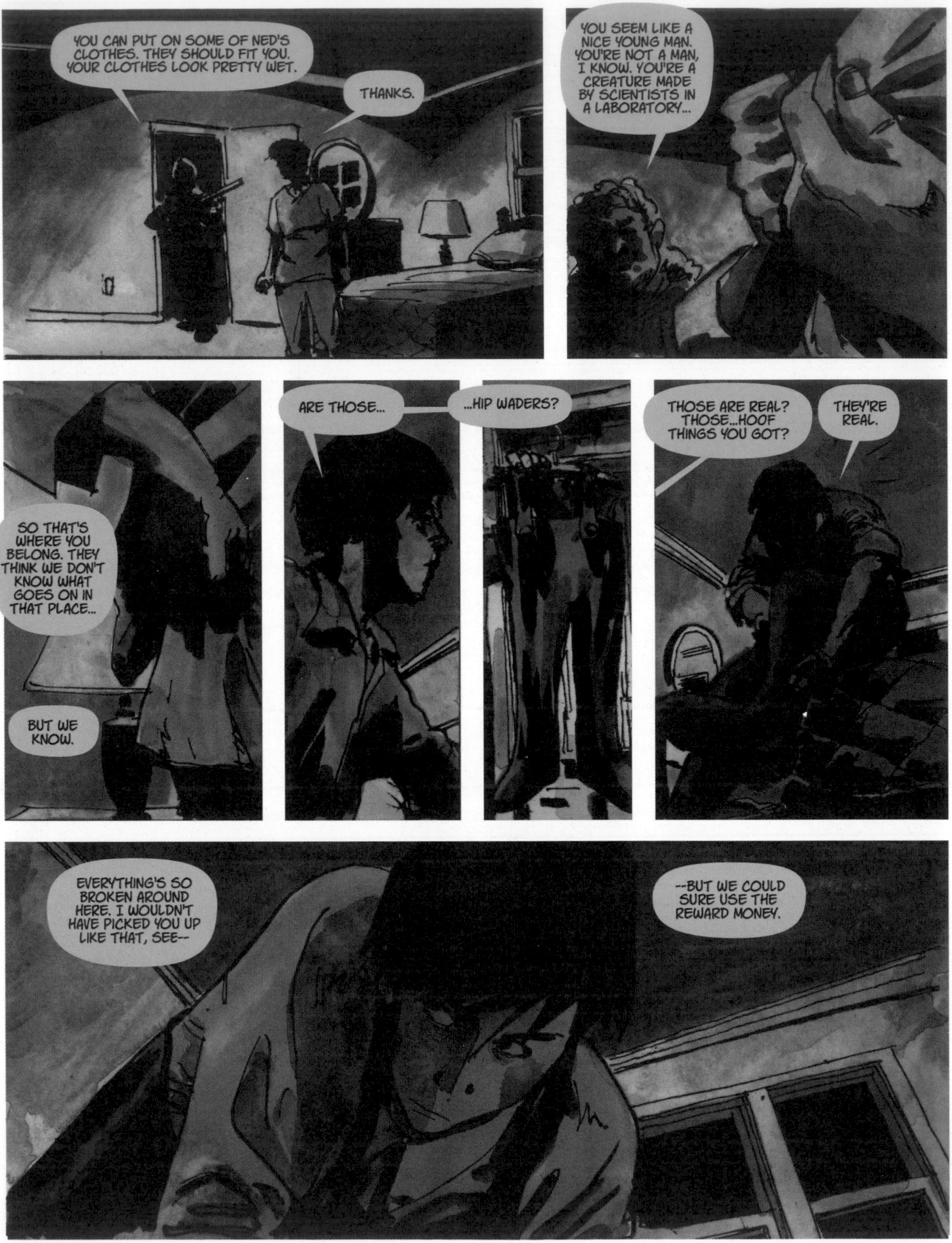
YOU CAN PUT ON SOME OF NED'S CLOTHES. THEY SHOULD FIT YOU. YOUR CLOTHES LOOK PRETTY WET.
THANKS.
YOU SEEM LIKE A NICE YOUNG MAN. YOU'RE NOT A MAN, I KNOW. YOU'RE A CREATURE MADE BY SCIENTISTS IN A LABORATORY...
SO THAT'S WHERE YOU BELONG. THEY THINK WE DON'T KNOW WHAT GOES ON IN THAT PLACE...
BUT WE KNOW.
ARE THOSE...
...HIP WADERS?
THOSE ARE REAL? THOSE...HOOF THINGS YOU GOT?
THEY'RE REAL.
EVERYTHING'S SO BROKEN AROUND HERE. I WOULDN'T HAVE PICKED YOU UP LIKE THAT, SEE--
--BUT WE COULD SURE USE THE REWARD MONEY.

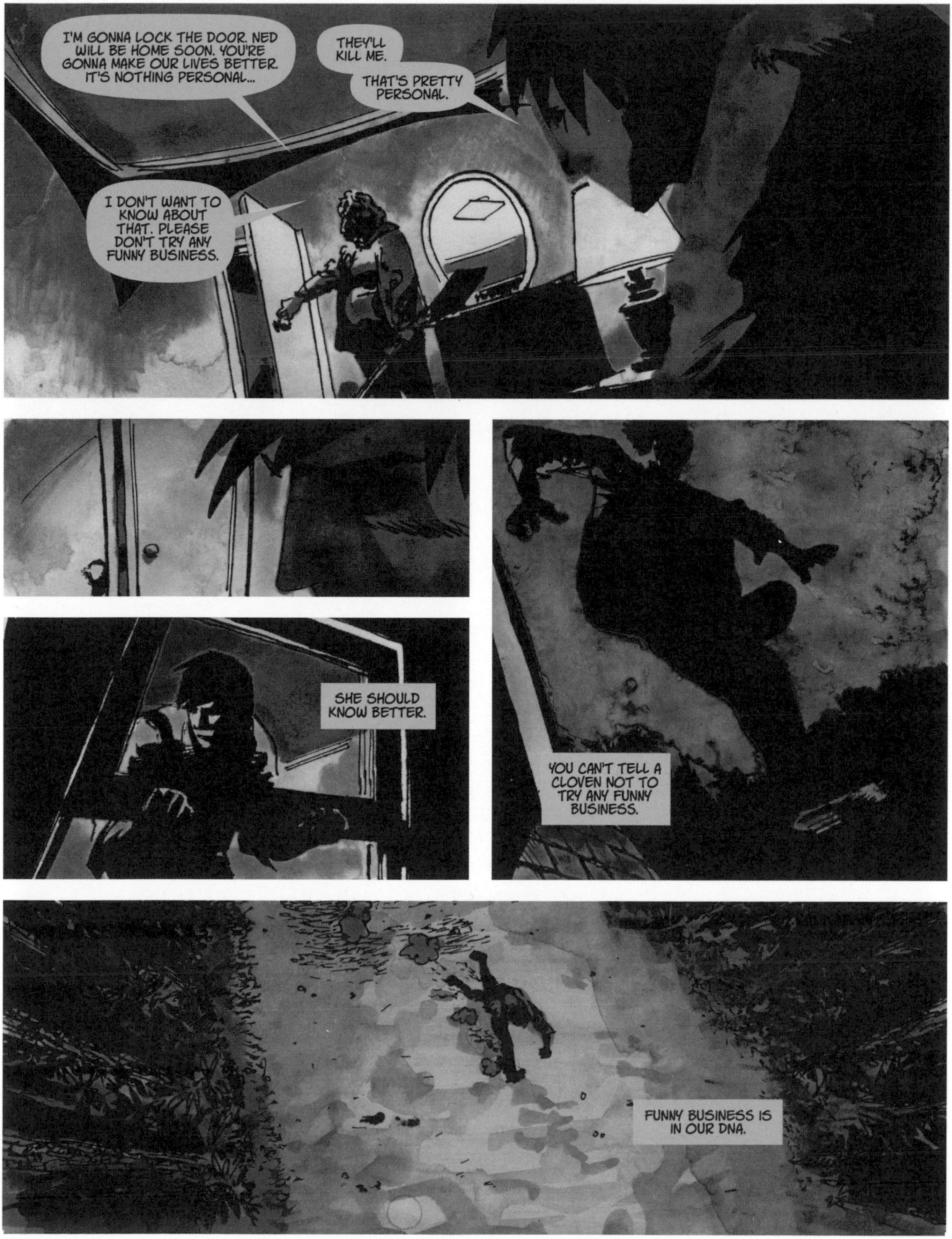
I'M GONNA LOCK THE DOOR. NED WILL BE HOME SOON. YOU'RE GONNA MAKE OUR LIVES BETTER. IT'S NOTHING PERSONAL...
THEY'LL KILL ME.
THAT'S PRETTY PERSONAL.
I DON'T WANT TO KNOW ABOUT THAT. PLEASE DON'T TRY ANY FUNNY BUSINESS.
SHE SHOULD KNOW BETTER.
YOU CAN'T TELL A CLOVEN NOT TO TRY ANY FUNNY BUSINESS.
FUNNY BUSINESS IS IN OUR DNA.

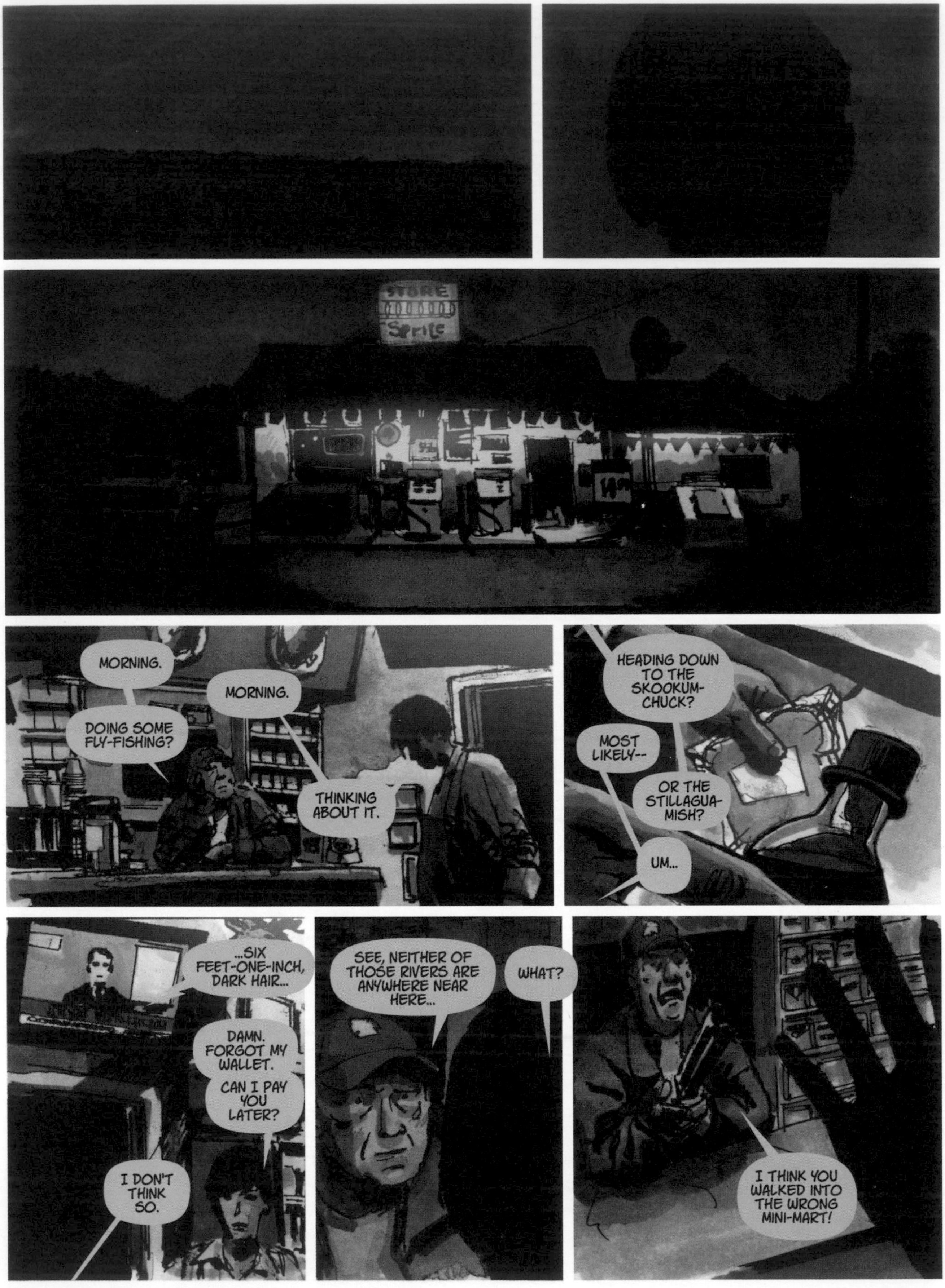
MORNING.
MORNING.
DOING SOME FLY-FISHING?
THINKING ABOUT IT.
HEADING DOWN TO THE SKOOKUM-CHUCK?
MOST LIKELY--
OR THE STILLAGUA-MISH?
UM...
...SIX FEET-ONE-INCH, DARK HAIR...
DAMN. FORGOT MY WALLET.
CAN I PAY YOU LATER?
I DON'T THINK SO.
SEE, NEITHER OF THOSE RIVERS ARE ANYWHERE NEAR HERE...
WHAT?
I THINK YOU WALKED INTO THE WRONG MINI-MART!

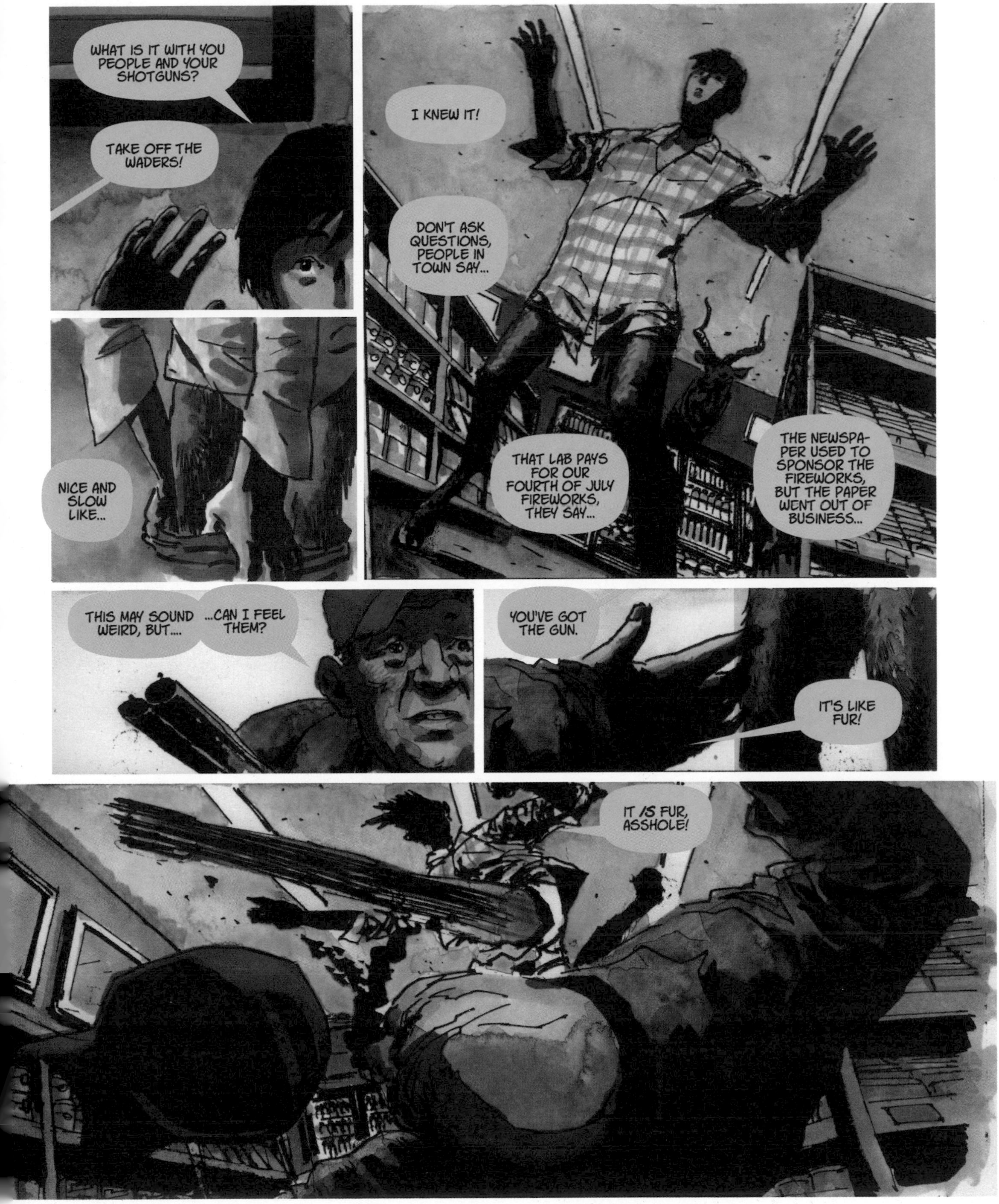
WHAT IS IT WITH YOU PEOPLE AND YOUR SHOTGUNS?
TAKE OFF THE WADERS!
NICE AND SLOW LIKE...
I KNEW IT!
DON'T ASK QUESTIONS, PEOPLE IN TOWN SAY...
THAT LAB PAYS FOR OUR FOURTH OF JULY FIREWORKS, THEY SAY...
THE NEWSPA-PER USED TO SPONSOR THE FIREWORKS, BUT THE PAPER WENT OUT OF BUSINESS...
THIS MAY SOUND WEIRD, BUT....
...CAN I FEEL THEM?
YOU'VE GOT THE GUN.
IT'S LIKE FUR!
IT *IS* FUR, ASSHOLE!

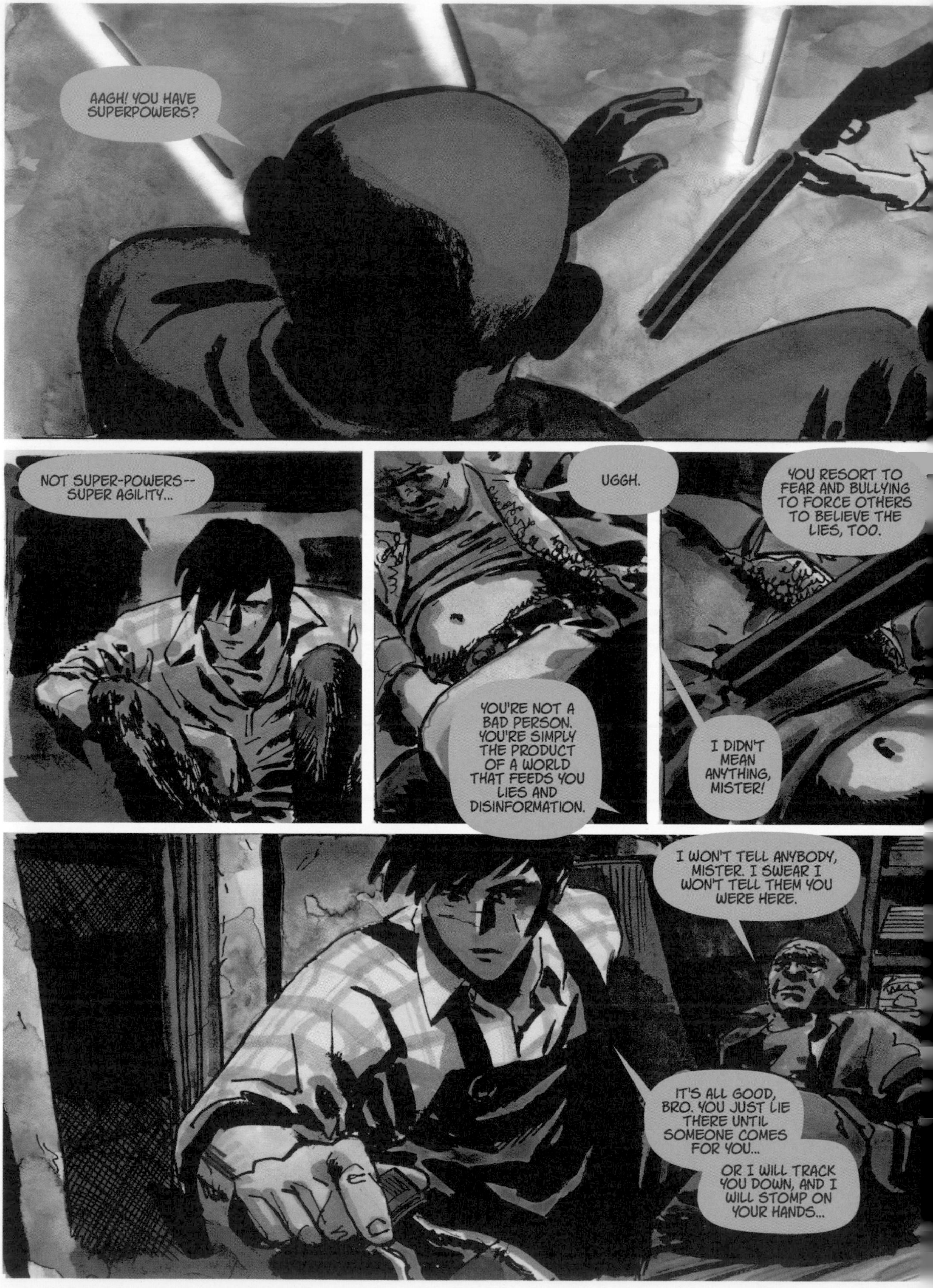
AAGH! YOU HAVE SUPERPOWERS?
NOT SUPER-POWERS--SUPER AGILITY...
UGGH.
YOU'RE NOT A BAD PERSON. YOU'RE SIMPLY THE PRODUCT OF A WORLD THAT FEEDS YOU LIES AND DISINFORMATION.
YOU RESORT TO FEAR AND BULLYING TO FORCE OTHERS TO BELIEVE THE LIES, TOO.
I DIDN'T MEAN ANYTHING, MISTER!
I WON'T TELL ANYBODY, MISTER. I SWEAR I WON'T TELL THEM YOU WERE HERE.
IT'S ALL GOOD, BRO. YOU JUST LIE THERE UNTIL SOMEONE COMES FOR YOU...
OR I WILL TRACK YOU DOWN, AND I WILL STOMP ON YOUR HANDS...

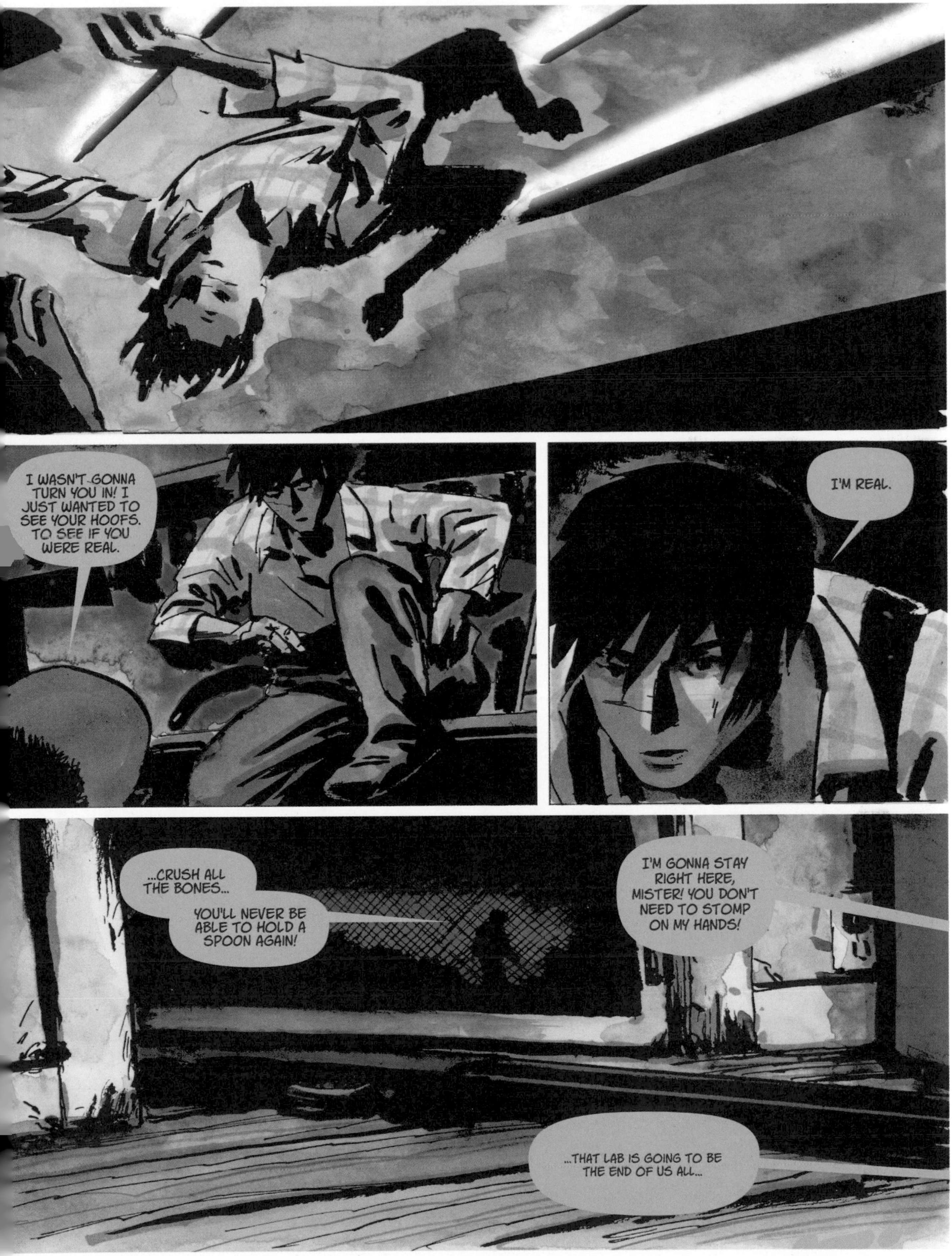
I WASN'T GONNA TURN YOU IN! I JUST WANTED TO SEE YOUR HOOFS. TO SEE IF YOU WERE REAL.
I'M REAL.
...CRUSH ALL THE BONES...
YOU'LL NEVER BE ABLE TO HOLD A SPOON AGAIN!
I'M GONNA STAY RIGHT HERE, MISTER! YOU DON'T NEED TO STOMP ON MY HANDS!
...THAT LAB IS GOING TO BE THE END OF US ALL...

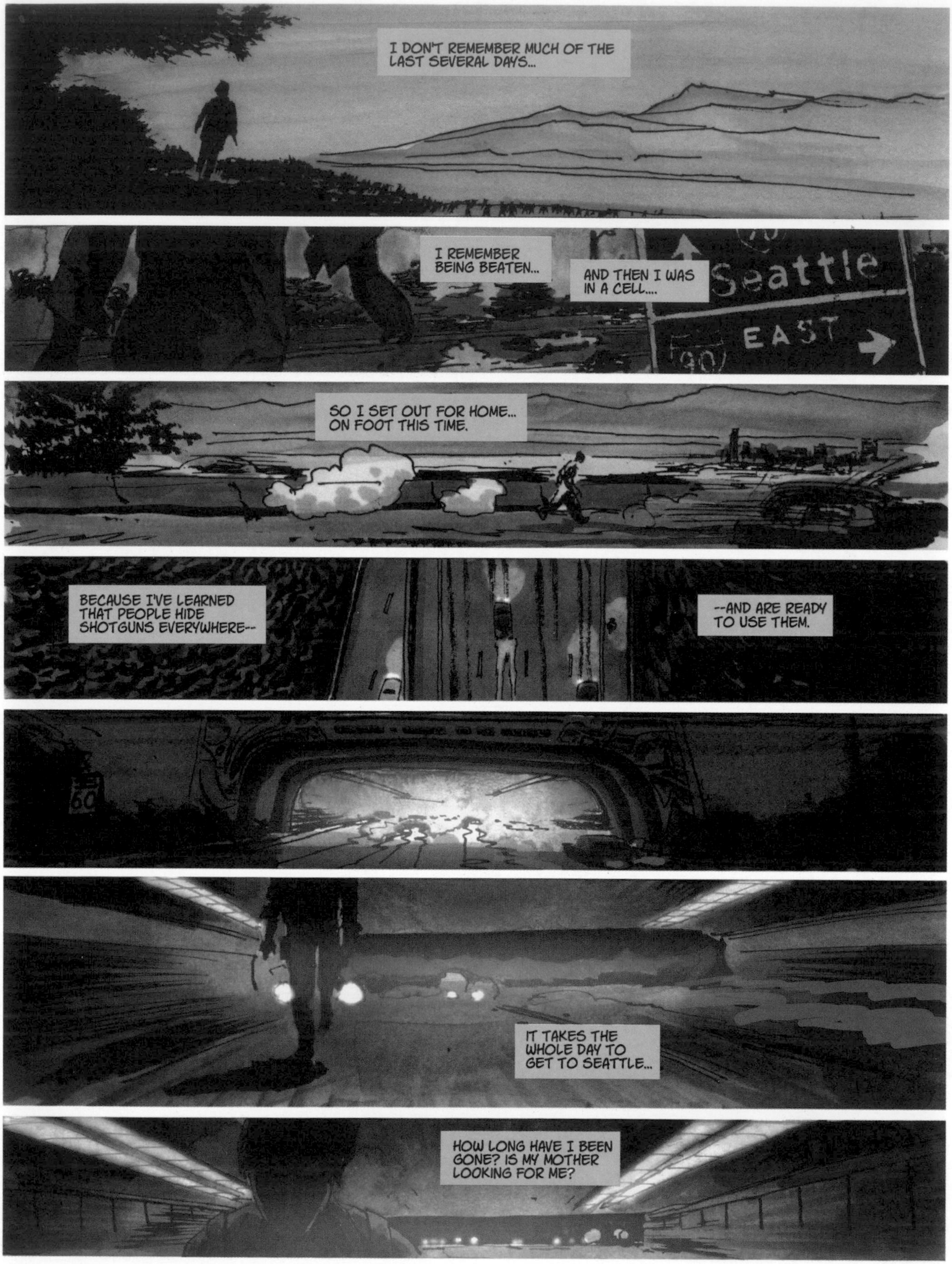
I DON'T REMEMBER MUCH OF THE LAST SEVERAL DAYS...
I REMEMBER BEING BEATEN...
AND THEN I WAS IN A CELL....
Seattle
EAST
90
SO I SET OUT FOR HOME... ON FOOT THIS TIME.
BECAUSE I'VE LEARNED THAT PEOPLE HIDE SHOTGUNS EVERYWHERE--
--AND ARE READY TO USE THEM.
60
IT TAKES THE WHOLE DAY TO GET TO SEATTLE...
HOW LONG HAVE I BEEN GONE? IS MY MOTHER LOOKING FOR ME?

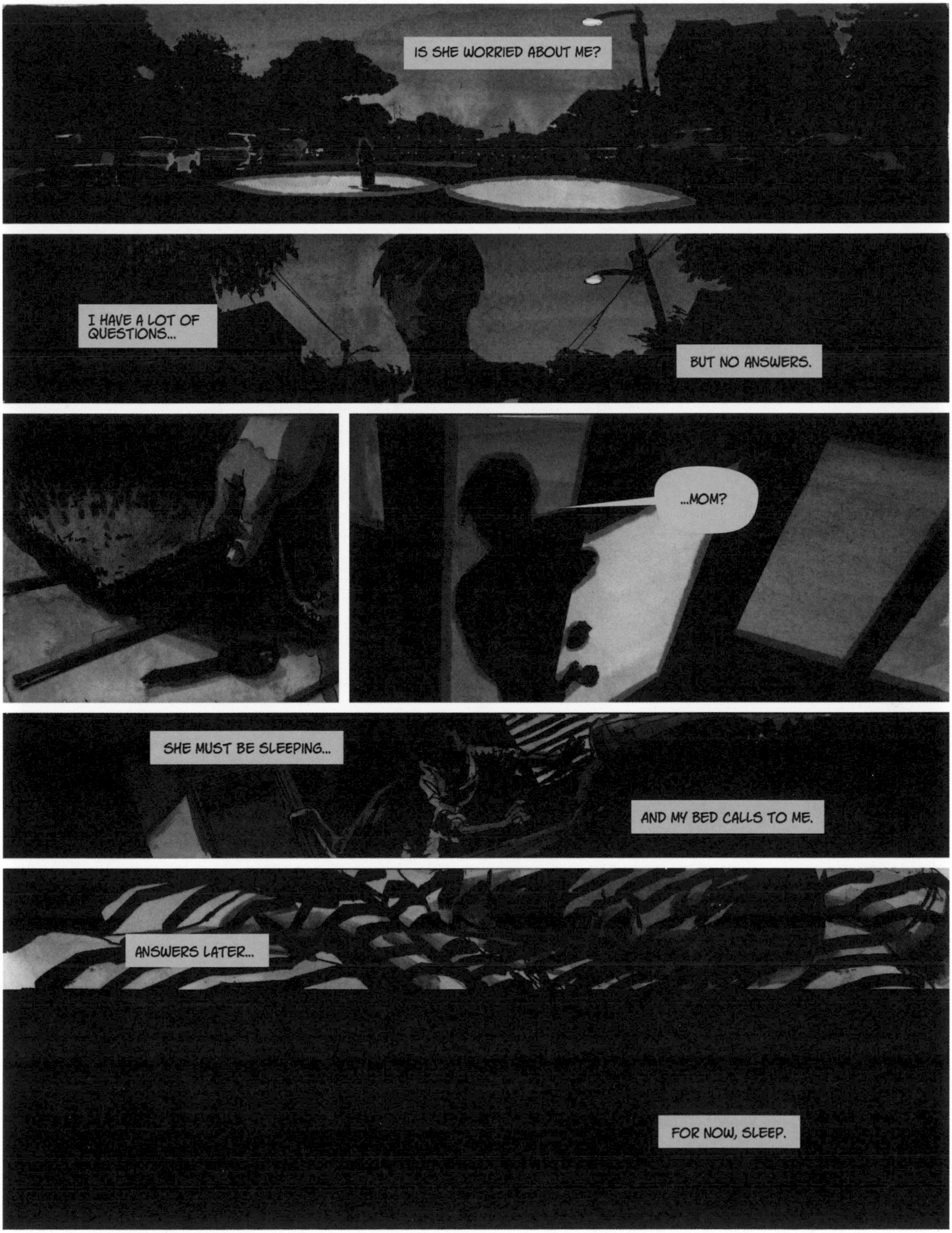
IS SHE WORRIED ABOUT ME?
I HAVE A LOT OF QUESTIONS...
BUT NO ANSWERS.
...MOM?
SHE MUST BE SLEEPING...
AND MY BED CALLS TO ME.
ANSWERS LATER...
FOR NOW, SLEEP.

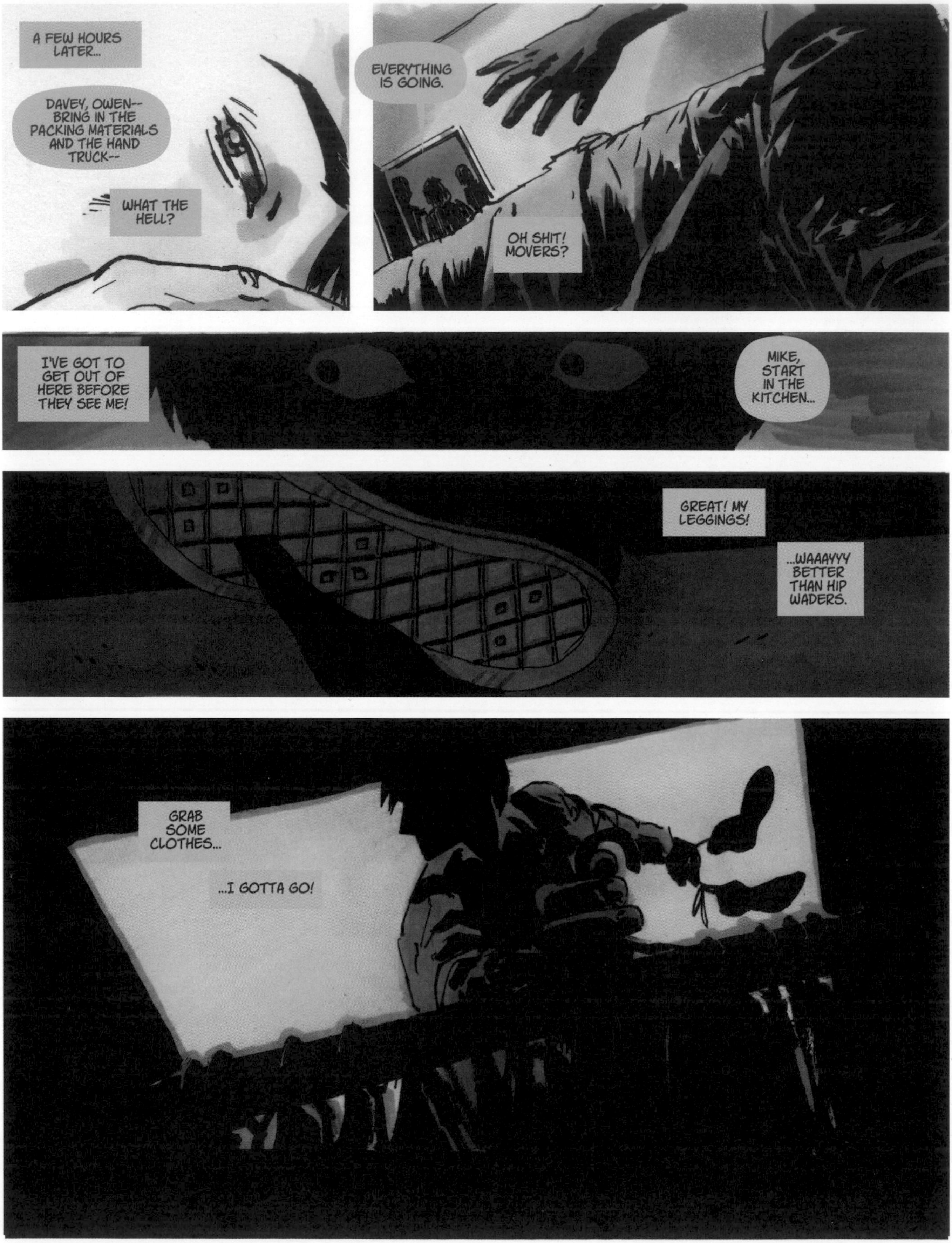
A FEW HOURS LATER...
DAVEY, OWEN--BRING IN THE PACKING MATERIALS AND THE HAND TRUCK--
WHAT THE HELL?
EVERYTHING IS GOING.
OH SHIT! MOVERS?
I'VE GOT TO GET OUT OF HERE BEFORE THEY SEE ME!
MIKE, START IN THE KITCHEN...
GREAT! MY LEGGINGS!
...WAAAYYY BETTER THAN HIP WADERS.
GRAB SOME CLOTHES...
...I GOTTA GO!

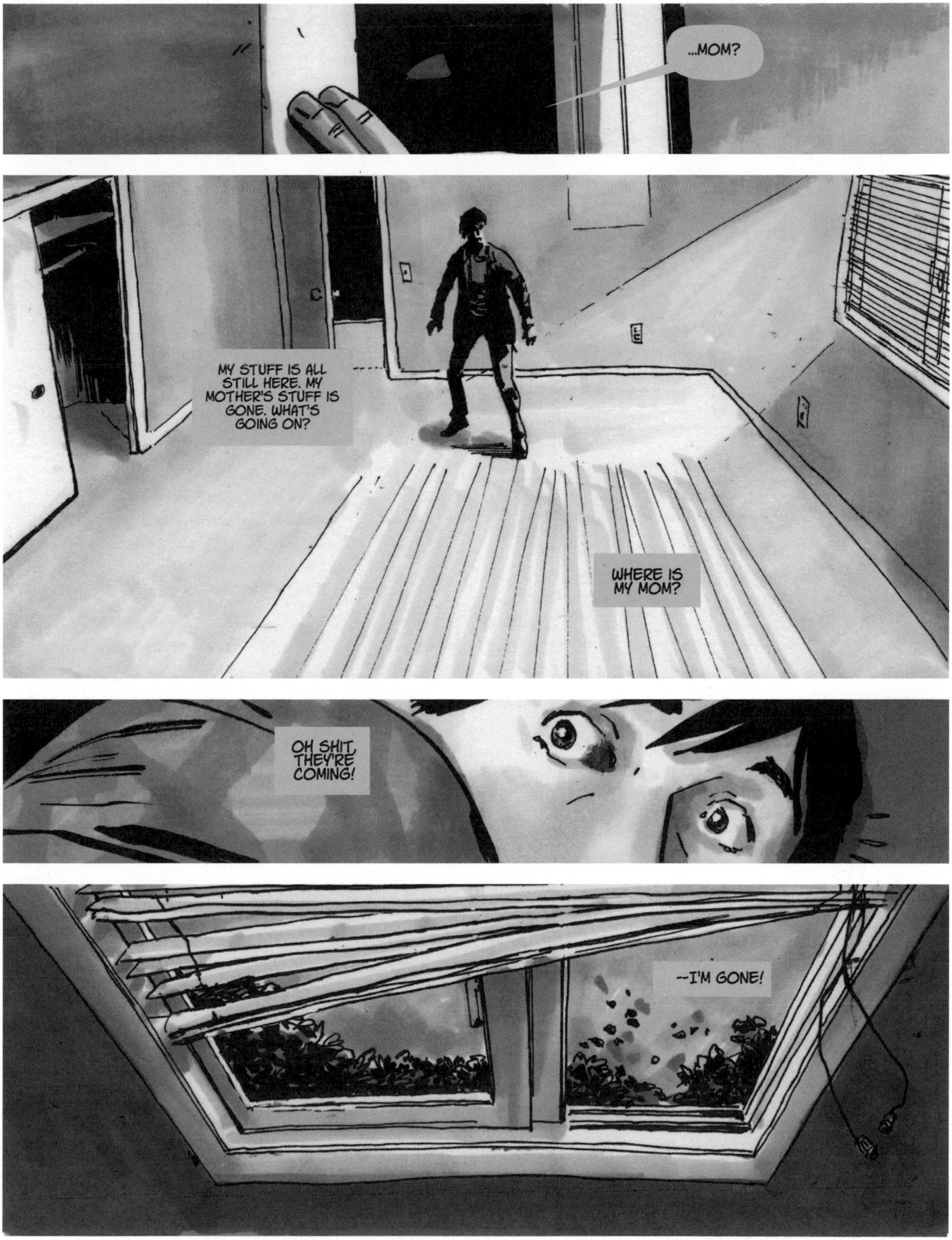
...MOM?
MY STUFF IS ALL STILL HERE. MY MOTHER'S STUFF IS GONE. WHAT'S GOING ON?
WHERE IS MY MOM?
OH SHIT, THEY'RE COMING!
--I'M GONE!

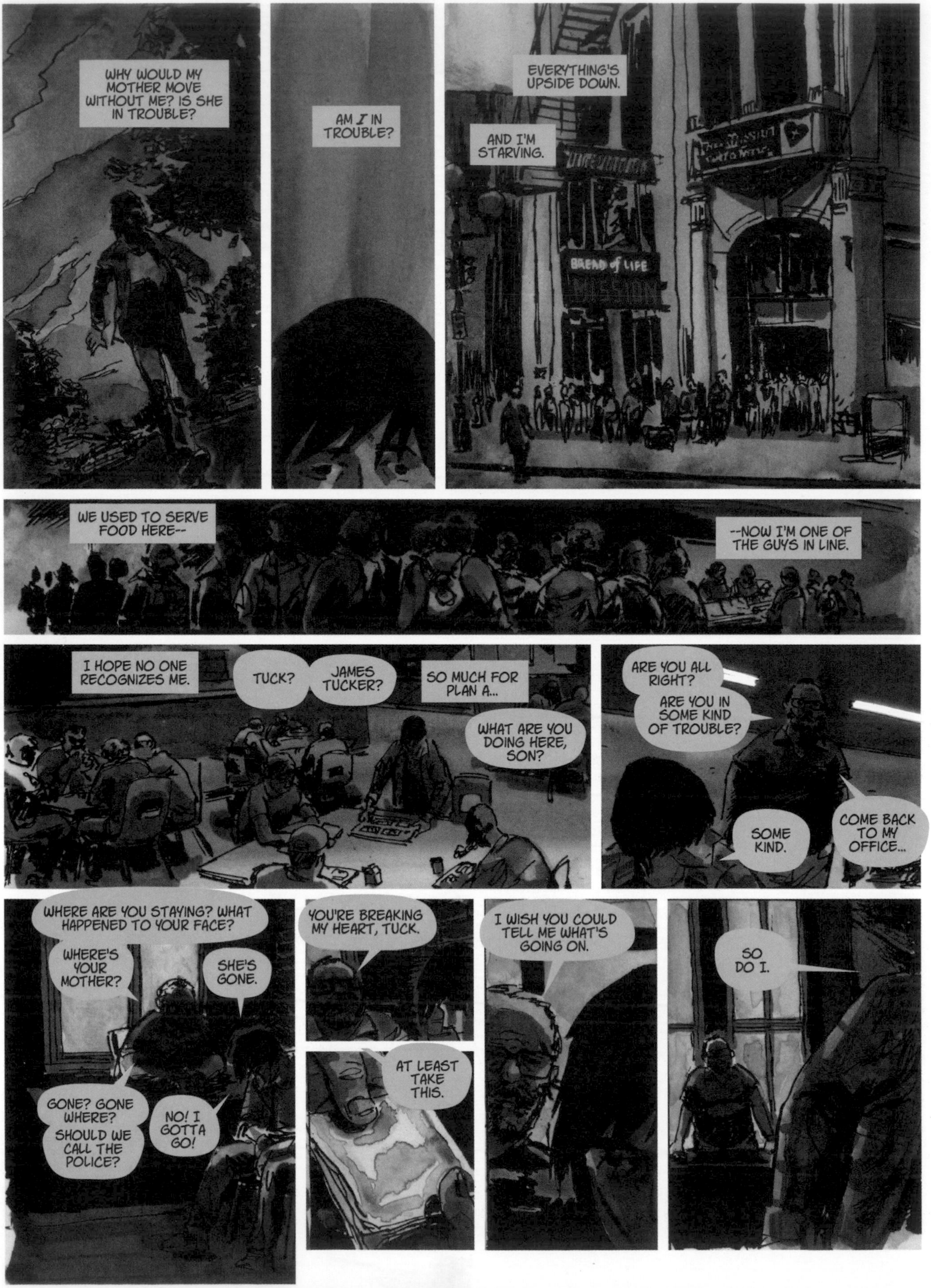
WHY WOULD MY MOTHER MOVE WITHOUT ME? IS SHE IN TROUBLE?
AM I IN TROUBLE?
EVERYTHING'S UPSIDE DOWN.
AND I'M STARVING.
BREAD of LIFE
WE USED TO SERVE FOOD HERE--
--NOW I'M ONE OF THE GUYS IN LINE.
I HOPE NO ONE RECOGNIZES ME.
TUCK?
JAMES TUCKER?
SO MUCH FOR PLAN A...
WHAT ARE YOU DOING HERE, SON?
ARE YOU ALL RIGHT?
ARE YOU IN SOME KIND OF TROUBLE?
SOME KIND.
COME BACK TO MY OFFICE...
WHERE ARE YOU STAYING? WHAT HAPPENED TO YOUR FACE?
WHERE'S YOUR MOTHER?
SHE'S GONE.
GONE? GONE WHERE?
SHOULD WE CALL THE POLICE?
NO! I GOTTA GO!
YOU'RE BREAKING MY HEART, TUCK.
AT LEAST TAKE THIS.
I WISH YOU COULD TELL ME WHAT'S GOING ON.
SO DO I.

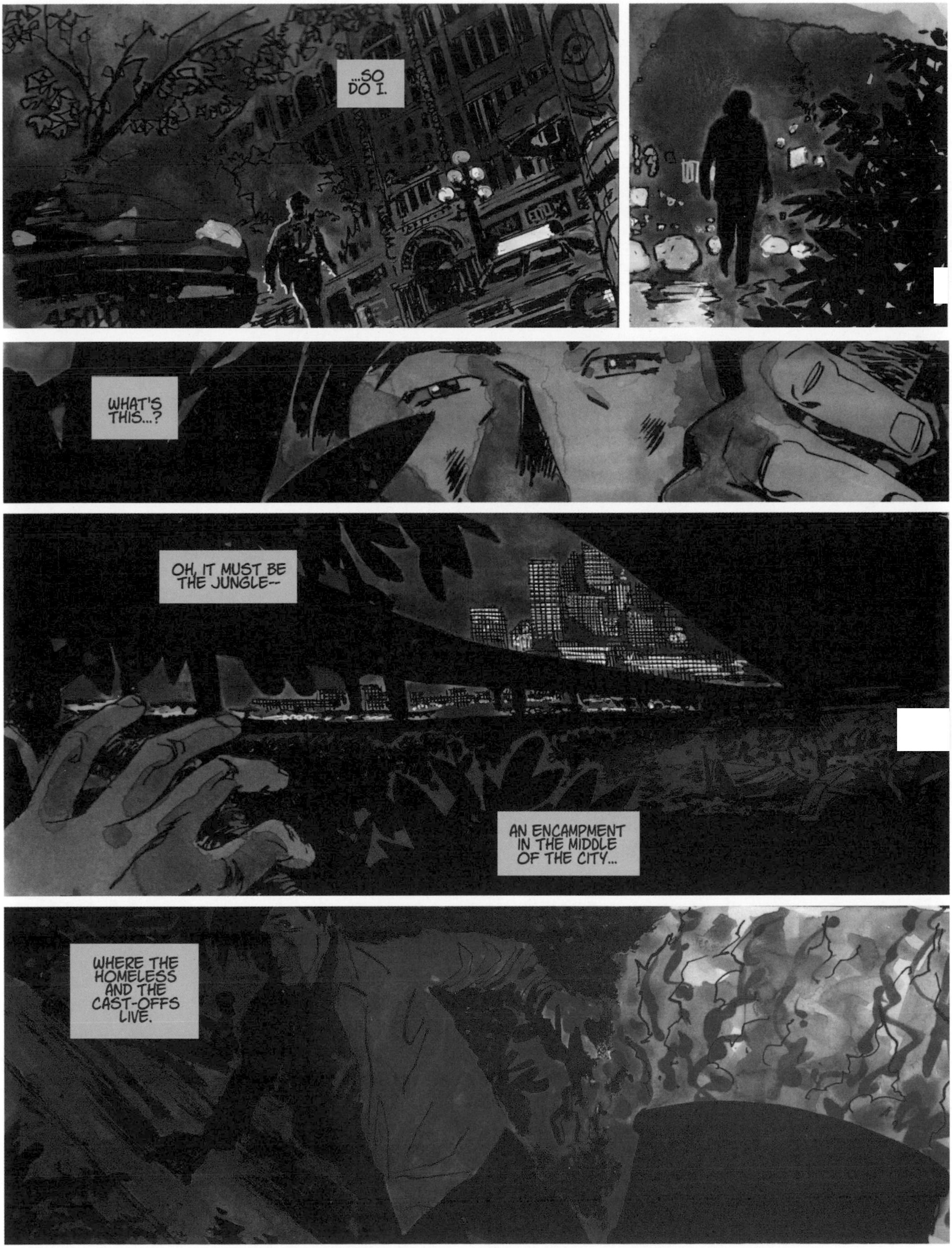
...SO DO I.
WHAT'S THIS...?
OH, IT MUST BE THE JUNGLE--
AN ENCAMPMENT IN THE MIDDLE OF THE CITY...
WHERE THE HOMELESS AND THE CAST-OFFS LIVE.

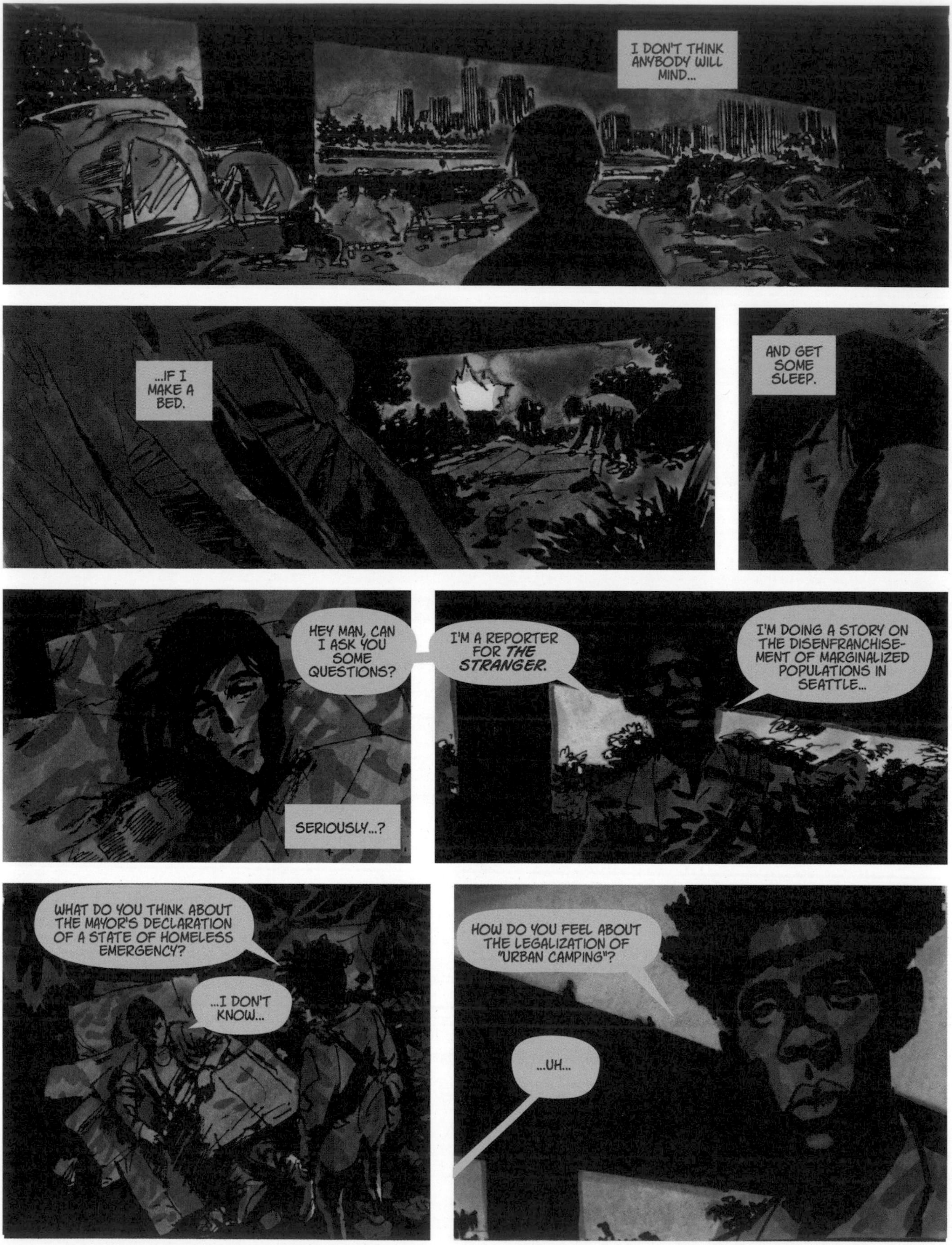
I DON'T THINK ANYBODY WILL MIND...
...IF I MAKE A BED.
AND GET SOME SLEEP.
HEY MAN, CAN I ASK YOU SOME QUESTIONS?
SERIOUSLY...?
I'M A REPORTER FOR THE STRANGER.
I'M DOING A STORY ON THE DISENFRANCHISEMENT OF MARGINALIZED POPULATIONS IN SEATTLE...
WHAT DO YOU THINK ABOUT THE MAYOR'S DECLARATION OF A STATE OF HOMELESS EMERGENCY?
...I DON'T KNOW...
HOW DO YOU FEEL ABOUT THE LEGALIZATION OF "URBAN CAMPING"?
...UH...

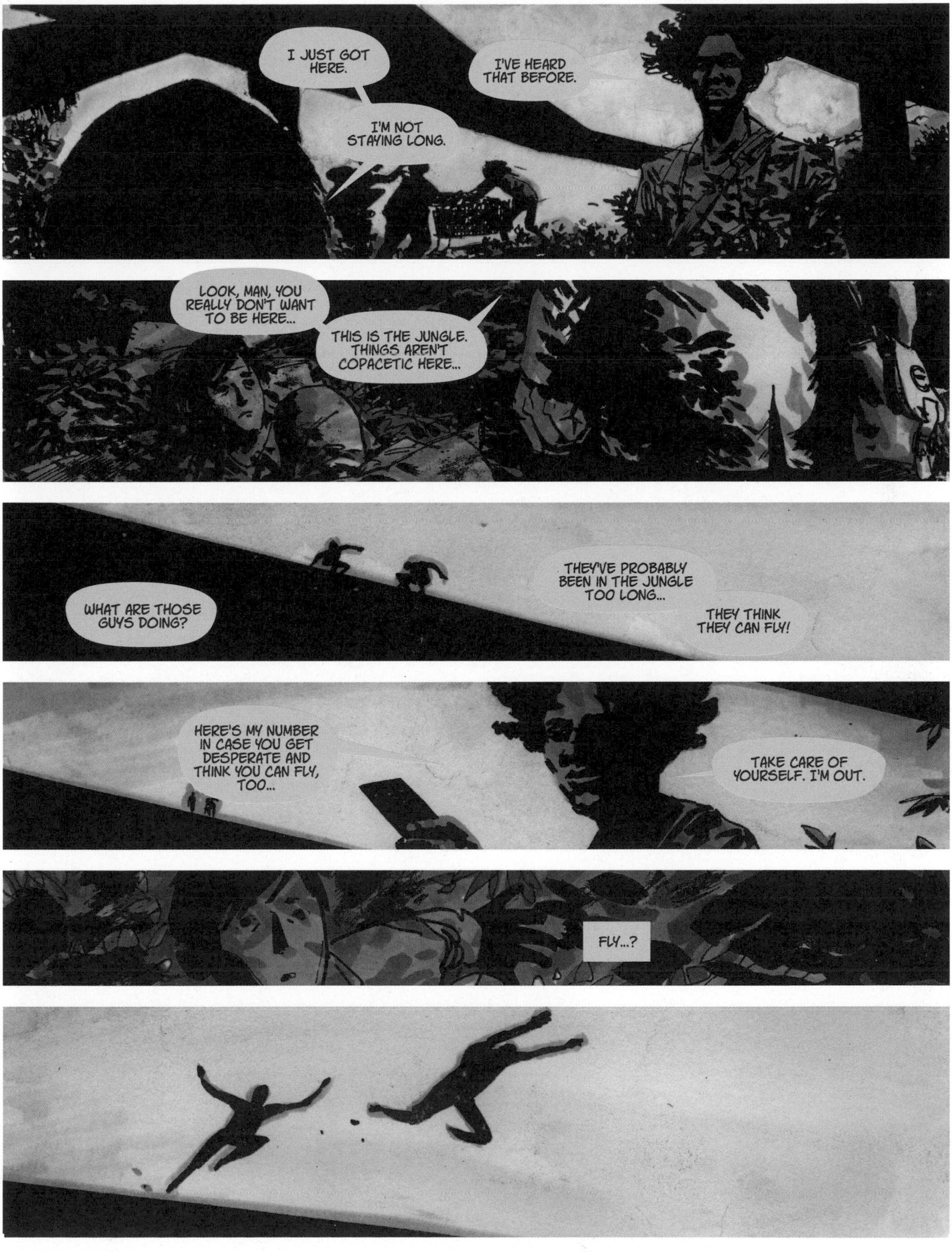
I JUST GOT HERE.
I'M NOT STAYING LONG.
I'VE HEARD THAT BEFORE.
LOOK, MAN, YOU REALLY DON'T WANT TO BE HERE...
THIS IS THE JUNGLE. THINGS AREN'T COPACETIC HERE...
WHAT ARE THOSE GUYS DOING?
THEY'VE PROBABLY BEEN IN THE JUNGLE TOO LONG...
THEY THINK THEY CAN FLY!
HERE'S MY NUMBER IN CASE YOU GET DESPERATE AND THINK YOU CAN FLY, TOO...
TAKE CARE OF YOURSELF. I'M OUT.
FLY...?

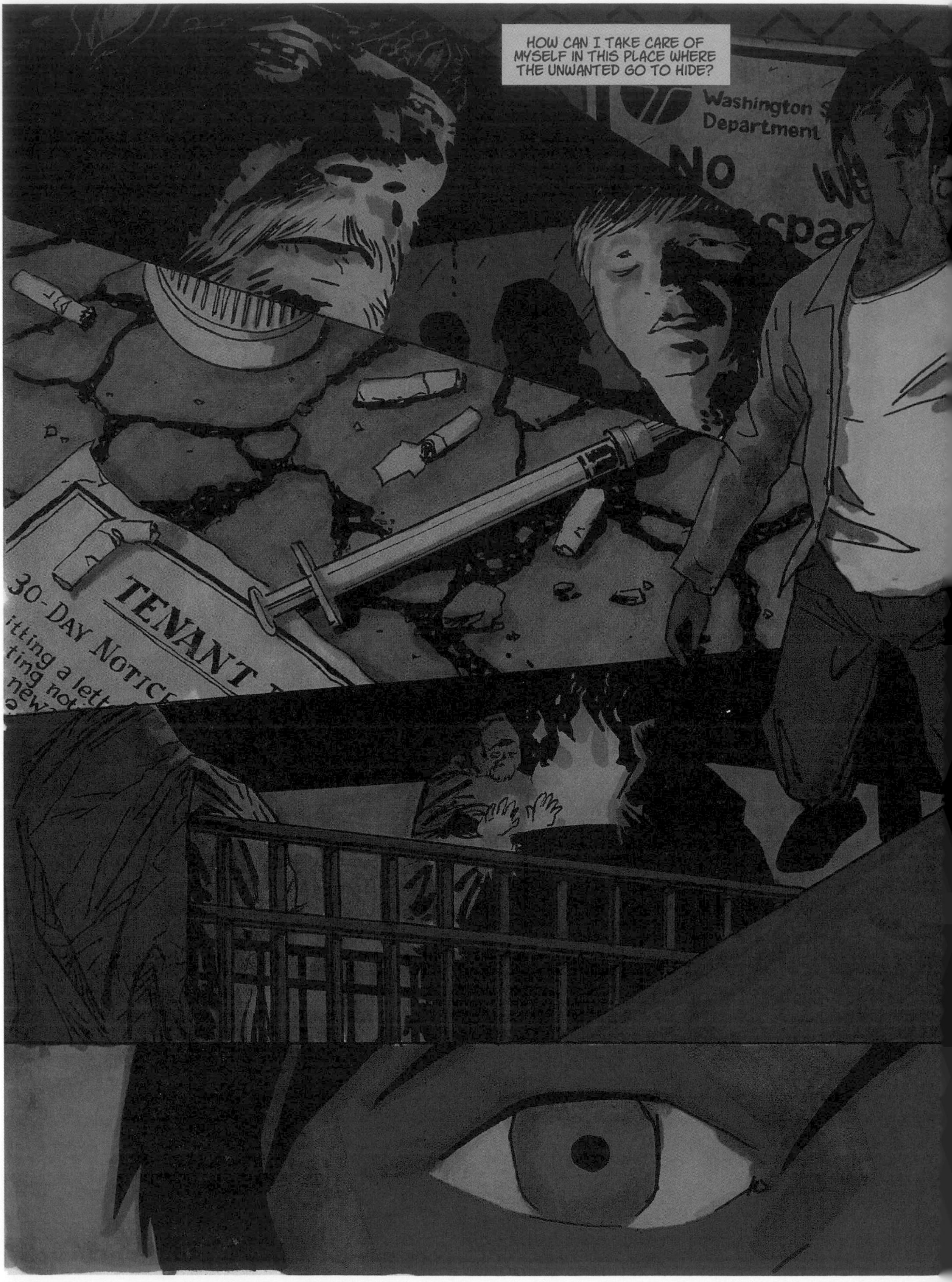
HOW CAN I TAKE CARE OF MYSELF IN THIS PLACE WHERE THE UNWANTED GO TO HIDE?
Department
No
TENANT

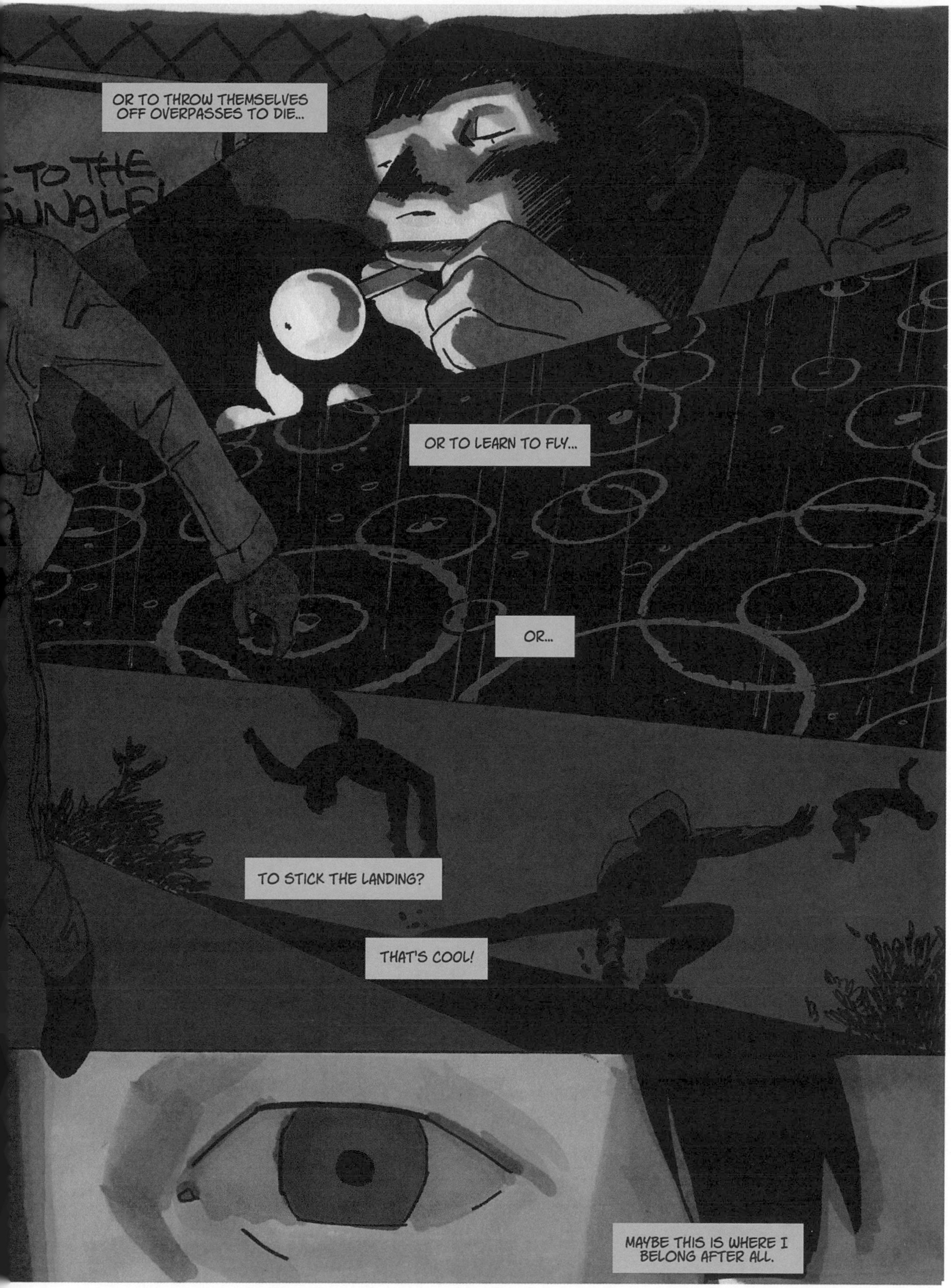

OR TO THROW THEMSELVES OFF OVERPASSES TO DIE...
TO THE
OR TO LEARN TO FLY...
OR...
TO STICK THE LANDING?
THAT'S COOL!
MAYBE THIS IS WHERE I BELONG AFTER ALL.

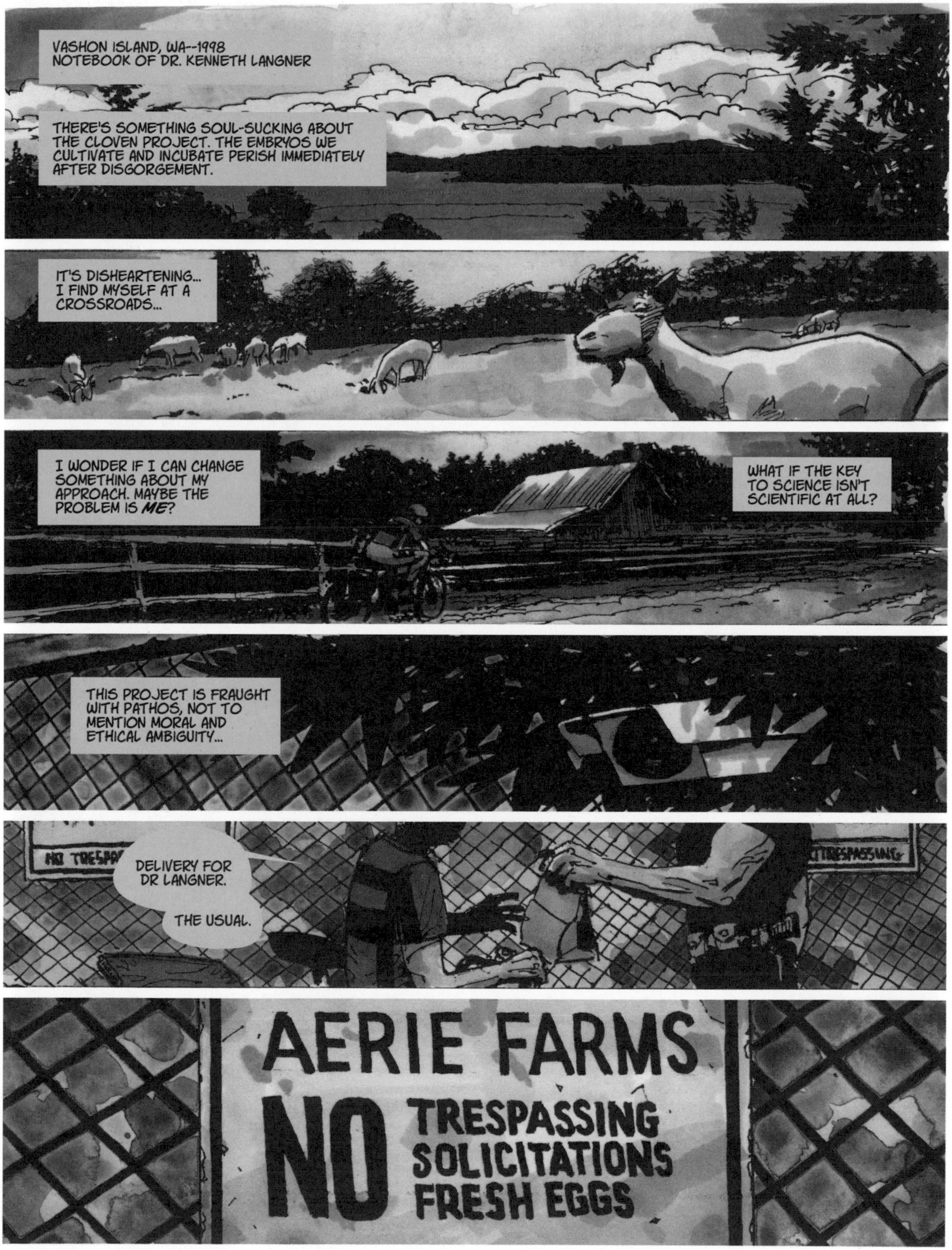
VASHON ISLAND, WA--1998
NOTEBOOK OF DR. KENNETH LANGNER
THERE'S SOMETHING SOUL-SUCKING ABOUT THE CLOVEN PROJECT. THE EMBRYOS WE CULTIVATE AND INCUBATE PERISH IMMEDIATELY AFTER DISGORGEMENT.
IT'S DISHEARTENING... I FIND MYSELF AT A CROSSROADS...
I WONDER IF I CAN CHANGE SOMETHING ABOUT MY APPROACH. MAYBE THE PROBLEM IS *ME*?
WHAT IF THE KEY TO SCIENCE ISN'T SCIENTIFIC AT ALL?
THIS PROJECT IS FRAUGHT WITH PATHOS, NOT TO MENTION MORAL AND ETHICAL AMBIGUITY...
DELIVERY FOR DR LANGNER.
THE USUAL.
AERIE FARMS
NO TRESPASSING
SOLICITATIONS
FRESH EGGS

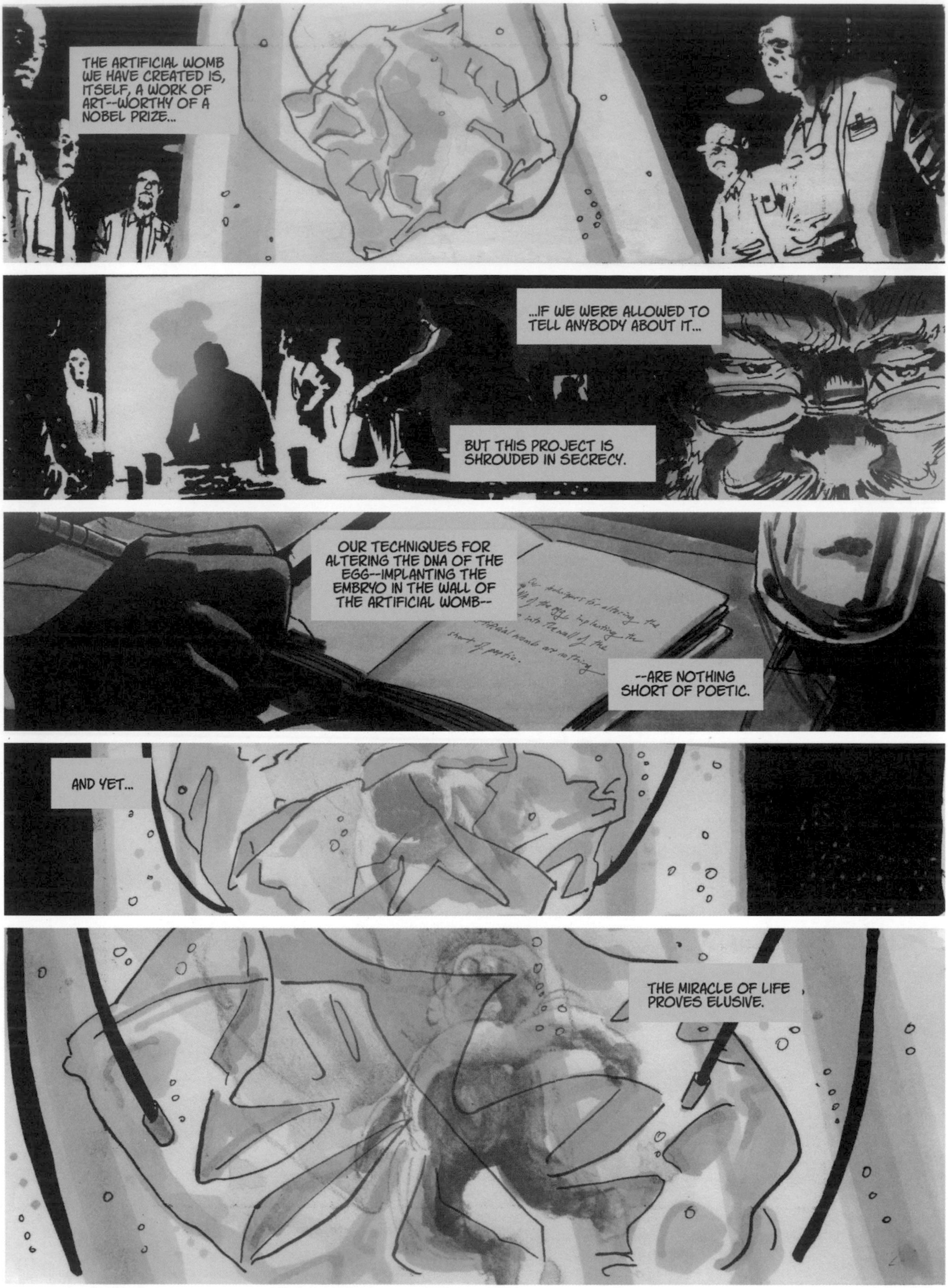
THE ARTIFICIAL WOMB WE HAVE CREATED IS, ITSELF, A WORK OF ART--WORTHY OF A NOBEL PRIZE...
...IF WE WERE ALLOWED TO TELL ANYBODY ABOUT IT...
BUT THIS PROJECT IS SHROUDED IN SECRECY.
OUR TECHNIQUES FOR ALTERING THE DNA OF THE EGG--IMPLANTING THE EMBRYO IN THE WALL OF THE ARTIFICIAL WOMB--
--ARE NOTHING SHORT OF POETIC.
AND YET...
THE MIRACLE OF LIFE PROVES ELUSIVE.

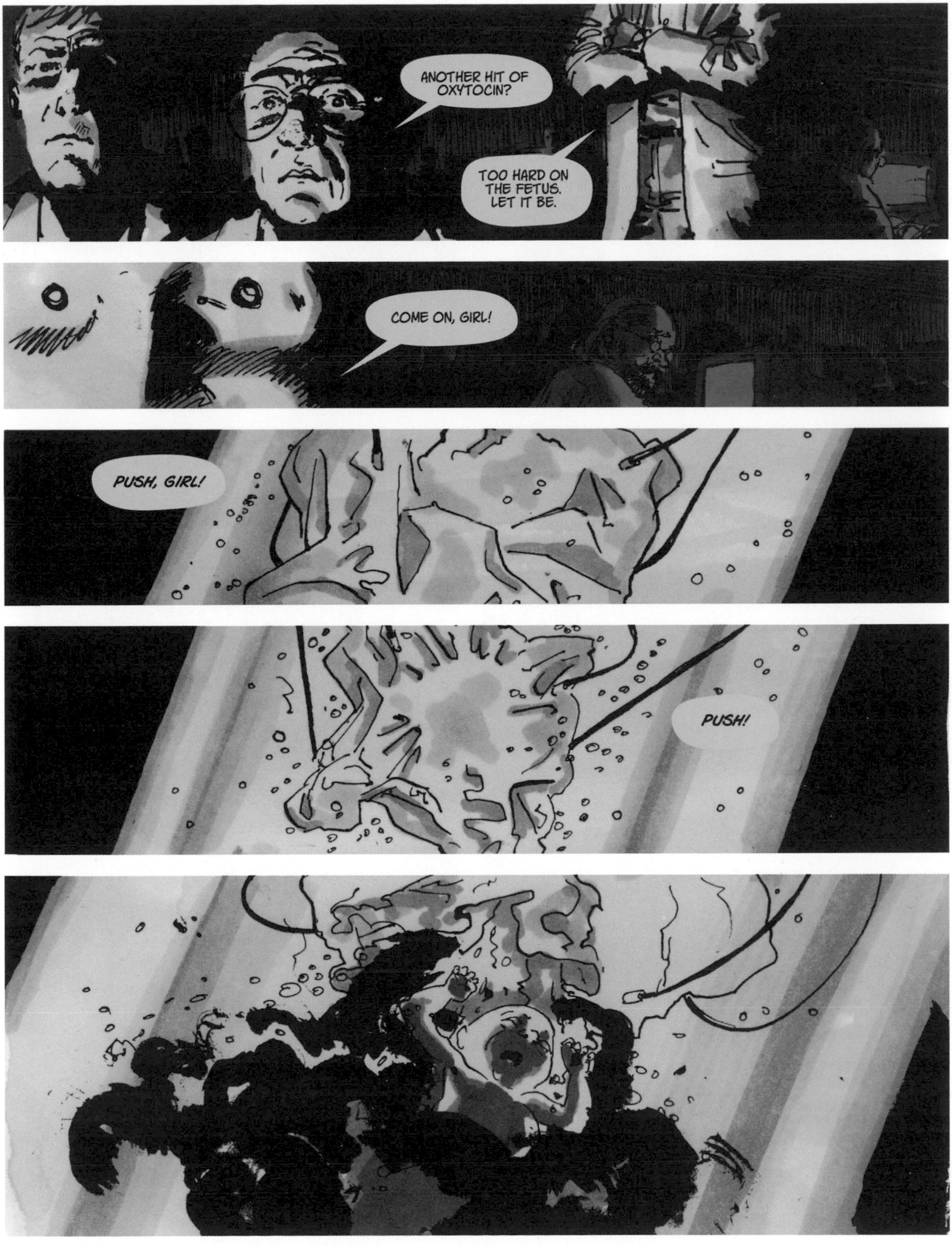
ANOTHER HIT OF OXYTOCIN?
TOO HARD ON THE FETUS. LET IT BE.
COME ON, GIRL!
PUSH, GIRL!
PUSH!

IT'S ALIVE!
THEIR LIVES ARE MEASURED IN MINUTES.
WHAT THE HELL?
HIT IT WITH THE PADDLES!
ANYTHING?
NOTHING.
DAMN.
WE'LL GET IT RIGHT EVENTUALLY, BOYS.

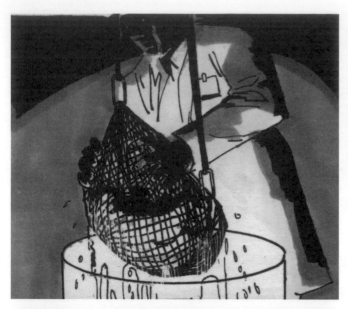

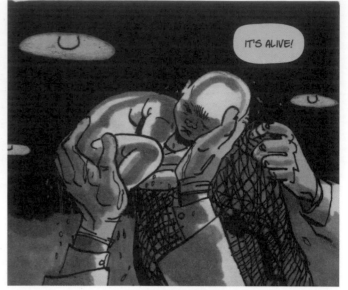

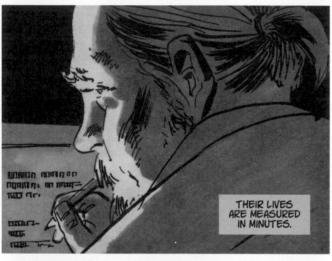

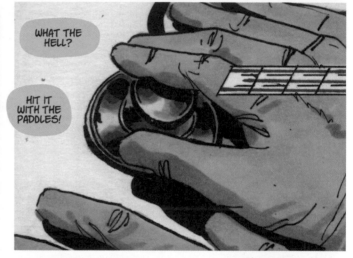

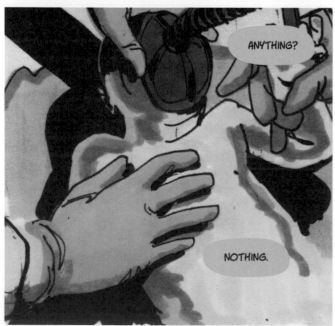

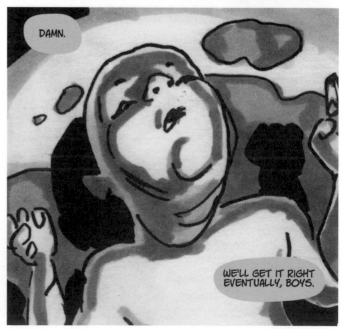

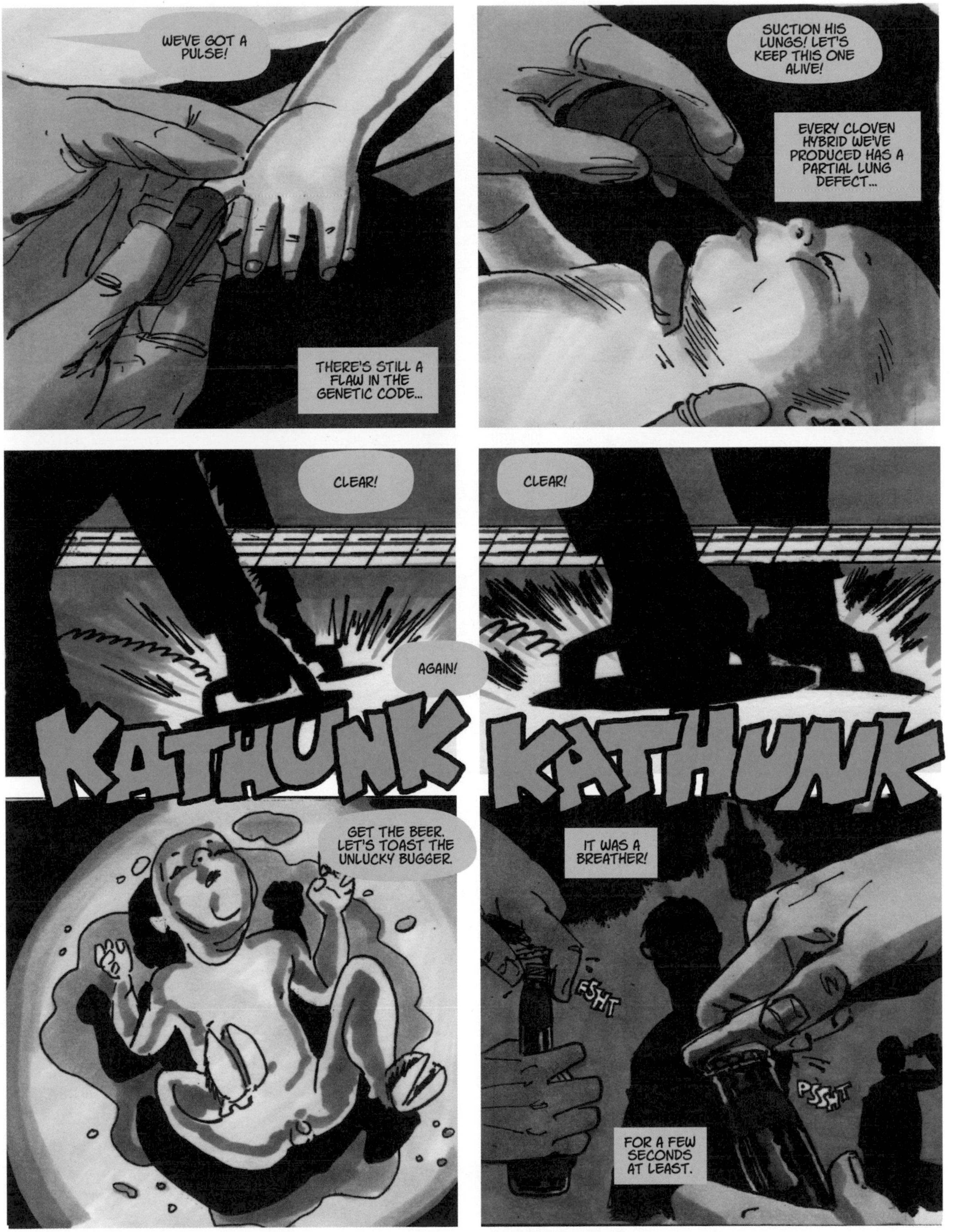
WE'VE GOT A PULSE!
THERE'S STILL A FLAW IN THE GENETIC CODE...
SUCTION HIS LUNGS! LET'S KEEP THIS ONE ALIVE!
EVERY CLOVEN HYBRID WE'VE PRODUCED HAS A PARTIAL LUNG DEFECT...
CLEAR!
KATHUNK
AGAIN!
CLEAR!
KATHUNK
GET THE BEER. LET'S TOAST THE UNLUCKY BUGGER.
IT WAS A BREATHER!
FSHT
PSSHT
FOR A FEW SECONDS AT LEAST.

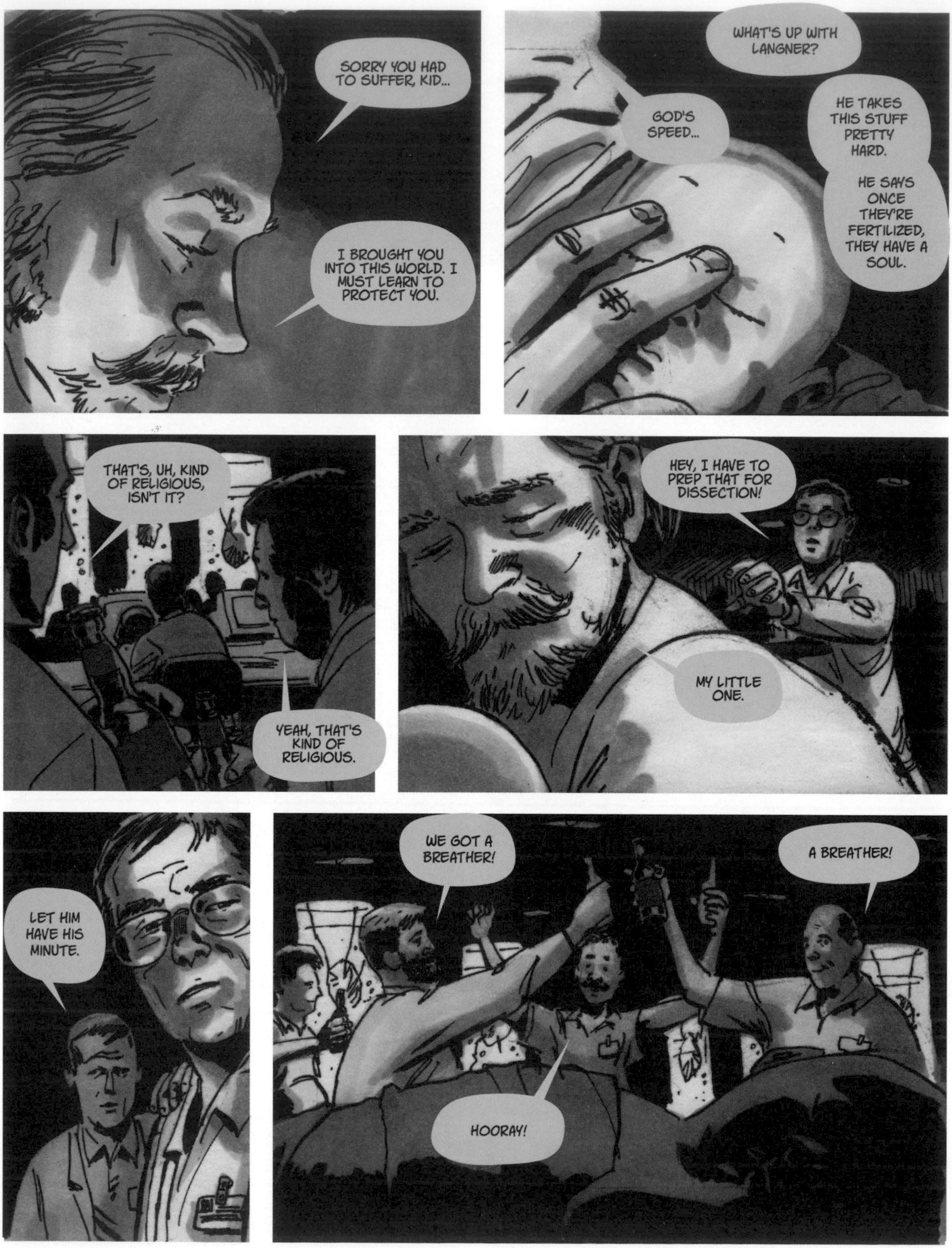
SORRY YOU HAD TO SUFFER, KID...
I BROUGHT YOU INTO THIS WORLD. I MUST LEARN TO PROTECT YOU.
WHAT'S UP WITH LANGNER?
GOD'S SPEED...
HE TAKES THIS STUFF PRETTY HARD.
HE SAYS ONCE THEY'RE FERTILIZED, THEY HAVE A SOUL.
THAT'S, UH, KIND OF RELIGIOUS, ISN'T IT?
YEAH, THAT'S KIND OF RELIGIOUS.
HEY, I HAVE TO PREP THAT FOR DISSECTION!
MY LITTLE ONE.
LET HIM HAVE HIS MINUTE.
WE GOT A BREATHER!
A BREATHER!
HOORAY!

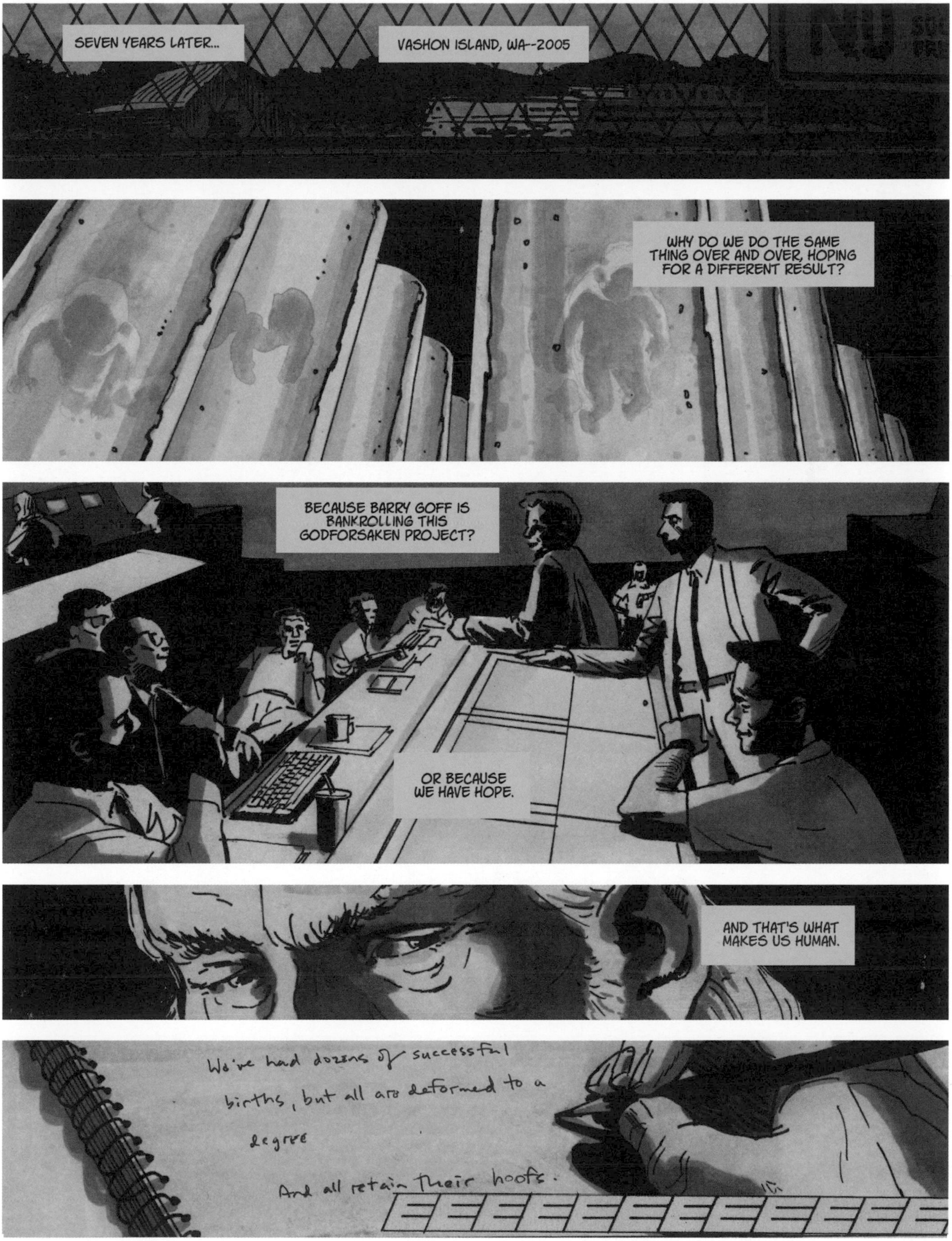
SEVEN YEARS LATER...
VASHON ISLAND, WA--2005
WHY DO WE DO THE SAME THING OVER AND OVER, HOPING FOR A DIFFERENT RESULT?
BECAUSE BARRY GOFF IS BANKROLLING THIS GODFORSAKEN PROJECT?
OR BECAUSE WE HAVE HOPE.
AND THAT'S WHAT MAKES US HUMAN.
We've had dozens of successful births, but all are deformed to a degree
And all retain their hoofs.
EEEEEEEEEEEE

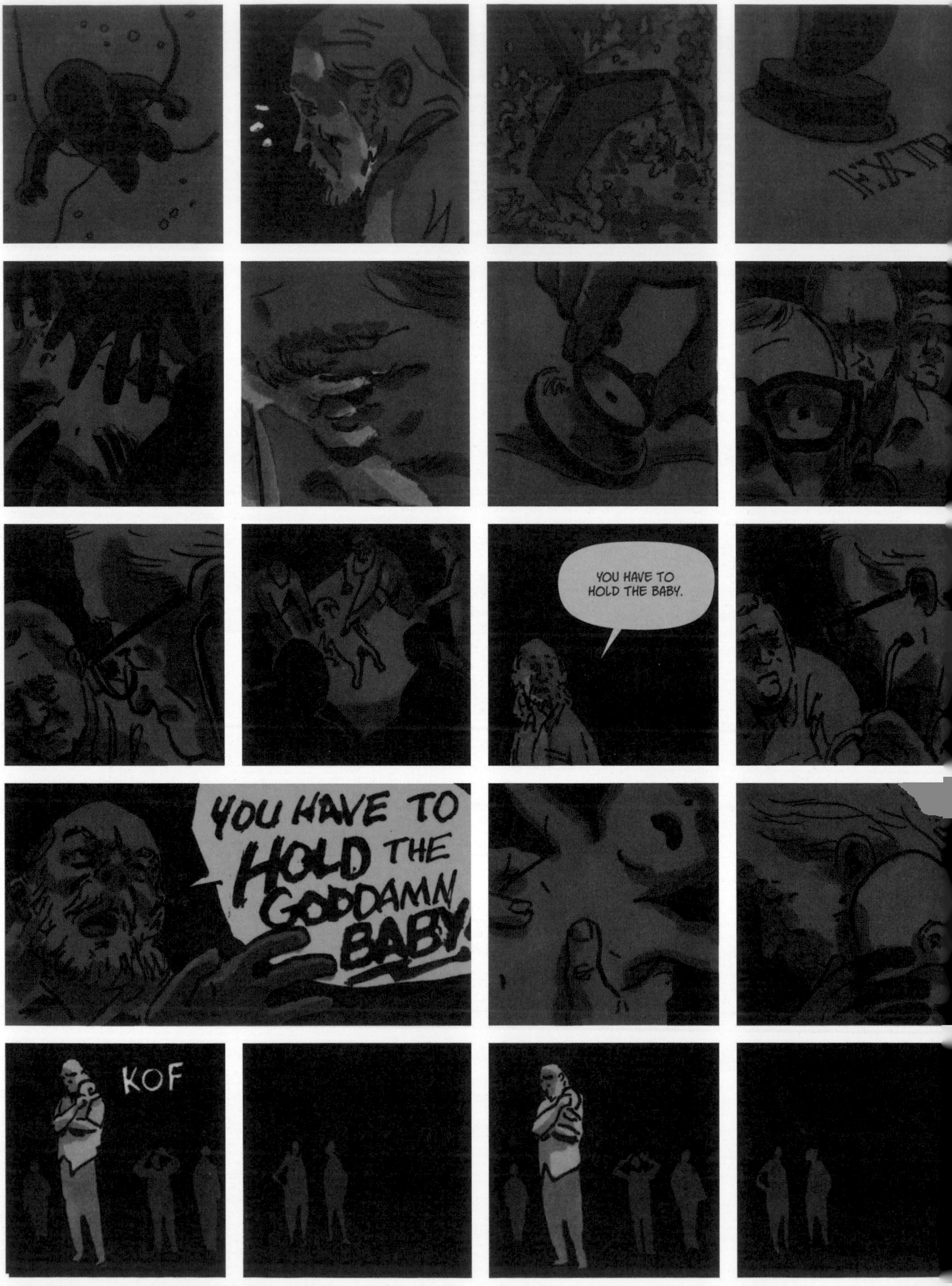

YOU HAVE TO HOLD THE BABY.
YOU HAVE TO HOLD THE GODDAMN BABY!
KOF

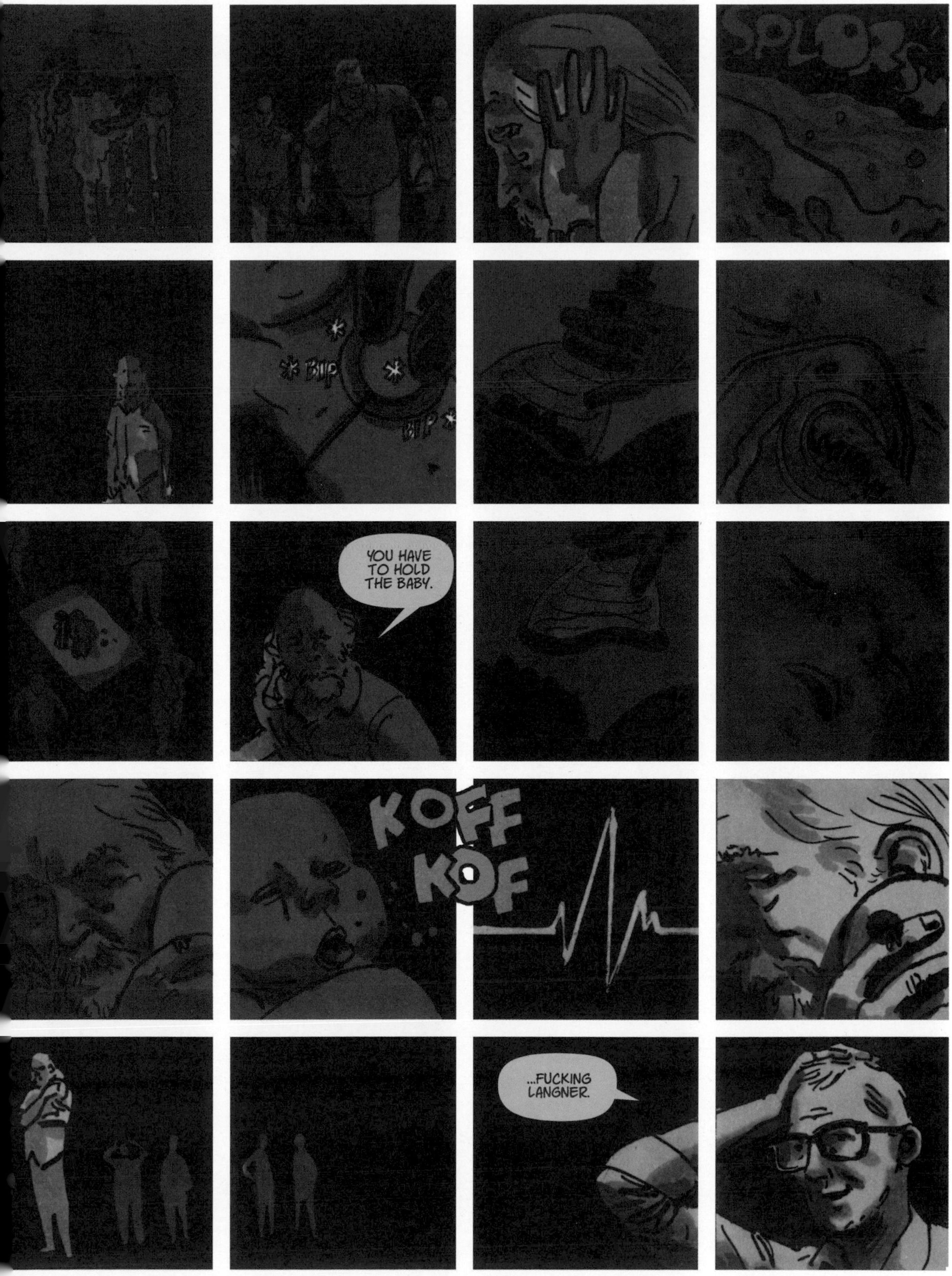
SPLOSH
* BLIP *
BLIP *
YOU HAVE TO HOLD THE BABY.
KOFF KOF
...FUCKING LANGNER.

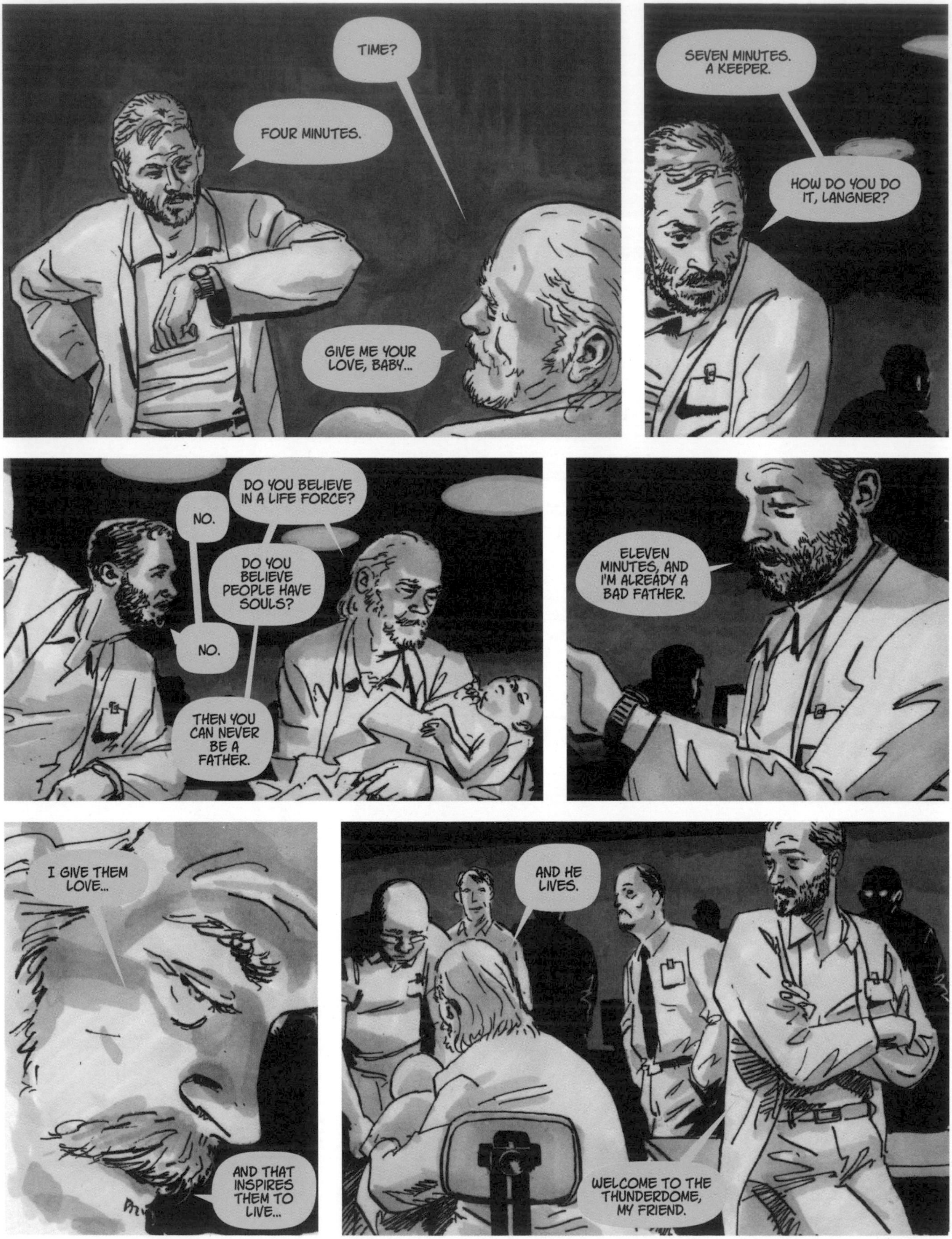
TIME?
FOUR MINUTES.
GIVE ME YOUR LOVE, BABY...
SEVEN MINUTES. A KEEPER.
HOW DO YOU DO IT, LANGNER?
DO YOU BELIEVE IN A LIFE FORCE?
NO.
DO YOU BELIEVE PEOPLE HAVE SOULS?
NO.
THEN YOU CAN NEVER BE A FATHER.
ELEVEN MINUTES, AND I'M ALREADY A BAD FATHER.
I GIVE THEM LOVE...
AND THAT INSPIRES THEM TO LIVE...
AND HE LIVES.
WELCOME TO THE THUNDERDOME, MY FRIEND.

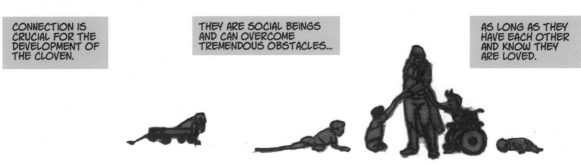

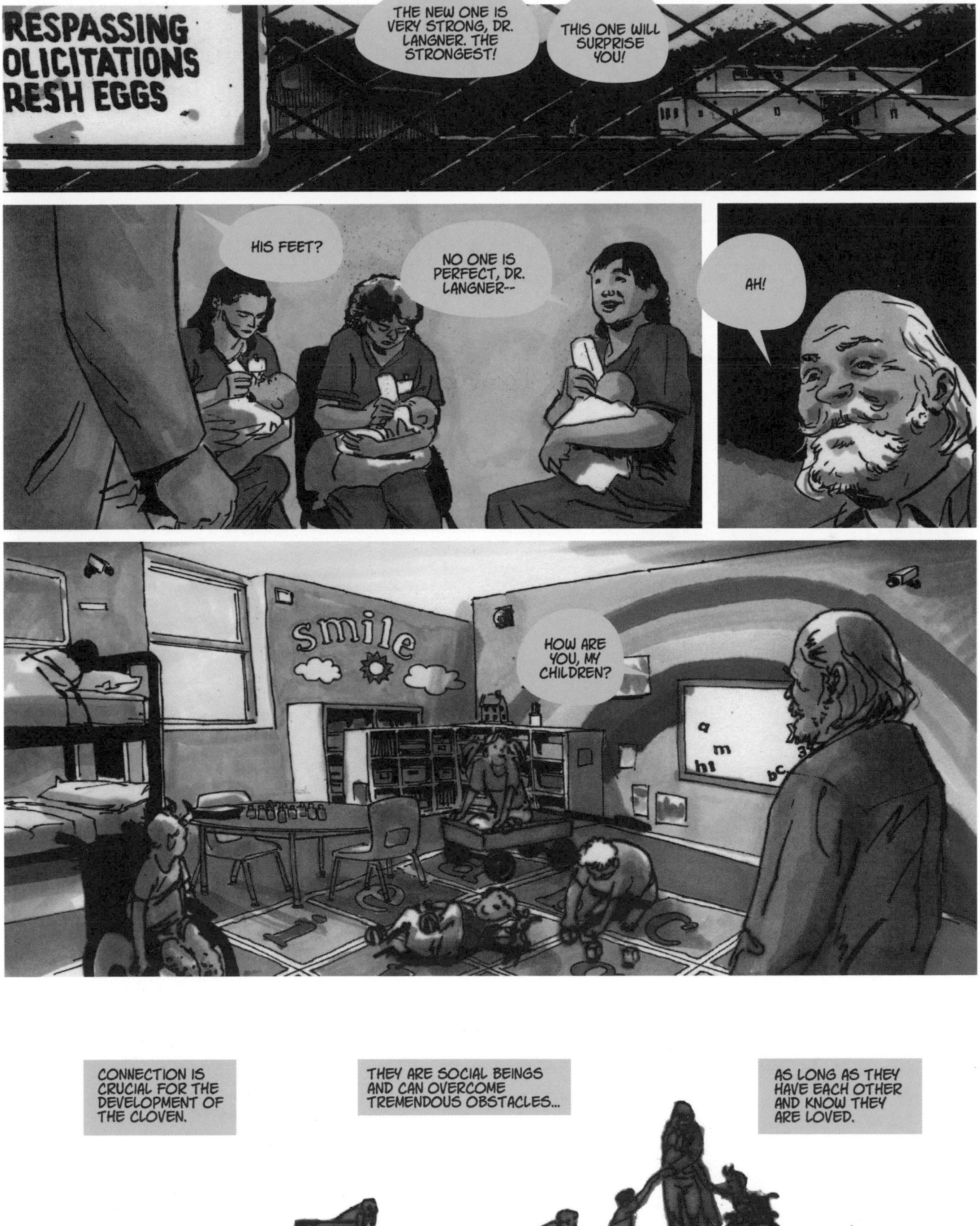
RESPASSING
OLICITATIONS
RESH EGGS
THE NEW ONE IS VERY STRONG, DR. LANGNER. THE STRONGEST!
THIS ONE WILL SURPRISE YOU!
HIS FEET?
NO ONE IS PERFECT, DR. LANGNER--
AH!
smile
HOW ARE YOU, MY CHILDREN?
CONNECTION IS CRUCIAL FOR THE DEVELOPMENT OF THE CLOVEN.
THEY ARE SOCIAL BEINGS AND CAN OVERCOME TREMENDOUS OBSTACLES...
AS LONG AS THEY HAVE EACH OTHER AND KNOW THEY ARE LOVED.

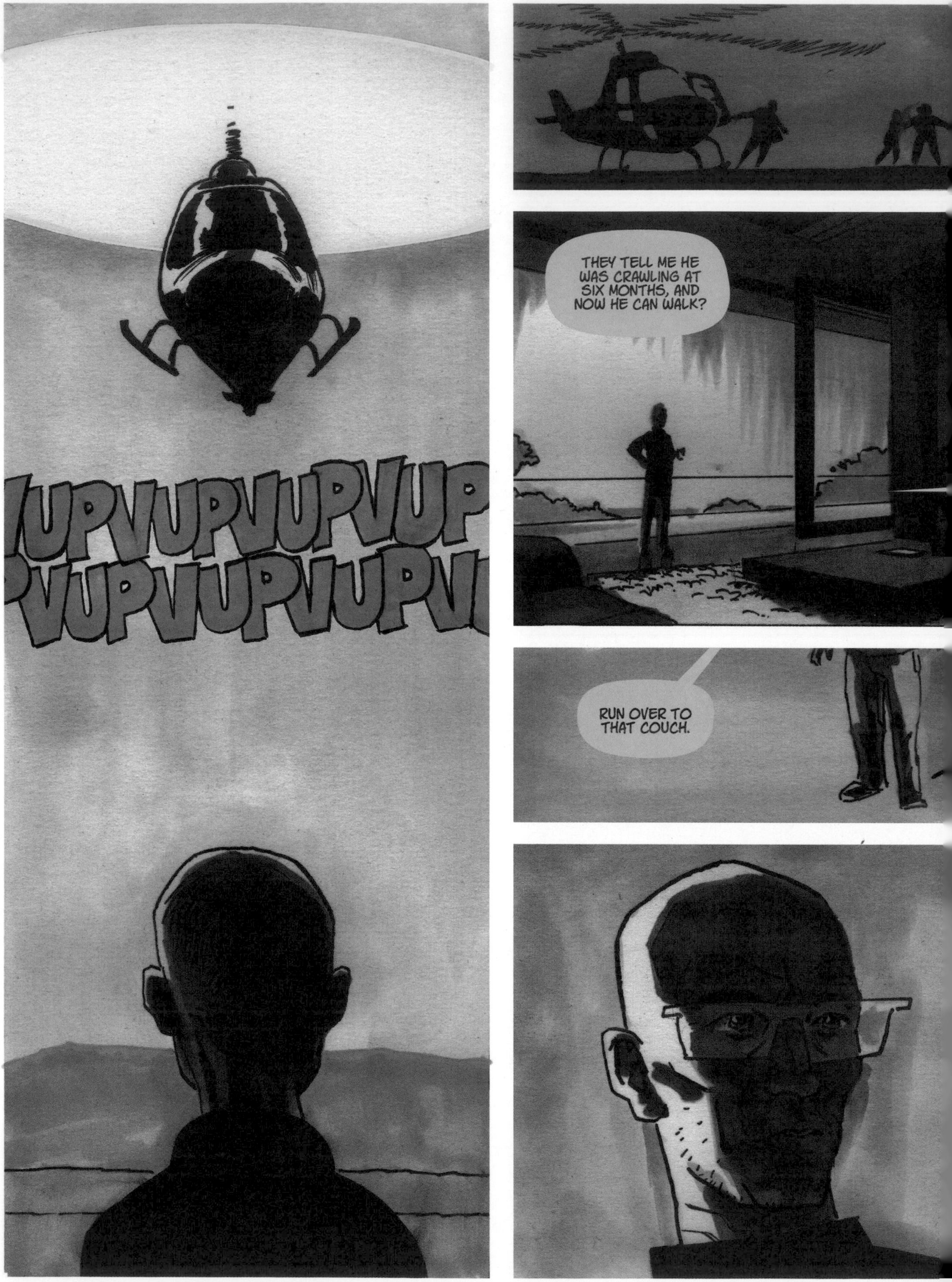

VUPVUPVUPVUP
VUPVUPVUPVU
THEY TELL ME HE WAS CRAWLING AT SIX MONTHS, AND NOW HE CAN WALK?
RUN OVER TO THAT COUCH.

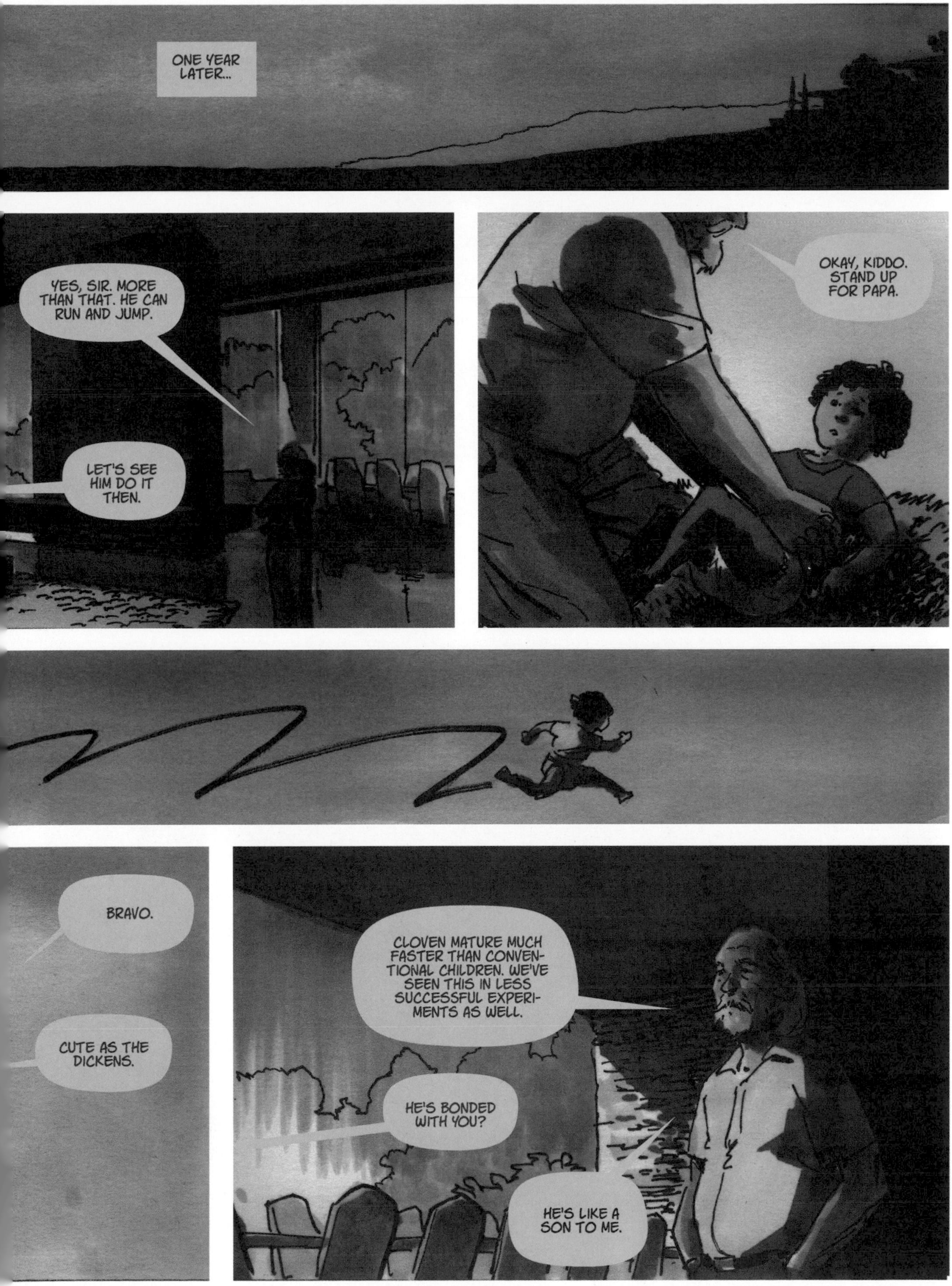
ONE YEAR LATER...
YES, SIR. MORE THAN THAT. HE CAN RUN AND JUMP.
LET'S SEE HIM DO IT THEN.
OKAY, KIDDO. STAND UP FOR PAPA.
BRAVO.
CUTE AS THE DICKENS.
CLOVEN MATURE MUCH FASTER THAN CONVEN-TIONAL CHILDREN. WE'VE SEEN THIS IN LESS SUCCESSFUL EXPERI-MENTS AS WELL.
HE'S BONDED WITH YOU?
HE'S LIKE A SON TO ME.

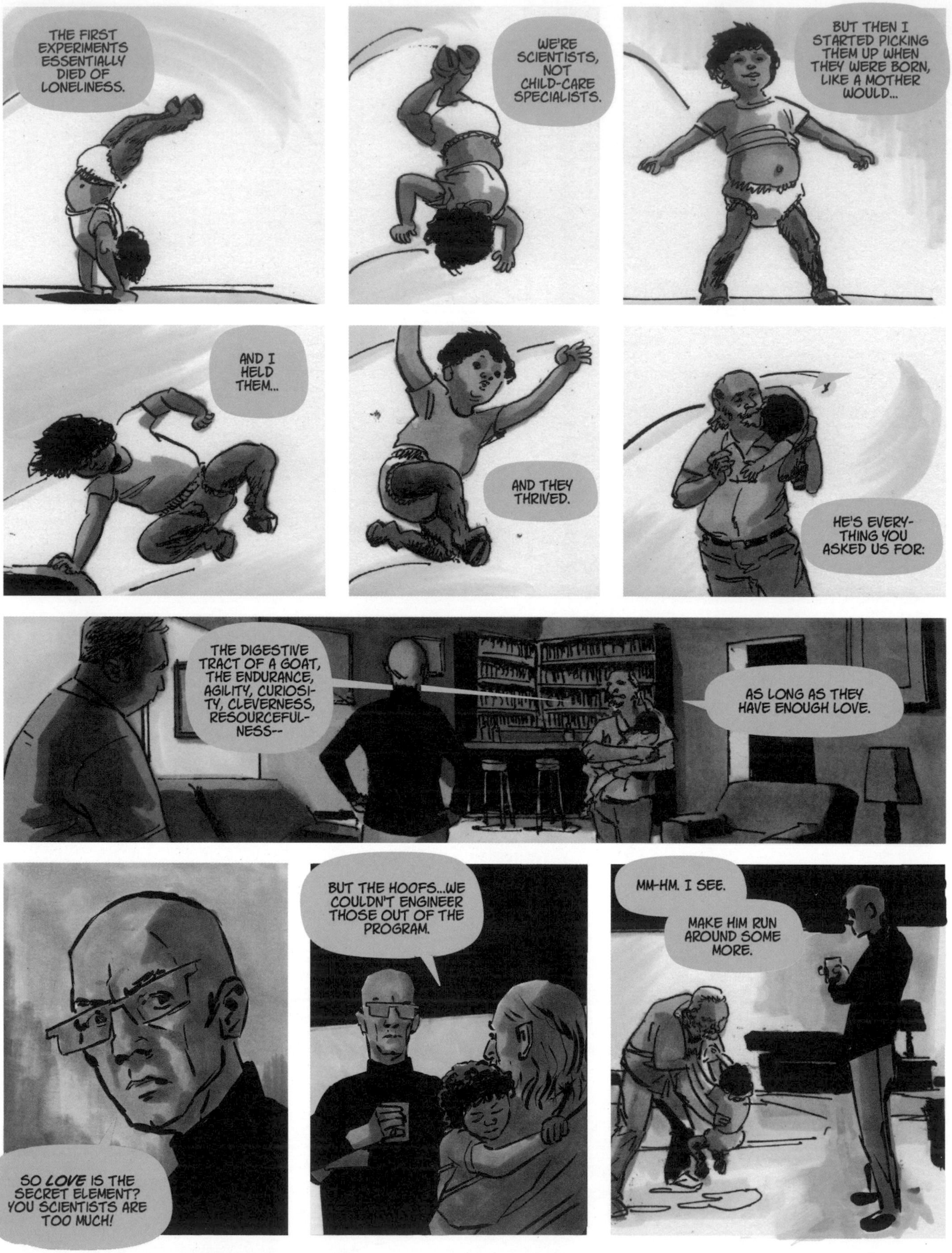
THE FIRST EXPERIMENTS ESSENTIALLY DIED OF LONELINESS.
WE'RE SCIENTISTS, NOT CHILD-CARE SPECIALISTS.
BUT THEN I STARTED PICKING THEM UP WHEN THEY WERE BORN, LIKE A MOTHER WOULD...
AND I HELD THEM...
AND THEY THRIVED.
HE'S EVERY-THING YOU ASKED US FOR:
THE DIGESTIVE TRACT OF A GOAT, THE ENDURANCE, AGILITY, CURIOSI-TY, CLEVERNESS, RESOURCEFUL-NESS--
AS LONG AS THEY HAVE ENOUGH LOVE.
SO LOVE IS THE SECRET ELEMENT? YOU SCIENTISTS ARE TOO MUCH!
BUT THE HOOFS...WE COULDN'T ENGINEER THOSE OUT OF THE PROGRAM.
MM-HM. I SEE.
MAKE HIM RUN AROUND SOME MORE.

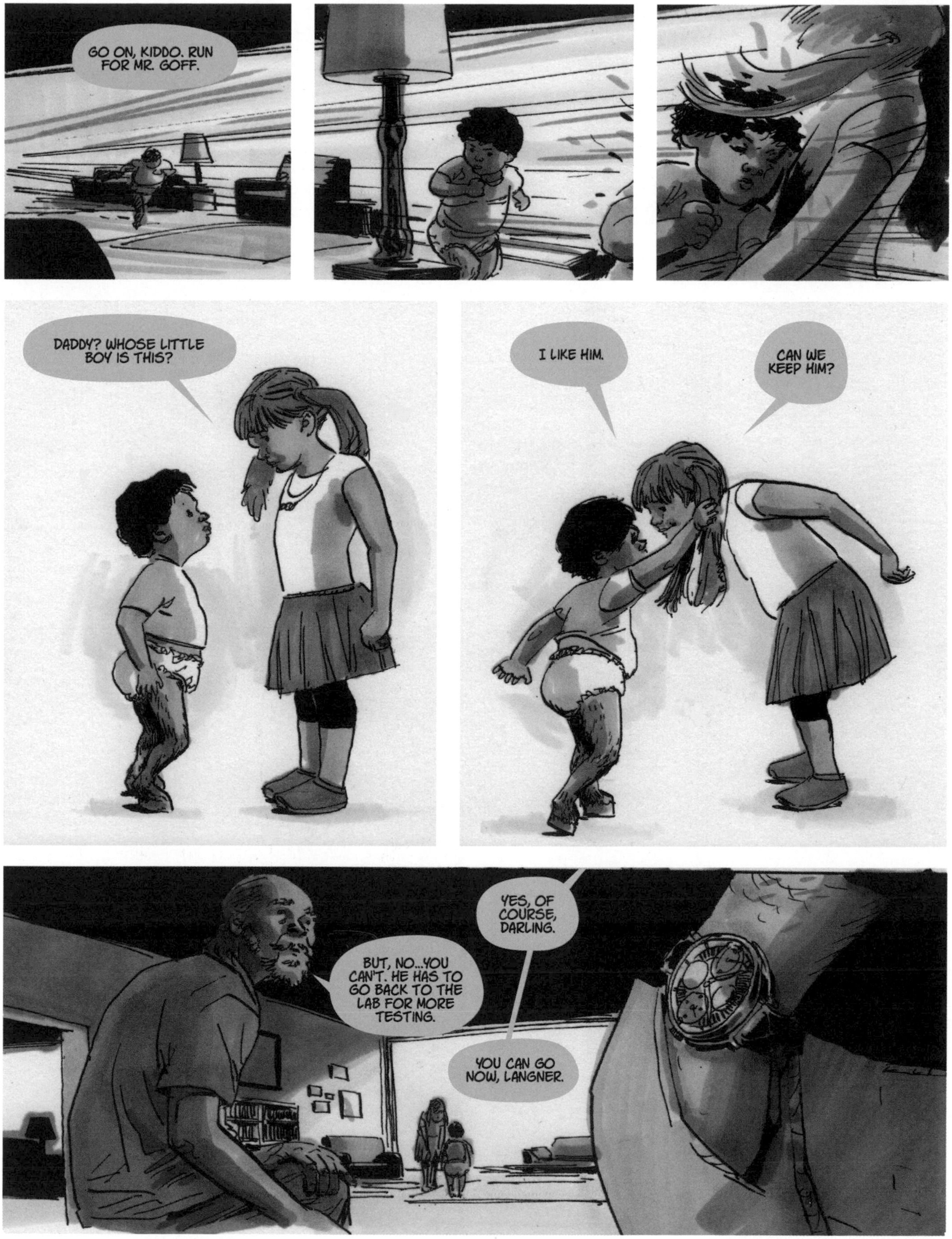
GO ON, KIDDO. RUN FOR MR. GOFF.
DADDY? WHOSE LITTLE BOY IS THIS?
I LIKE HIM.
CAN WE KEEP HIM?
YES, OF COURSE, DARLING.
BUT, NO...YOU CAN'T. HE HAS TO GO BACK TO THE LAB FOR MORE TESTING.
YOU CAN GO NOW, LANGNER.

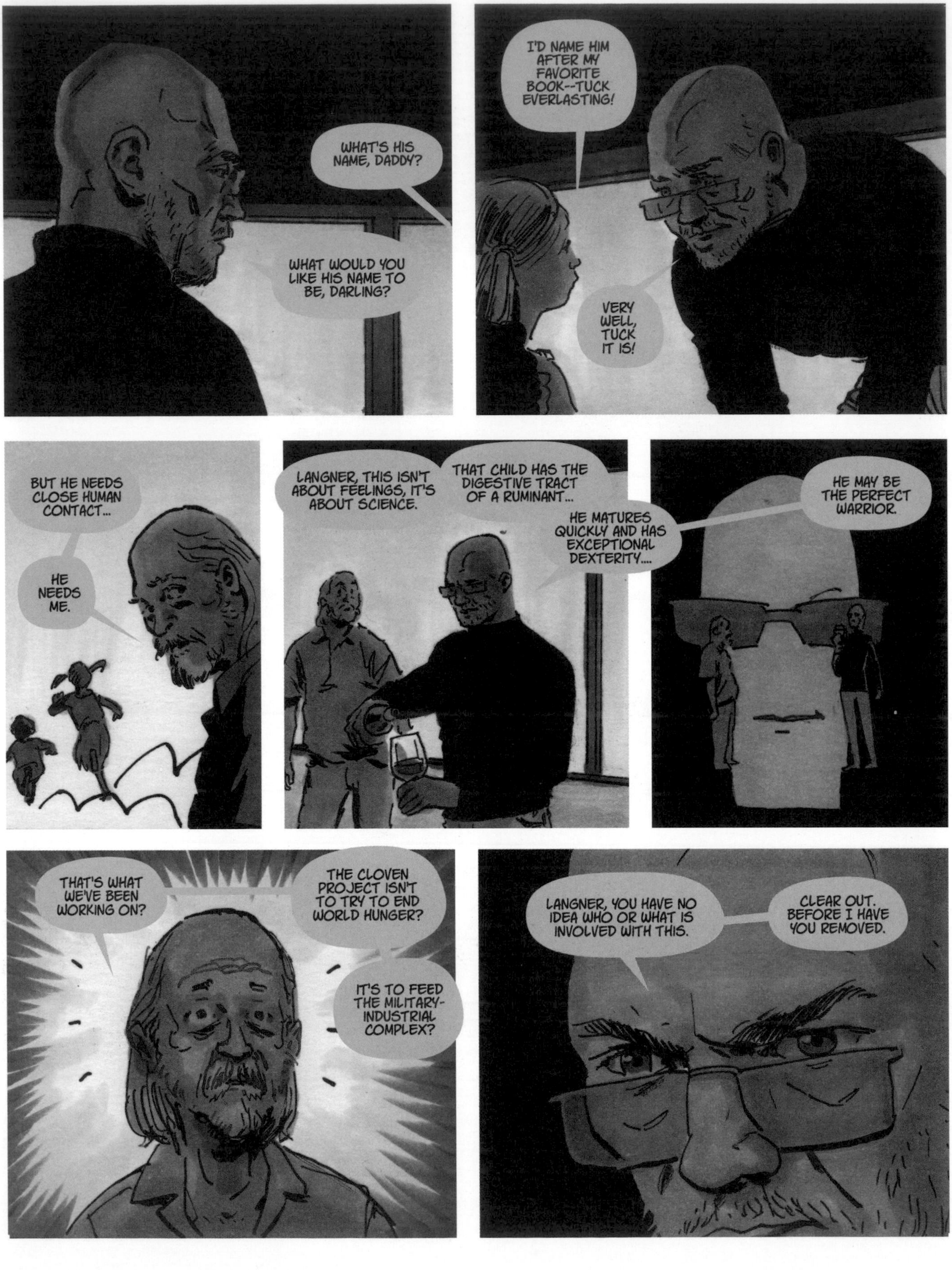
WHAT'S HIS NAME, DADDY?
WHAT WOULD YOU LIKE HIS NAME TO BE, DARLING?
I'D NAME HIM AFTER MY FAVORITE BOOK--TUCK EVERLASTING!
VERY WELL, TUCK IT IS!
BUT HE NEEDS CLOSE HUMAN CONTACT...
HE NEEDS ME.
LANGNER, THIS ISN'T ABOUT FEELINGS, IT'S ABOUT SCIENCE.
THAT CHILD HAS THE DIGESTIVE TRACT OF A RUMINANT...
HE MATURES QUICKLY AND HAS EXCEPTIONAL DEXTERITY....
HE MAY BE THE PERFECT WARRIOR.
THAT'S WHAT WE'VE BEEN WORKING ON?
THE CLOVEN PROJECT ISN'T TO TRY TO END WORLD HUNGER?
IT'S TO FEED THE MILITARY-INDUSTRIAL COMPLEX?
LANGNER, YOU HAVE NO IDEA WHO OR WHAT IS INVOLVED WITH THIS.
CLEAR OUT. BEFORE I HAVE YOU REMOVED.

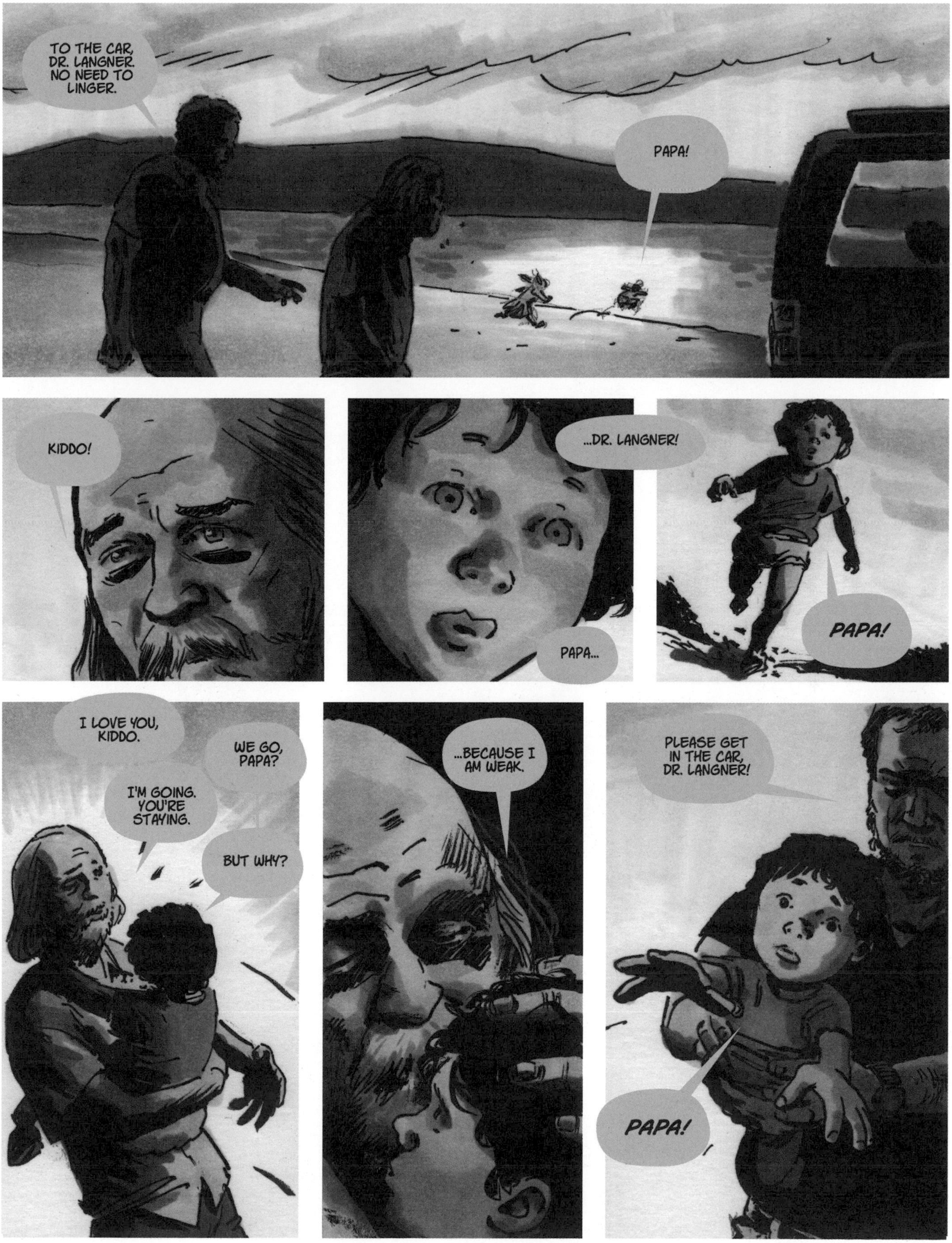
TO THE CAR, DR. LANGNER. NO NEED TO LINGER.
PAPA!
KIDDO!
...DR. LANGNER!
PAPA...
PAPA!
I LOVE YOU, KIDDO.
WE GO, PAPA?
I'M GOING. YOU'RE STAYING.
BUT WHY?
...BECAUSE I AM WEAK.
PLEASE GET IN THE CAR, DR. LANGNER!
PAPA!

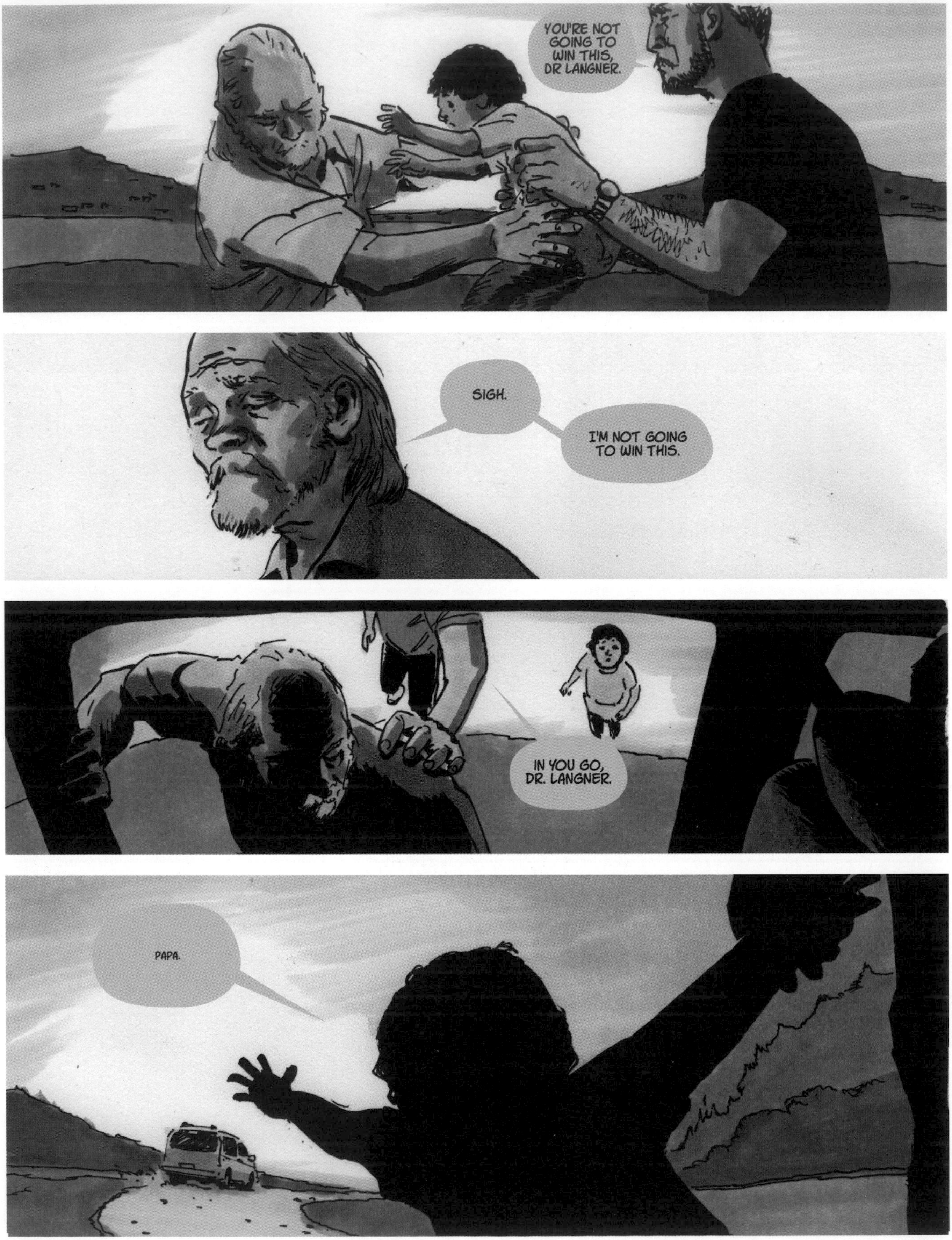
YOU'RE NOT GOING TO WIN THIS, DR LANGNER.
SIGH.
I'M NOT GOING TO WIN THIS.
IN YOU GO, DR. LANGNER.
PAPA.

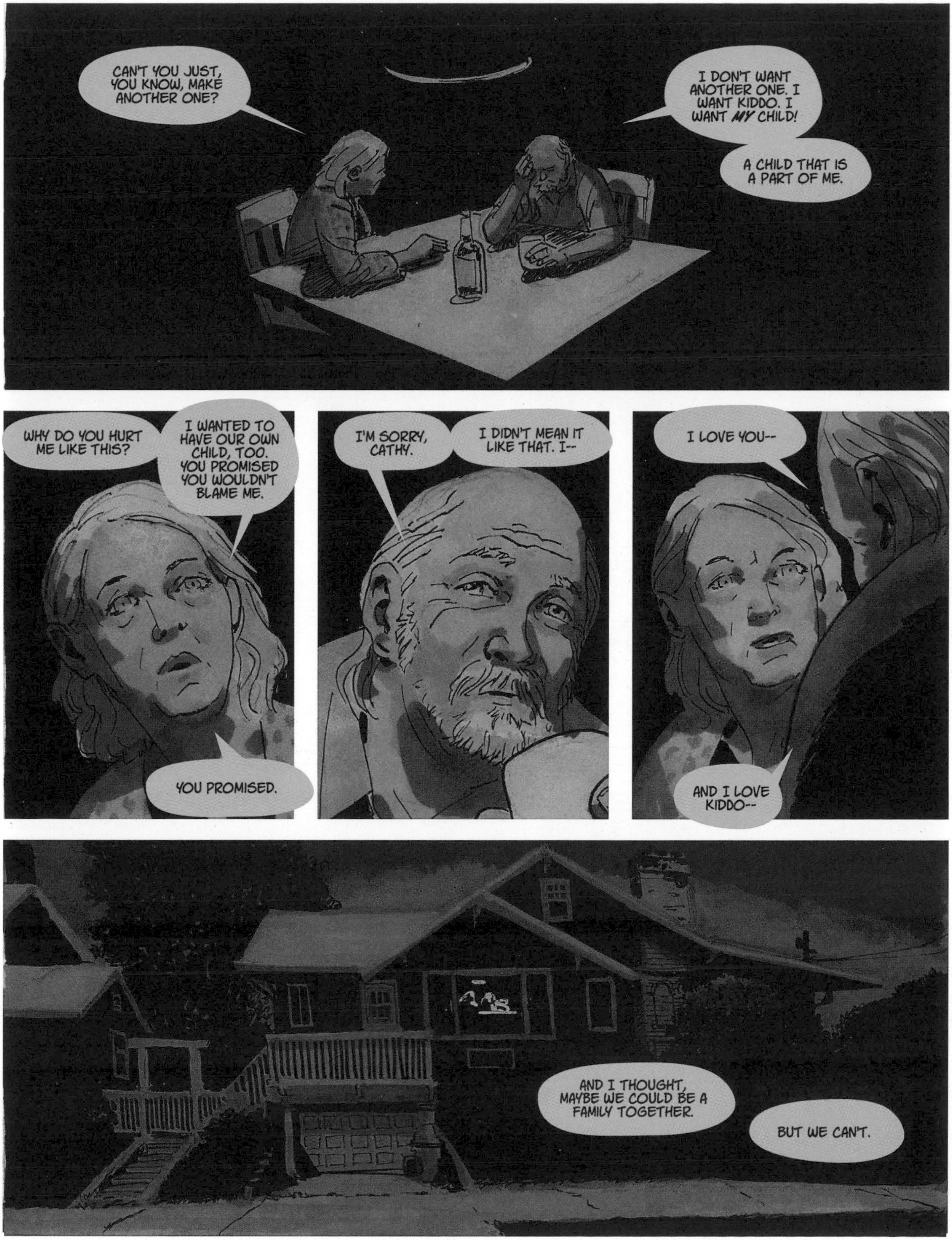

CAN'T YOU JUST, YOU KNOW, MAKE ANOTHER ONE?
I DON'T WANT ANOTHER ONE. I WANT KIDDO. I WANT *MY* CHILD!
A CHILD THAT IS A PART OF ME.
WHY DO YOU HURT ME LIKE THIS?
I WANTED TO HAVE OUR OWN CHILD, TOO. YOU PROMISED YOU WOULDN'T BLAME ME.
YOU PROMISED.
I'M SORRY, CATHY.
I DIDN'T MEAN IT LIKE THAT. I--
I LOVE YOU--
AND I LOVE KIDDO--
AND I THOUGHT, MAYBE WE COULD BE A FAMILY TOGETHER.
BUT WE CAN'T.

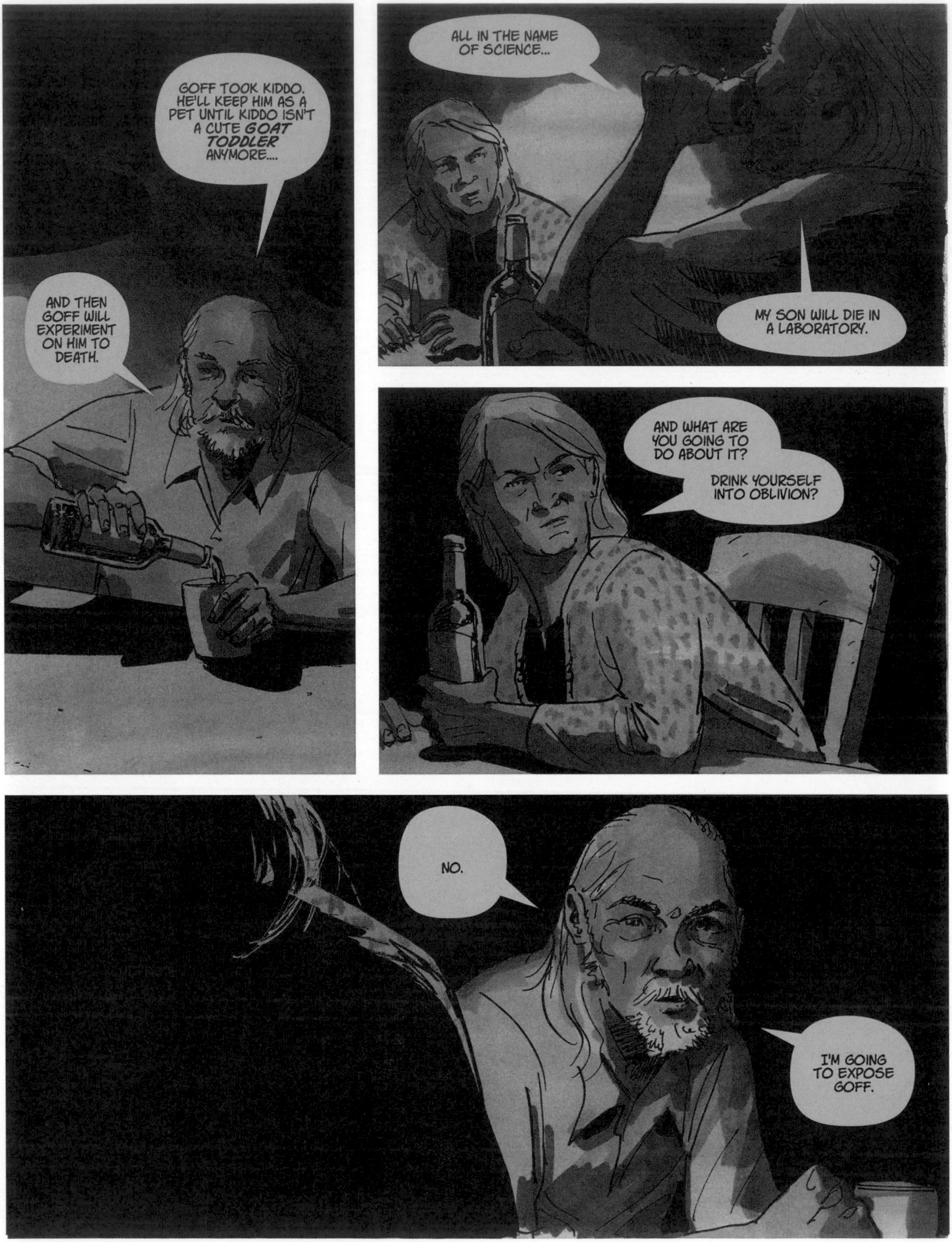
GOFF TOOK KIDDO. HE'LL KEEP HIM AS A PET UNTIL KIDDO ISN'T A CUTE *GOAT TODDLER* ANYMORE....
AND THEN GOFF WILL EXPERIMENT ON HIM TO DEATH.
ALL IN THE NAME OF SCIENCE...
MY SON WILL DIE IN A LABORATORY.
AND WHAT ARE YOU GOING TO DO ABOUT IT?
DRINK YOURSELF INTO OBLIVION?
NO.
I'M GOING TO EXPOSE GOFF.

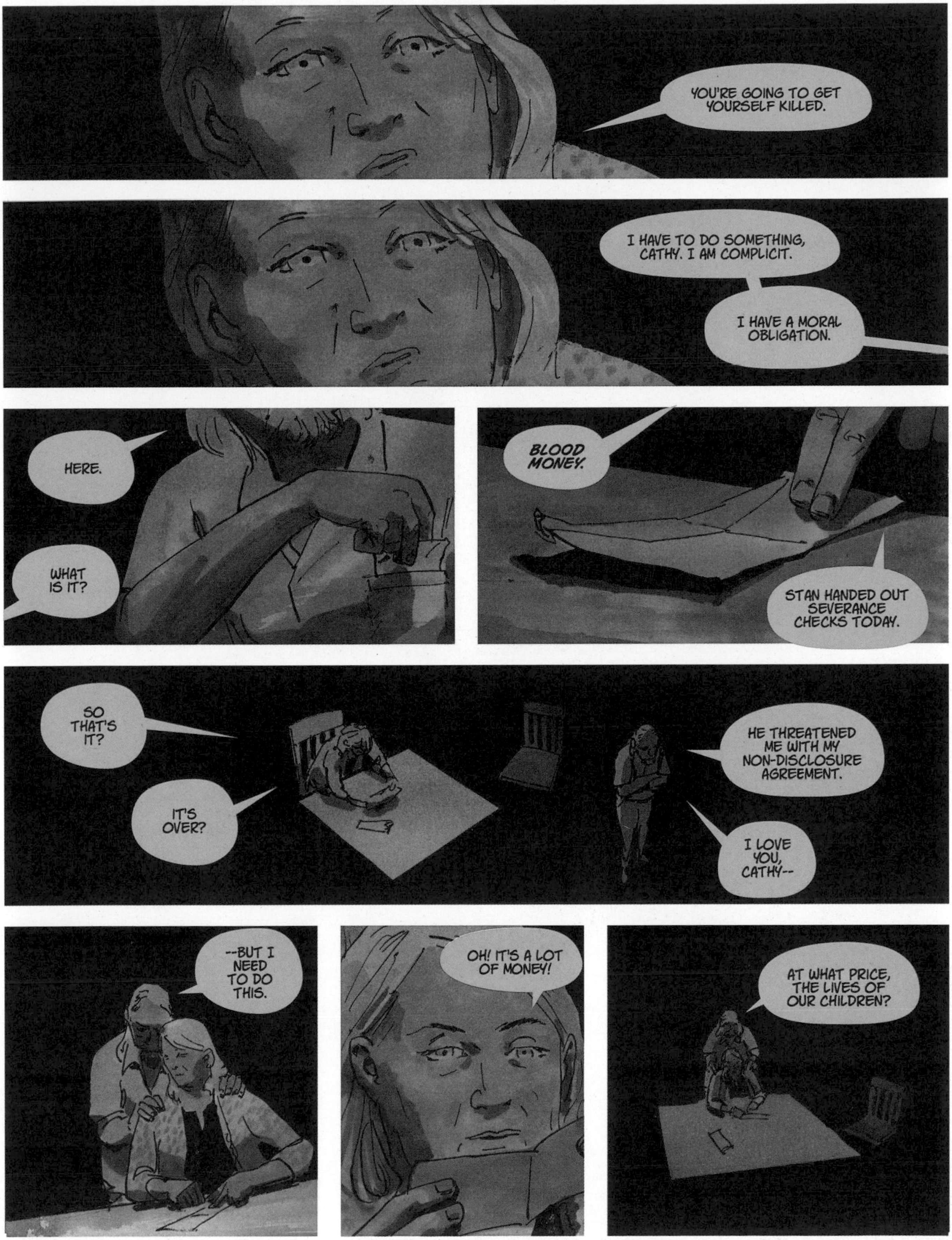
YOU'RE GOING TO GET YOURSELF KILLED.
I HAVE TO DO SOMETHING, CATHY. I AM COMPLICIT.
I HAVE A MORAL OBLIGATION.
HERE.
WHAT IS IT?
BLOOD MONEY.
STAN HANDED OUT SEVERANCE CHECKS TODAY.
SO THAT'S IT?
IT'S OVER?
HE THREATENED ME WITH MY NON-DISCLOSURE AGREEMENT.
I LOVE YOU, CATHY--
--BUT I NEED TO DO THIS.
OH! IT'S A LOT OF MONEY!
AT WHAT PRICE, THE LIVES OF OUR CHILDREN?

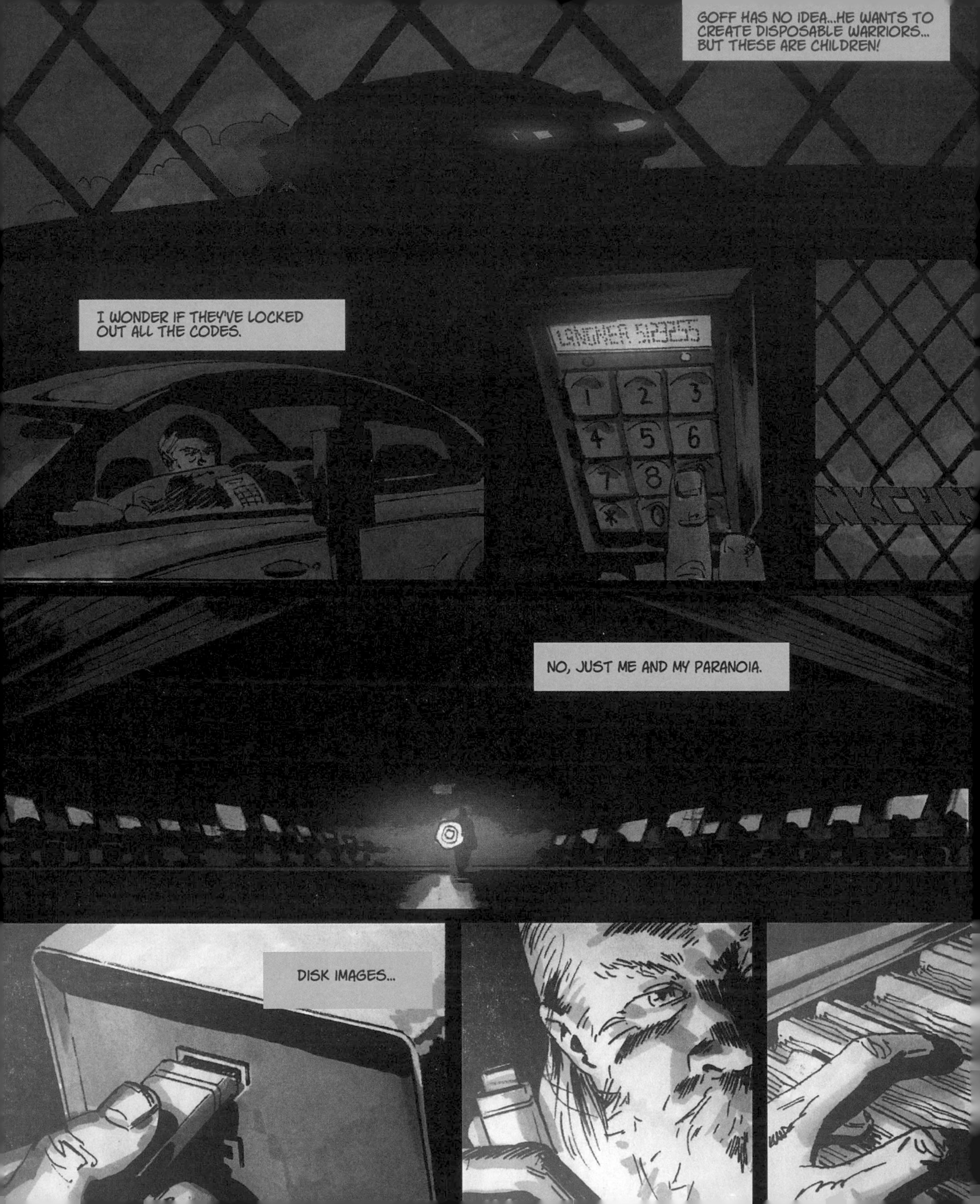
GOFF HAS NO IDEA...HE WANTS TO CREATE DISPOSABLE WARRIORS... BUT THESE ARE CHILDREN!
I WONDER IF THEY'VE LOCKED OUT ALL THE CODES.
NO, JUST ME AND MY PARANOIA.
DISK IMAGES...

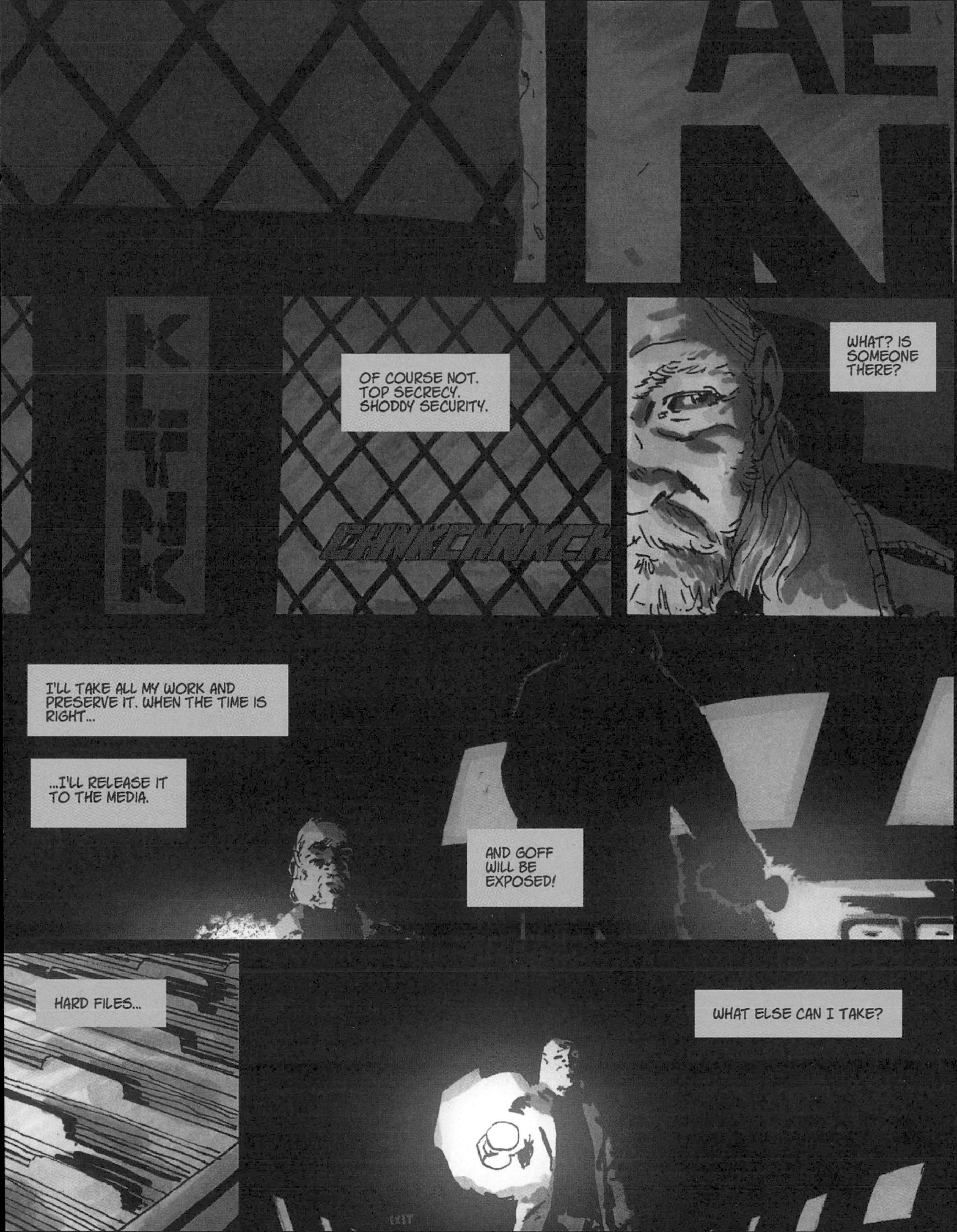
KLTNK
OF COURSE NOT. TOP SECRECY. SHODDY SECURITY.
CHNKCHNKCH
WHAT? IS SOMEONE THERE?
I'LL TAKE ALL MY WORK AND PRESERVE IT. WHEN THE TIME IS RIGHT...
...I'LL RELEASE IT TO THE MEDIA.
AND GOFF WILL BE EXPOSED!
HARD FILES...
WHAT ELSE CAN I TAKE?

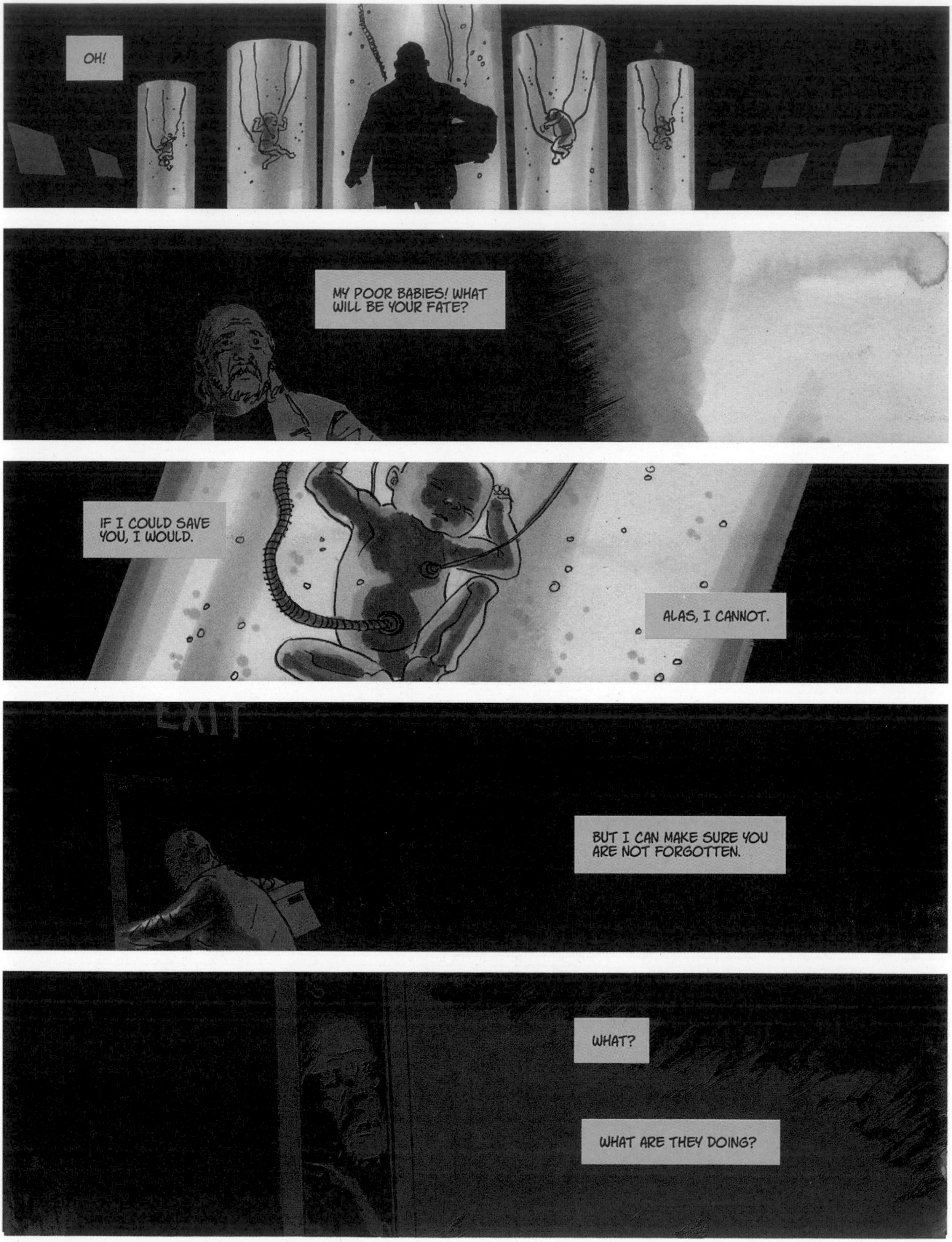
OH!
MY POOR BABIES! WHAT WILL BE YOUR FATE?
IF I COULD SAVE YOU, I WOULD.
ALAS, I CANNOT.
EXIT
BUT I CAN MAKE SURE YOU ARE NOT FORGOTTEN.
WHAT?
WHAT ARE THEY DOING?

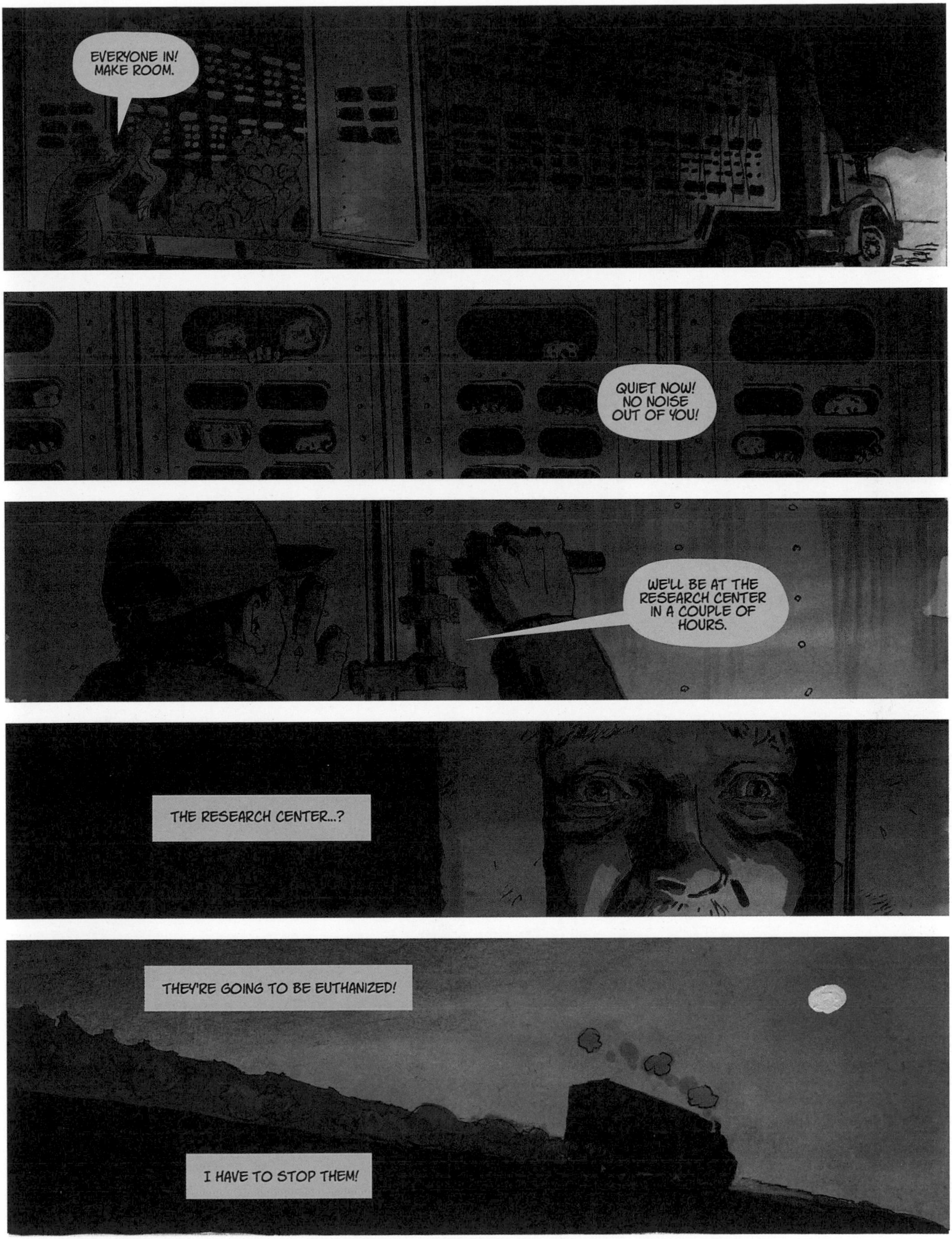
EVERYONE IN! MAKE ROOM.
QUIET NOW! NO NOISE OUT OF YOU!
WE'LL BE AT THE RESEARCH CENTER IN A COUPLE OF HOURS.
THE RESEARCH CENTER...?
THEY'RE GOING TO BE EUTHANIZED!
I HAVE TO STOP THEM!

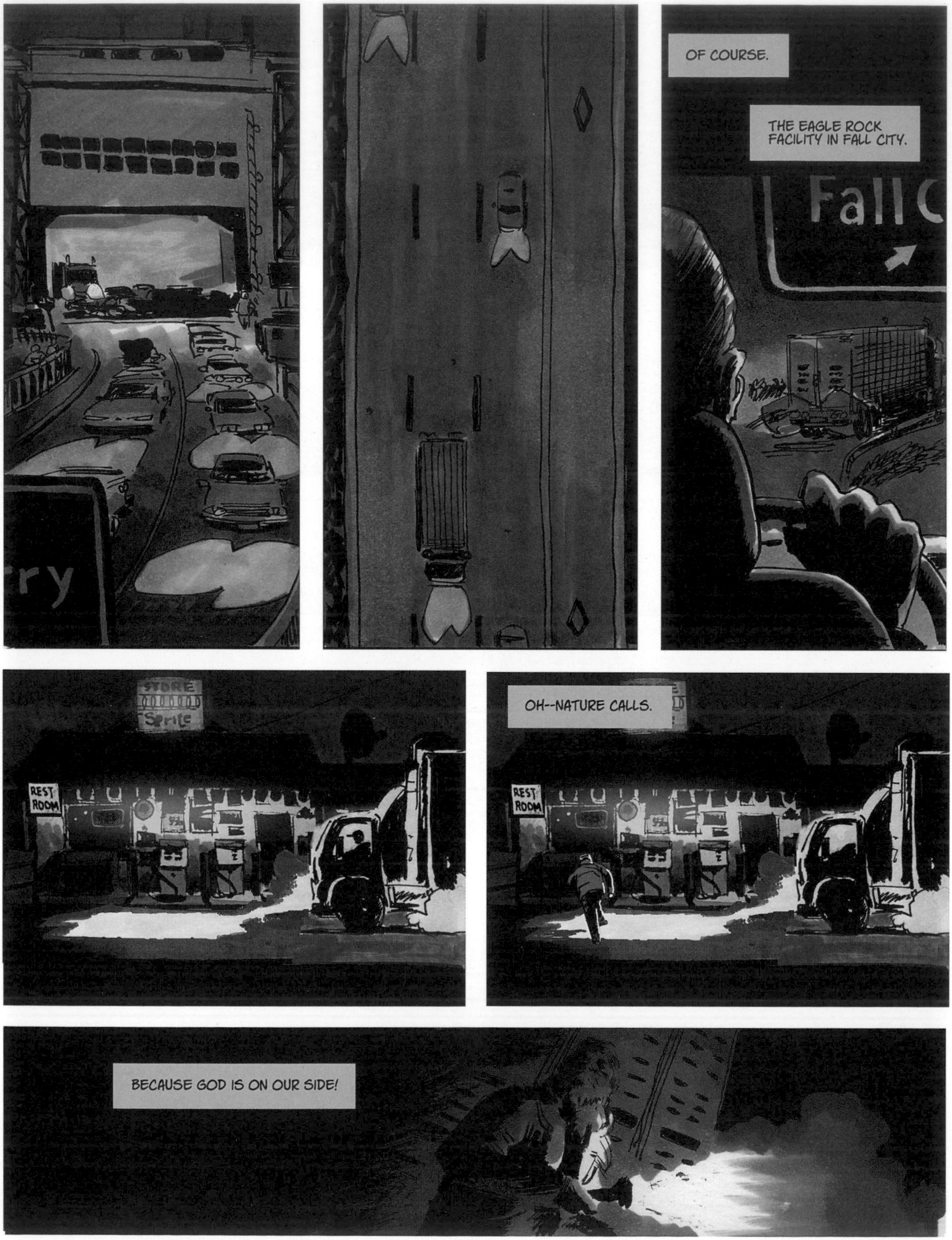
rry
OF COURSE.
THE EAGLE ROCK FACILITY IN FALL CITY.
Fall C
STORE
Sprite
REST ROOM
OH--NATURE CALLS.
REST ROOM
BECAUSE GOD IS ON OUR SIDE!

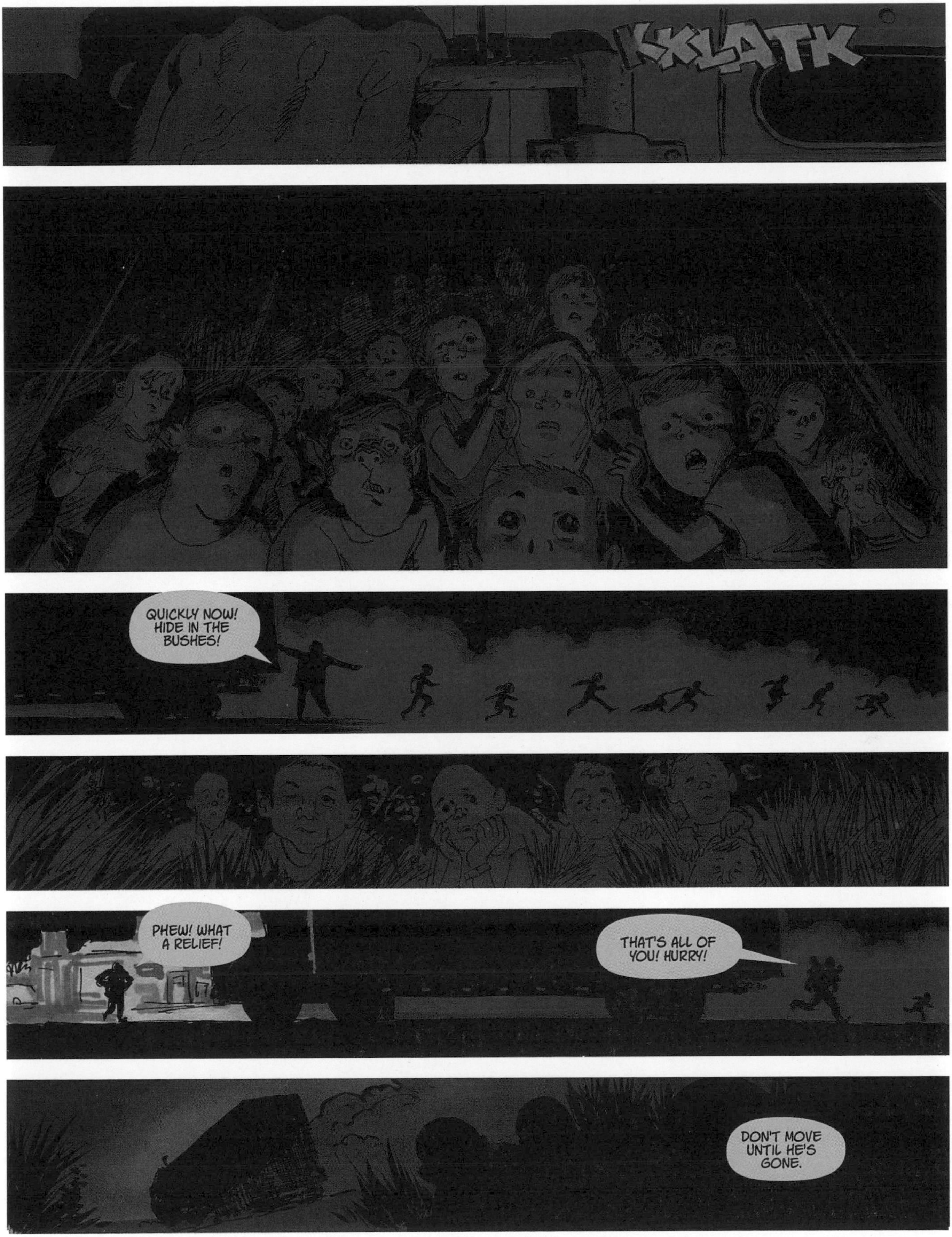
KKLATK
QUICKLY NOW! HIDE IN THE BUSHES!
PHEW! WHAT A RELIEF!
THAT'S ALL OF YOU! HURRY!
DON'T MOVE UNTIL HE'S GONE.

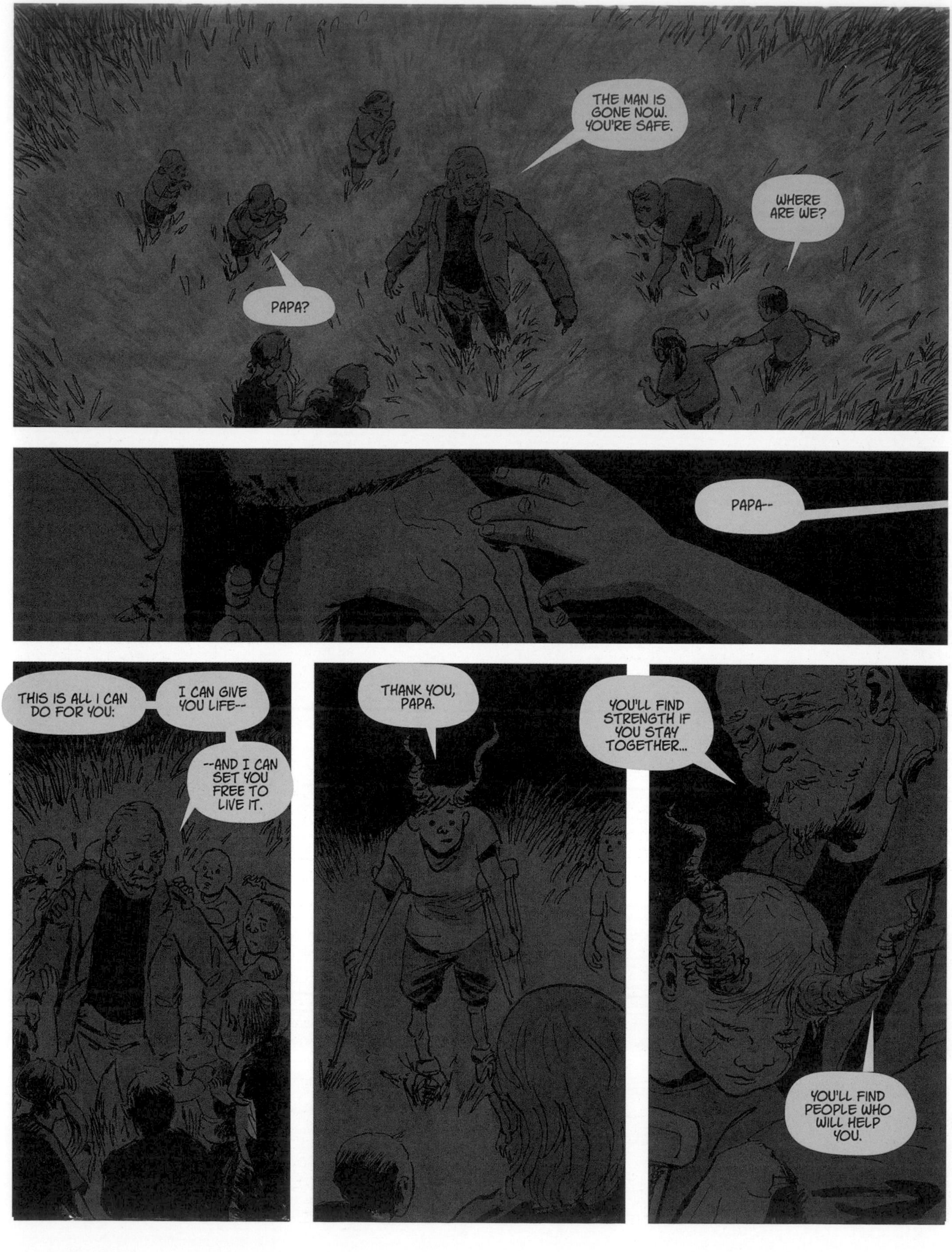
THE MAN IS GONE NOW. YOU'RE SAFE.
WHERE ARE WE?
PAPA?
PAPA--
THIS IS ALL I CAN DO FOR YOU:
I CAN GIVE YOU LIFE--
--AND I CAN SET YOU FREE TO LIVE IT.
THANK YOU, PAPA.
YOU'LL FIND STRENGTH IF YOU STAY TOGETHER...
YOU'LL FIND PEOPLE WHO WILL HELP YOU.

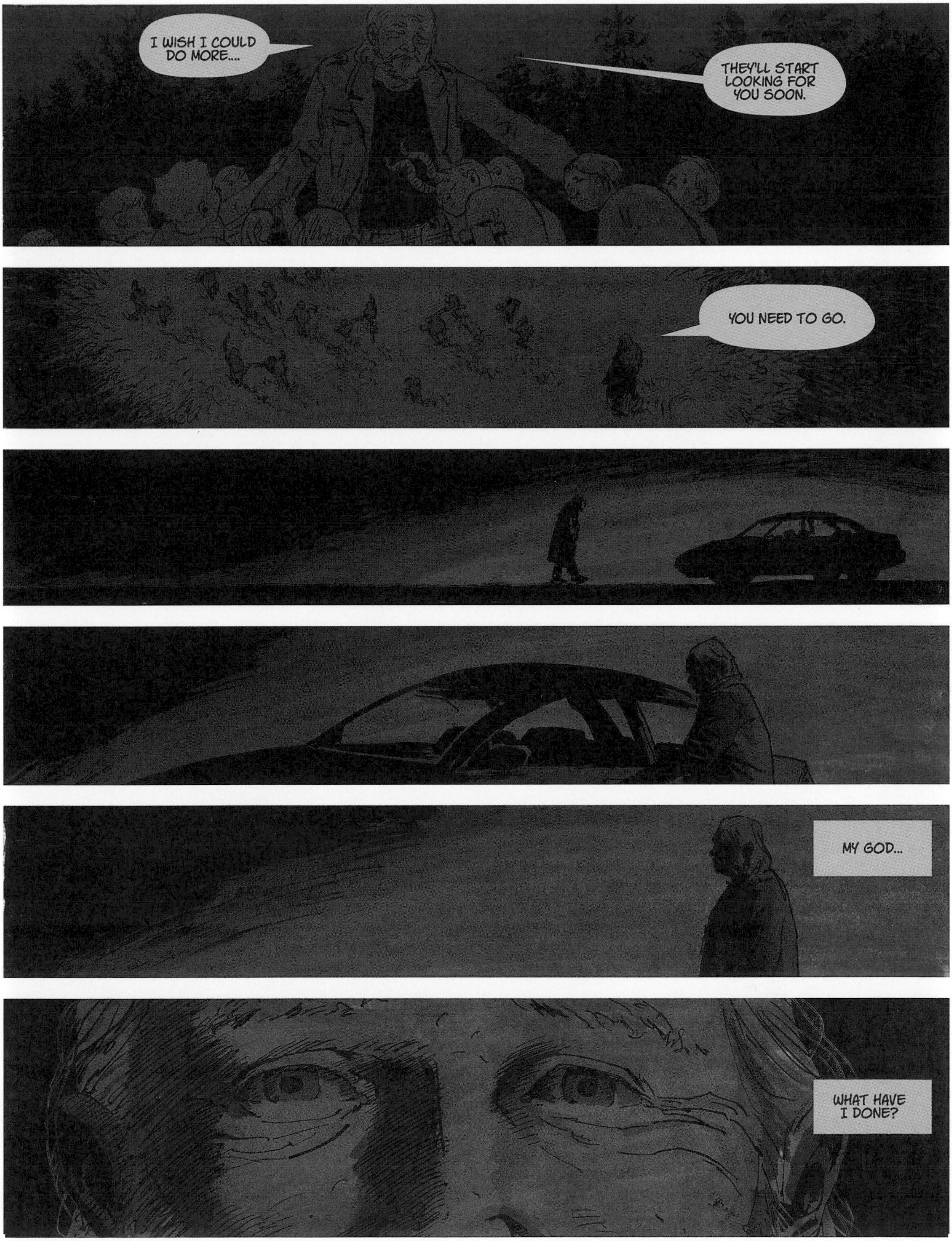
I WISH I COULD DO MORE....
THEY'LL START LOOKING FOR YOU SOON.
YOU NEED TO GO.
MY GOD...
WHAT HAVE I DONE?

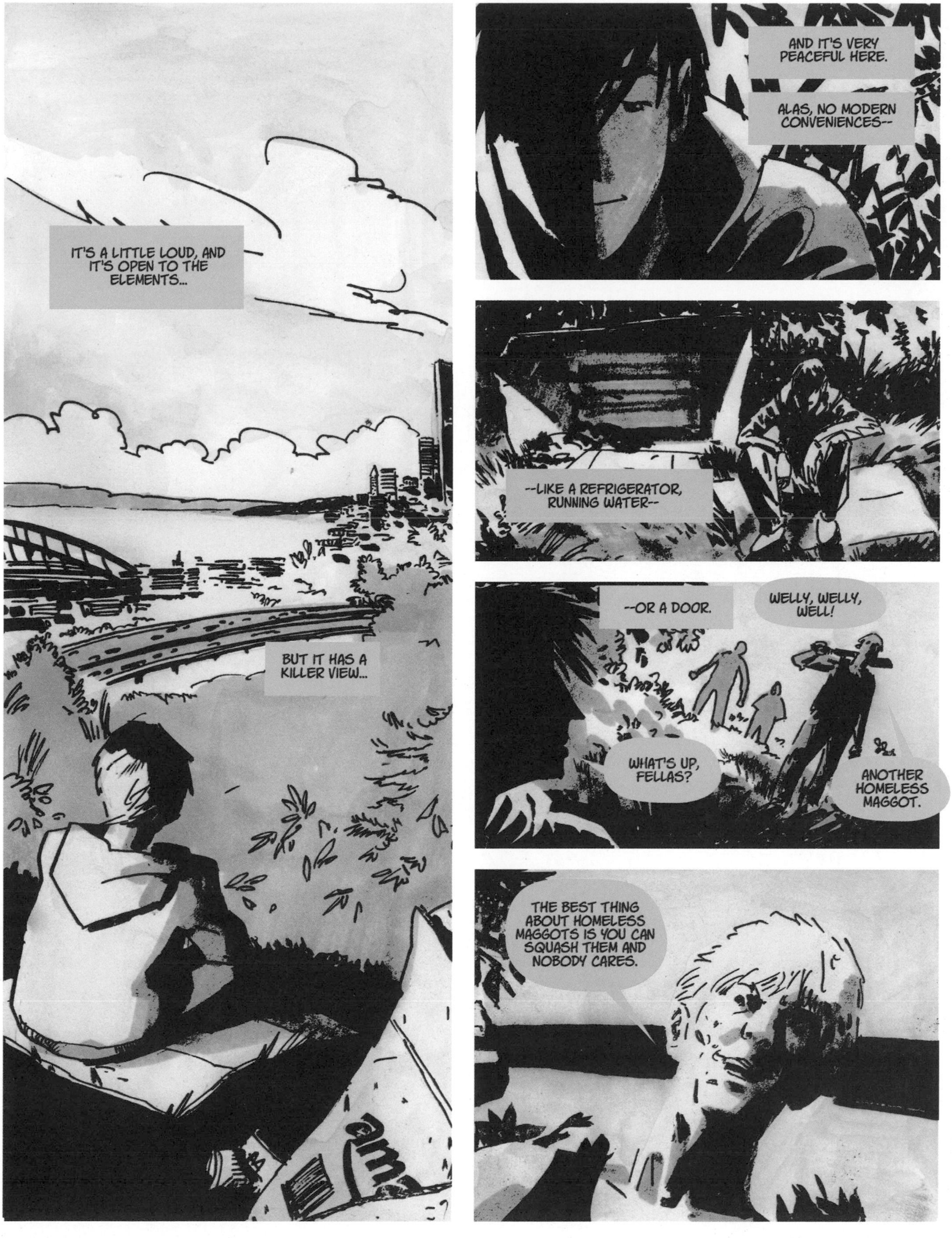

IT'S A LITTLE LOUD, AND IT'S OPEN TO THE ELEMENTS...
BUT IT HAS A KILLER VIEW...
AND IT'S VERY PEACEFUL HERE.
ALAS, NO MODERN CONVENIENCES--
--LIKE A REFRIGERATOR, RUNNING WATER--
--OR A DOOR.
WELLY, WELLY, WELL!
WHAT'S UP, FELLAS?
ANOTHER HOMELESS MAGGOT.
THE BEST THING ABOUT HOMELESS MAGGOTS IS YOU CAN SQUASH THEM AND NOBODY CARES.

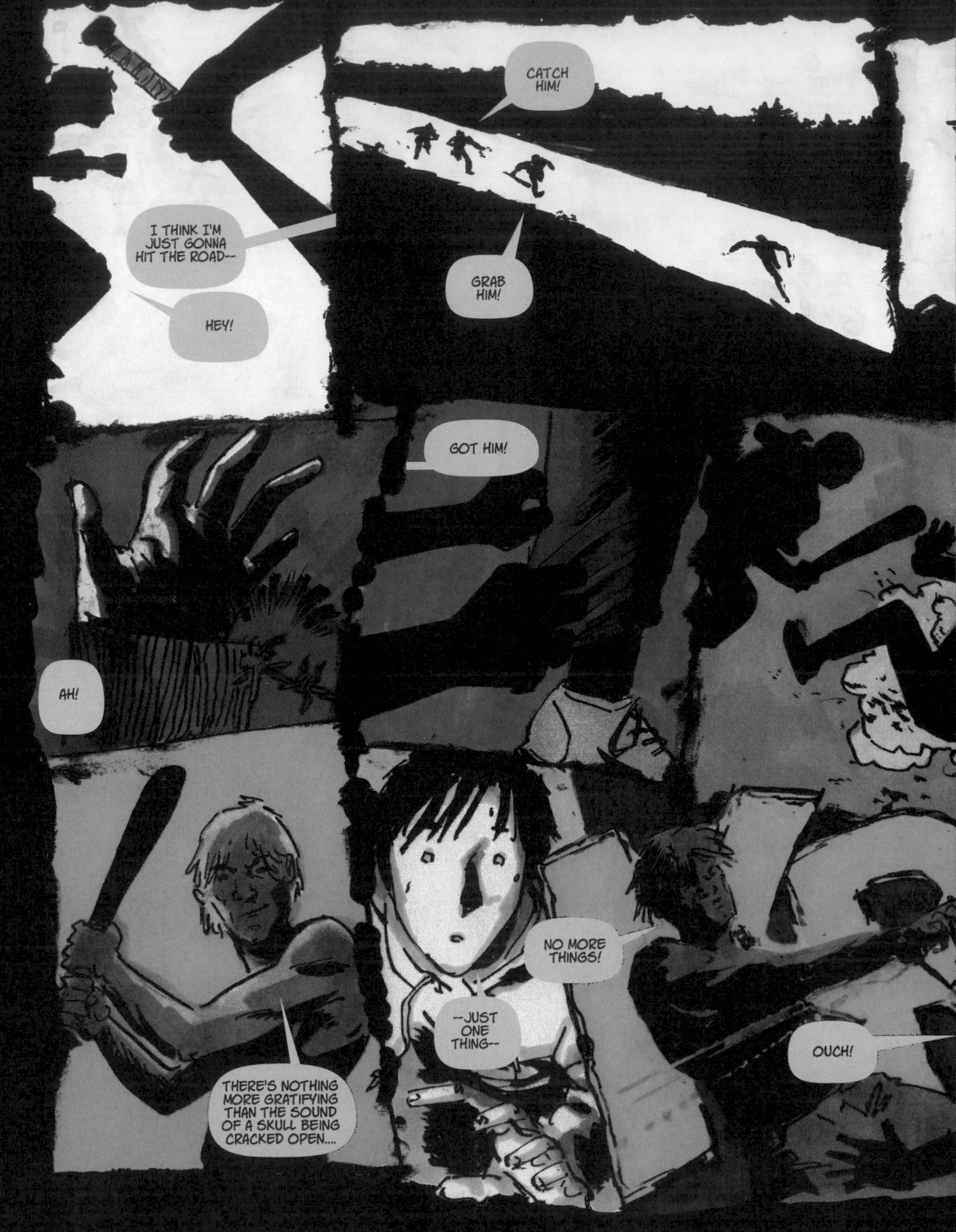
I THINK I'M JUST GONNA HIT THE ROAD--
HEY!
CATCH HIM!
GRAB HIM!
GOT HIM!
AH!
THERE'S NOTHING MORE GRATIFYING THAN THE SOUND OF A SKULL BEING CRACKED OPEN....
--JUST ONE THING--
NO MORE THINGS!
OUCH!

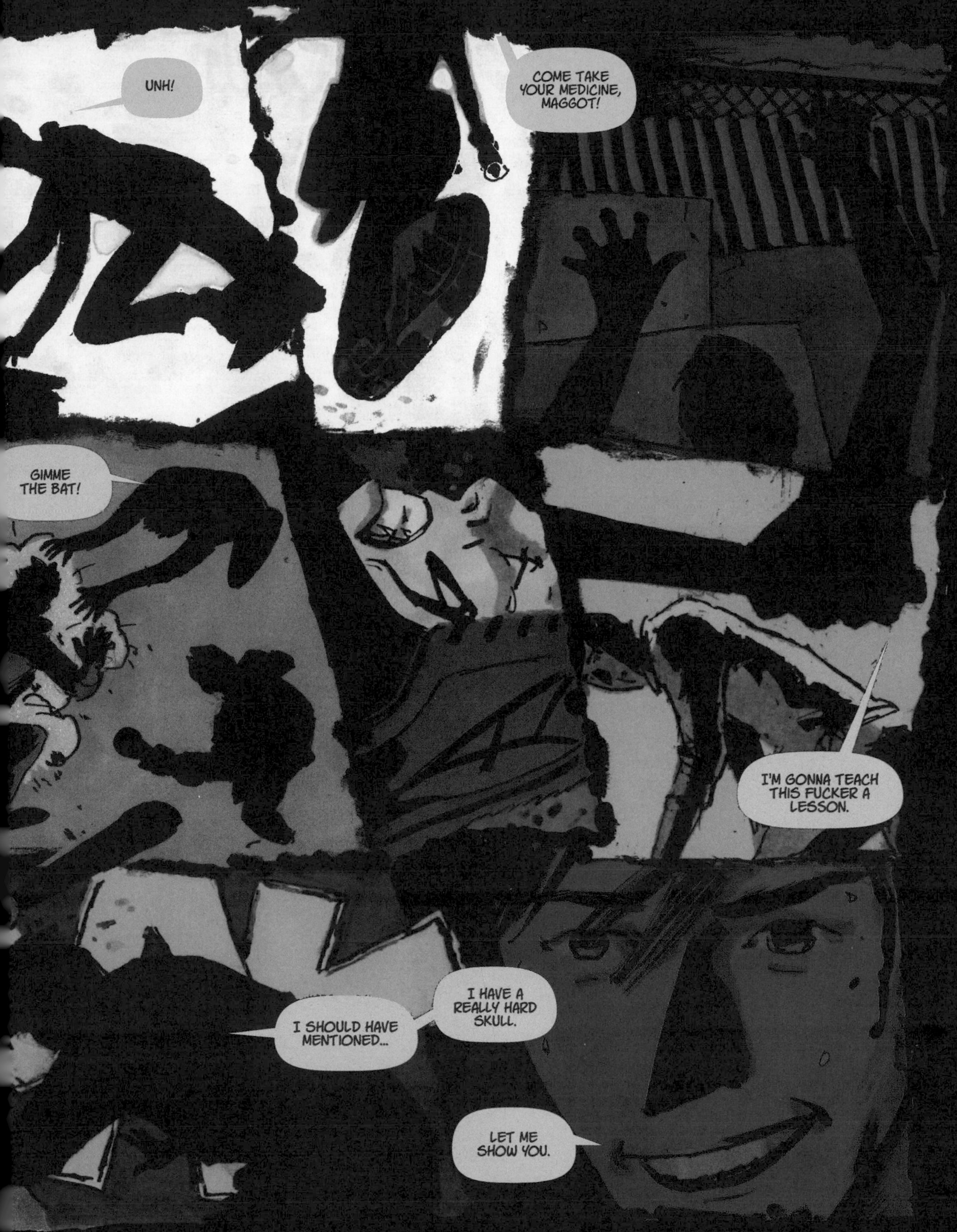
UNH!
COME TAKE YOUR MEDICINE, MAGGOT!
GIMME THE BAT!
I'M GONNA TEACH THIS FUCKER A LESSON.
I SHOULD HAVE MENTIONED...
I HAVE A REALLY HARD SKULL.
LET ME SHOW YOU.

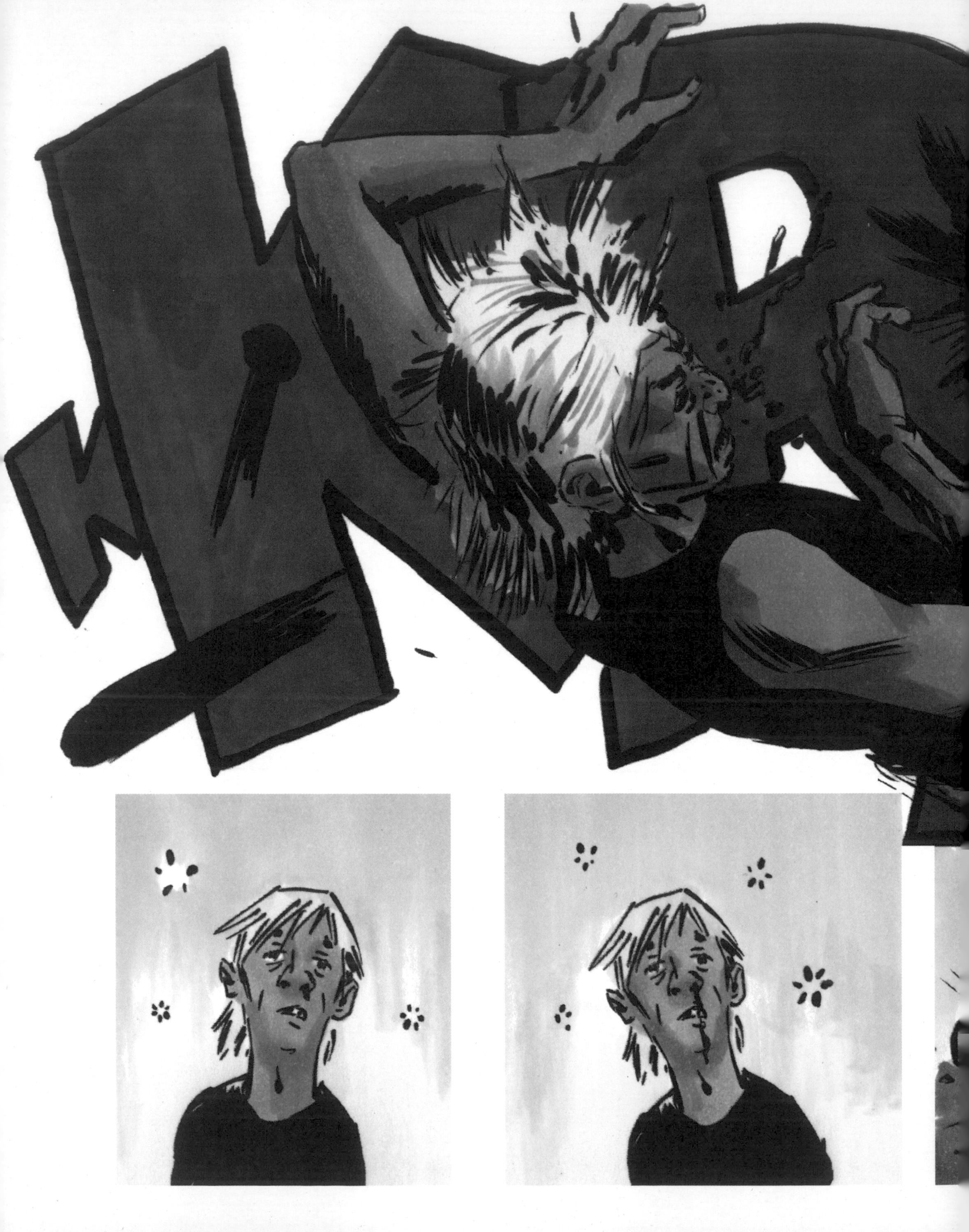

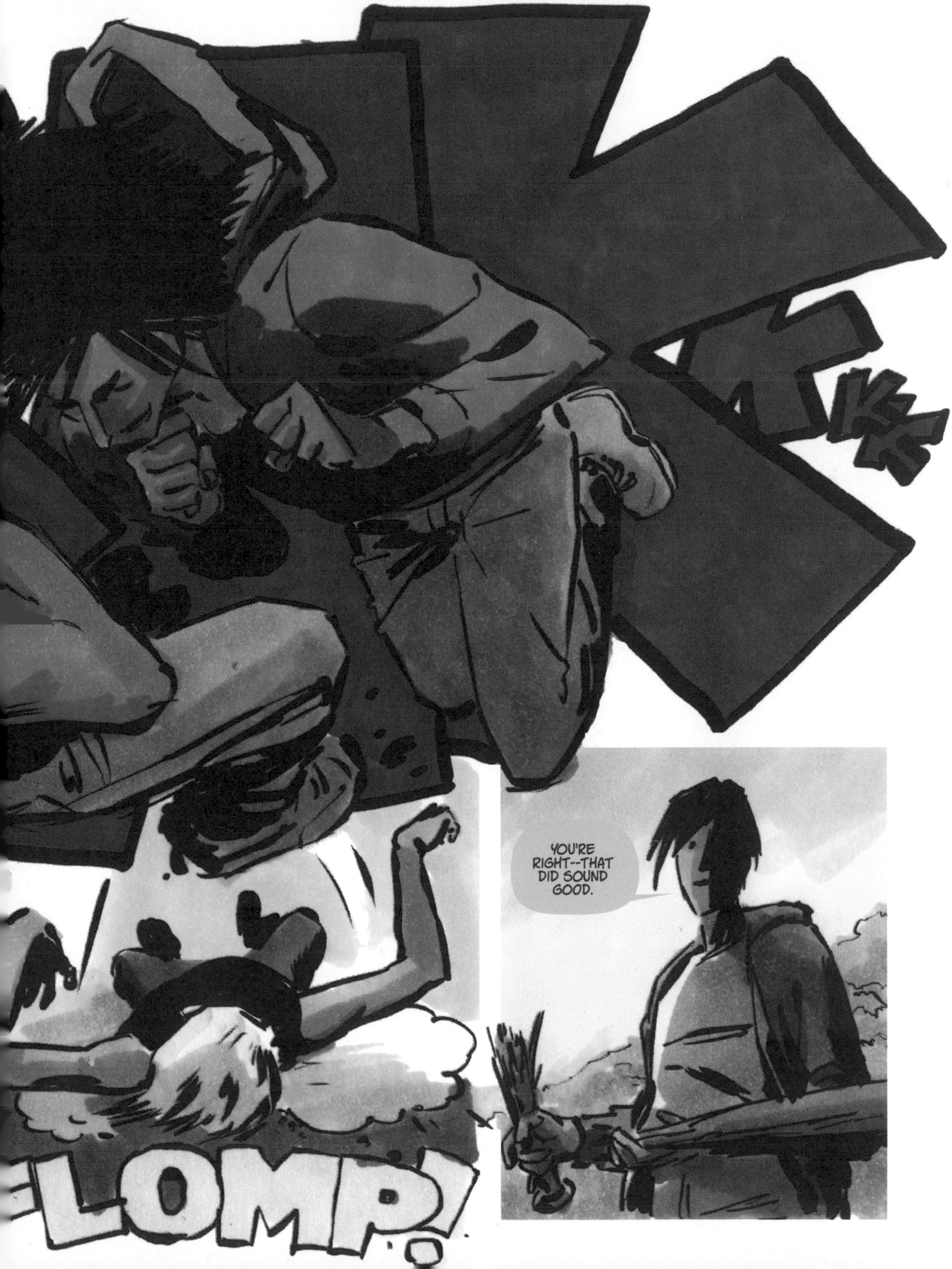
LOMP!
YOU'RE RIGHT--THAT DID SOUND GOOD.

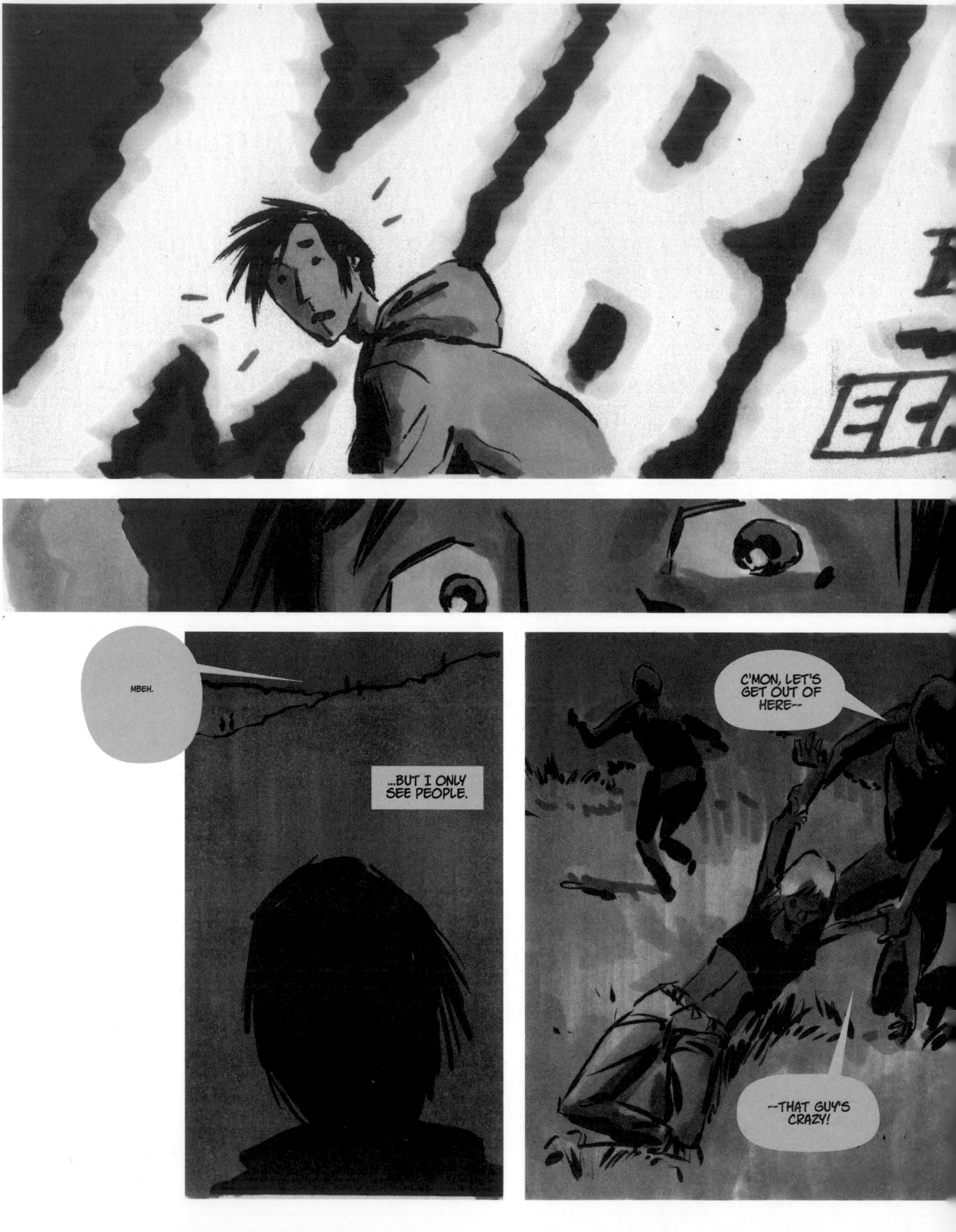
MBEH.
...BUT I ONLY SEE PEOPLE.
C'MON, LET'S GET OUT OF HERE--
--THAT GUY'S CRAZY!

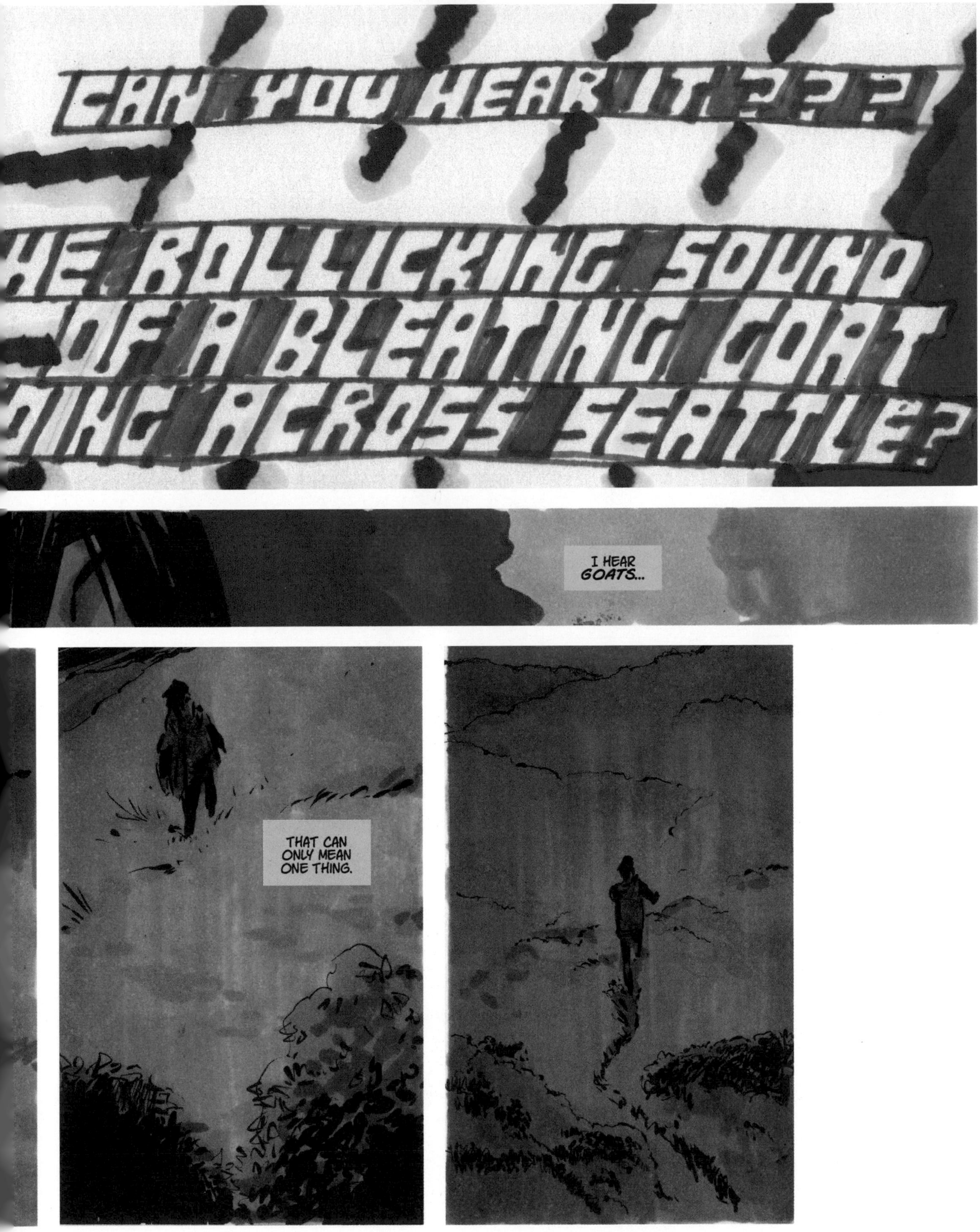
CAN YOU HEAR IT ???!
HE ROLLICKING SOUND
OF A BLEATING GOAT
OING ACROSS SEATTLE?
I HEAR *GOATS*...
THAT CAN ONLY MEAN ONE THING.

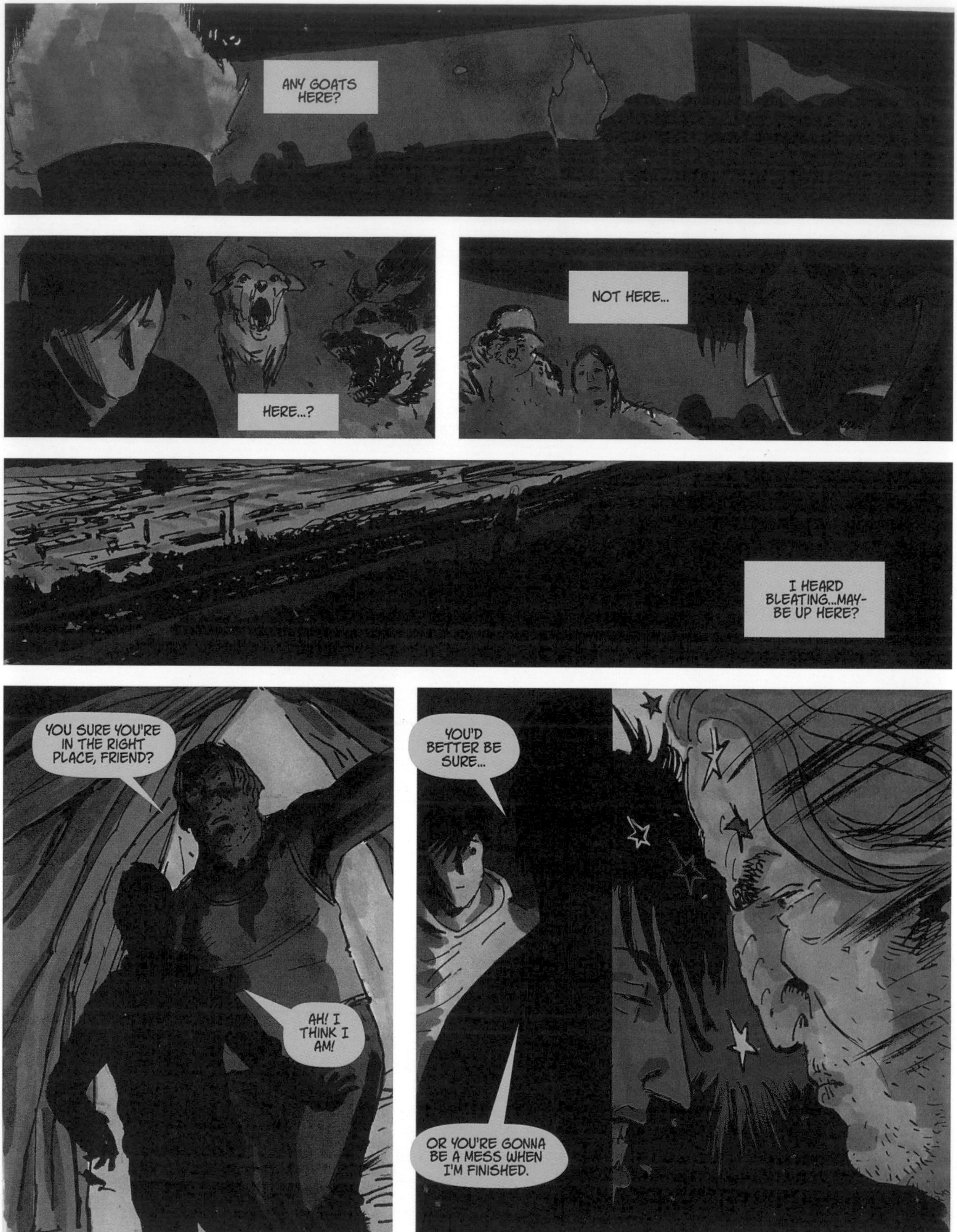
ANY GOATS HERE?
HERE...?
NOT HERE...
I HEARD BLEATING...MAY-BE UP HERE?
YOU SURE YOU'RE IN THE RIGHT PLACE, FRIEND?
AH! I THINK I AM!
YOU'D BETTER BE SURE...
OR YOU'RE GONNA BE A MESS WHEN I'M FINISHED.

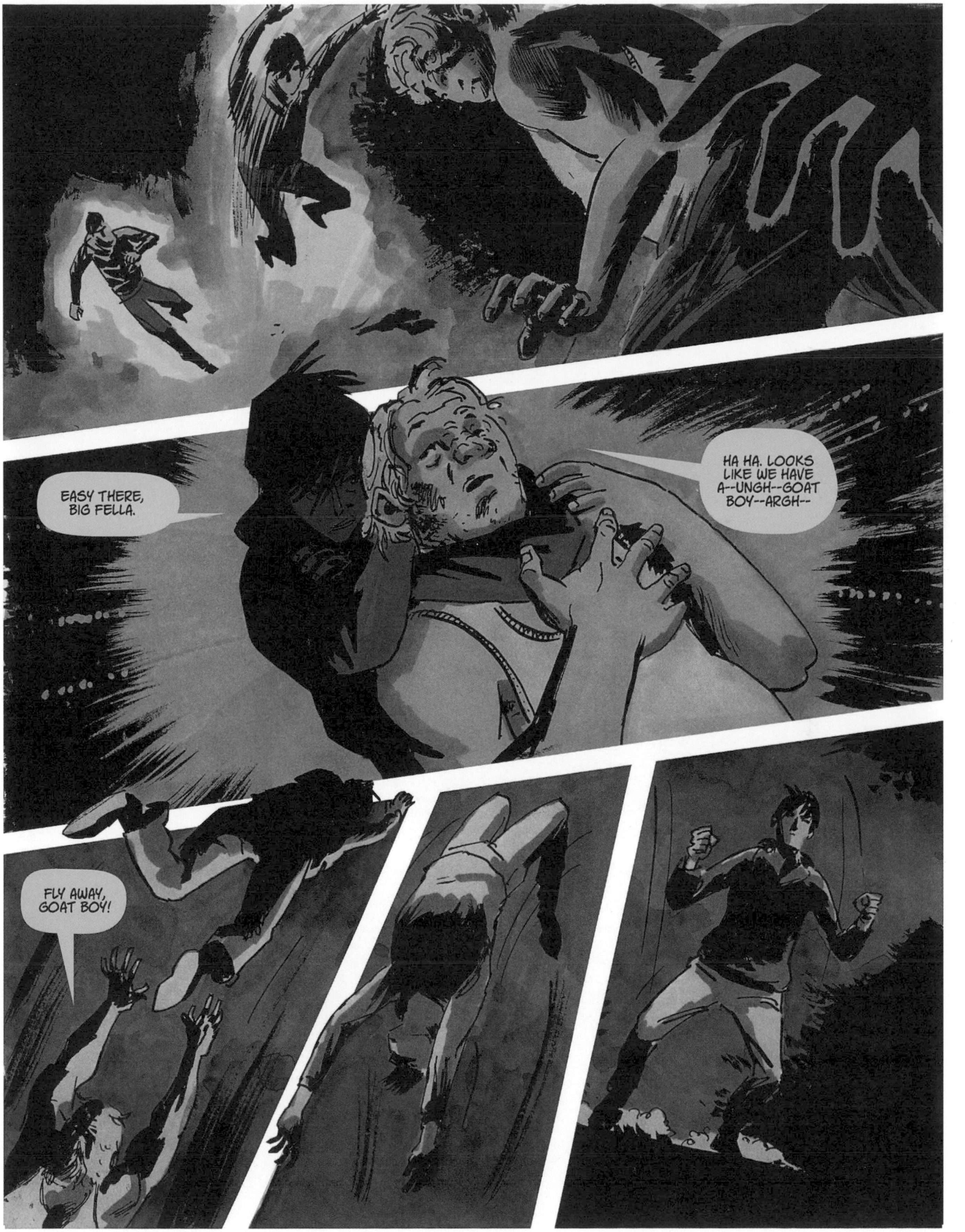
EASY THERE, BIG FELLA.
HA HA. LOOKS LIKE WE HAVE A--UNGH--GOAT BOY--ARGH--
FLY AWAY, GOAT BOY!

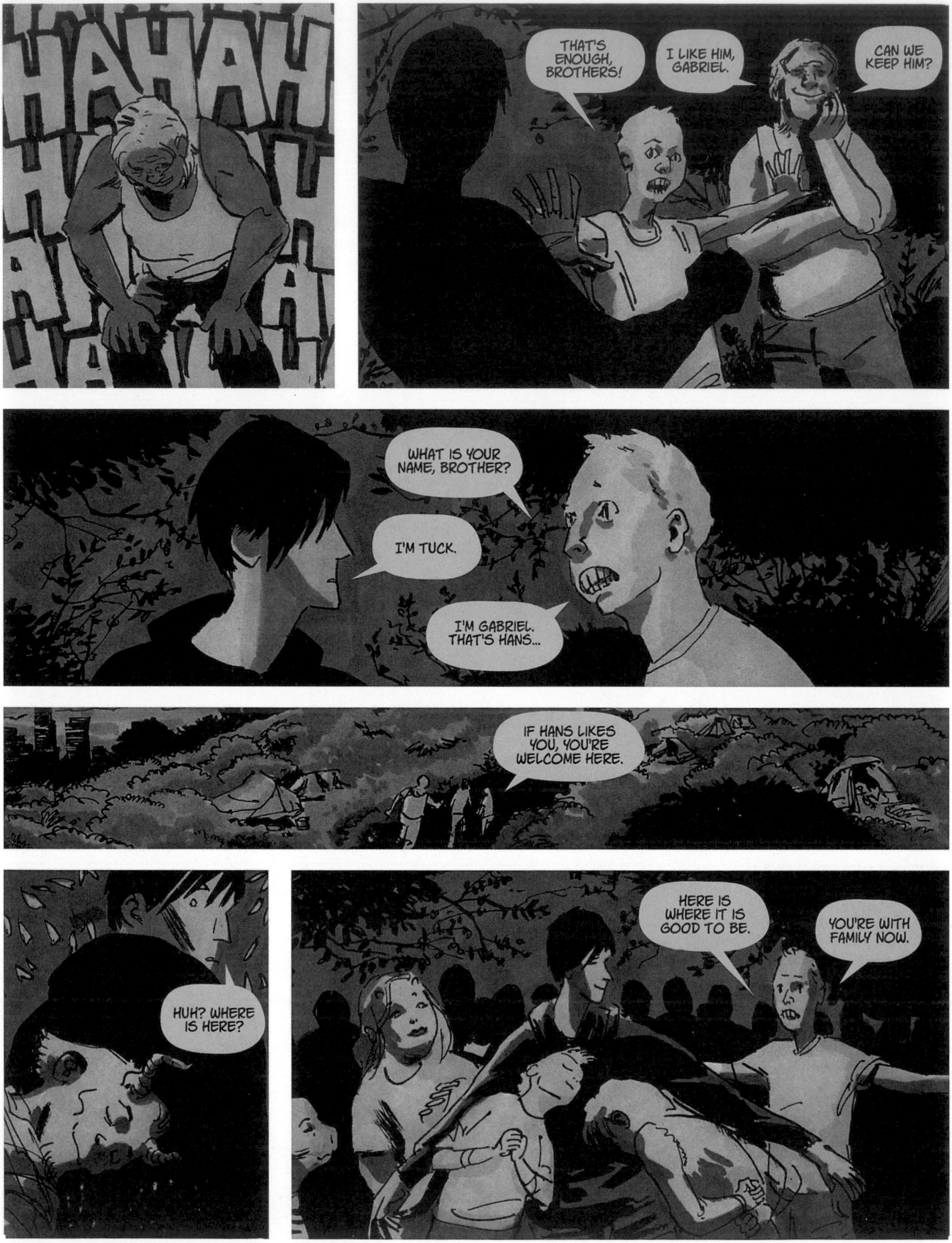
HAHAH
THAT'S ENOUGH, BROTHERS!
I LIKE HIM, GABRIEL.
CAN WE KEEP HIM?
WHAT IS YOUR NAME, BROTHER?
I'M TUCK.
I'M GABRIEL. THAT'S HANS...
IF HANS LIKES YOU, YOU'RE WELCOME HERE.
HUH? WHERE IS HERE?
HERE IS WHERE IT IS GOOD TO BE.
YOU'RE WITH FAMILY NOW.

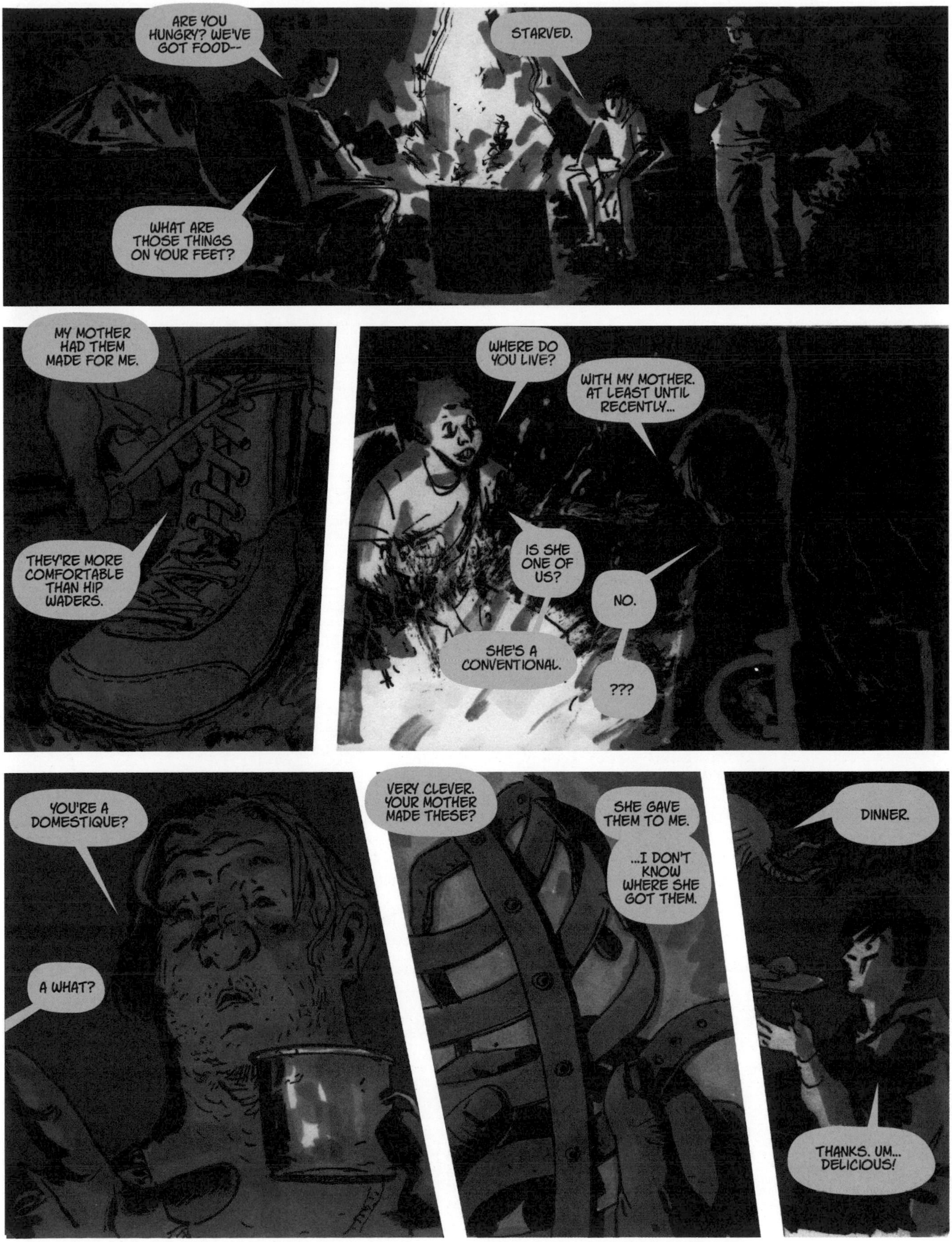
ARE YOU HUNGRY? WE'VE GOT FOOD--
STARVED.
WHAT ARE THOSE THINGS ON YOUR FEET?
MY MOTHER HAD THEM MADE FOR ME.
THEY'RE MORE COMFORTABLE THAN HIP WADERS.
WHERE DO YOU LIVE?
WITH MY MOTHER. AT LEAST UNTIL RECENTLY...
IS SHE ONE OF US?
NO.
SHE'S A CONVENTIONAL.
???
YOU'RE A DOMESTIQUE?
A WHAT?
VERY CLEVER. YOUR MOTHER MADE THESE?
SHE GAVE THEM TO ME.
...I DON'T KNOW WHERE SHE GOT THEM.
DINNER.
THANKS. UM... DELICIOUS!

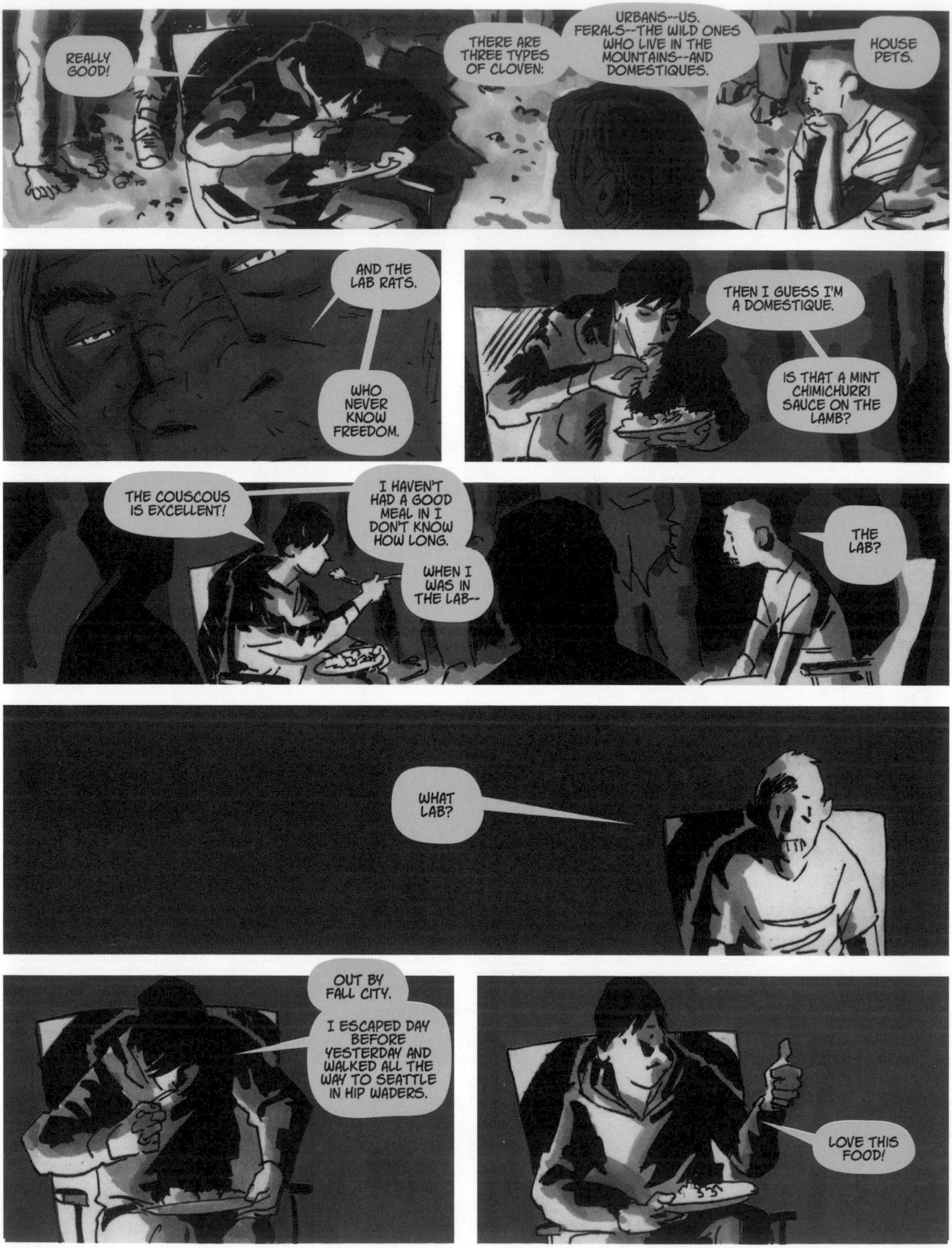
REALLY GOOD!
THERE ARE THREE TYPES OF CLOVEN:
URBANS--US. FERALS--THE WILD ONES WHO LIVE IN THE MOUNTAINS--AND DOMESTIQUES.
HOUSE PETS.
AND THE LAB RATS.
WHO NEVER KNOW FREEDOM.
THEN I GUESS I'M A DOMESTIQUE.
IS THAT A MINT CHIMICHURRI SAUCE ON THE LAMB?
THE COUSCOUS IS EXCELLENT!
I HAVEN'T HAD A GOOD MEAL IN I DON'T KNOW HOW LONG.
WHEN I WAS IN THE LAB--
THE LAB?
WHAT LAB?
OUT BY FALL CITY.
I ESCAPED DAY BEFORE YESTERDAY AND WALKED ALL THE WAY TO SEATTLE IN HIP WADERS.
LOVE THIS FOOD!

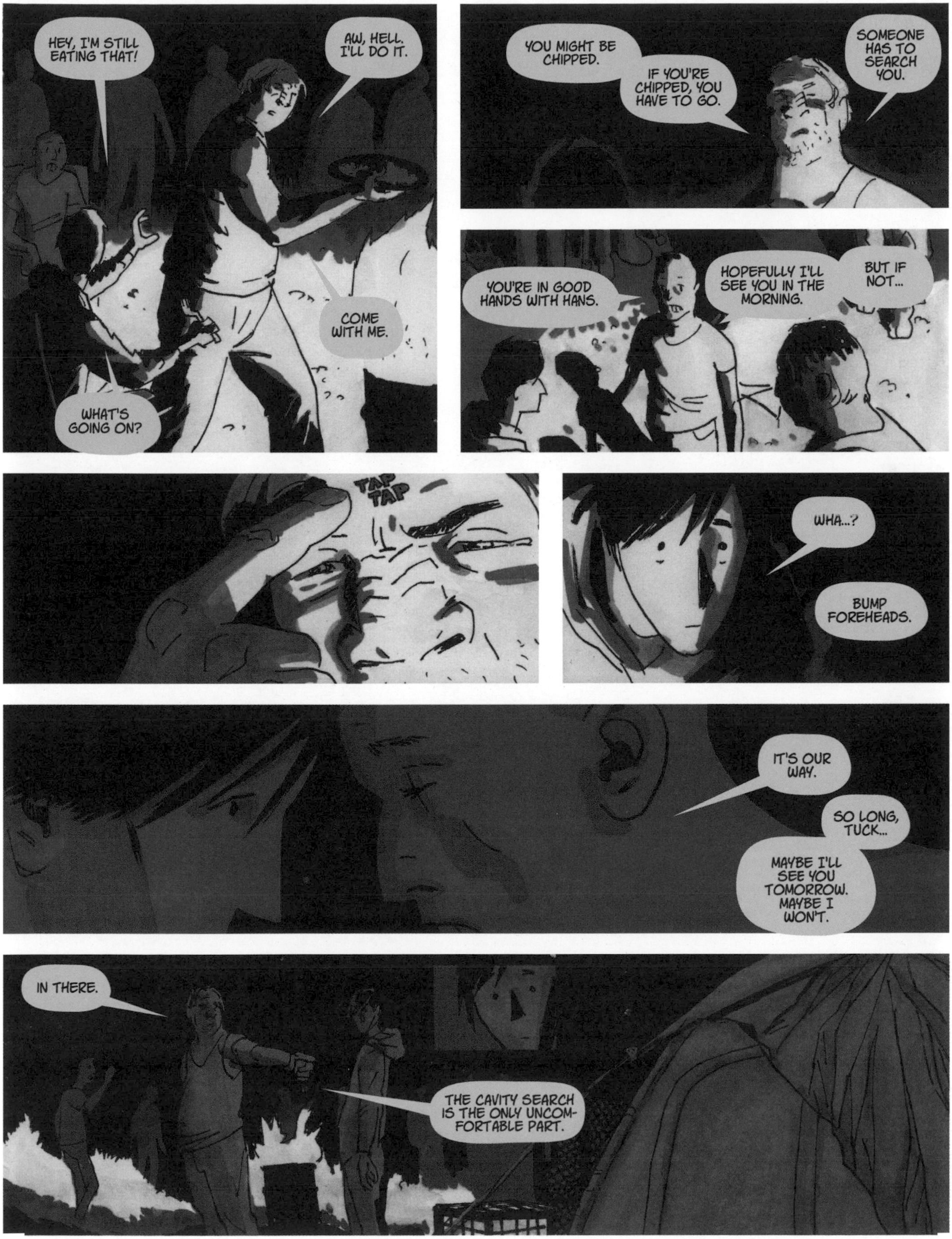
HEY, I'M STILL EATING THAT!
AW, HELL. I'LL DO IT.
COME WITH ME.
WHAT'S GOING ON?
YOU MIGHT BE CHIPPED.
IF YOU'RE CHIPPED, YOU HAVE TO GO.
SOMEONE HAS TO SEARCH YOU.
YOU'RE IN GOOD HANDS WITH HANS.
HOPEFULLY I'LL SEE YOU IN THE MORNING.
BUT IF NOT...
TAP TAP
WHA...?
BUMP FOREHEADS.
IT'S OUR WAY.
SO LONG, TUCK...
MAYBE I'LL SEE YOU TOMORROW. MAYBE I WON'T.
IN THERE.
THE CAVITY SEARCH IS THE ONLY UNCOMFORTABLE PART.

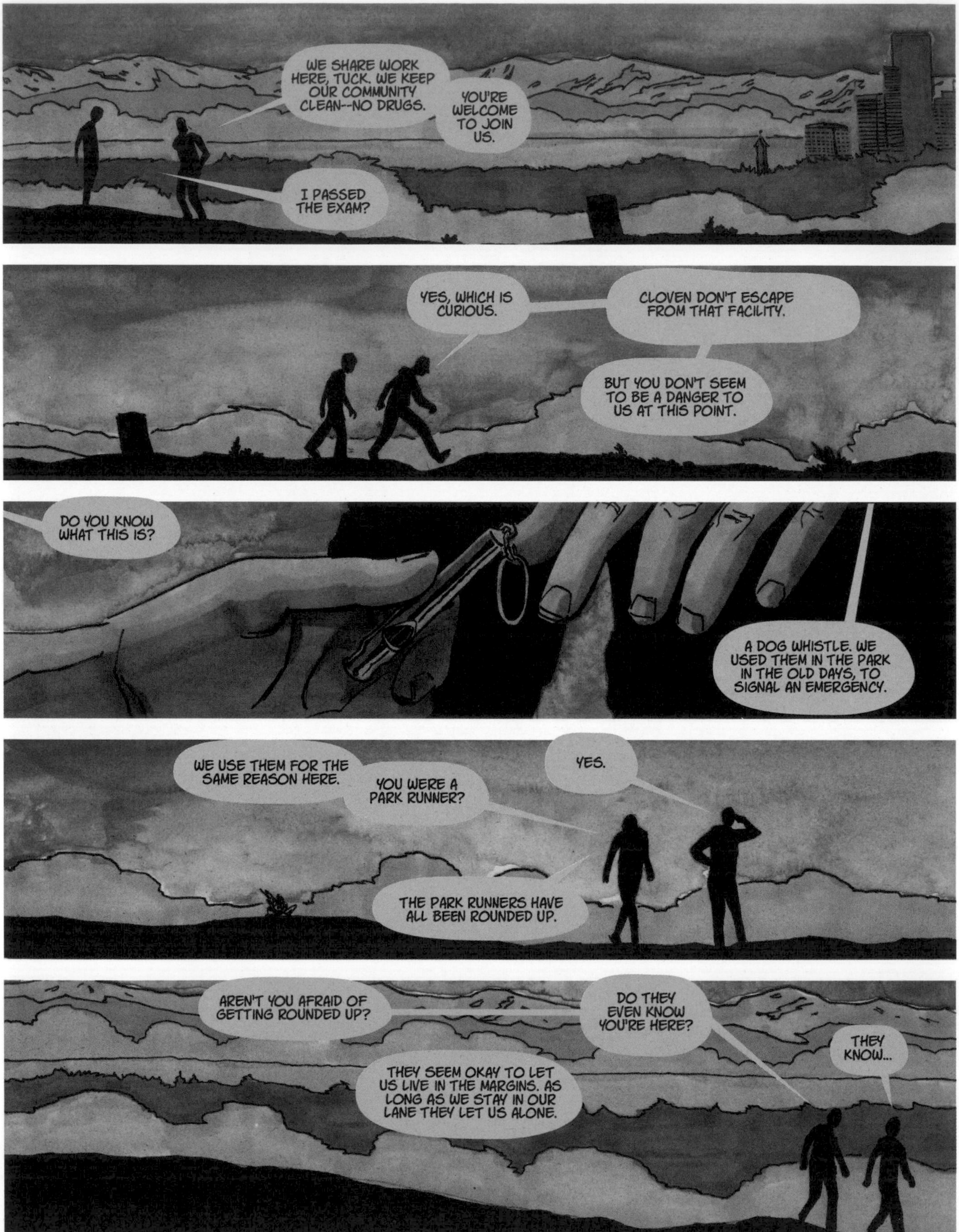
WE SHARE WORK HERE, TUCK. WE KEEP OUR COMMUNITY CLEAN--NO DRUGS.
YOU'RE WELCOME TO JOIN US.
I PASSED THE EXAM?
YES, WHICH IS CURIOUS.
CLOVEN DON'T ESCAPE FROM THAT FACILITY.
BUT YOU DON'T SEEM TO BE A DANGER TO US AT THIS POINT.
DO YOU KNOW WHAT THIS IS?
A DOG WHISTLE. WE USED THEM IN THE PARK IN THE OLD DAYS, TO SIGNAL AN EMERGENCY.
WE USE THEM FOR THE SAME REASON HERE.
YOU WERE A PARK RUNNER?
YES.
THE PARK RUNNERS HAVE ALL BEEN ROUNDED UP.
AREN'T YOU AFRAID OF GETTING ROUNDED UP?
DO THEY EVEN KNOW YOU'RE HERE?
THEY SEEM OKAY TO LET US LIVE IN THE MARGINS. AS LONG AS WE STAY IN OUR LANE THEY LET US ALONE.
THEY KNOW...

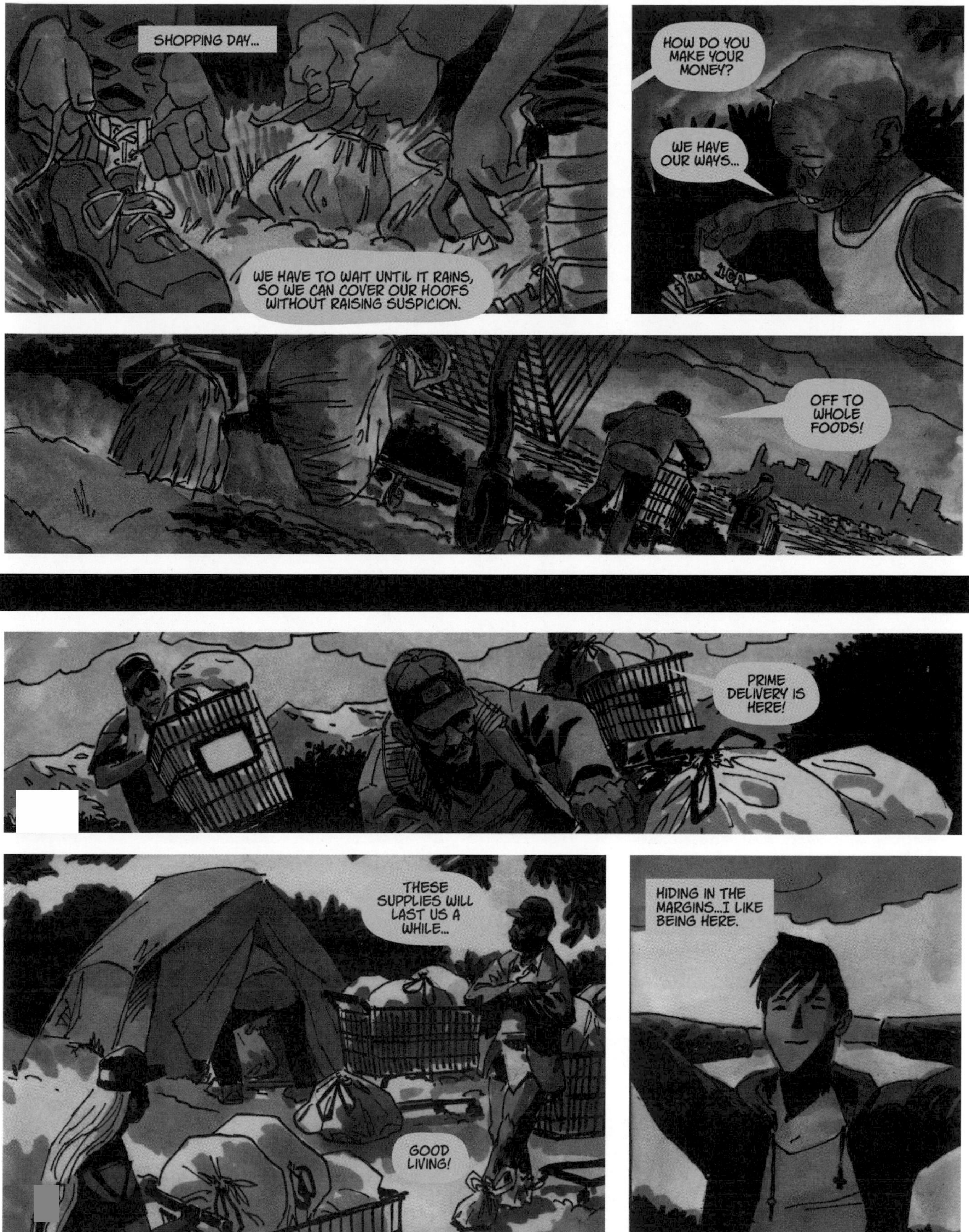
SHOPPING DAY...
WE HAVE TO WAIT UNTIL IT RAINS, SO WE CAN COVER OUR HOOFS WITHOUT RAISING SUSPICION.
HOW DO YOU MAKE YOUR MONEY?
WE HAVE OUR WAYS...
OFF TO WHOLE FOODS!
PRIME DELIVERY IS HERE!
THESE SUPPLIES WILL LAST US A WHILE...
GOOD LIVING!
HIDING IN THE MARGINS...I LIKE BEING HERE.

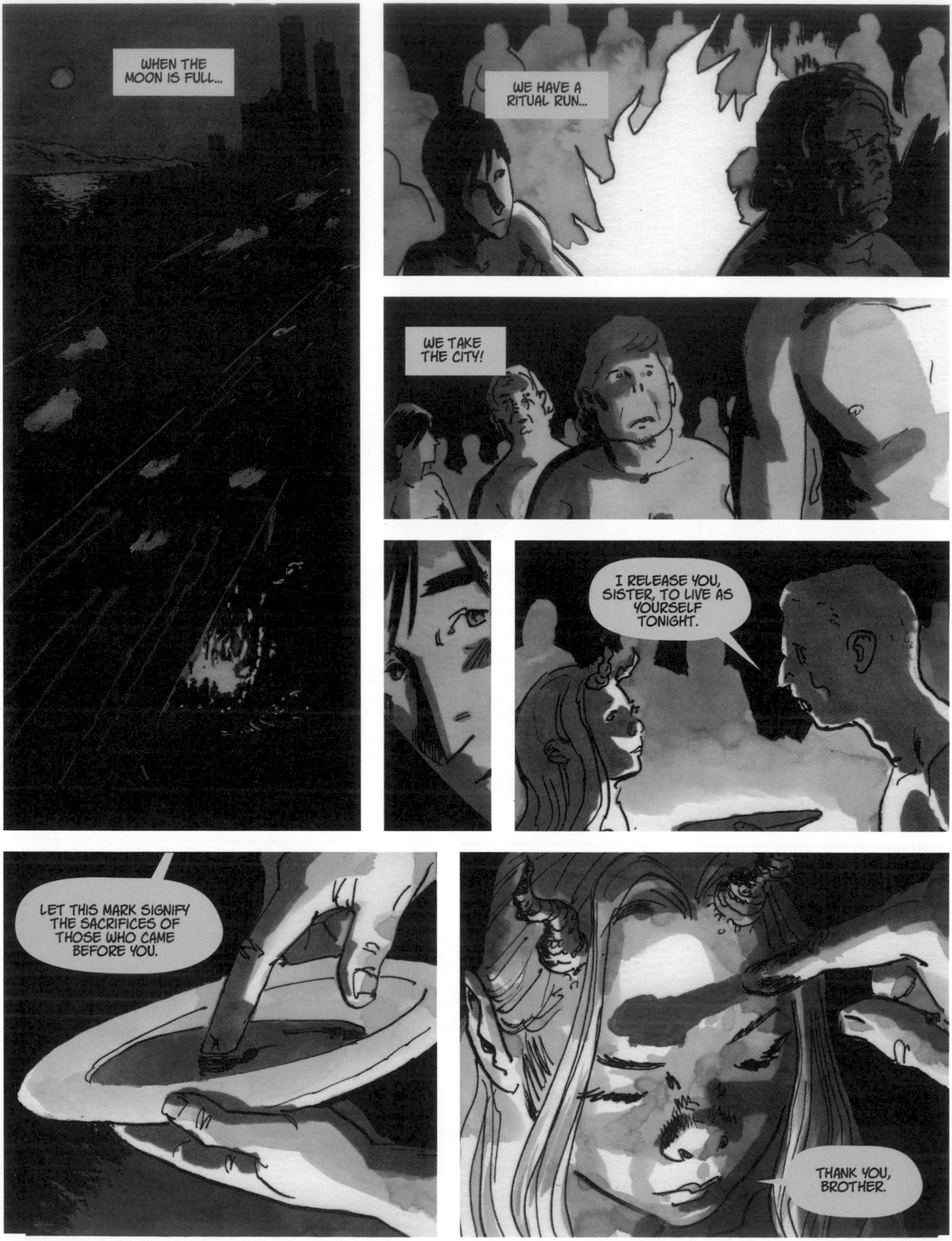
WHEN THE MOON IS FULL...
WE HAVE A RITUAL RUN...
WE TAKE THE CITY!
I RELEASE YOU, SISTER, TO LIVE AS YOURSELF TONIGHT.
LET THIS MARK SIGNIFY THE SACRIFICES OF THOSE WHO CAME BEFORE YOU.
THANK YOU, BROTHER.

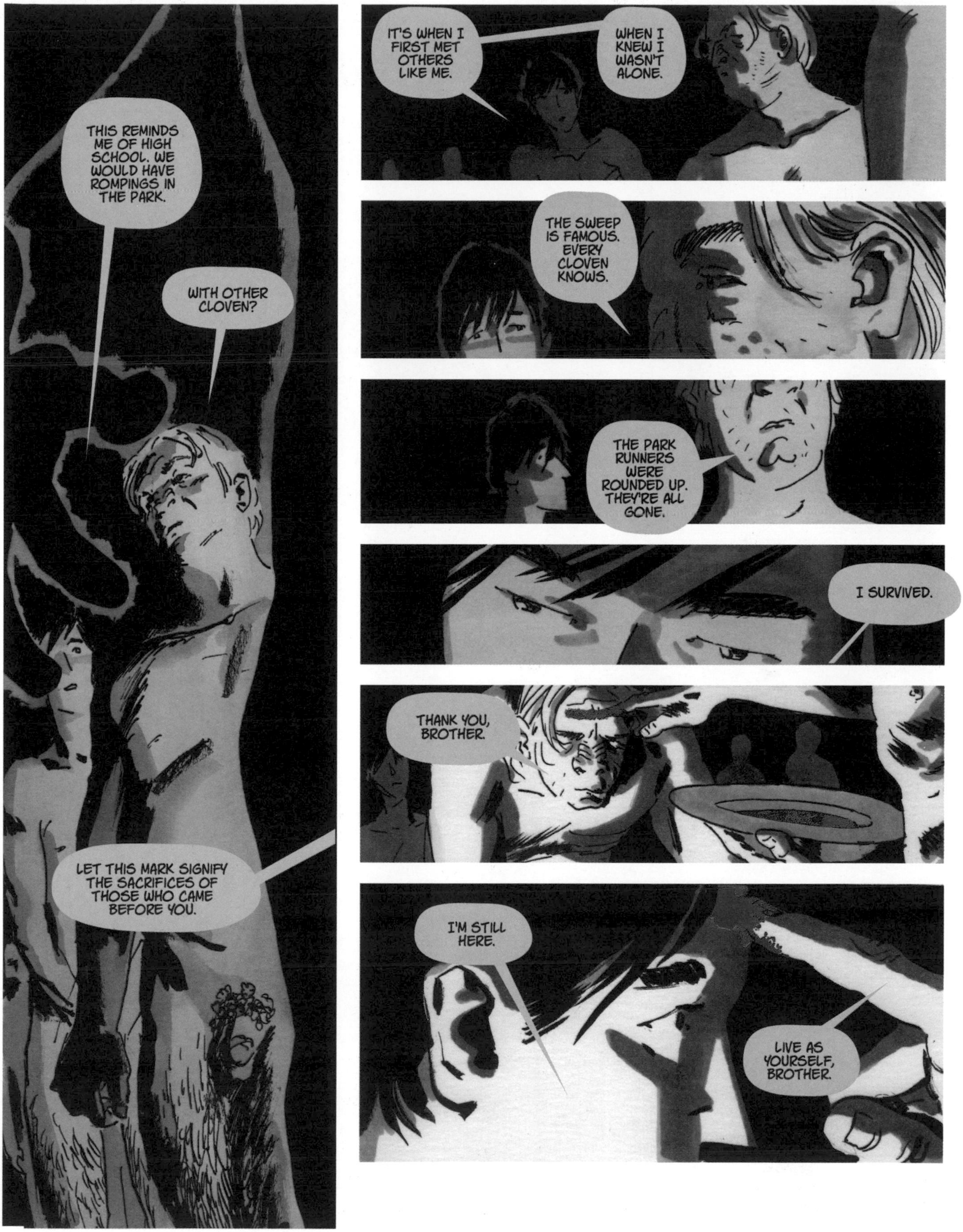

THIS REMINDS ME OF HIGH SCHOOL. WE WOULD HAVE ROMPINGS IN THE PARK.
WITH OTHER CLOVEN?
LET THIS MARK SIGNIFY THE SACRIFICES OF THOSE WHO CAME BEFORE YOU.
IT'S WHEN I FIRST MET OTHERS LIKE ME.
WHEN I KNEW I WASN'T ALONE.
THE SWEEP IS FAMOUS. EVERY CLOVEN KNOWS.
THE PARK RUNNERS WERE ROUNDED UP. THEY'RE ALL GONE.
I SURVIVED.
THANK YOU, BROTHER.
I'M STILL HERE.
LIVE AS YOURSELF, BROTHER.

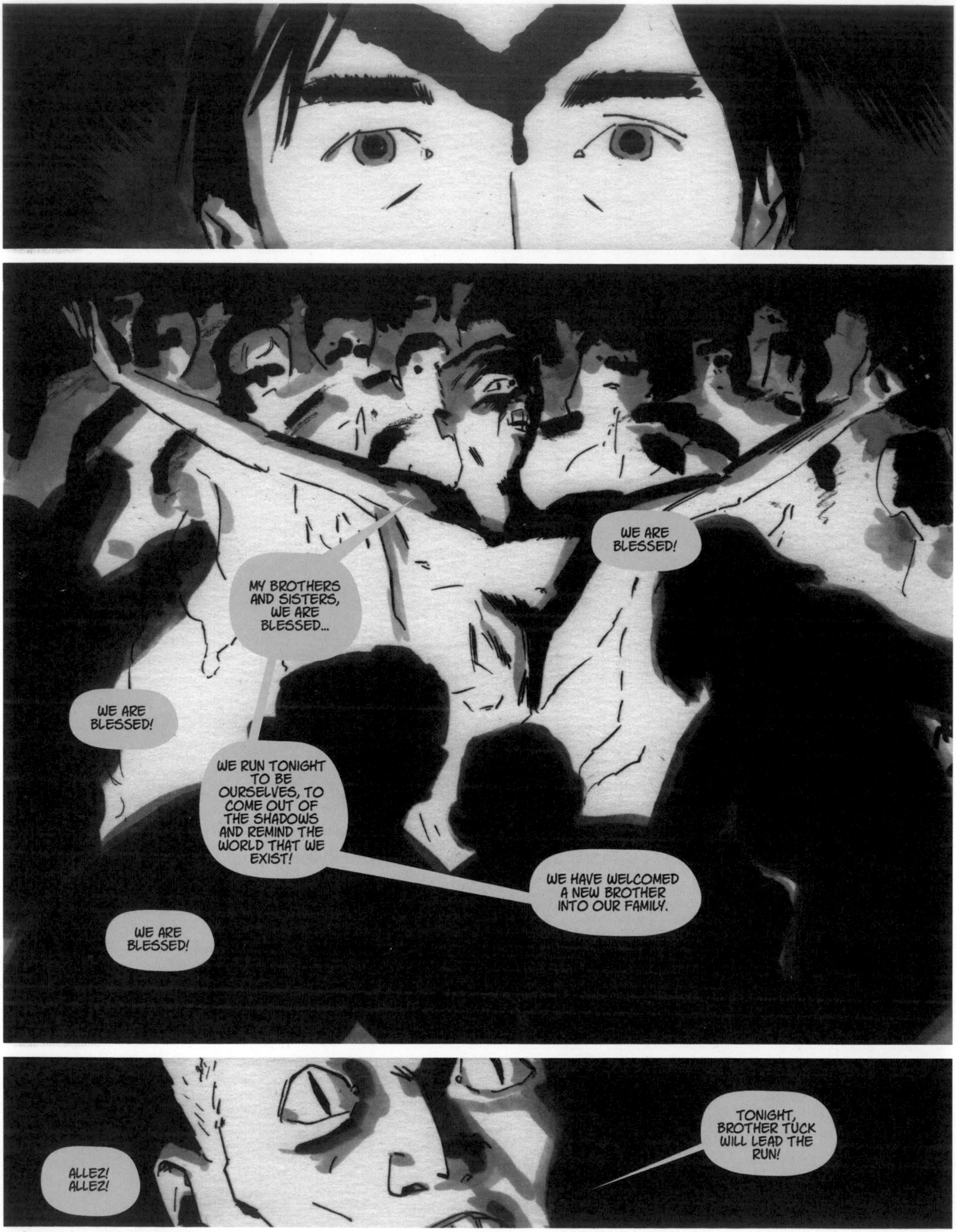
MY BROTHERS AND SISTERS, WE ARE BLESSED...
WE ARE BLESSED!
WE ARE BLESSED!
WE RUN TONIGHT TO BE OURSELVES, TO COME OUT OF THE SHADOWS AND REMIND THE WORLD THAT WE EXIST!
WE HAVE WELCOMED A NEW BROTHER INTO OUR FAMILY.
WE ARE BLESSED!
TONIGHT, BROTHER TUCK WILL LEAD THE RUN!
ALLEZ! ALLEZ!

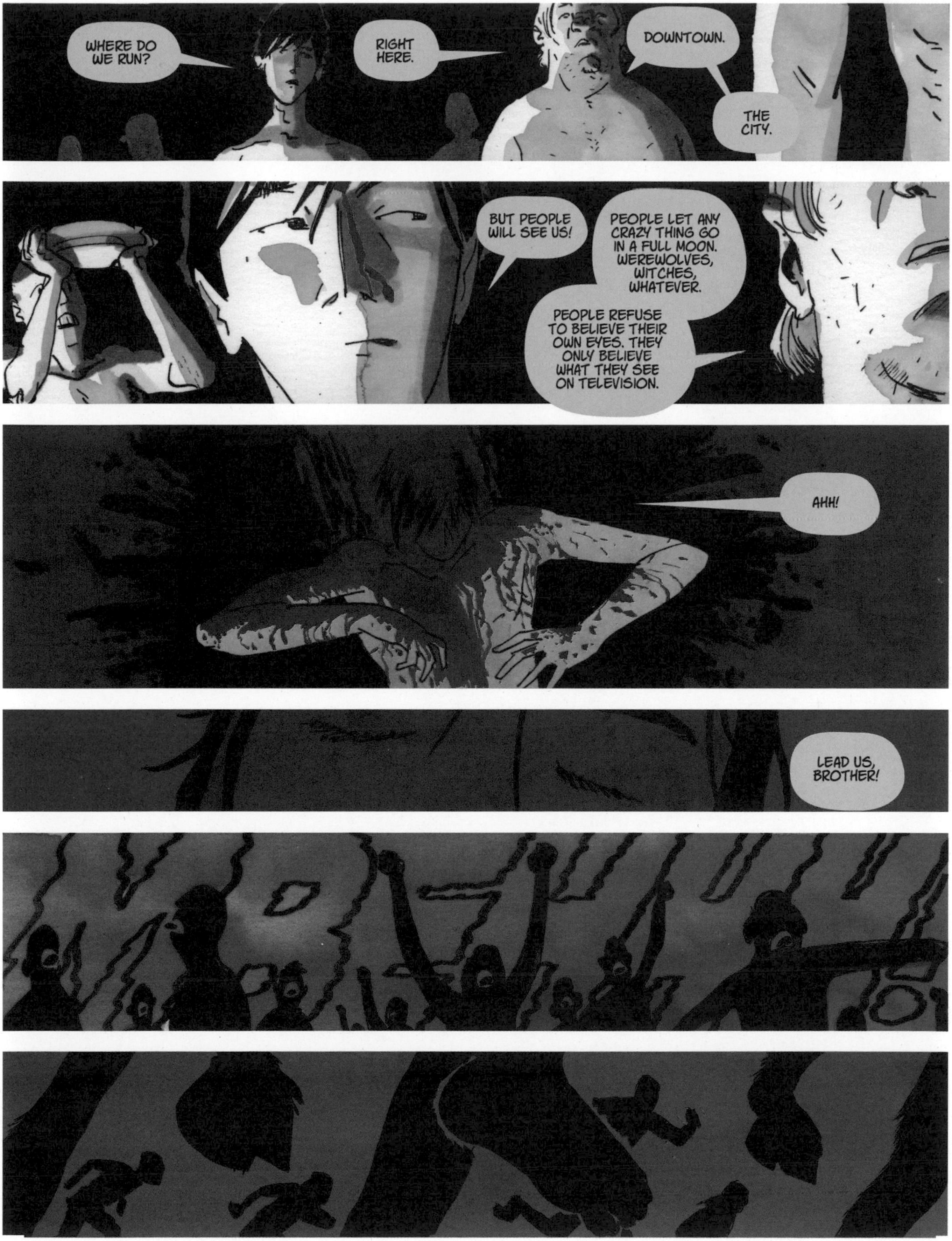
WHERE DO WE RUN?
RIGHT HERE.
DOWNTOWN.
THE CITY.
BUT PEOPLE WILL SEE US!
PEOPLE LET ANY CRAZY THING GO IN A FULL MOON. WEREWOLVES, WITCHES, WHATEVER.
PEOPLE REFUSE TO BELIEVE THEIR OWN EYES. THEY ONLY BELIEVE WHAT THEY SEE ON TELEVISION.
AHH!
LEAD US, BROTHER!

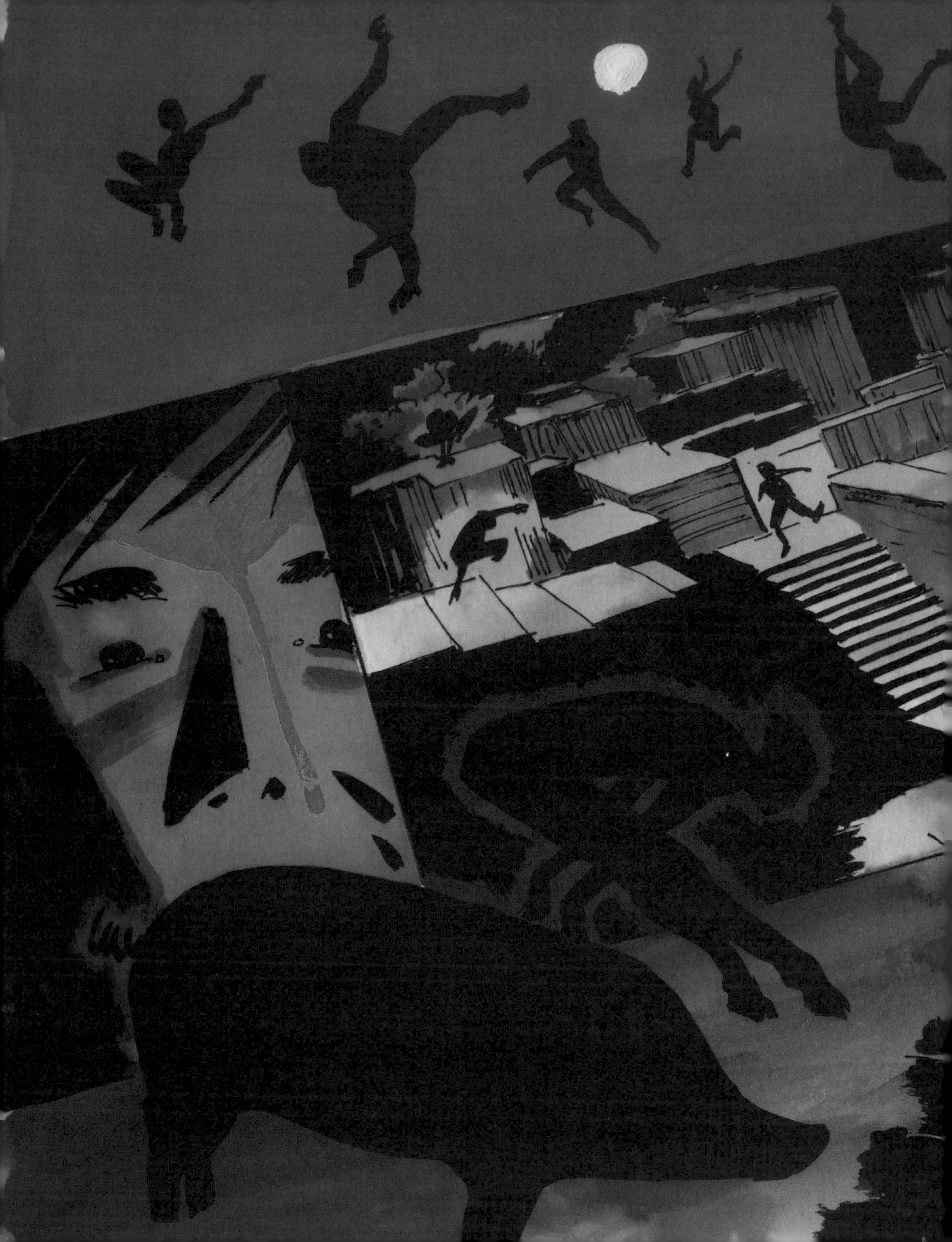

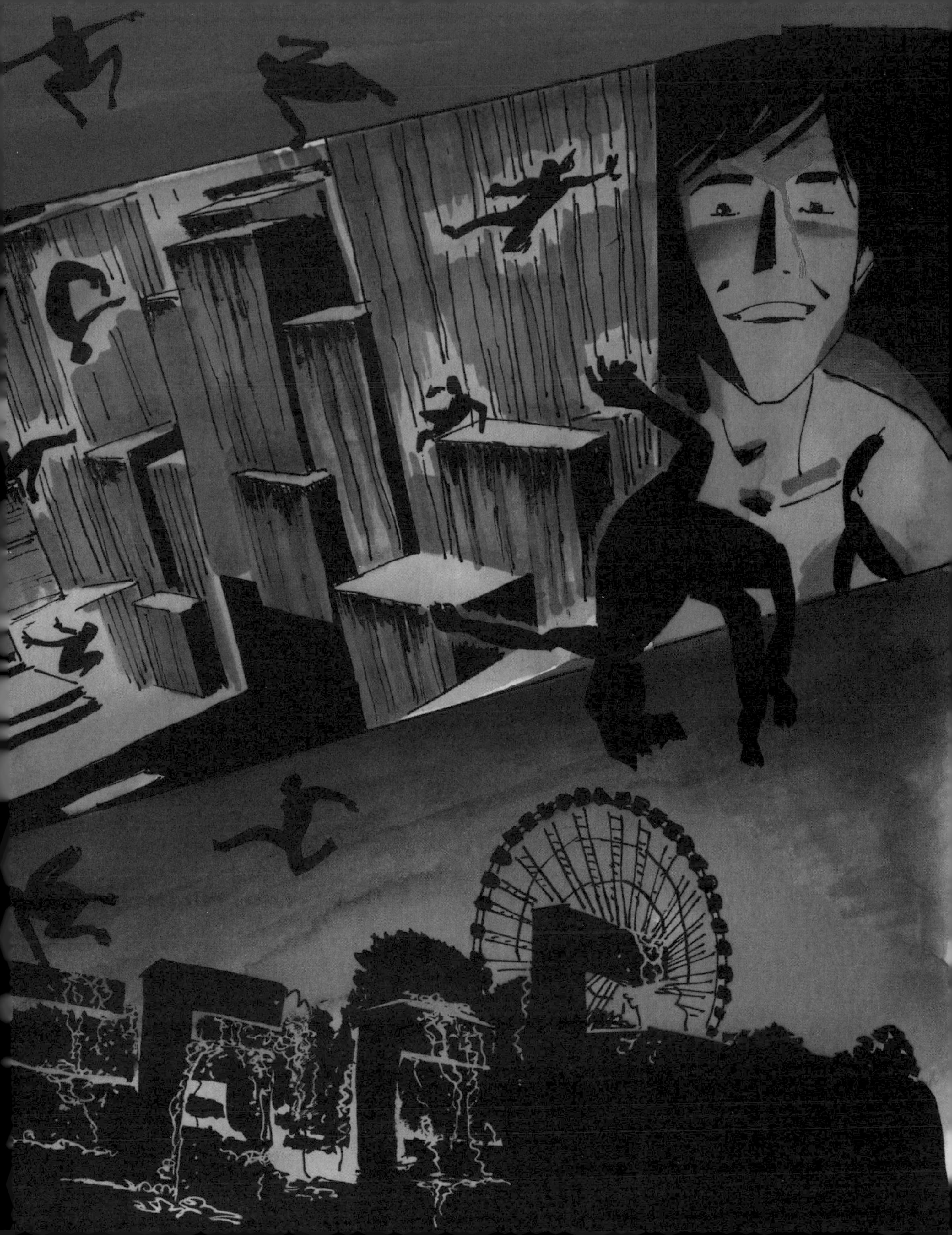

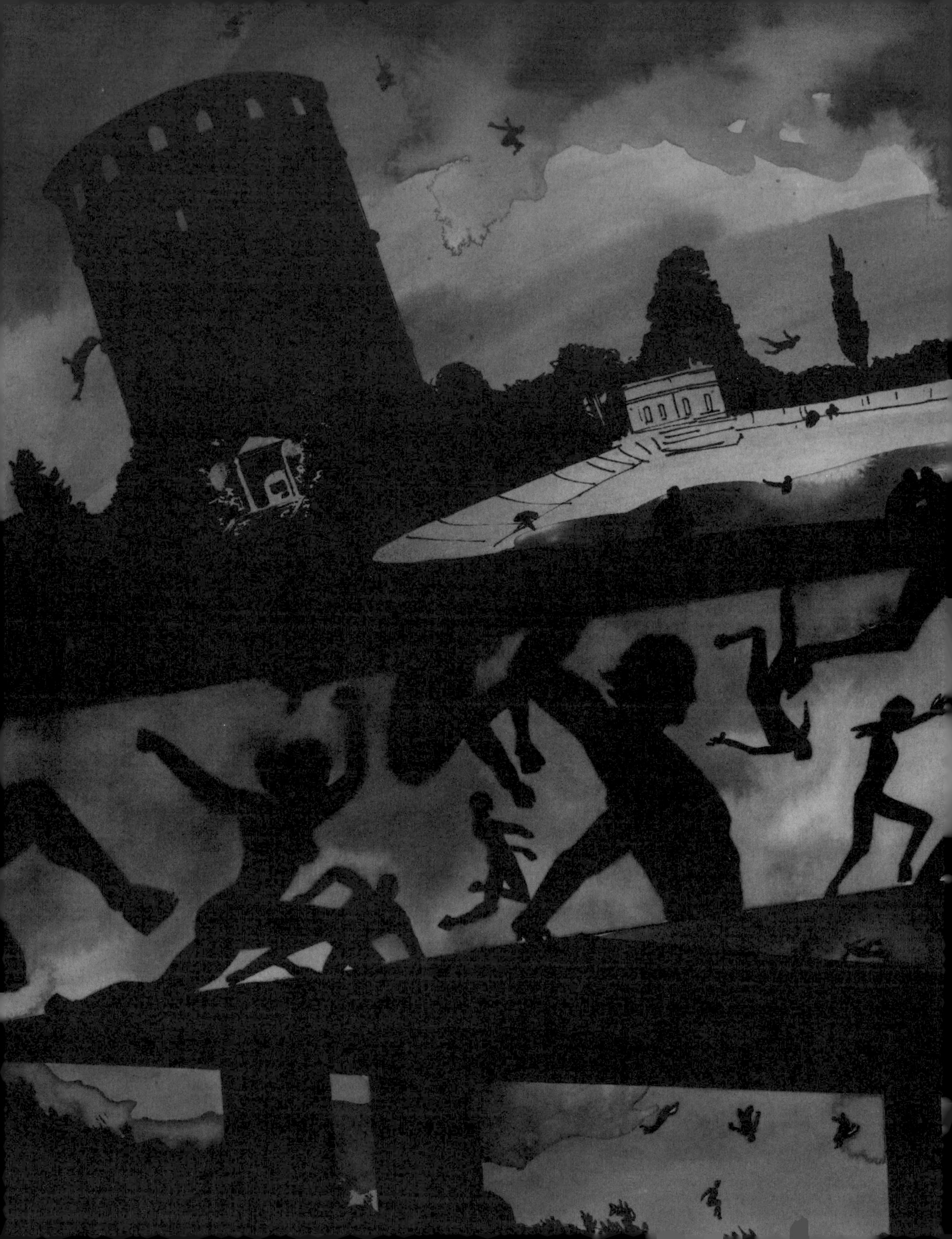

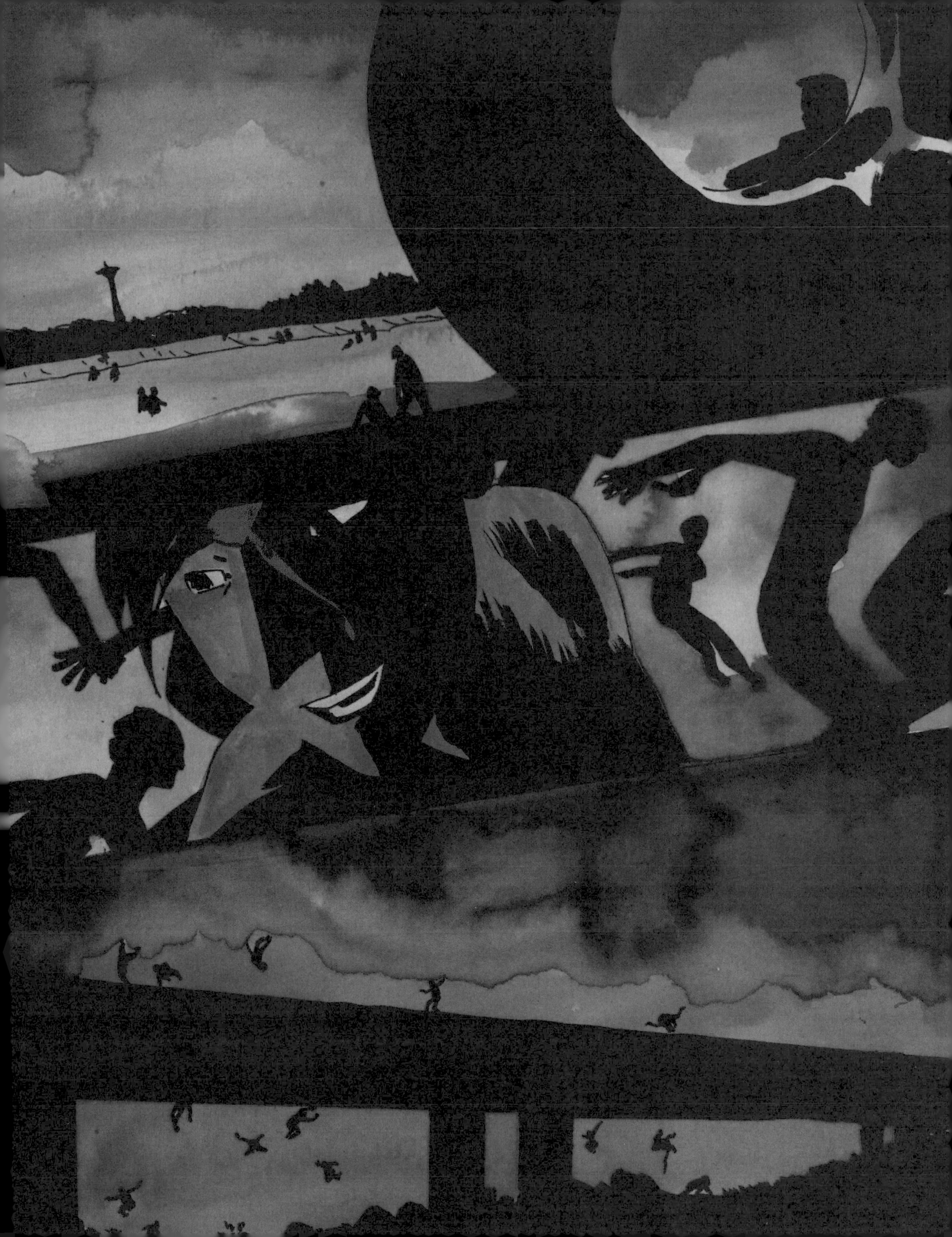

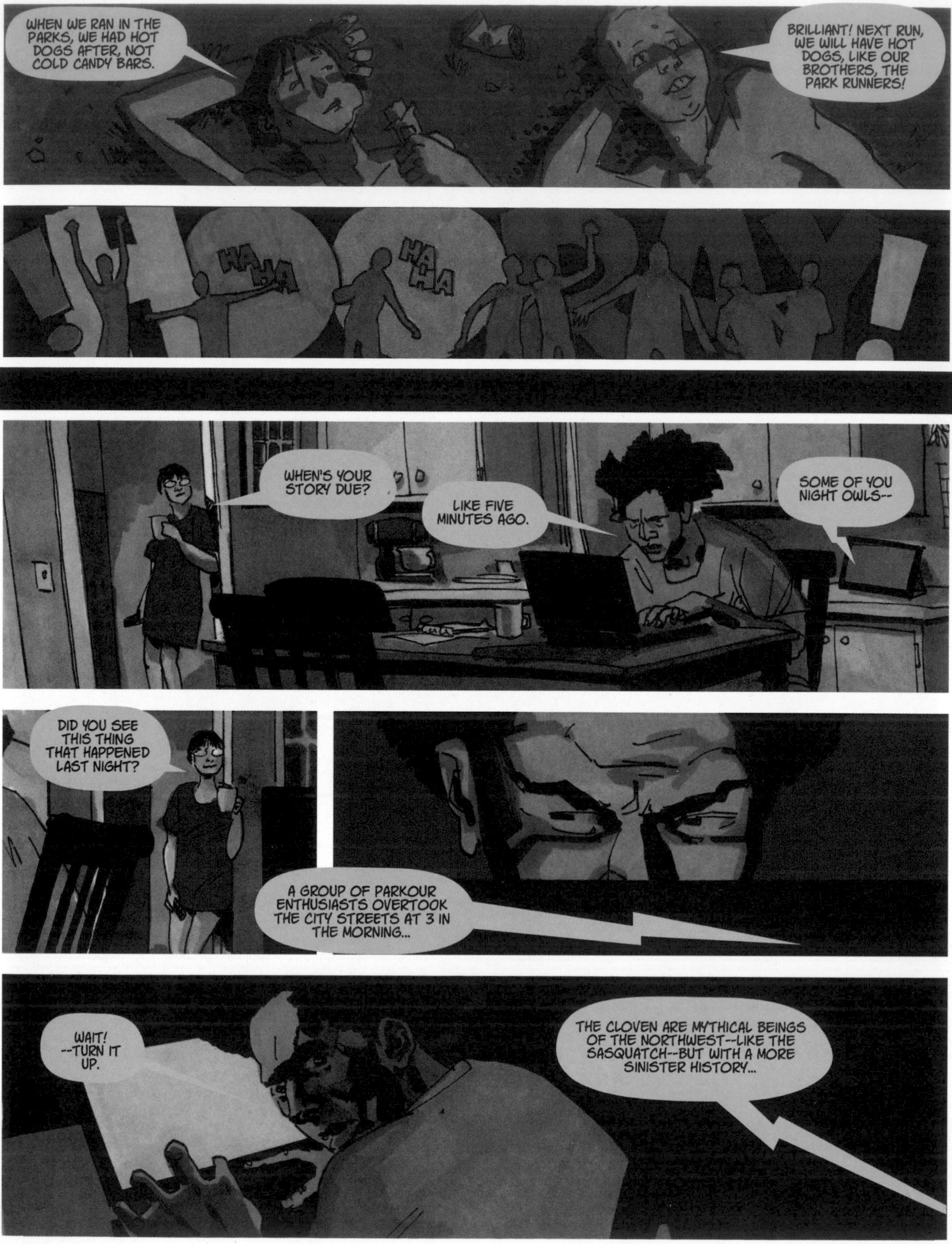
WHEN WE RAN IN THE PARKS, WE HAD HOT DOGS AFTER, NOT COLD CANDY BARS.
BRILLIANT! NEXT RUN, WE WILL HAVE HOT DOGS, LIKE OUR BROTHERS, THE PARK RUNNERS!
HA HA
HA HA
WHEN'S YOUR STORY DUE?
LIKE FIVE MINUTES AGO.
SOME OF YOU NIGHT OWLS--
DID YOU SEE THIS THING THAT HAPPENED LAST NIGHT?
A GROUP OF PARKOUR ENTHUSIASTS OVERTOOK THE CITY STREETS AT 3 IN THE MORNING...
WAIT! --TURN IT UP.
THE CLOVEN ARE MYTHICAL BEINGS OF THE NORTHWEST--LIKE THE SASQUATCH--BUT WITH A MORE SINISTER HISTORY...

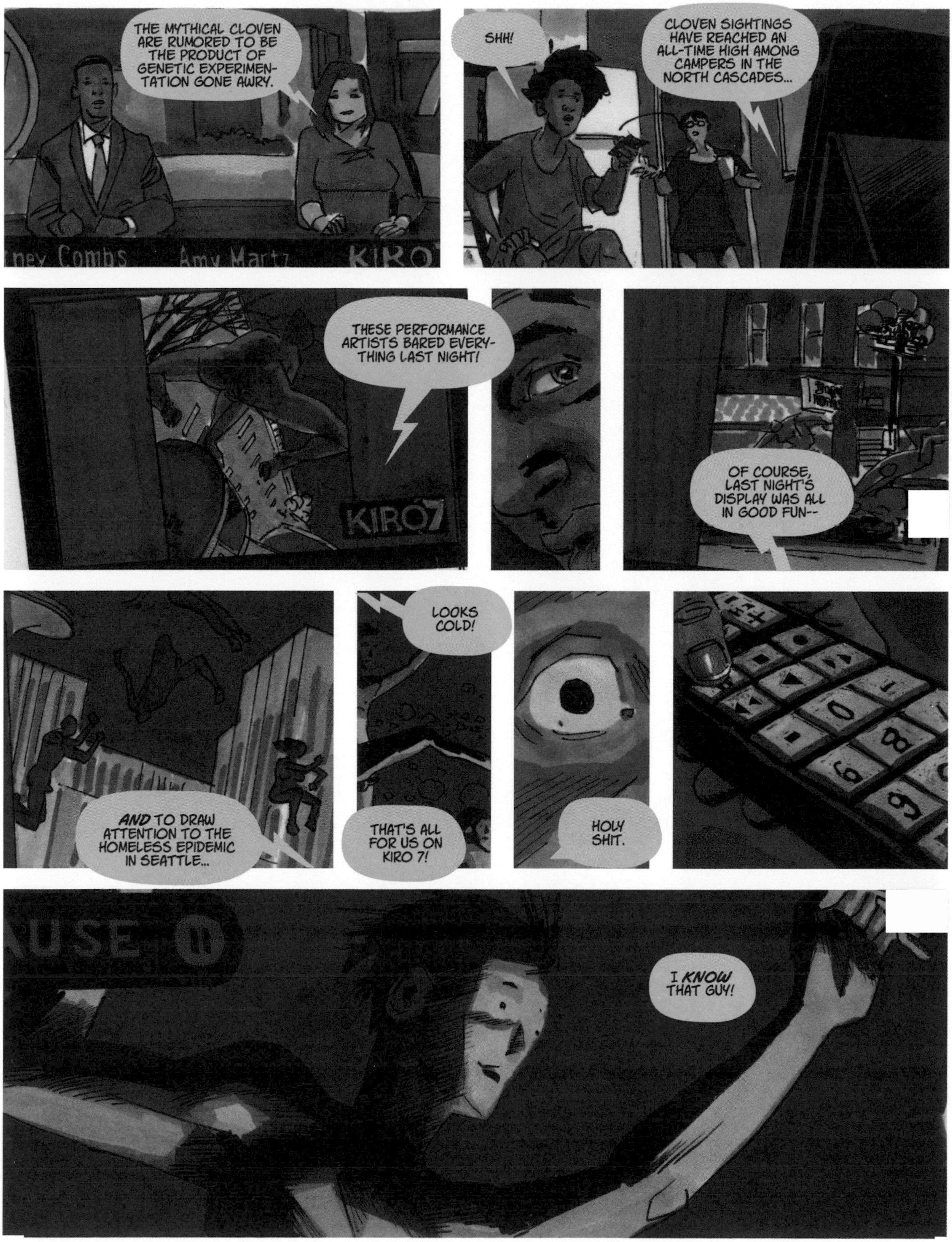
THE MYTHICAL CLOVEN ARE RUMORED TO BE THE PRODUCT OF GENETIC EXPERIMEN-TATION GONE AWRY.
Amy Martz
KIRO
SHH!
CLOVEN SIGHTINGS HAVE REACHED AN ALL-TIME HIGH AMONG CAMPERS IN THE NORTH CASCADES...
THESE PERFORMANCE ARTISTS BARED EVERY-THING LAST NIGHT!
KIRO7
OF COURSE, LAST NIGHT'S DISPLAY WAS ALL IN GOOD FUN--
AND TO DRAW ATTENTION TO THE HOMELESS EPIDEMIC IN SEATTLE...
LOOKS COLD!
THAT'S ALL FOR US ON KIRO 7!
HOLY SHIT.
I KNOW THAT GUY!

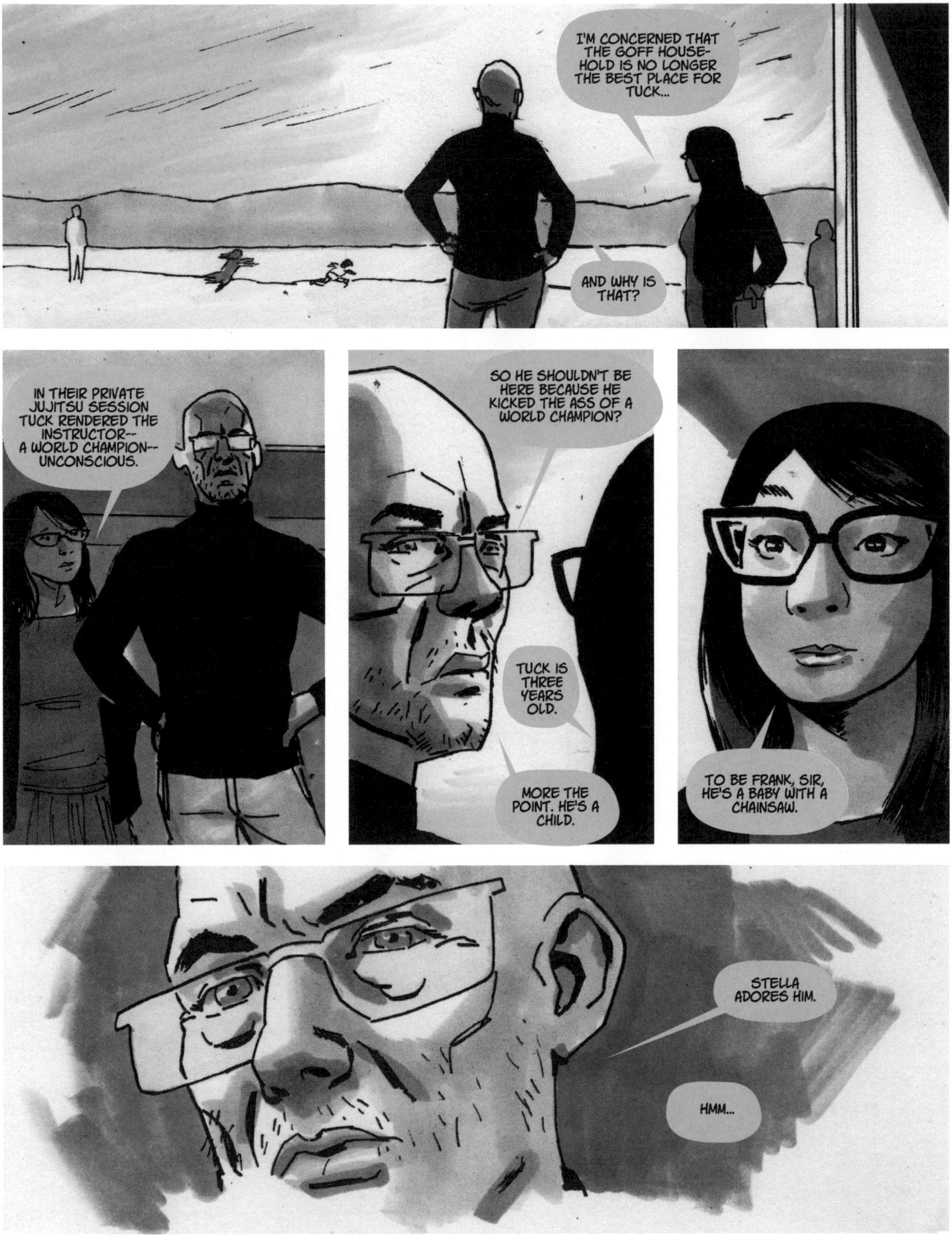
I'M CONCERNED THAT THE GOFF HOUSE-HOLD IS NO LONGER THE BEST PLACE FOR TUCK...
AND WHY IS THAT?
IN THEIR PRIVATE JUJITSU SESSION TUCK RENDERED THE INSTRUCTOR-- A WORLD CHAMPION-- UNCONSCIOUS.
SO HE SHOULDN'T BE HERE BECAUSE HE KICKED THE ASS OF A WORLD CHAMPION?
TUCK IS THREE YEARS OLD.
MORE THE POINT. HE'S A CHILD.
TO BE FRANK, SIR, HE'S A BABY WITH A CHAINSAW.
STELLA ADORES HIM.
HMM...

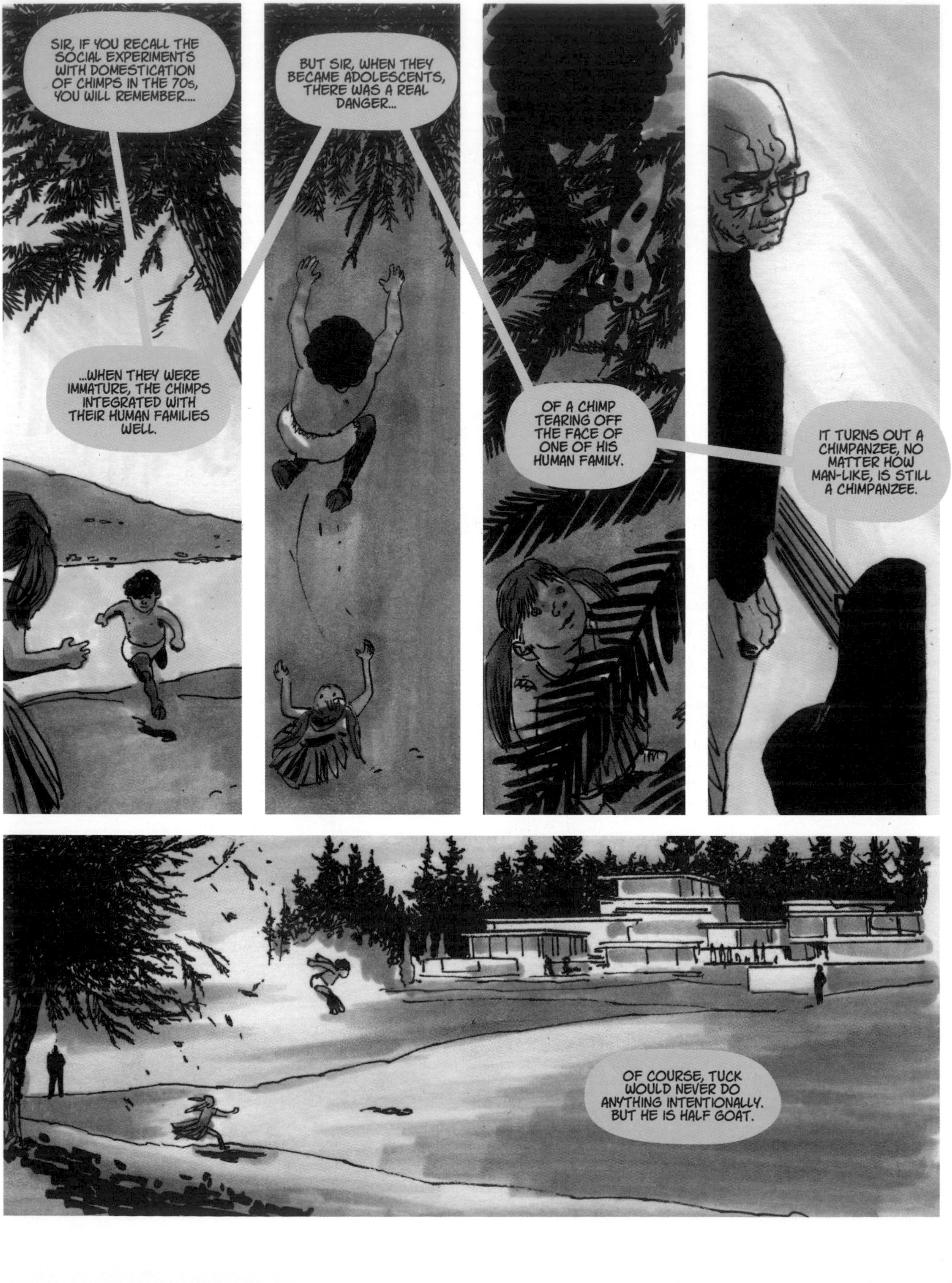
SIR, IF YOU RECALL THE SOCIAL EXPERIMENTS WITH DOMESTICATION OF CHIMPS IN THE 70s, YOU WILL REMEMBER....
...WHEN THEY WERE IMMATURE, THE CHIMPS INTEGRATED WITH THEIR HUMAN FAMILIES WELL.
BUT SIR, WHEN THEY BECAME ADOLESCENTS, THERE WAS A REAL DANGER...
OF A CHIMP TEARING OFF THE FACE OF ONE OF HIS HUMAN FAMILY.
IT TURNS OUT A CHIMPANZEE, NO MATTER HOW MAN-LIKE, IS STILL A CHIMPANZEE.
OF COURSE, TUCK WOULD NEVER DO ANYTHING INTENTIONALLY. BUT HE IS HALF GOAT.

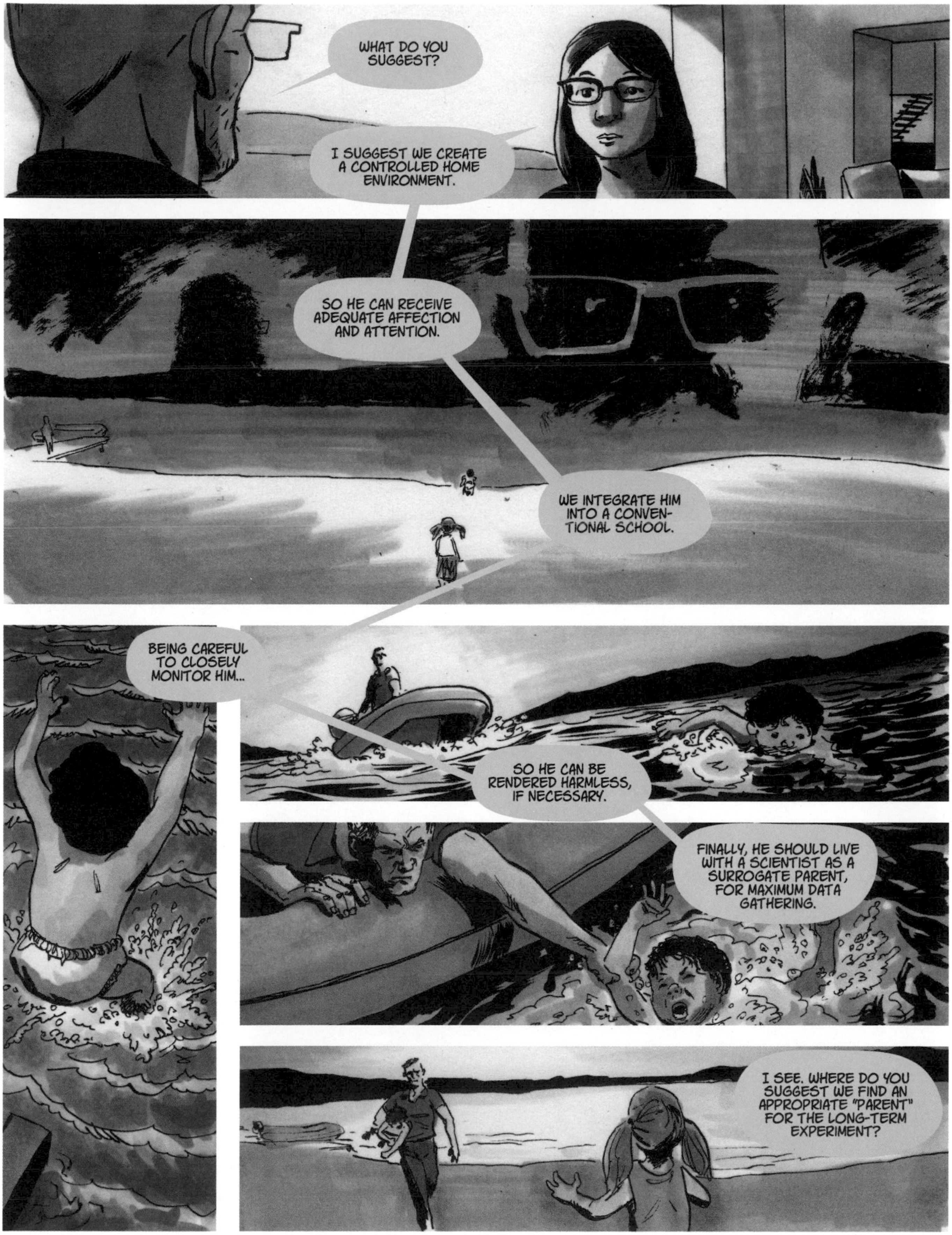
WHAT DO YOU SUGGEST?
I SUGGEST WE CREATE A CONTROLLED HOME ENVIRONMENT.
SO HE CAN RECEIVE ADEQUATE AFFECTION AND ATTENTION.
WE INTEGRATE HIM INTO A CONVEN-TIONAL SCHOOL.
BEING CAREFUL TO CLOSELY MONITOR HIM...
SO HE CAN BE RENDERED HARMLESS, IF NECESSARY.
FINALLY, HE SHOULD LIVE WITH A SCIENTIST AS A SURROGATE PARENT, FOR MAXIMUM DATA GATHERING.
I SEE. WHERE DO YOU SUGGEST WE FIND AN APPROPRIATE "PARENT" FOR THE LONG-TERM EXPERIMENT?

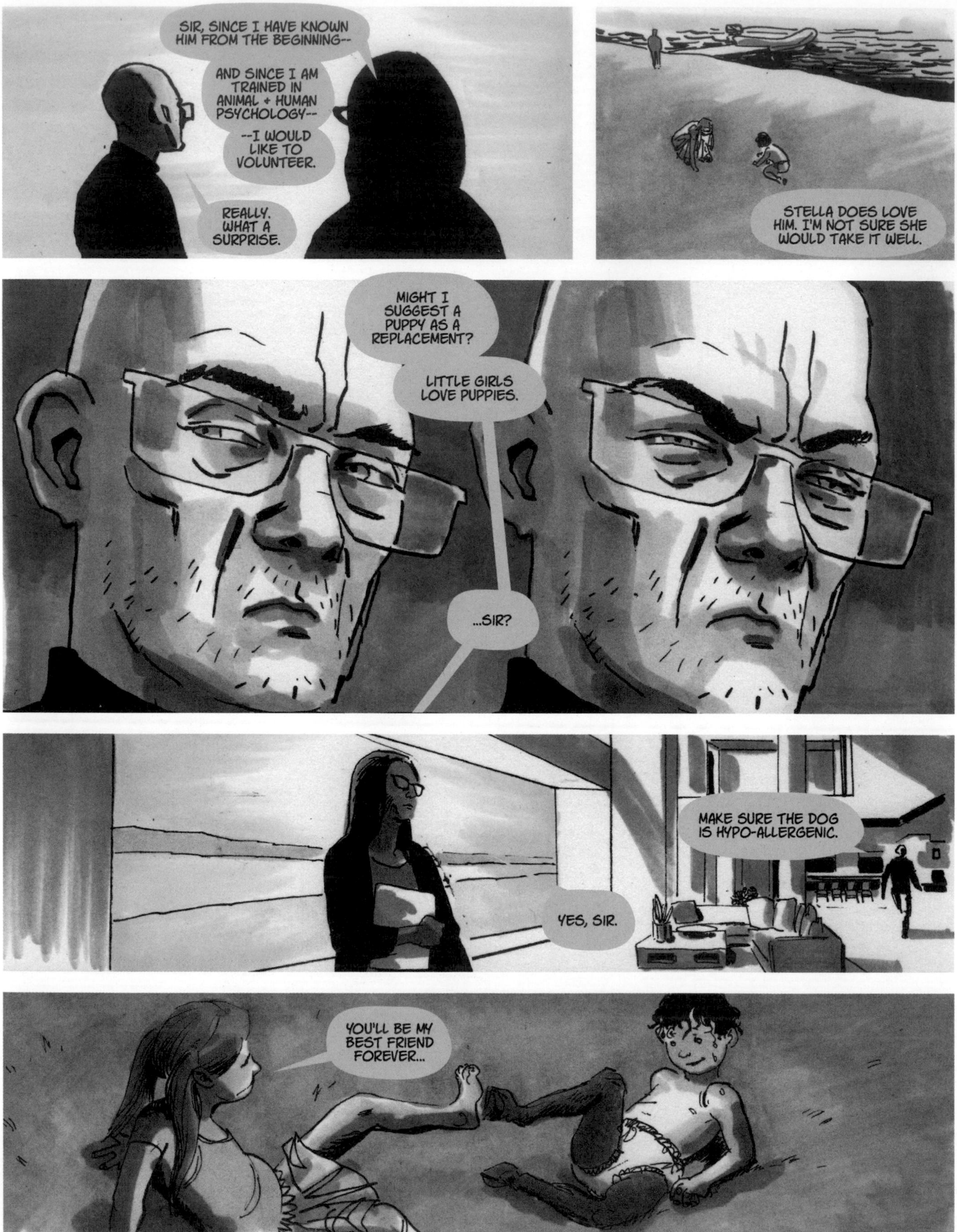
SIR, SINCE I HAVE KNOWN HIM FROM THE BEGINNING--
AND SINCE I AM TRAINED IN ANIMAL & HUMAN PSYCHOLOGY--
--I WOULD LIKE TO VOLUNTEER.
REALLY. WHAT A SURPRISE.
STELLA DOES LOVE HIM. I'M NOT SURE SHE WOULD TAKE IT WELL.
MIGHT I SUGGEST A PUPPY AS A REPLACEMENT?
LITTLE GIRLS LOVE PUPPIES.
...SIR?
MAKE SURE THE DOG IS HYPO-ALLERGENIC.
YES, SIR.
YOU'LL BE MY BEST FRIEND FOREVER...

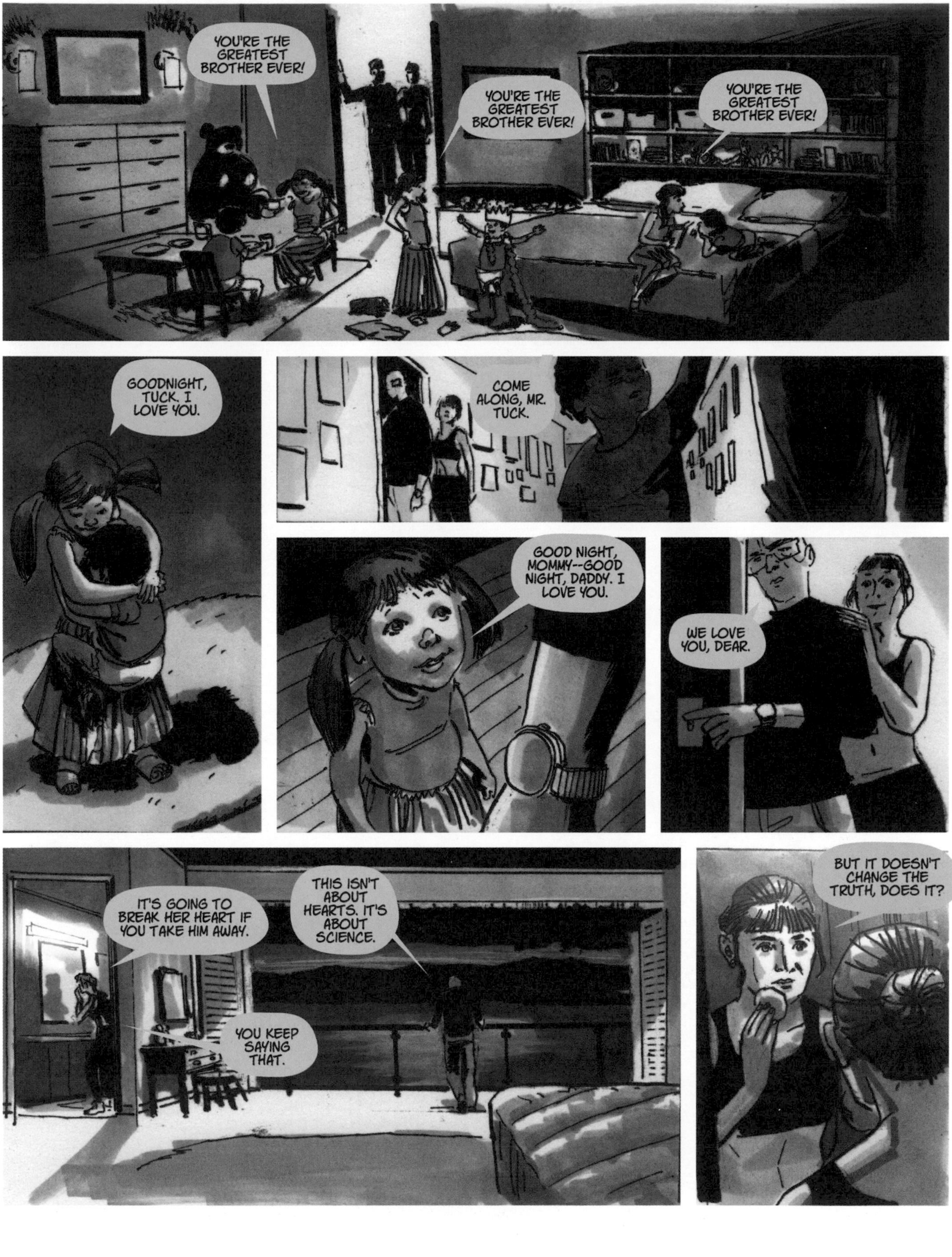

YOU'RE THE GREATEST BROTHER EVER!
YOU'RE THE GREATEST BROTHER EVER!
YOU'RE THE GREATEST BROTHER EVER!
GOODNIGHT, TUCK. I LOVE YOU.
COME ALONG, MR. TUCK.
GOOD NIGHT, MOMMY--GOOD NIGHT, DADDY. I LOVE YOU.
WE LOVE YOU, DEAR.
IT'S GOING TO BREAK HER HEART IF YOU TAKE HIM AWAY.
THIS ISN'T ABOUT HEARTS. IT'S ABOUT SCIENCE.
YOU KEEP SAYING THAT.
BUT IT DOESN'T CHANGE THE TRUTH, DOES IT?

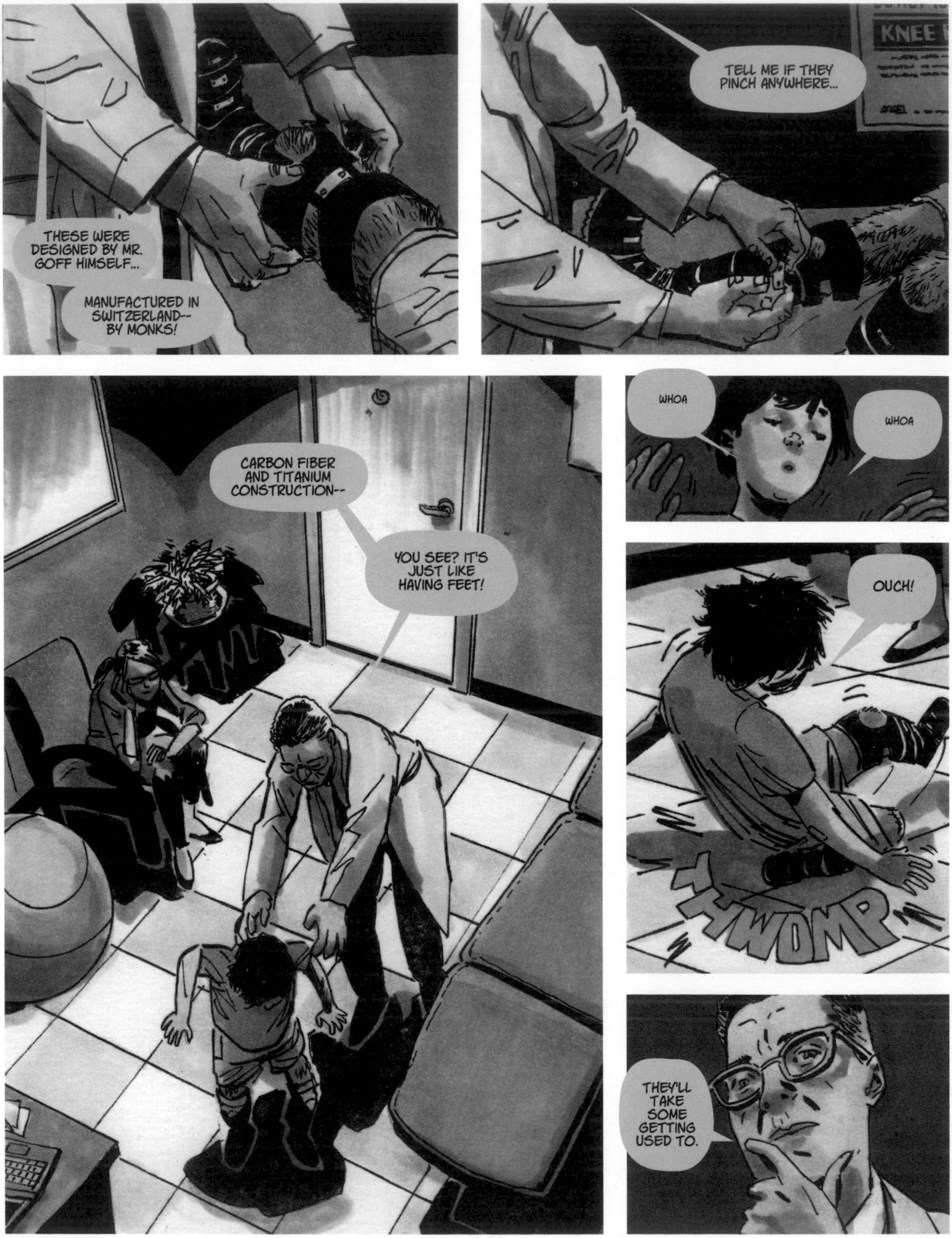
THESE WERE DESIGNED BY MR. GOFF HIMSELF...
MANUFACTURED IN SWITZERLAND-- BY MONKS!
TELL ME IF THEY PINCH ANYWHERE...
CARBON FIBER AND TITANIUM CONSTRUCTION--
YOU SEE? IT'S JUST LIKE HAVING FEET!
WHOA
WHOA
OUCH!
THWOMP
THEY'LL TAKE SOME GETTING USED TO.

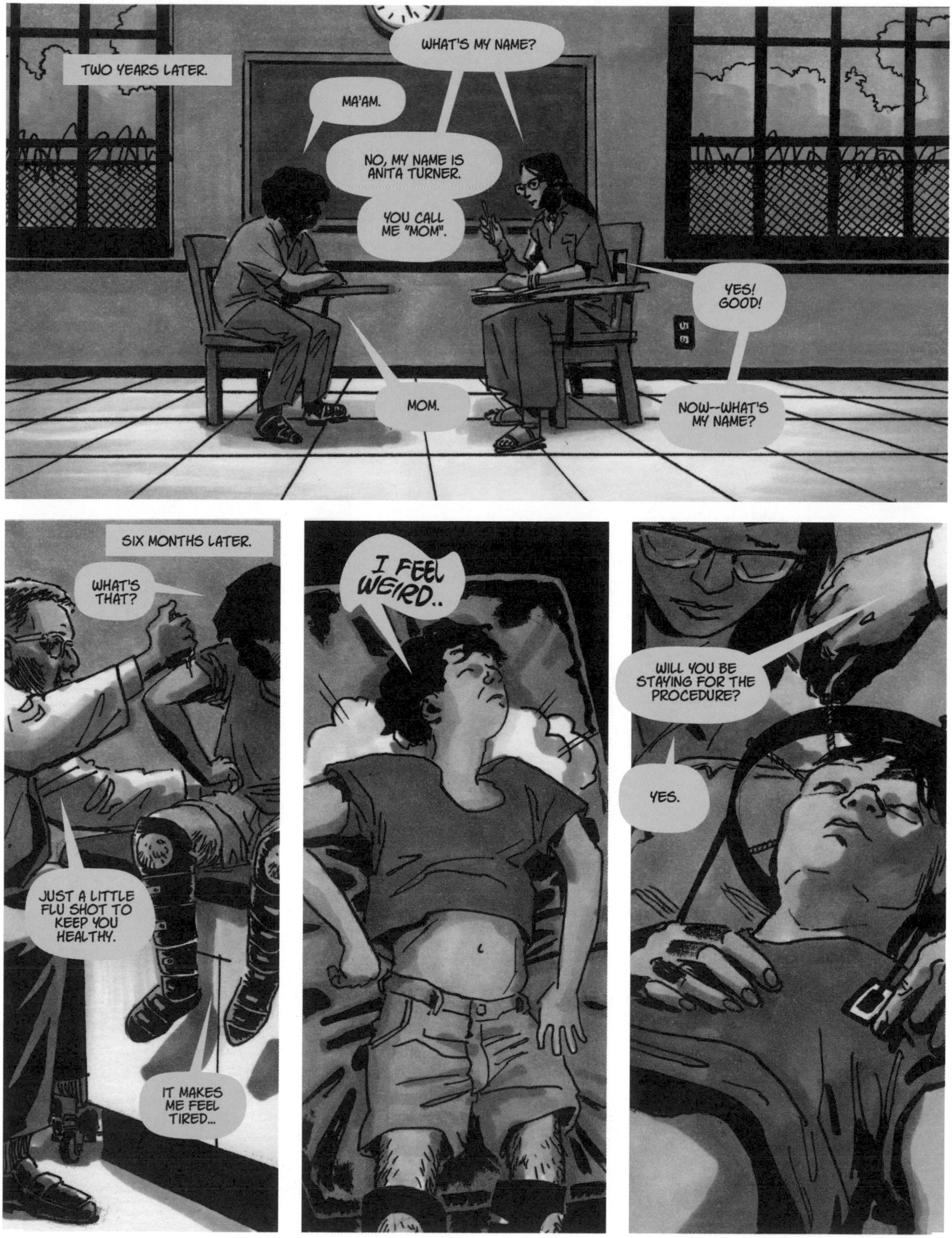
TWO YEARS LATER.
WHAT'S MY NAME?
MA'AM.
NO, MY NAME IS ANITA TURNER.
YOU CALL ME "MOM".
MOM.
YES! GOOD!
NOW--WHAT'S MY NAME?
SIX MONTHS LATER.
WHAT'S THAT?
JUST A LITTLE FLU SHOT TO KEEP YOU HEALTHY.
IT MAKES ME FEEL TIRED...
I FEEL WEIRD..
WILL YOU BE STAYING FOR THE PROCEDURE?
YES.

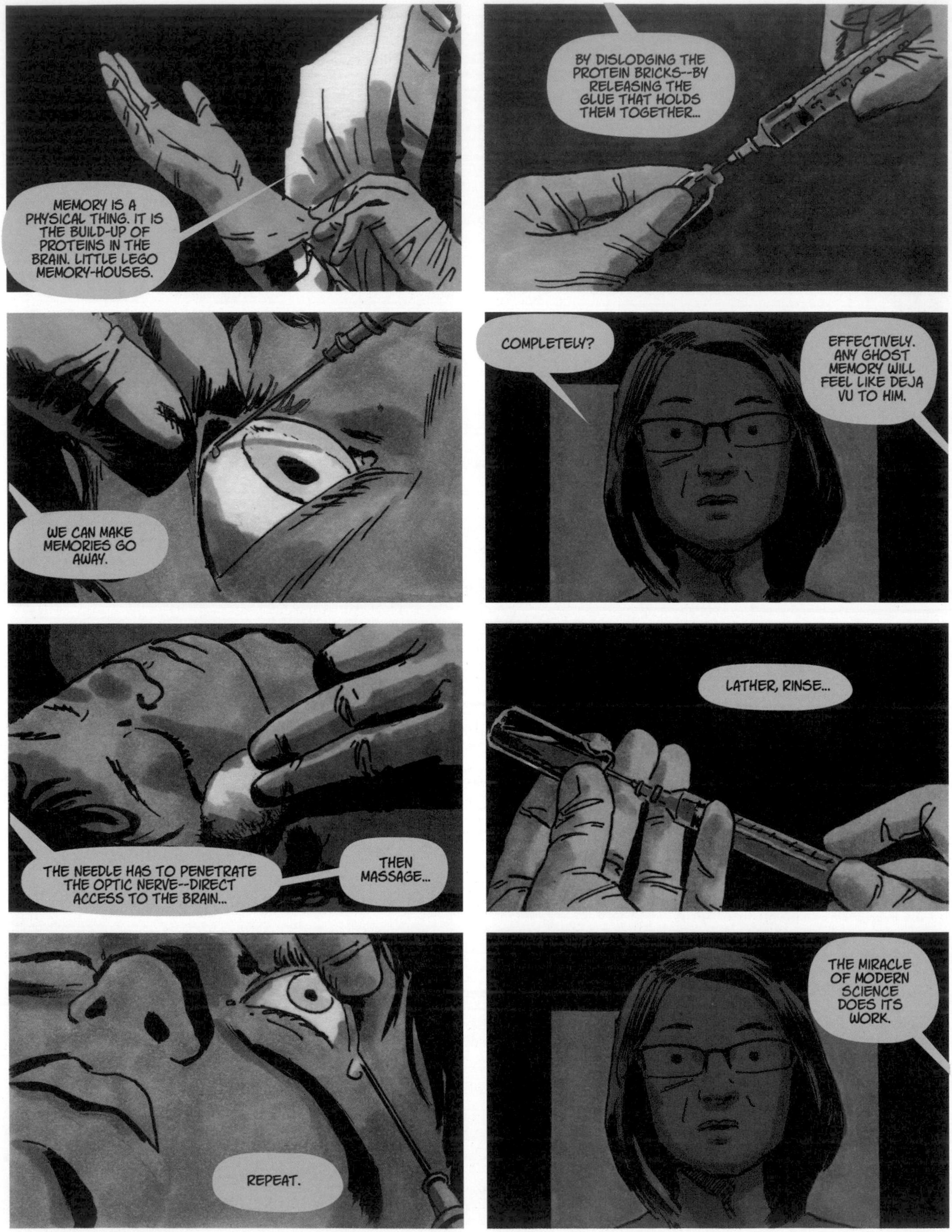
MEMORY IS A PHYSICAL THING. IT IS THE BUILD-UP OF PROTEINS IN THE BRAIN. LITTLE LEGO MEMORY-HOUSES.
BY DISLODGING THE PROTEIN BRICKS--BY RELEASING THE GLUE THAT HOLDS THEM TOGETHER...
WE CAN MAKE MEMORIES GO AWAY.
COMPLETELY?
EFFECTIVELY. ANY GHOST MEMORY WILL FEEL LIKE DEJA VU TO HIM.
THE NEEDLE HAS TO PENETRATE THE OPTIC NERVE--DIRECT ACCESS TO THE BRAIN...
THEN MASSAGE...
LATHER, RINSE...
REPEAT.
THE MIRACLE OF MODERN SCIENCE DOES ITS WORK.

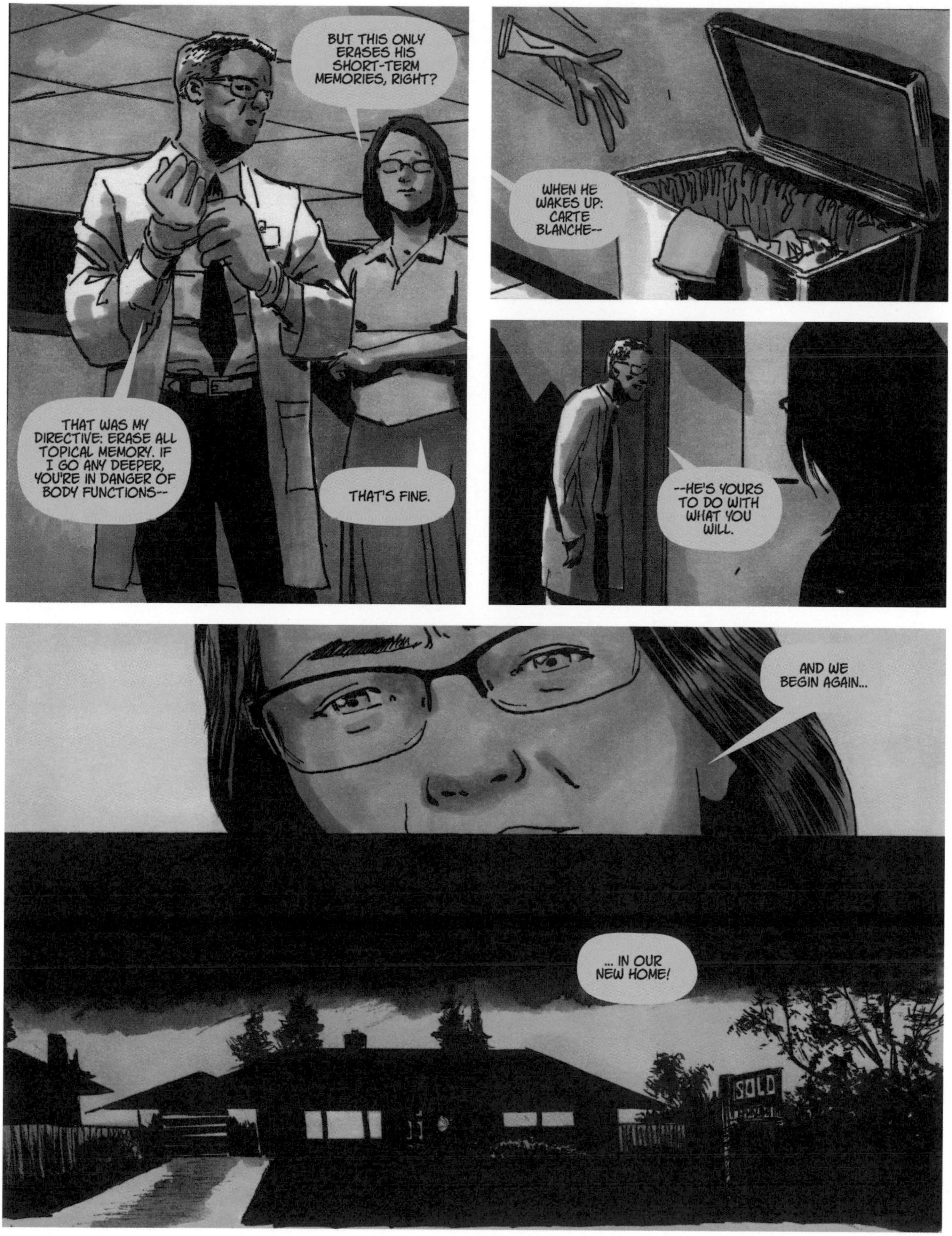
BUT THIS ONLY ERASES HIS SHORT-TERM MEMORIES, RIGHT?
THAT WAS MY DIRECTIVE: ERASE ALL TOPICAL MEMORY. IF I GO ANY DEEPER, YOU'RE IN DANGER OF BODY FUNCTIONS--
THAT'S FINE.
WHEN HE WAKES UP: CARTE BLANCHE--
--HE'S YOURS TO DO WITH WHAT YOU WILL.
AND WE BEGIN AGAIN...
... IN OUR NEW HOME!
SOLD

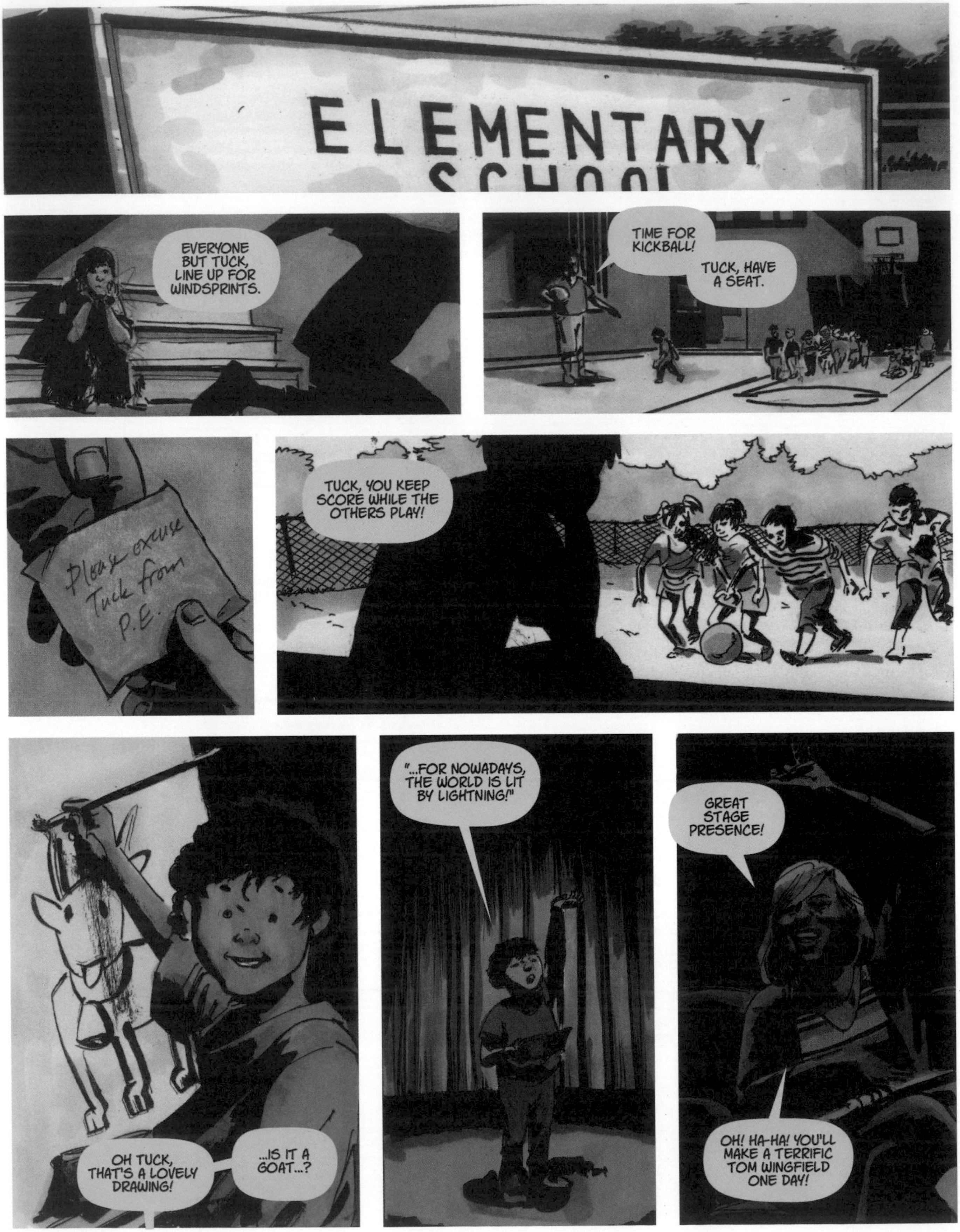
ELEMENTARY
SCHOOL
EVERYONE BUT TUCK, LINE UP FOR WINDSPRINTS.
TIME FOR KICKBALL!
TUCK, HAVE A SEAT.
Please excuse Tuck from P.E.
TUCK, YOU KEEP SCORE WHILE THE OTHERS PLAY!
OH TUCK, THAT'S A LOVELY DRAWING!
...IS IT A GOAT...?
"...FOR NOWADAYS, THE WORLD IS LIT BY LIGHTNING!"
GREAT STAGE PRESENCE!
OH! HA-HA! YOU'LL MAKE A TERRIFIC TOM WINGFIELD ONE DAY!

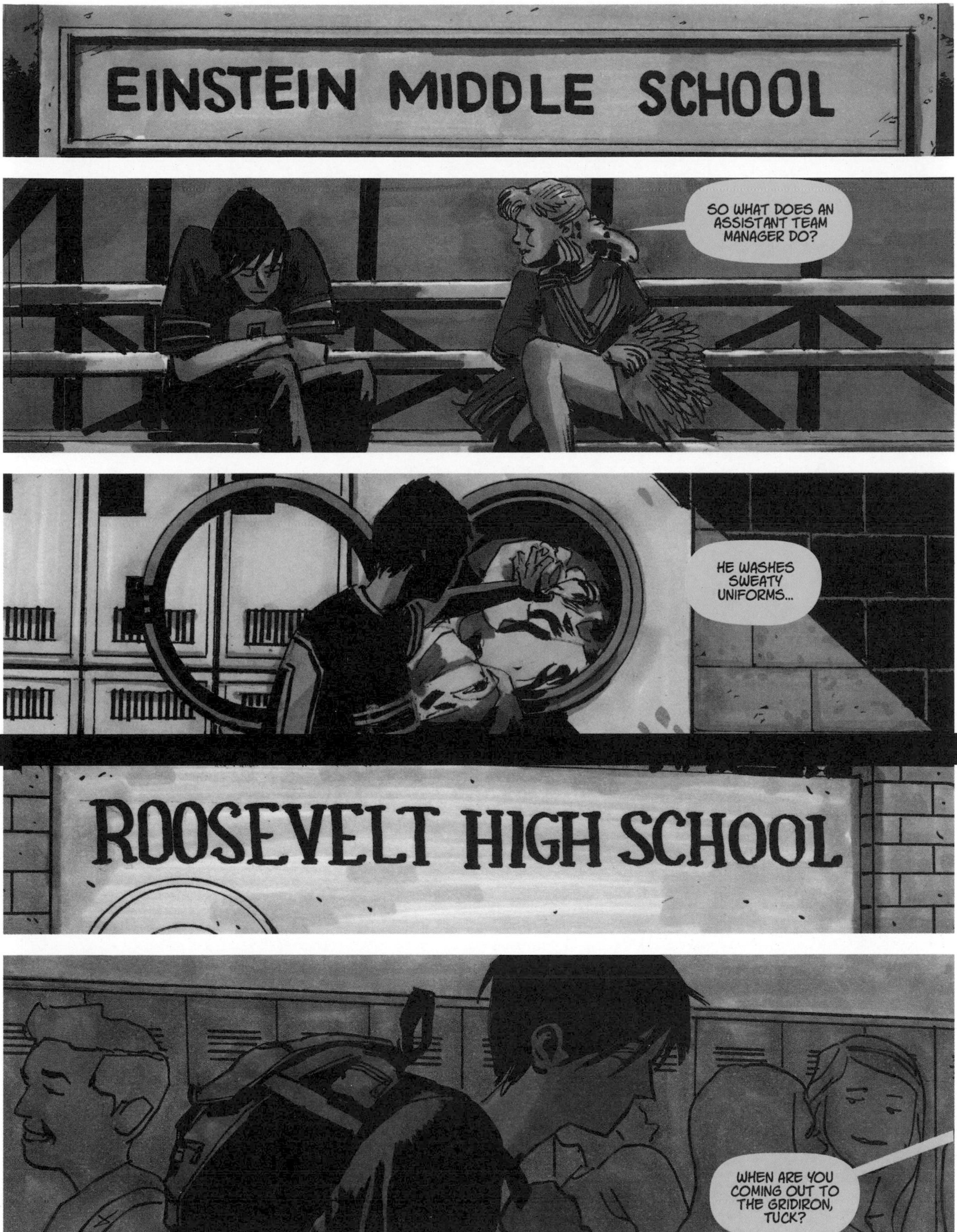
EINSTEIN MIDDLE SCHOOL
SO WHAT DOES AN ASSISTANT TEAM MANAGER DO?
HE WASHES SWEATY UNIFORMS...
ROOSEVELT HIGH SCHOOL
WHEN ARE YOU COMING OUT TO THE GRIDIRON, TUCK?

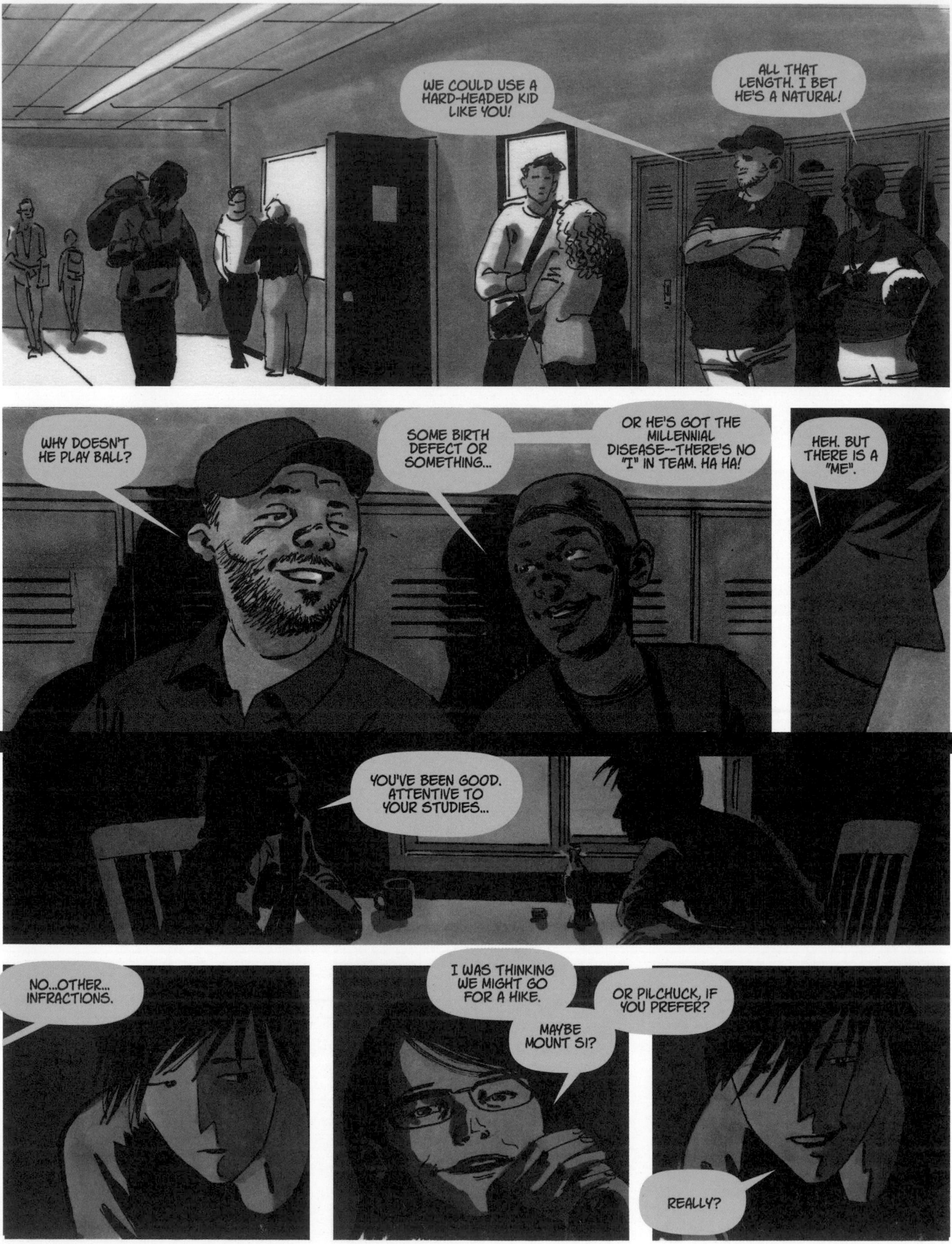
WE COULD USE A HARD-HEADED KID LIKE YOU!
ALL THAT LENGTH. I BET HE'S A NATURAL!
WHY DOESN'T HE PLAY BALL?
SOME BIRTH DEFECT OR SOMETHING...
OR HE'S GOT THE MILLENNIAL DISEASE--THERE'S NO "I" IN TEAM. HA HA!
HEH. BUT THERE IS A "ME".
YOU'VE BEEN GOOD. ATTENTIVE TO YOUR STUDIES...
NO...OTHER... INFRACTIONS.
I WAS THINKING WE MIGHT GO FOR A HIKE.
MAYBE MOUNT SI?
OR PILCHUCK, IF YOU PREFER?
REALLY?

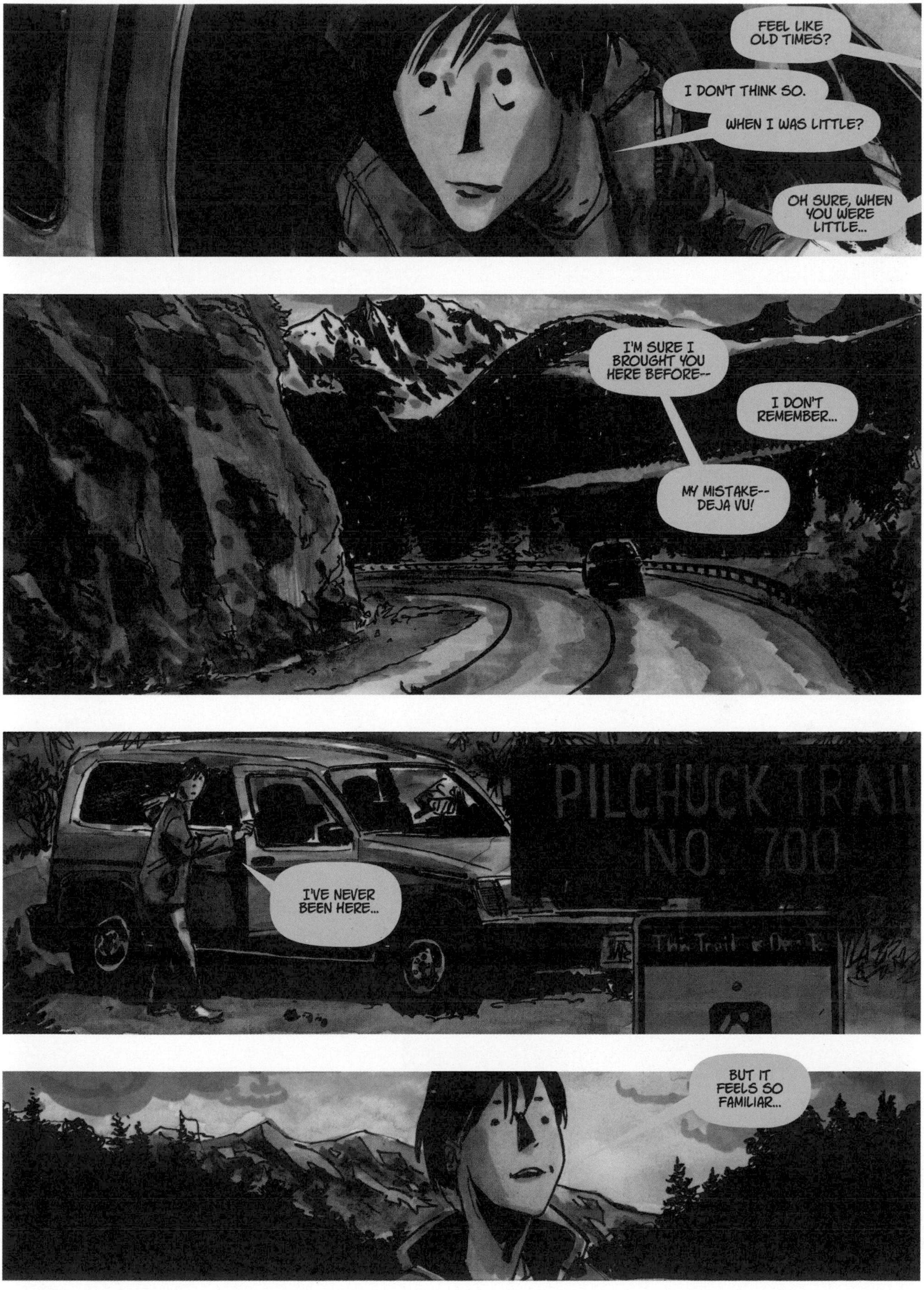
FEEL LIKE OLD TIMES?
I DON'T THINK SO.
WHEN I WAS LITTLE?
OH SURE, WHEN YOU WERE LITTLE...
I'M SURE I BROUGHT YOU HERE BEFORE--
I DON'T REMEMBER...
MY MISTAKE-- DEJA VU!
PILCHUCK TRAI
NO. 700
I'VE NEVER BEEN HERE...
BUT IT FEELS SO FAMILIAR...

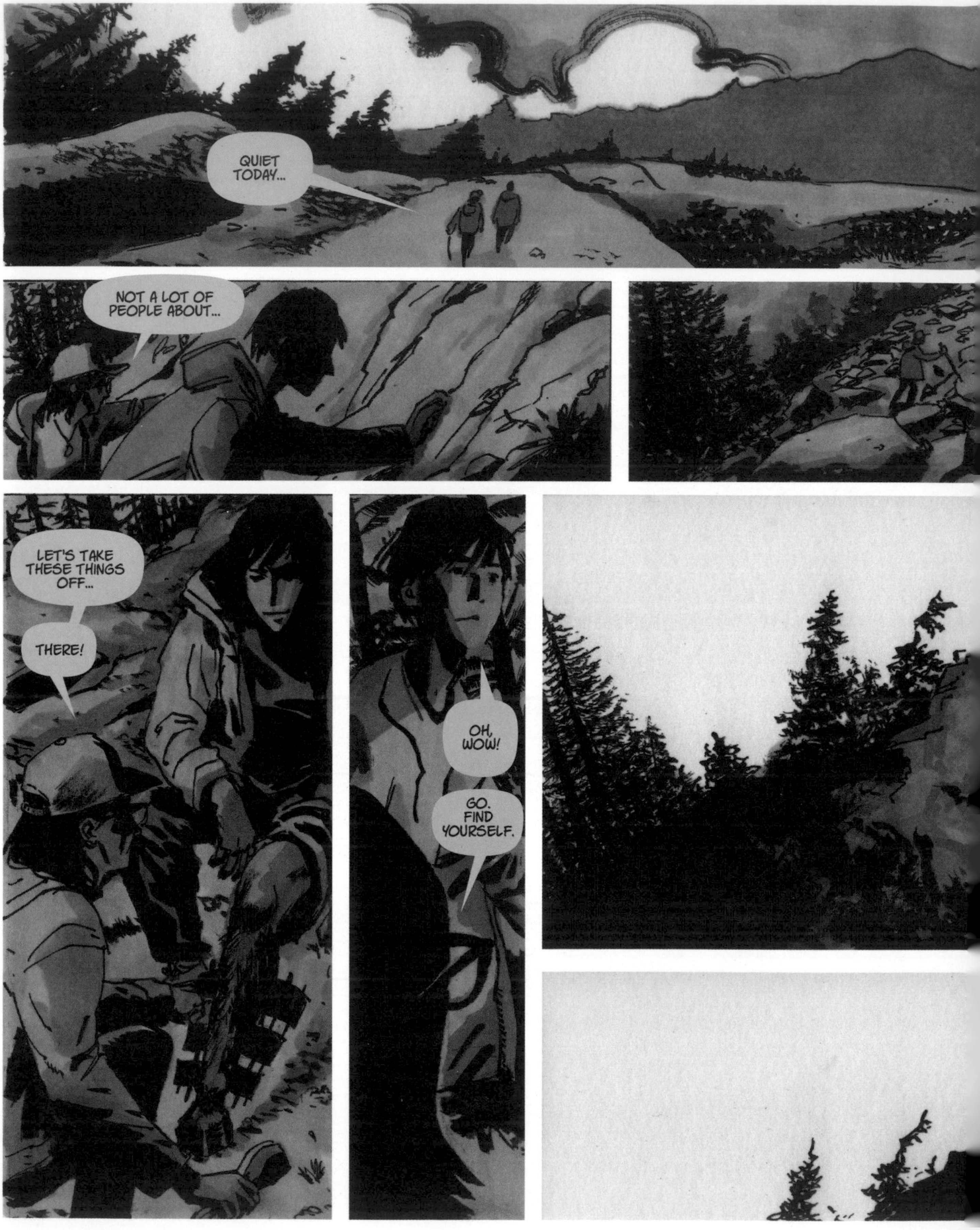
QUIET TODAY...
NOT A LOT OF PEOPLE ABOUT...
LET'S TAKE THESE THINGS OFF...
THERE!
OH, WOW!
GO. FIND YOURSELF.

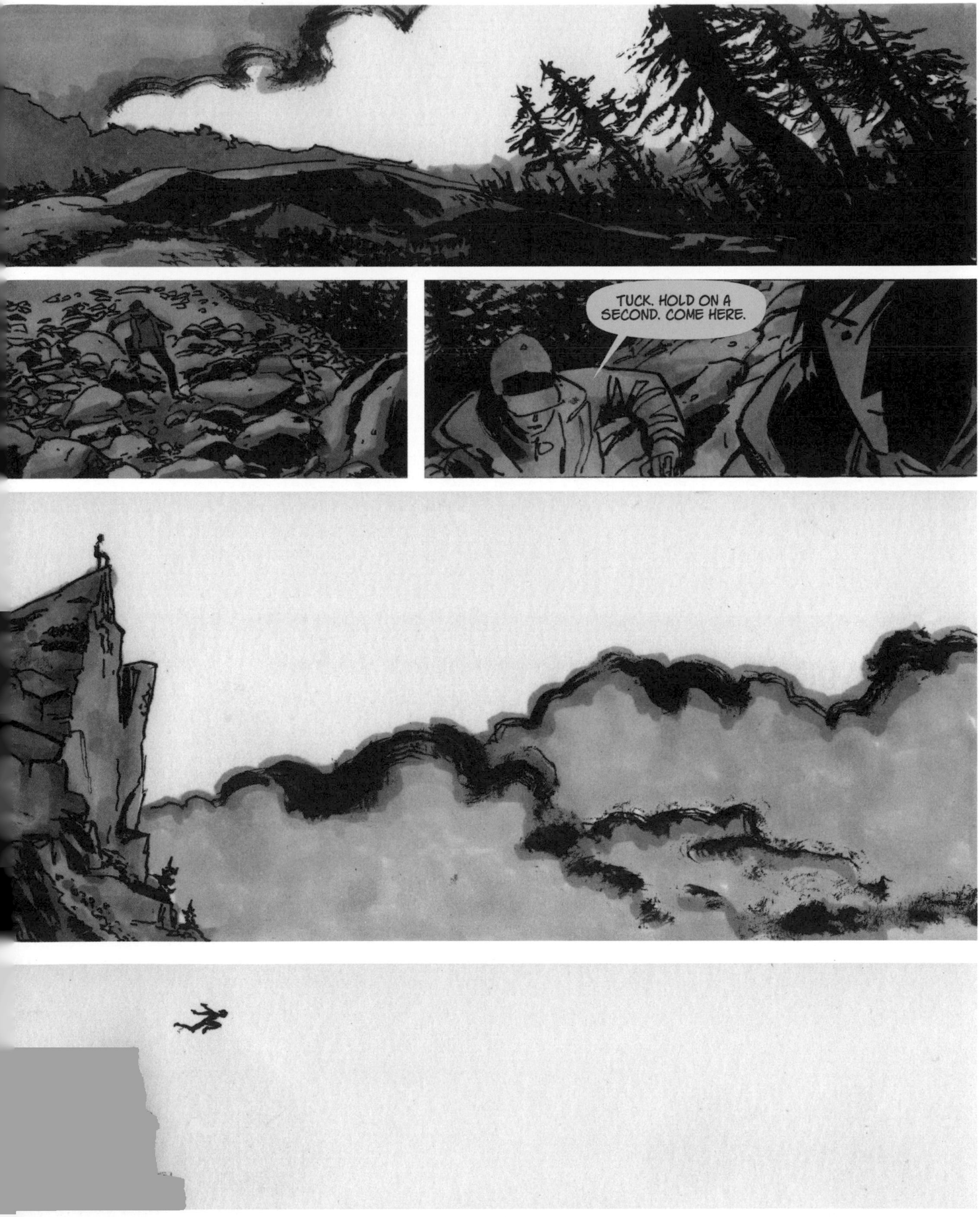
TUCK. HOLD ON A SECOND. COME HERE.

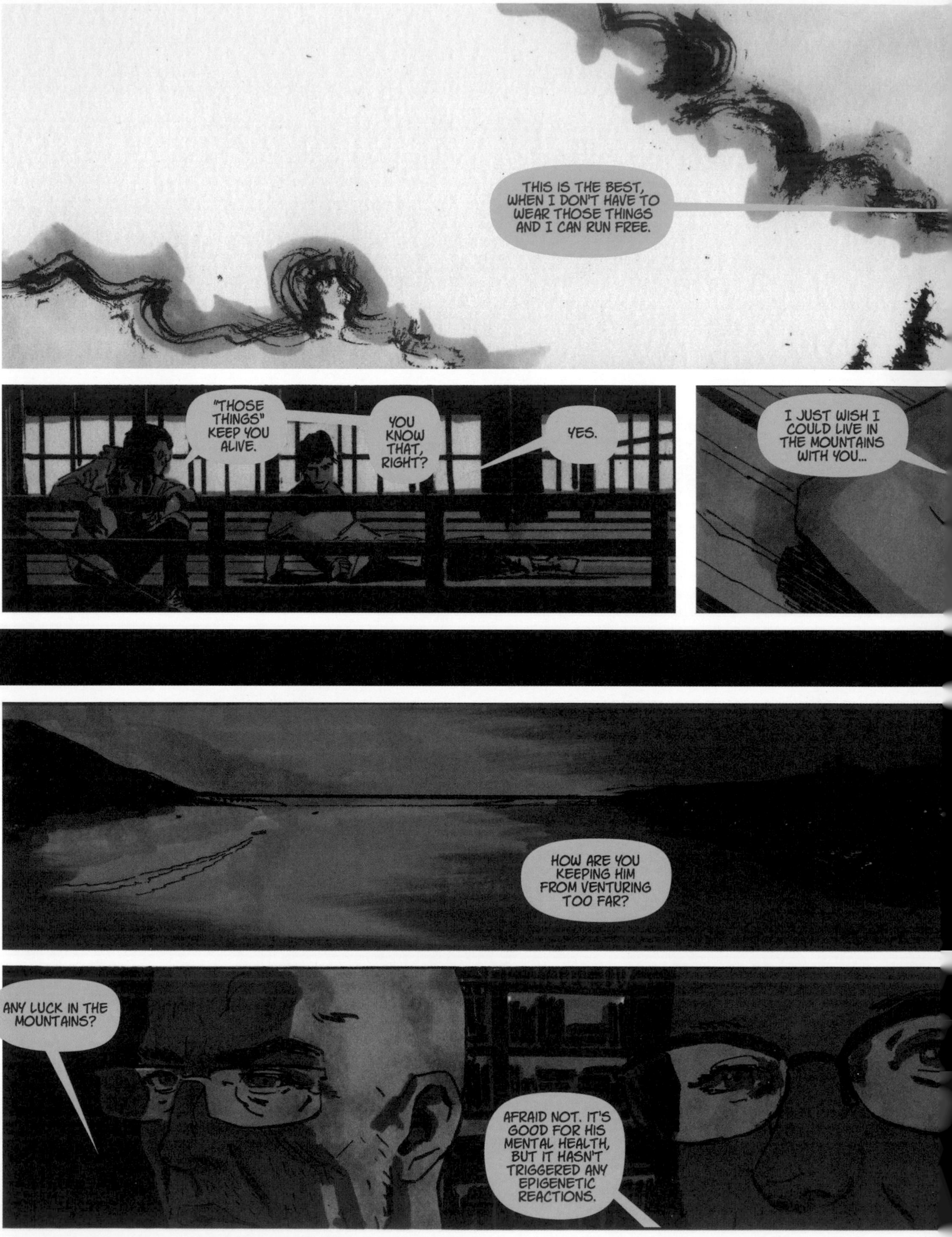
THIS IS THE BEST, WHEN I DON'T HAVE TO WEAR THOSE THINGS AND I CAN RUN FREE.
"THOSE THINGS" KEEP YOU ALIVE.
YOU KNOW THAT, RIGHT?
YES.
I JUST WISH I COULD LIVE IN THE MOUNTAINS WITH YOU...
HOW ARE YOU KEEPING HIM FROM VENTURING TOO FAR?
ANY LUCK IN THE MOUNTAINS?
AFRAID NOT. IT'S GOOD FOR HIS MENTAL HEALTH, BUT IT HASN'T TRIGGERED ANY EPIGENETIC REACTIONS.

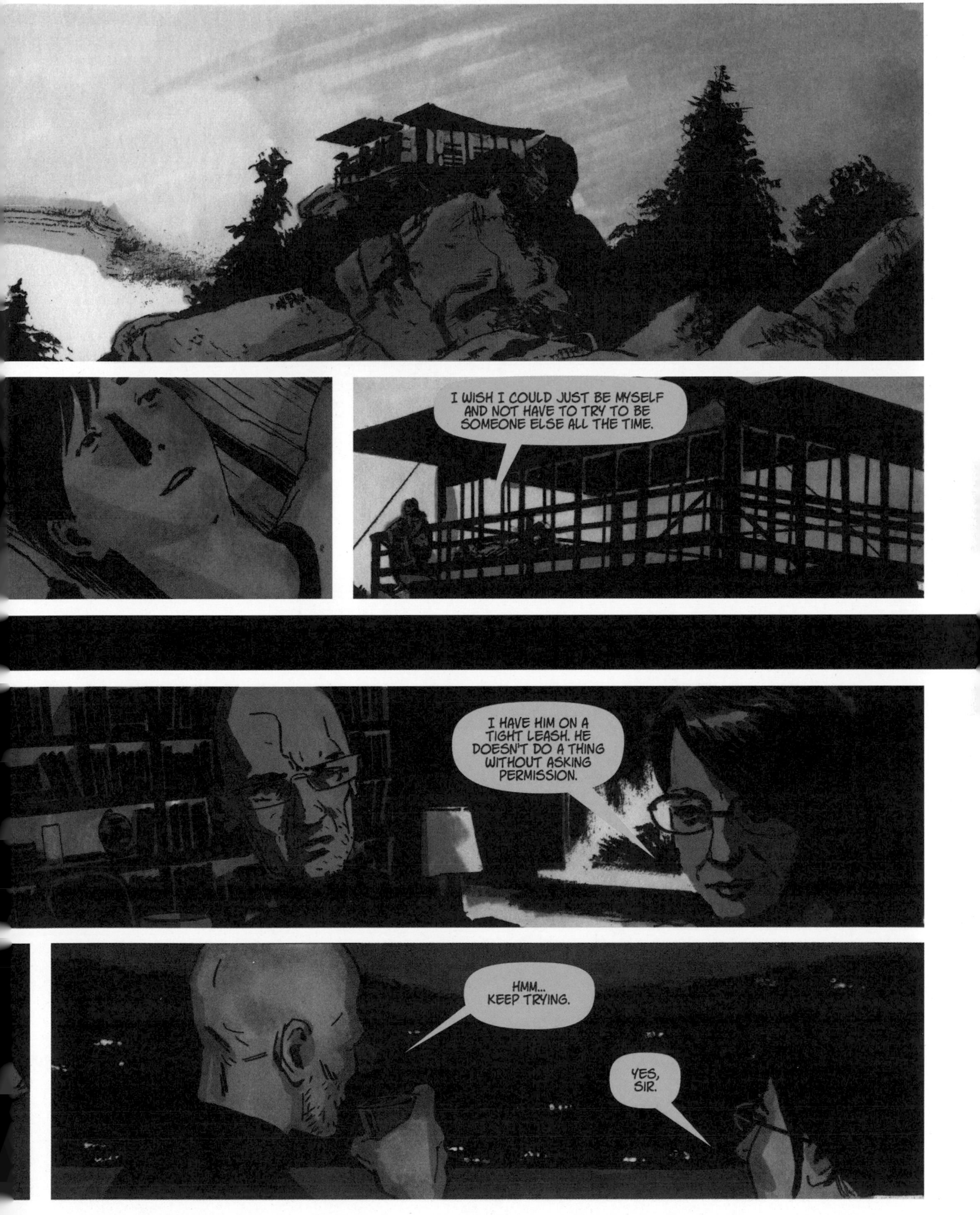
I WISH I COULD JUST BE MYSELF AND NOT HAVE TO TRY TO BE SOMEONE ELSE ALL THE TIME.
I HAVE HIM ON A TIGHT LEASH. HE DOESN'T DO A THING WITHOUT ASKING PERMISSION.
HMM... KEEP TRYING.
YES, SIR.

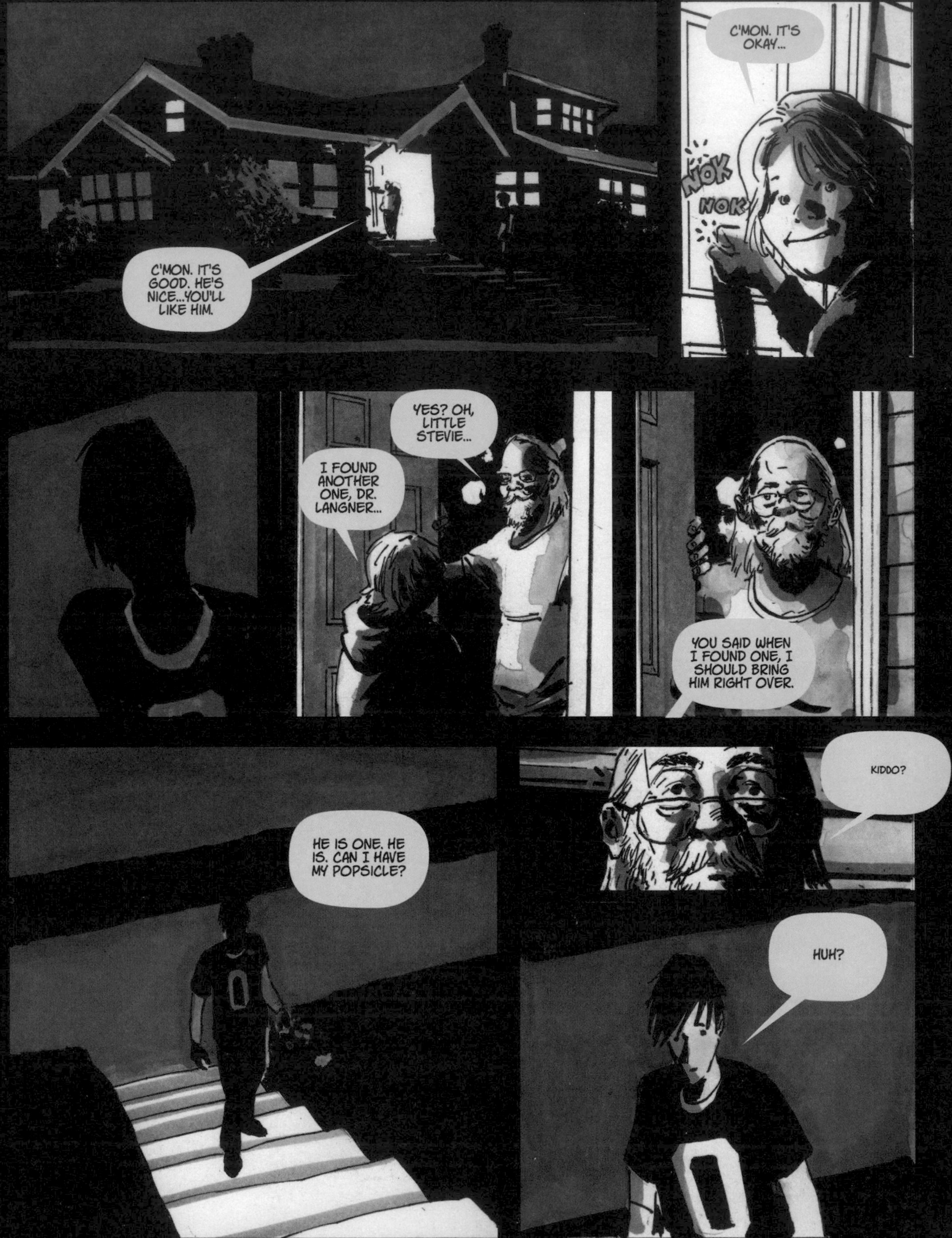
C'MON. IT'S GOOD. HE'S NICE...YOU'LL LIKE HIM.
C'MON. IT'S OKAY...
NOK
NOK
YES? OH, LITTLE STEVIE...
I FOUND ANOTHER ONE, DR. LANGNER...
YOU SAID WHEN I FOUND ONE, I SHOULD BRING HIM RIGHT OVER.
HE IS ONE. HE IS. CAN I HAVE MY POPSICLE?
KIDDO?
HUH?

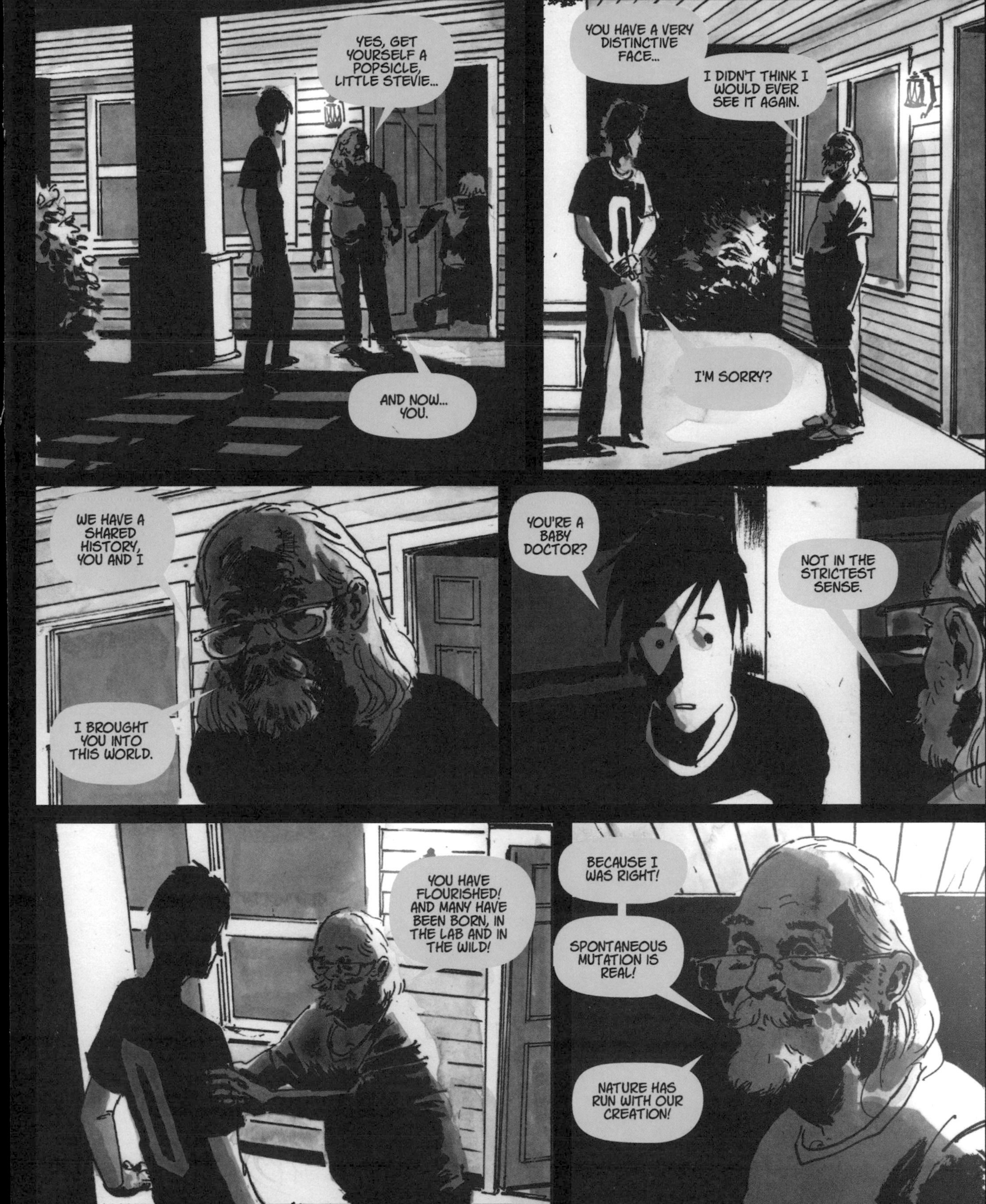

YES, GET YOURSELF A POPSICLE, LITTLE STEVIE...
AND NOW... YOU.
YOU HAVE A VERY DISTINCTIVE FACE...
I DIDN'T THINK I WOULD EVER SEE IT AGAIN.
I'M SORRY?
WE HAVE A SHARED HISTORY, YOU AND I
I BROUGHT YOU INTO THIS WORLD.
YOU'RE A BABY DOCTOR?
NOT IN THE STRICTEST SENSE.
YOU HAVE FLOURISHED! AND MANY HAVE BEEN BORN, IN THE LAB AND IN THE WILD!
BECAUSE I WAS RIGHT!
SPONTANEOUS MUTATION IS REAL!
NATURE HAS RUN WITH OUR CREATION!

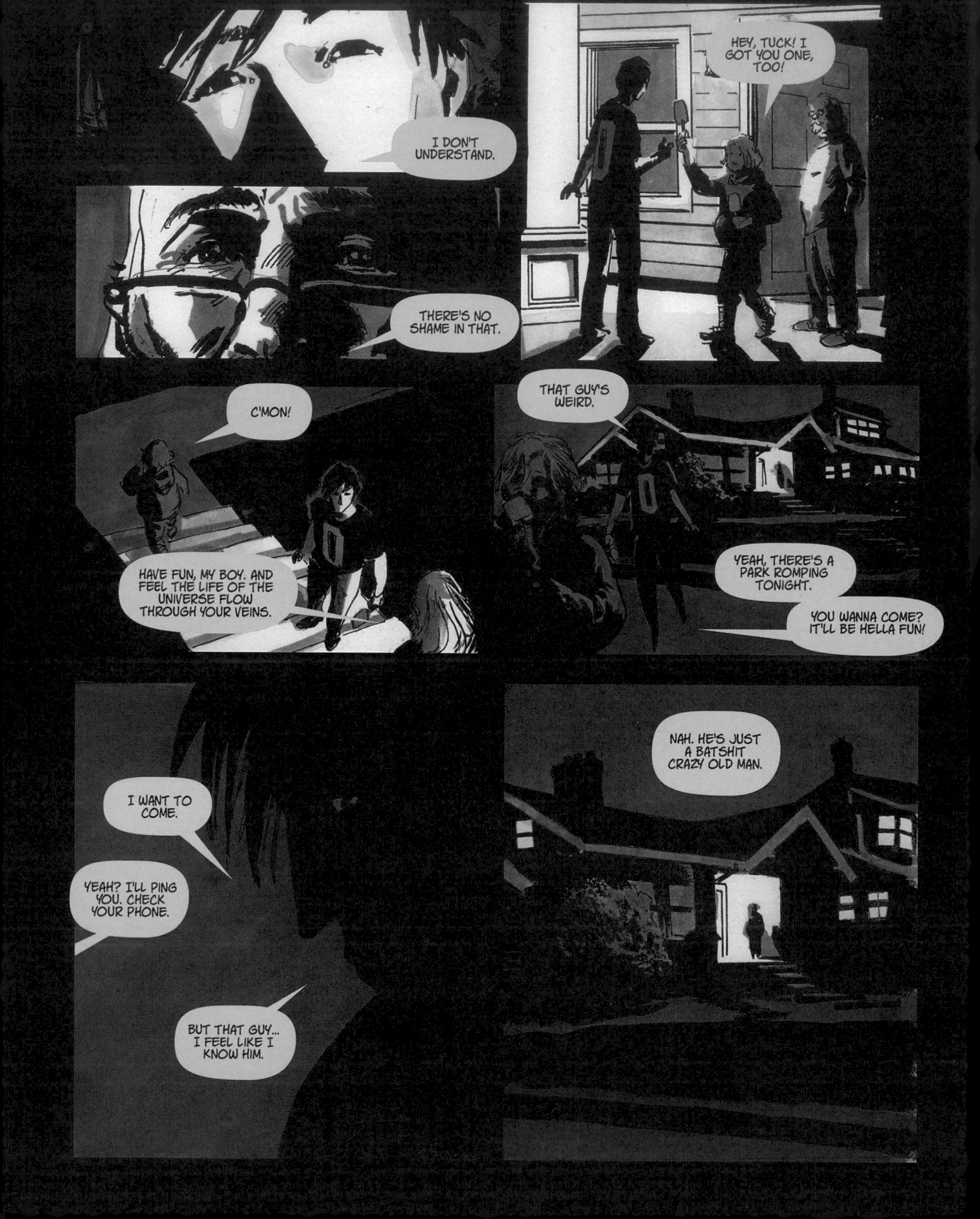
I DON'T UNDERSTAND.
THERE'S NO SHAME IN THAT.
HEY, TUCK! I GOT YOU ONE, TOO!
C'MON!
HAVE FUN, MY BOY. AND FEEL THE LIFE OF THE UNIVERSE FLOW THROUGH YOUR VEINS.
THAT GUY'S WEIRD.
YEAH, THERE'S A PARK ROMPING TONIGHT.
YOU WANNA COME? IT'LL BE HELLA FUN!
I WANT TO COME.
YEAH? I'LL PING YOU. CHECK YOUR PHONE.
BUT THAT GUY... I FEEL LIKE I KNOW HIM.
NAH. HE'S JUST A BATSHIT CRAZY OLD MAN.

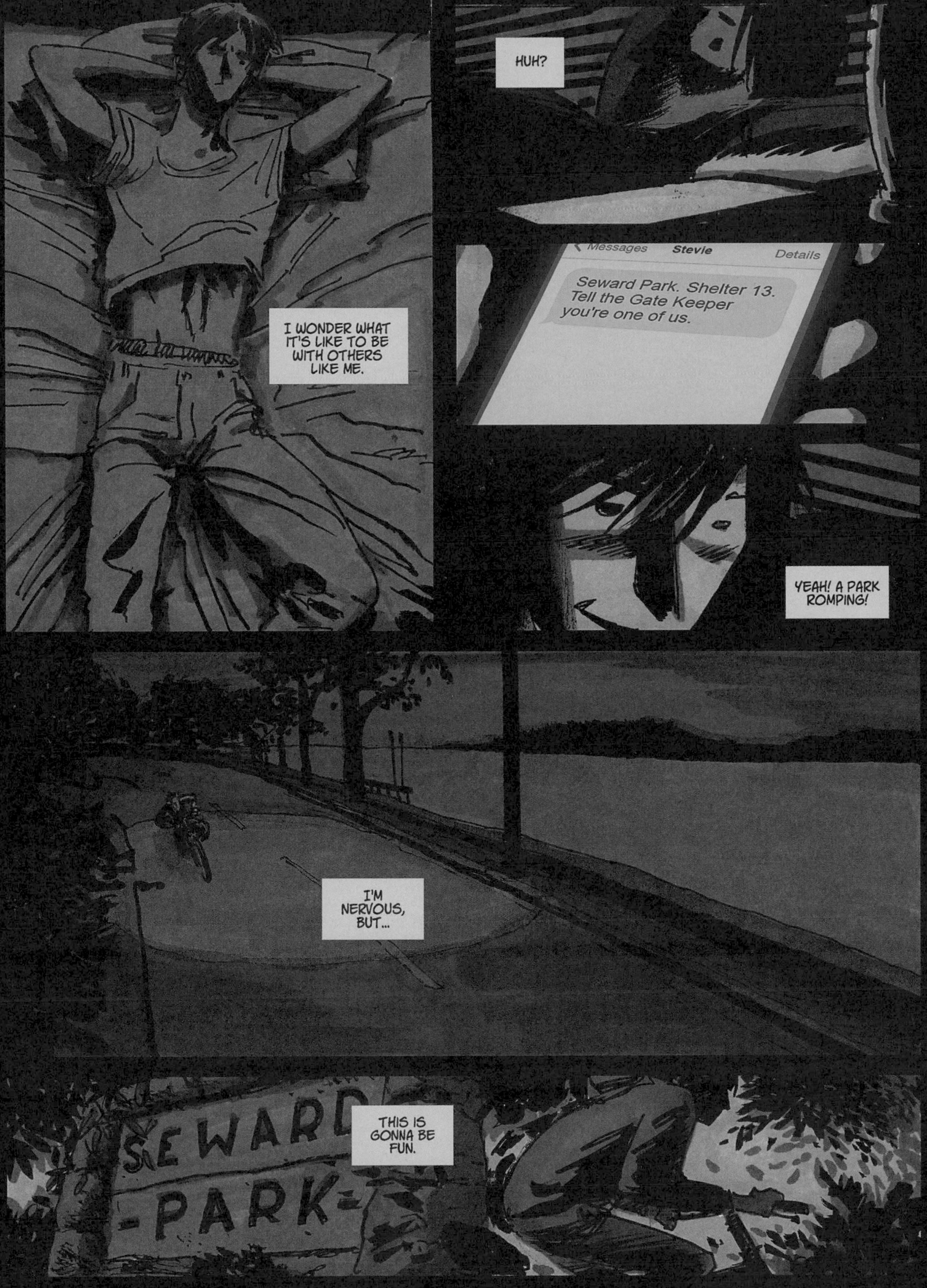
I WONDER WHAT IT'S LIKE TO BE WITH OTHERS LIKE ME.
HUH?
Messages
Stevie
Details
Seward Park. Shelter 13. Tell the Gate Keeper you're one of us.
YEAH! A PARK ROMPING!
I'M NERVOUS, BUT...
SEWARD
-PARK-
THIS IS GONNA BE FUN.

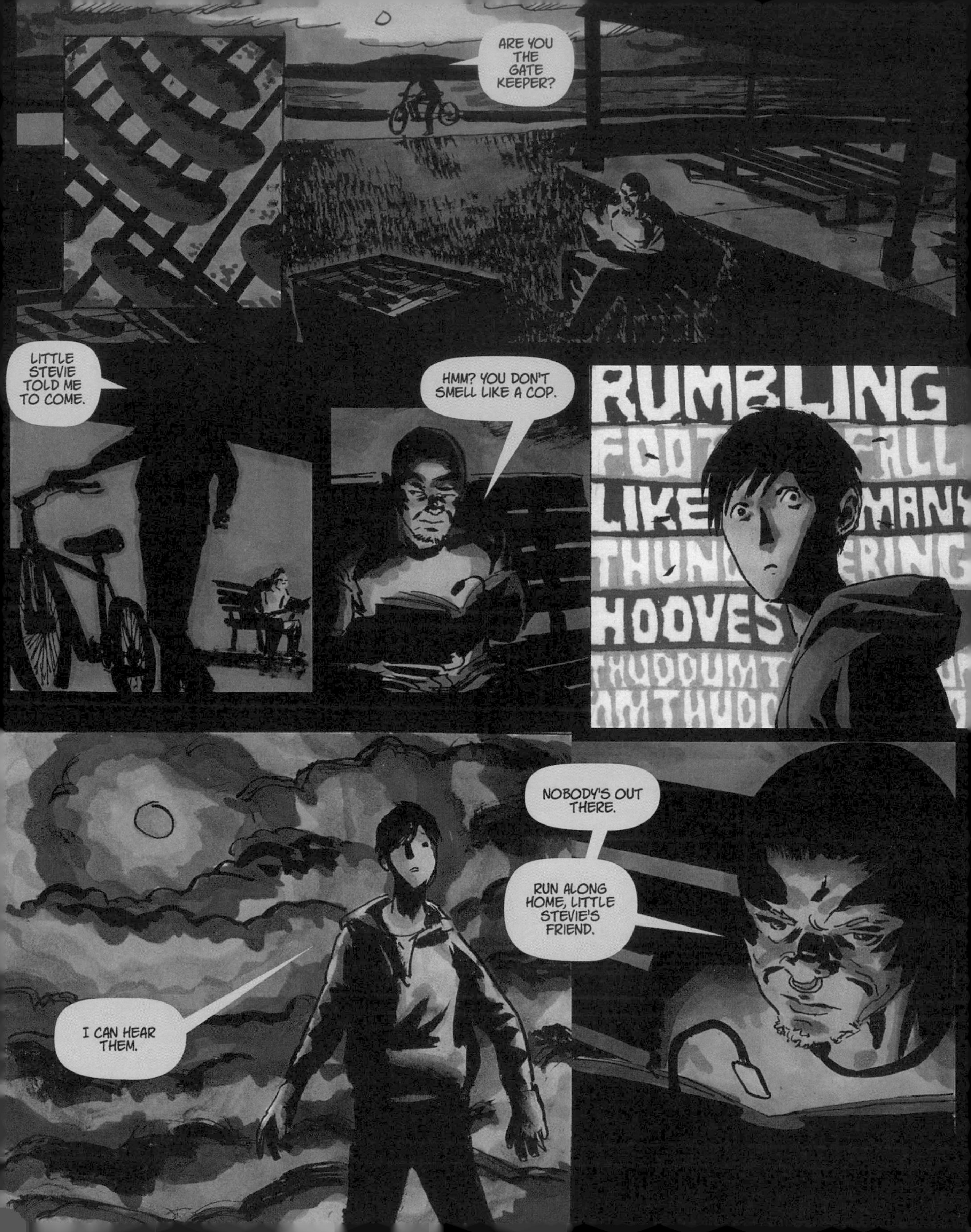
ARE YOU THE GATE KEEPER?
LITTLE STEVIE TOLD ME TO COME.
HMM? YOU DON'T SMELL LIKE A COP.
RUMBLING
FOOT FALL
LIKE MANY
THUNDERING
HOOVES
THUDDUMTHUDDUM
I CAN HEAR THEM.
NOBODY'S OUT THERE.
RUN ALONG HOME, LITTLE STEVIE'S FRIEND.

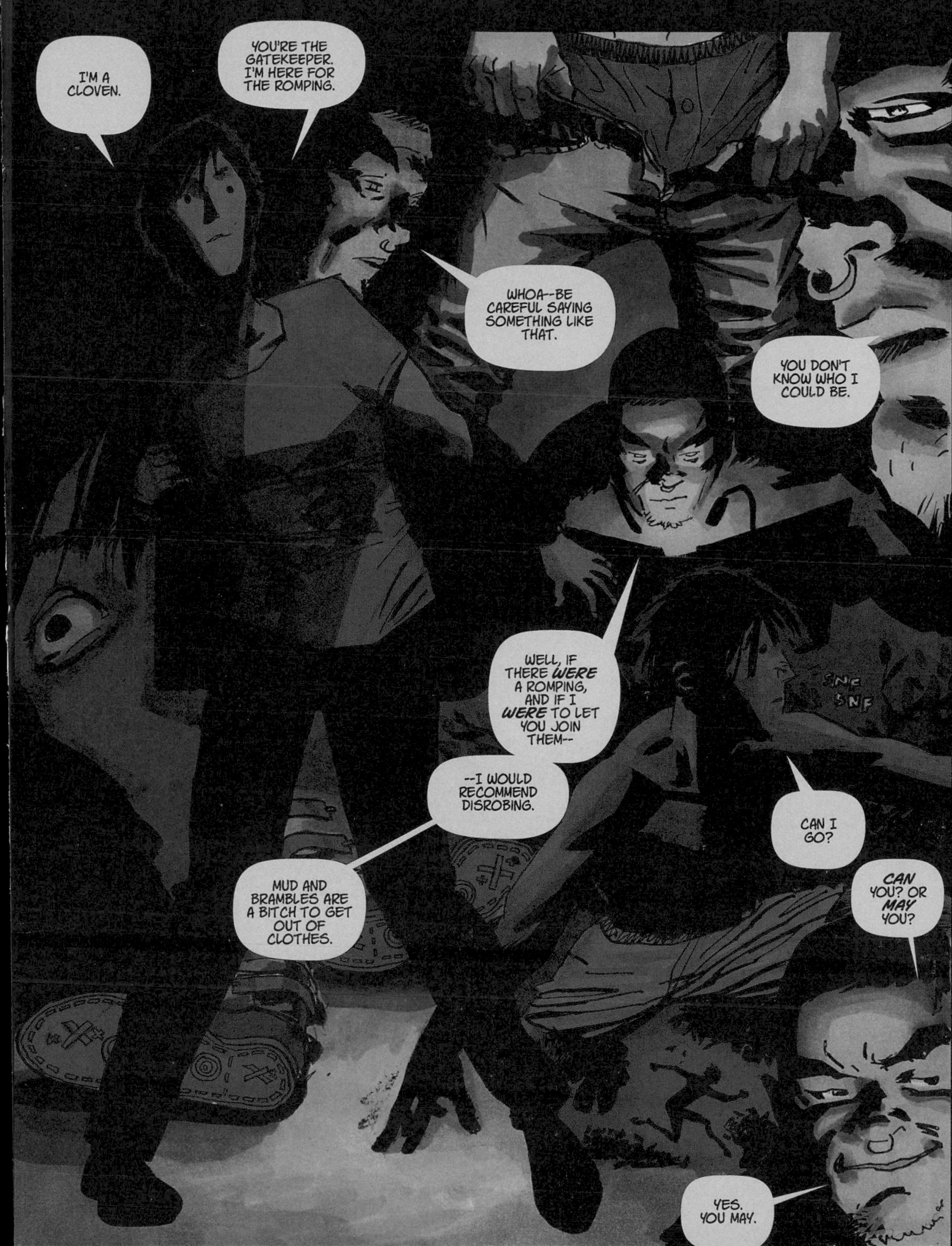
I'M A CLOVEN.
YOU'RE THE GATEKEEPER. I'M HERE FOR THE ROMPING.
WHOA--BE CAREFUL SAYING SOMETHING LIKE THAT.
YOU DON'T KNOW WHO I COULD BE.
WELL, IF THERE *WERE* A ROMPING, AND IF I *WERE* TO LET YOU JOIN THEM--
--I WOULD RECOMMEND DISROBING.
MUD AND BRAMBLES ARE A BITCH TO GET OUT OF CLOTHES.
SNF SNF
CAN I GO?
CAN YOU? OR *MAY* YOU?
YES. YOU MAY.

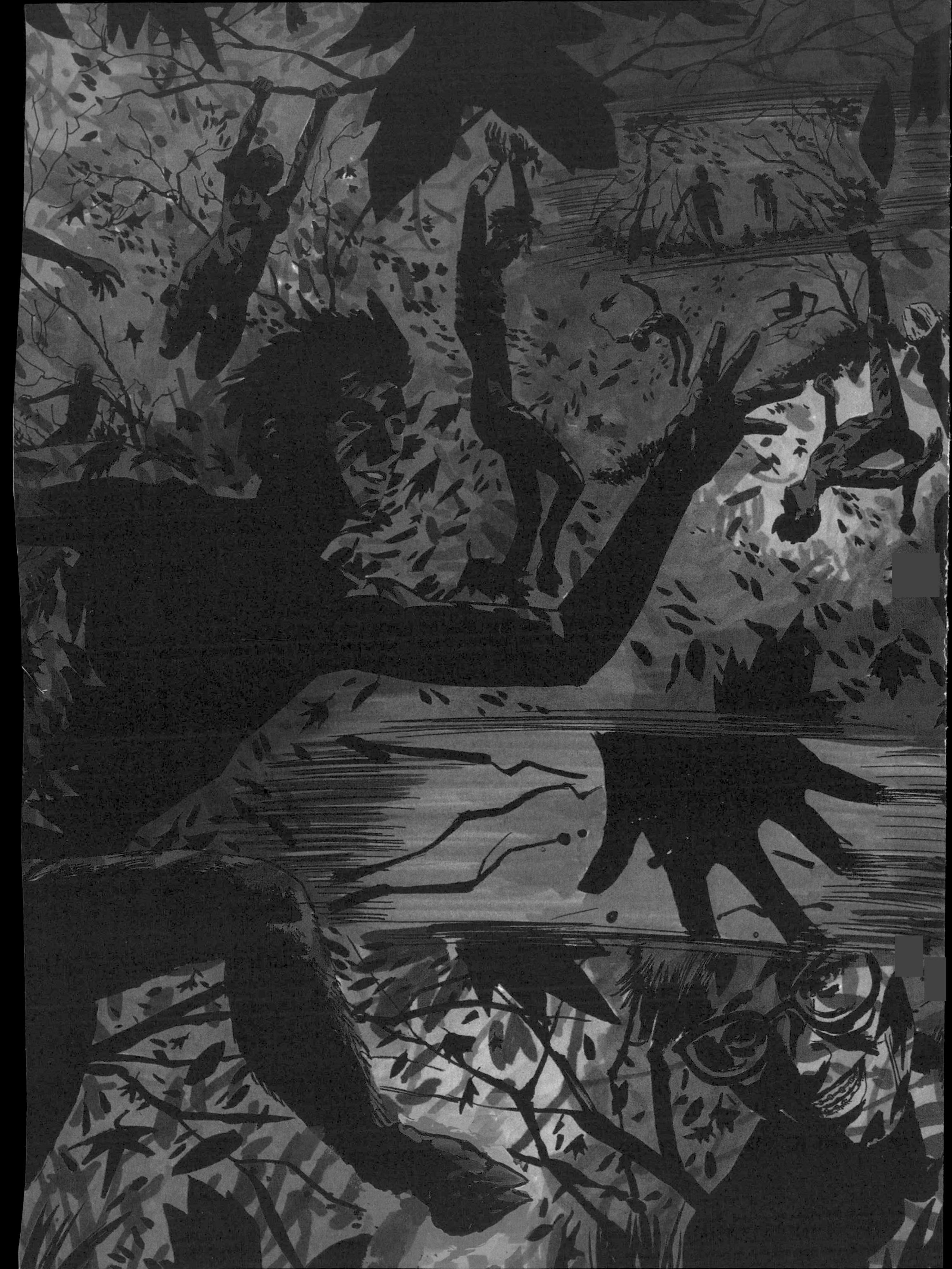

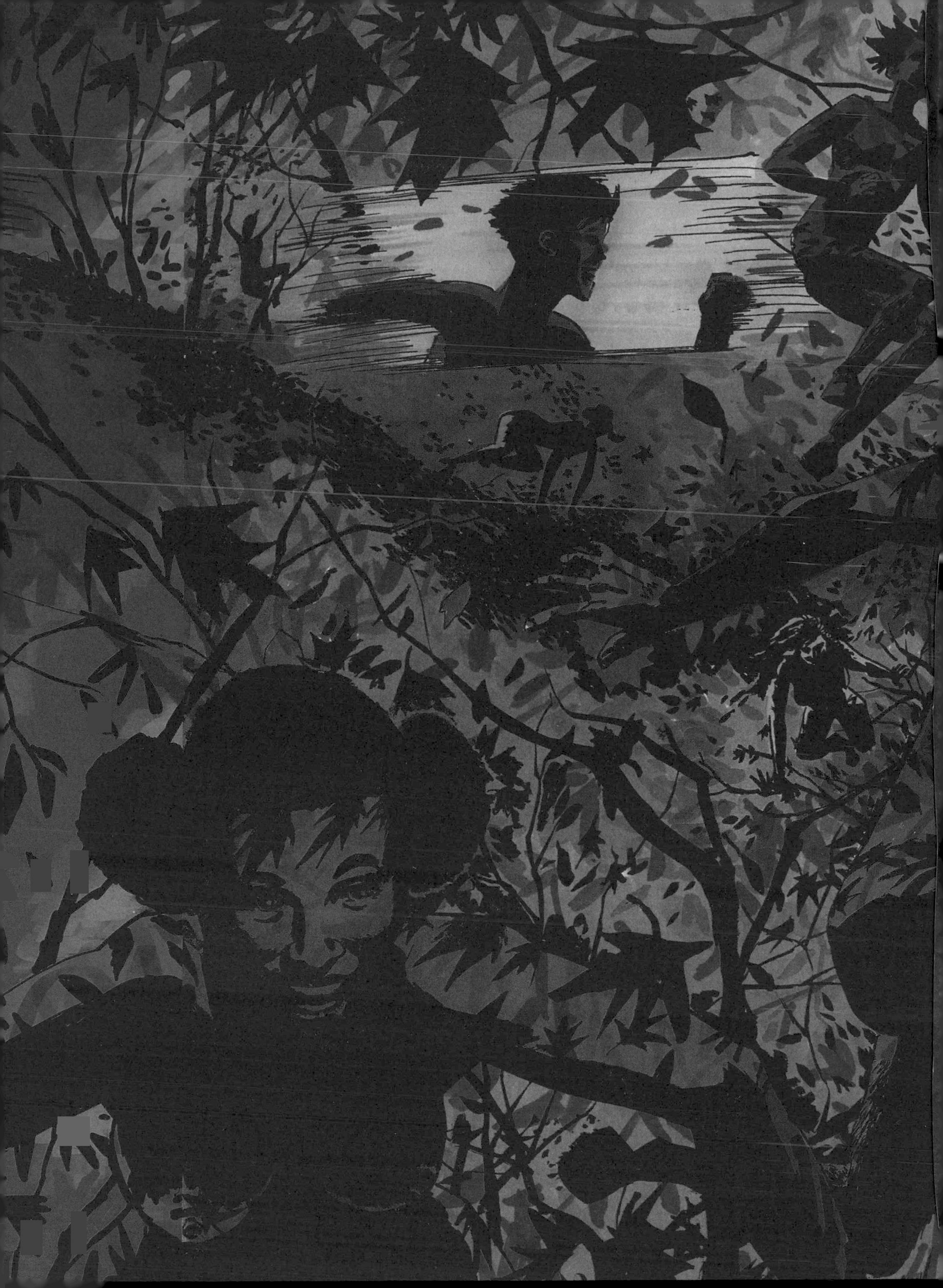

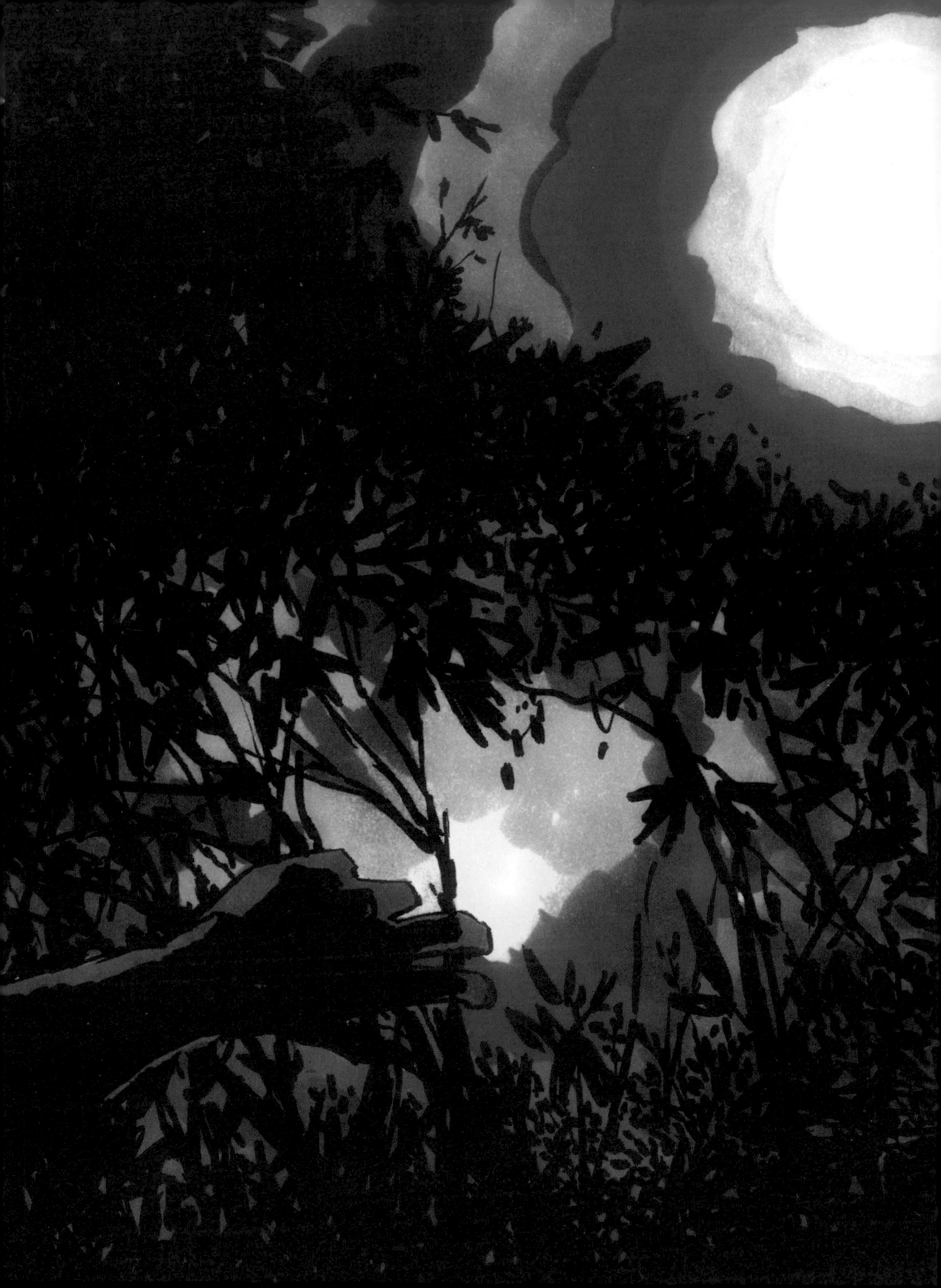

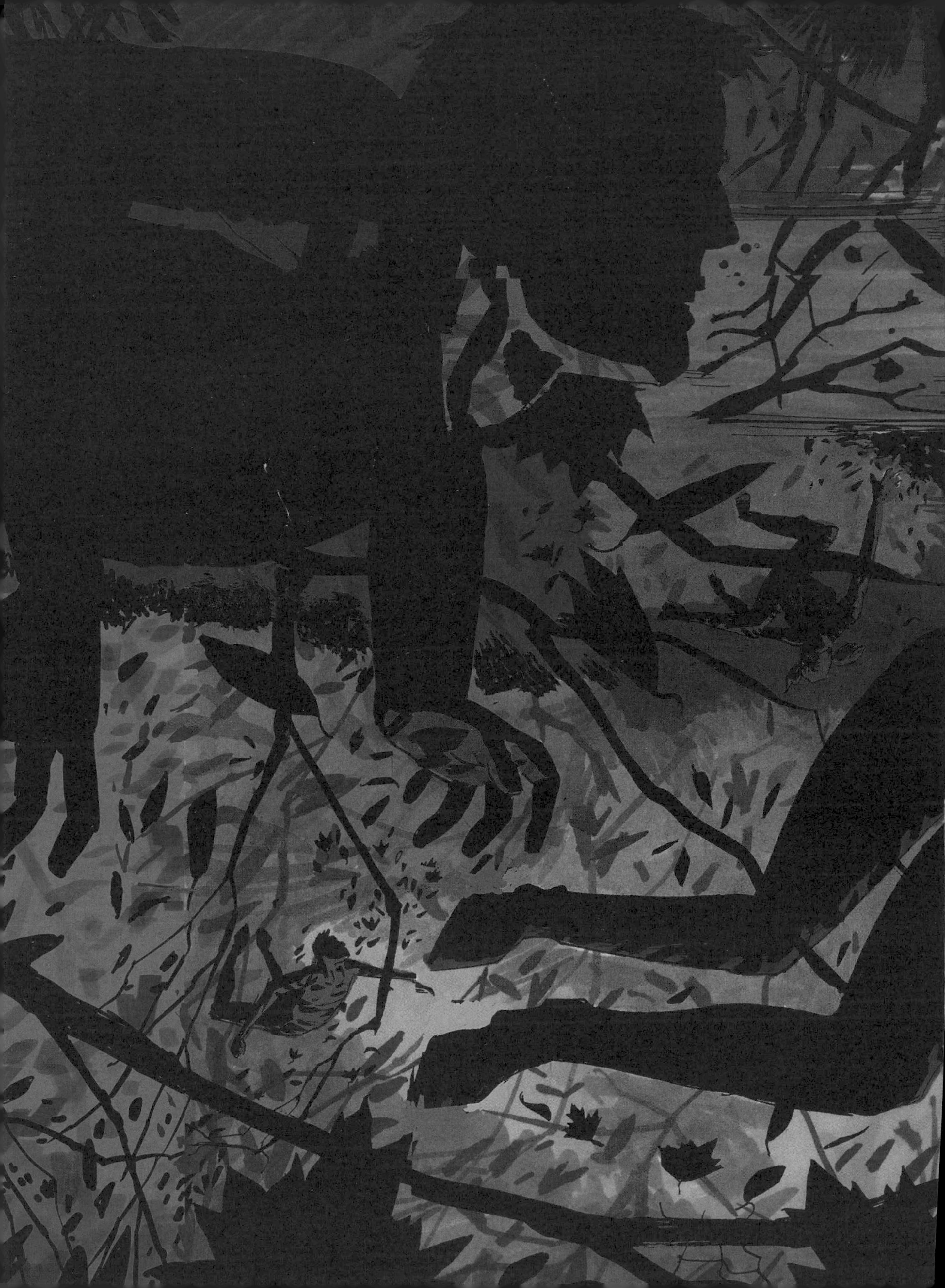

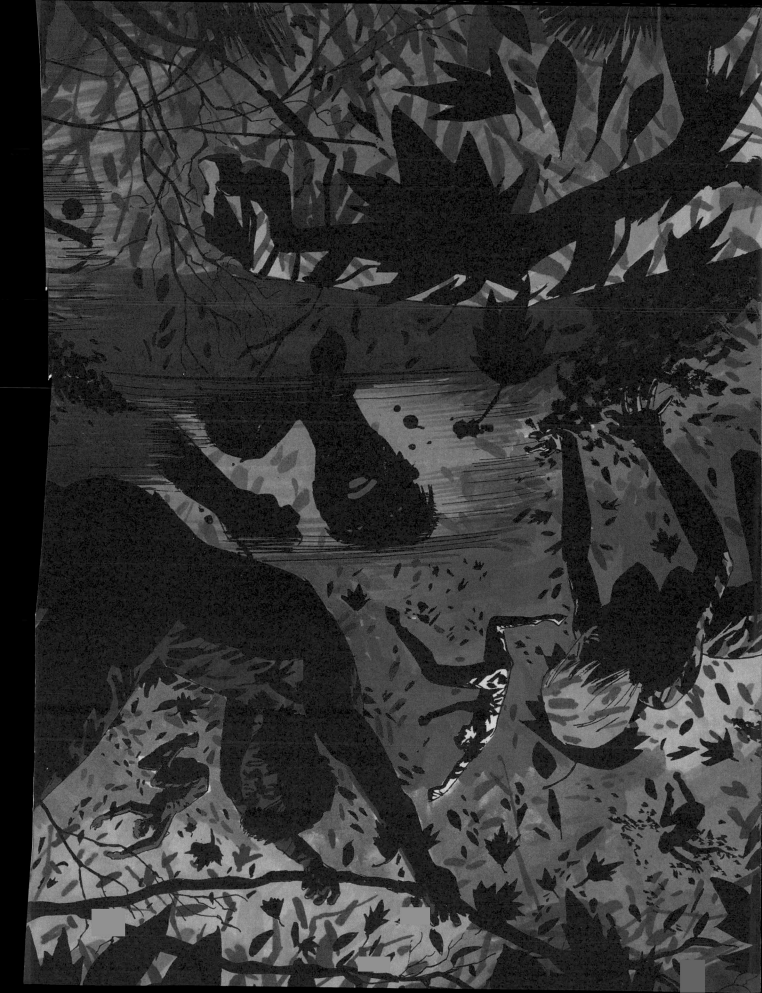

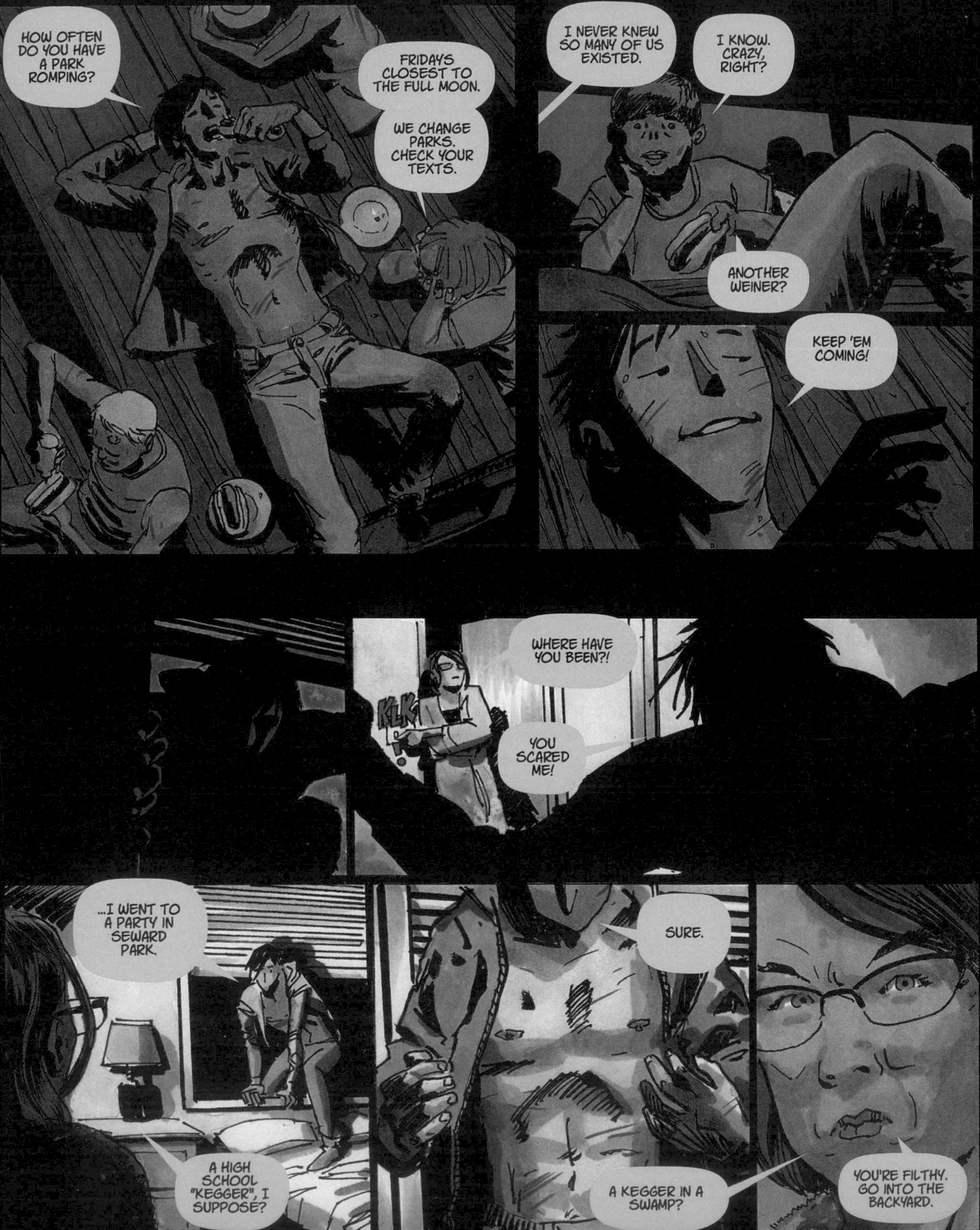
HOW OFTEN DO YOU HAVE A PARK ROMPING?
FRIDAYS CLOSEST TO THE FULL MOON.
WE CHANGE PARKS. CHECK YOUR TEXTS.
I NEVER KNEW SO MANY OF US EXISTED.
I KNOW. CRAZY, RIGHT?
ANOTHER WEINER?
KEEP 'EM COMING!
KLIK
WHERE HAVE YOU BEEN?!
YOU SCARED ME!
...I WENT TO A PARTY IN SEWARD PARK.
A HIGH SCHOOL "KEGGER", I SUPPOSE?
SURE.
A KEGGER IN A SWAMP?
YOU'RE FILTHY. GO INTO THE BACKYARD.

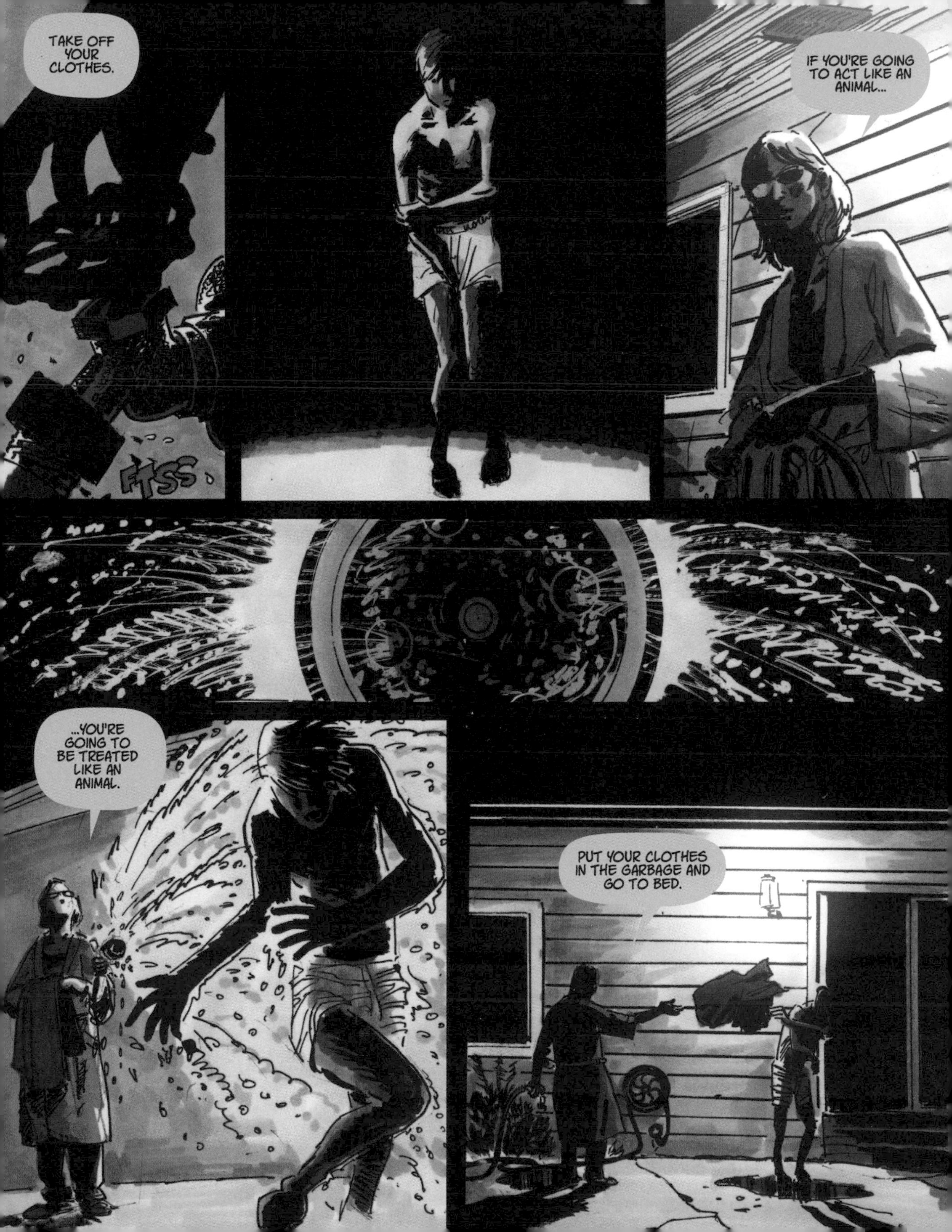
TAKE OFF YOUR CLOTHES.
FTSS
IF YOU'RE GOING TO ACT LIKE AN ANIMAL...
...YOU'RE GOING TO BE TREATED LIKE AN ANIMAL.
PUT YOUR CLOTHES IN THE GARBAGE AND GO TO BED.

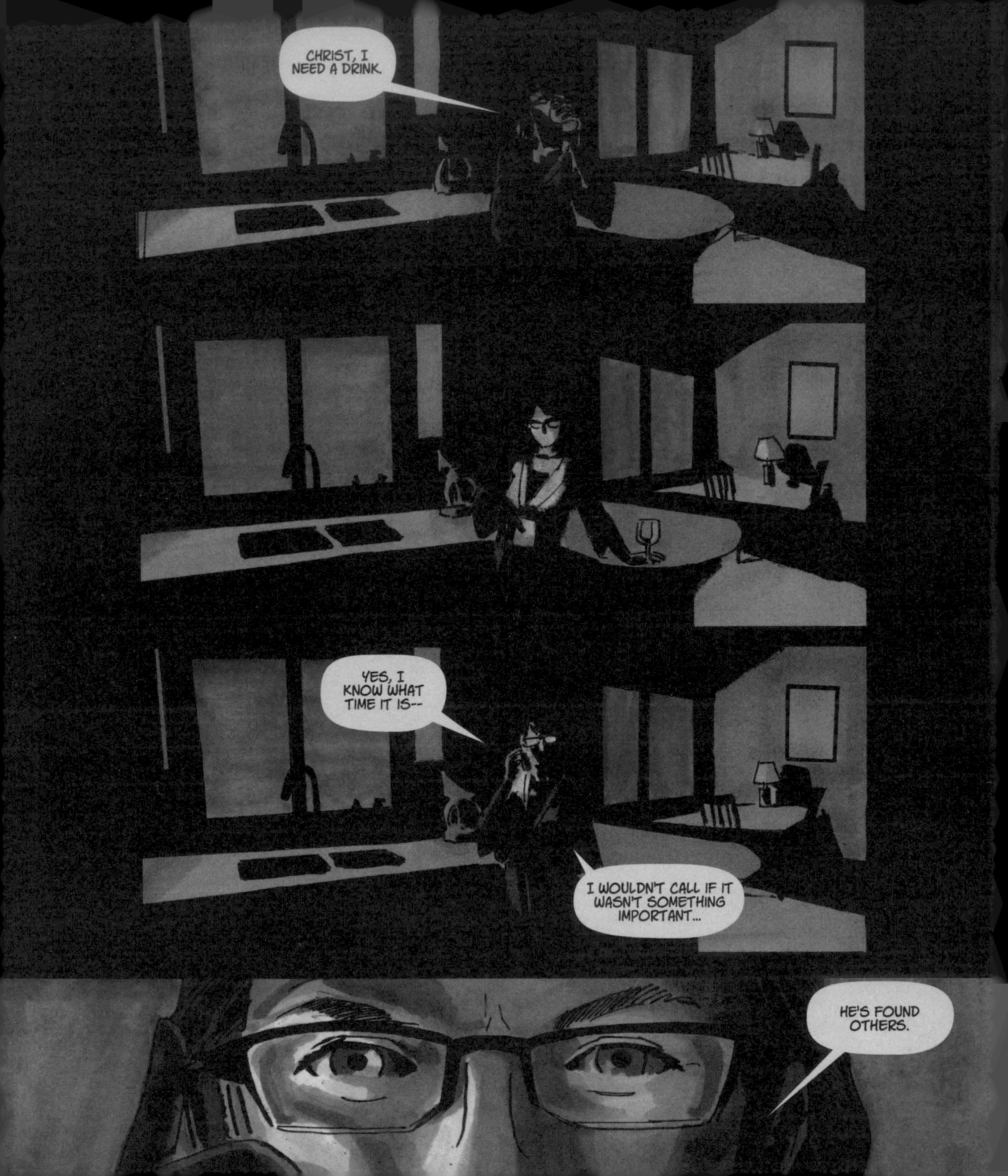
CHRIST, I NEED A DRINK.
YES, I KNOW WHAT TIME IT IS--
I WOULDN'T CALL IF IT WASN'T SOMETHING IMPORTANT...
HE'S FOUND OTHERS.

GARTH STEIN is a *New York Times*-bestselling author, filmmaker, and playwright based in Seattle. He is the winner of several literary awards, including two PNBA Awards. The author of two plays and four novels, his book, *The Art of Racing in the Rain*, has sold over six million copies worldwide, been produced as a stage play, a children's book series, and a film starring Kevin Costner, Amanda Seyfried, and Milo Ventimiglia.

MATTHEW SOUTHWORTH is a comic artist, musician, and writer based in Seattle. He is the co-creator (along with Greg Rucka) of the comic book series *Stumptown*, as well as an Executive Producer of ABC's *Stumptown* TV series. He has worked for Marvel, DC, and Dark Horse Comics, and was the lead vocalist and guitarist of the Seattle rock band, the Capillaries.

AUTHORS' NOTE: Linguisticians have understandably questioned the use of "hoofs" instead of "hooves" as the plural form of "hoof" in this edition: while both forms are acceptable in today's language, "hooves" is the more commonly used. However, the authors have deferred to Dr. Kenneth Langner's consistent use of "hoofs" in his laboratory notes and journal entries. In fact, Dr. Langner addressed the issue himself in a 1997 journal entry: "I will use the plural form, 'hoofs,' instead of the common form, 'hooves,' to indicate that the hoof of a Cloven is slightly but significantly different from the hoof of a common ungulate, as a Cloven hoof retains some man-like qualities in terms of bone structure and ligament attachment." GS/MS